THE CAT STAR CHRONICLES

CHERYL BROOKS

sourcebooks
casablanca

Published by Sourcebooks Casablanca, an imprint of Sourcebooks, Inc.
P.O. Box 4410, Naperville, Illinois 60567-4410
(630) 961-3900
FAX: (630) 961-2168
www.sourcebooks.com

Printed and bound in the United States of America
QW 10 9 8 7 6 5 4 3 2 1

Dedicated to my dear husband
for all of his support,
encouragement, and love.

Prologue

MANX KNEW SHE WAS WATCHING HIM. THE GENTLE BREEZE that blew across the deck and sent her erotic scent wafting down toward the lake confirmed it. He stretched upward with his head thrown back, inhaling deeply as he felt his body respond. Within moments, her scent intensified; she was not only aroused, but, judging from the strength of her enticing aroma, she was also naked; there was nothing between them but the cool night air. His mind took that image and savored it—her soft breasts, her hard nipples—and even across the distance that separated them, he could sense the wet heat between her thighs, could almost hear her body calling out to him, and his cock turned to stone.

He closed his eyes and imagined her coming to him, her touch gentle on his skin, her fingers teasing him to a feverish pitch. She was the most intoxicating female he had ever encountered, and he knew that soon, he would mate with her. But for now, he held back, sensing her shyness and knowing just how tenuous his own existence was. He might be captured at any moment and taken from her, though it was easy to ignore that fact when his body was demanding release.

Reaching down, he touched his rigid penis, the orgasm-inducing fluid already beginning to ooze from the star-like coronal points of the head. Pleasuring oneself was almost unheard of among his kind—few Zetithian males were even capable—and though he knew that males of other species engaged in such practices regularly, he'd seldom felt the need for it until encountering her. This woman's scent was particularly potent, and she did things to him no other woman had ever done; made him reckless when he'd been so cautious in the past, made him want to risk everything for the chance to sheathe himself with her and give her joy.

For now, he could only imagine holding her in his arms. As his eyes closed again, he dreamed of her soft lips kissing his stiff shaft, her hot mouth sucking the snard from his testicles, and her entire body crashing into orgasm just from tasting it. He could almost see her deep, auburn hair shimmering in the moonlight, light that was even now caressing her skin as he longed to do himself. He didn't know the color of her eyes—hadn't been close enough yet to discover that secret—but he knew how they would gaze up at him, heavy-lidded with desire, but soft with the expression of her love.

And she *would* love him; he was certain of that. He'd watched her down by the lake while she created her stunning works of art. She imparted the love she felt for those creatures onto the canvas, just as she had with the image she'd painted of him. He'd felt that when he first viewed the portrait; something in the gentle brushstrokes made him feel that she had actually swept her hands over his back, down to his waist and thighs. She had somehow captured not only his image, but her feelings toward him—furtive, tentative, and definitely intrigued.

His cock was slick with his fluid—fluid that he hoped would affect her just as it had affected the women of his world—and his hands tightened around his cock, pumping faster, seeming to pull him forward as though seeking her out. Turning his profile toward her, he let her see what she was doing to him, and he felt a sudden gush of his fluids at the thought of her eyes on him. In his mind, these were no longer his hands, but hers, wrapping him in a firm tunnel, squeezing him hard, tightening so that he had to push even harder to slide through them.

He felt his balls tighten and his breathing grew coarse and ragged as he began purring—whether she could hear him or not. Widening his stance, he let his head fall back, his long, black curls tickling his backside the way hers would as she passed behind him. He wanted to know the feel of her, the taste of her. He knew her eyes were on him, their heated gaze exploring his body—and, knowing that he didn't need to be secretive any longer, he was no longer silent, letting his grunts of effort be as loud as they needed to be, letting her know what she was doing to him.

At last he felt it: the unmistakable signal of impending climax. With an accompanying roar that echoed across the still lake, his balls repeatedly squeezed out his snard in long, powerful arcs. He imagined it hitting her succulent breasts, her beautiful face, and her softly parted lips, and as she tasted it, he could almost see her expression of joy.

As he took in a deep, cleansing breath, he smiled. She had seen him, and he could smell her climax even from where he stood—could even hear her soft sighs of ecstasy. She would be his mate. It was only a matter of time.

Chapter 1

"DRUSILLA, *DARLING*," RALPH DRAWLED. "YOU SIMPLY *MUST* get away for a time. That horrid beast had no right to treat you in such a callous manner, and I have just the place for you, too—have already booked your passage! A quiet lake, cool woods, solitude, and the most fabulous birds your heart could desire."

This description didn't include a place to live, as Drusilla was quick to point out.

"Oh, but the house is absolutely charming!" he assured her. "All the amenities, and no worries, my dear. Everything taken care of to ensure your comfort."

Drusilla smiled grimly. "And just where is this paradise?" The last jaunt Ralph had sent her on had been a major fiasco—unbearable heat, no indoor plumbing, and, worst of all, no birds. Being a renowned wildlife artist, she simply *had* to have birds, and waterfowl, in particular, since they were her specialty.

"Barada Seven," he replied. "Charming natives, though not attractive in any way—quite hideous, actually—but very eager to please. Primitive living conditions, of course—small villages scattered along the coastline, very little technology—but apparently, along with the birds, their claim to fame is something called fuuslak juice, which is supposed to make even the sourest disposition turn positively sunny. They've only recently begun to develop their offworld tourist industry and will do their utmost to make your stay memorable."

"Memorable doesn't necessarily mean good," Drusilla said under her breath.

"What was that, dear?" Ralph asked, his most winning smile reaching out to her from the viewscreen. "I don't believe I caught that last bit."

Drusilla smiled back, but she wasn't fooled. Ralph always heard her mutterings. She knew this because he tended to repeat them—rarely to her, but nearly always to his friends, who then made a list of them; some had become catchphrases within the art world. Authorship was rarely traced back to her—that credit was nearly always given to Ralph—but she recognized one of her own comments when she heard it. "Nothing important, Ralph," she replied. "I'm sure Barada will be a bird-watching paradise."

"And I promise you'll forget all about Drab Dave and come back all fresh and new!" Ralph paused, tapping his elegant chin reflectively. "If only I knew of *someone* who could be waiting for you when you return. I must give it some thought."

Since the "Drab Dave" episode had been the result of one of Ralph's carefully casual introductions, Drusilla doubted that the next one would be any different. Ralph might have been the head of London's largest and most prestigious art gallery, which put him in the way of meeting art lovers from all over the galaxy, but most of his friends preferred a different sort of companionship than she was able to provide. This, unfortunately, had turned out to be the case with Dave. He'd liked the idea of his name being connected with that of a famous artist, but that was about the *only* way he wanted to be connected with her.

"You do that, Ralph," she said, knowing that her approval wasn't a requirement. One of the joys of Ralph's existence was in pairing up buyers with the perfect painting, but he was also an enthusiastic match-maker—and though, in Drusilla's opinion, he wasn't any good at it, it didn't affect his dedication. How Ralph, of all people, could have made such a blatant error when he introduced her to Dave was beyond her.

"Oh, I will," he promised. Running a careless hand through his perfectly styled blond locks, he added, "Should be *someone* around here who likes auburn hair and green eyes... Perhaps whoever buys that Tehern painting—you know, the one that looks just like you?"

"Ralph," Drusilla said patiently, "that *is* a painting of me." As an art dealer, Ralph should have known this, but since Tehern was a Cubist, Drusilla would have been astonished if anyone else ever realized it—let alone wanted to meet her as a result.

Laughing delightedly, he trilled, "How silly of me not to remember that! You know, I'm surprised you haven't modeled for more artists. I think you're the loveliest woman of my acquaintance."

"Why, thank you, Ralph," Drusilla said promptly, though she didn't believe a word of it. "That's very sweet of you." Drusilla had heard too many remarks from her mother about being skinny to ever consider herself in that light—and Tehern's painting had done nothing to alter her opinion. In it, she looked more like a collection of sticks with a large red brick perched on top than a woman, and her jade-green eyes had simply looked like… well, two blocks of jade—but with a flattering hexagonal cut, as Tehern had been quick to point out to her. She hadn't done any modeling since then, though an Impressionist from Io had once asked very nicely. Her reply had been just as polite, but since Ionian Impressionism focused entirely upon nudes—and Drusilla had no desire to be depicted as a *nude* stick person—she refused, though she did allow him to buy her a drink. This was a mistake in itself because, when they've been imbibing freely, Ionians tend to demonstrate just why it is that they prefer painting nudes. Following that episode, Drusilla made a mental note never to visit Io.

"So, what about it, Drusie?" Ralph said brightly. "Going to go to Barada?"

Drusilla hated to admit it, but there was no reason not to. She was used to traveling to distant locales in search of subjects for her paintings and didn't even have a plant that would need watering while she was gone. And there was that thing with Dave… She might have to disappear for *months* to live that one down.

"Sure, Ralph," she replied. "Just tell me the rest of it."

"Well, now, you'll need to take your paints—I'll have the canvases shipped on ahead, of course. And be sure to take your swimsuit, though if my information is correct, you could swim in the nude and no one would see you," he tittered. "They speak the Standard Tongue, so you won't need a translator, though it *is* a second language for them. Oh, and there's no need for insect repellent. No biting flies or mosquitoes of any kind! Can you imagine?"

Since Drusilla had been nearly eaten alive by bugs in many of the places she'd visited to paint the waterfowl, she found this hard to believe. "No, I can't," she replied, deciding to take some repellent along with her anyway. "But it sounds wonderful."

"And you haven't even *seen* the birds yet!" he exclaimed, his enthusiasm growing. "They're absolutely gorgeous!" This was really all Drusilla needed to hear to get her hooked on the plan. Her idea of heaven was to lie beside a lake and watch birds all day long. Not very exciting to others, perhaps, but it was something she enjoyed.

"I'm sure they are," she said. "And thank you, Ralph. You're a peach."

Smiling gleefully, he said, "I'll send you the rest of the info in a moment. It'll be fabulous. Have a wonderful trip!"

"I'll do that," she replied as he rang off.

Drusilla leaned back in her chair with a sigh. Getting away was a good idea, and one she should have thought of herself. Ralph, bless his heart, looked after her far better than she did. There were times when she didn't eat more than a few bites for days on end if she was caught up in a painting, and she often went to bed with her arm stiff and sore from holding the brush. She sometimes secretly wished to be like normal people and find enjoyment doing something else, but art was her life, her passion, and it wouldn't let her go long enough to discover any other interests—or even realize that her current boyfriend preferred the company of other men.

Glancing around her studio, Drusilla noted that, unlike her new destination, when it came to comforts and amenities, it could boast very few; all it really had to recommend itself was good light and plenty of space.

She rarely ventured out unless she was going off to paint and wondered if it was even possible for her to take a vacation—a true vacation where she didn't feel the need to do at least a quick sketch of every bird she laid eyes on. She'd been to a casino once at the instigation of some friends, and while she'd come away a good deal richer than when she arrived, she didn't understand the appeal. Drusilla had tried other leisure activities and knew that while other people enjoyed myriad pleasures, she'd yet to find even one that could compare with the rush of excitement she felt when she caught a fleeting glimpse of brilliant plumage hidden among the green leaves of a forest or gracing the surface of a quiet pond. Her friends often teased her about her artistic temperament, but they didn't understand it—and sometimes, neither did she.

Her parents hadn't known what to make of her, and Drusilla felt no urge to have a family of her own, knowing that they wouldn't understand her any better than anyone else did. She had more in common with other artists, but, like her, they were often too caught up in their own work to fall in love.

So it was that at thirty-four, Drusilla Chevrault was completely unattached and unlikely to ever become a wife to anyone—which was okay with her, if only she didn't have the sneaking suspicion that something was missing…

———

Arriving on Barada Seven, Drusilla was at once struck by the beauty of the planet and the homeliness of its inhabitants. The mountains in the distance were snow-capped and breathtaking, the sky was a brilliant shade of purple, which was reflected in the vast ocean, and the riotous green of the jungle promised birds galore, but the people looked like skinny, wart-covered, orange toads. Drusilla wondered how they managed to talk with mouths nearly the full width of their heads and tongues that were forked like a snake's, but what was even more remarkable was how nimble their fingers were. She was fascinated by them—had never seen any species that could move so quickly, their hands almost a blur whenever dexterity was required.

"You guys must paint really fast," she said to the Baradan who was checking her passport.

When he grinned at her, his face seemed to split in half. "We do many things quickly," he said—and left it at that. It might have been a suggestive remark, or a very true one, Drusilla didn't know, but she had an idea that this might be the reason there were no mosquitoes on Barada; they'd all been slapped out of existence long ago.

One attribute the natives did have was pleasant, almost musical voices. The males varied from bass to tenor, the females from alto to soprano, and, if you closed your eyes, you could imagine you were being addressed by the most beautiful creatures in the galaxy. Their style of dress was simple—tiny little shorts for the males and shorts with a scarf tied around the upper torso for the females—and while this provided an easy way to differentiate the sexes, it did nothing to enhance their attractiveness. Drusilla decided that where she would be staying, she wouldn't be around them enough to ever become accustomed to their appearance, but thought that, given their beautiful voices, it might be possible with time.

After assuring the officials that she had no weapons in her possession, she exchanged some standard credits for the local currency, called triplaks, which appeared to be nothing more than carved pebbles, and received her visitor's permit along with a complimentary cup of fuuslak juice. It might not have improved her disposition appreciably, but it did have a pleasant taste and seemed to wash away the fatigue of her journey, leaving her feeling refreshed and revitalized.

Upon leaving the thatched hut that served as immigration office, spaceport control tower, and welcome center, she was immediately swarmed by a throng of Baradan women and children. All were dressed in the scant native style, and several of the children had rat-like monkeys perched on their shoulders.

"Would you like some fruit?" one of the children asked. "Only one triplak for six bolaka fruits." Upon hearing this, one of the women gasped and waved her hands in a delicate dance, after which the child added, "I misspoke; that will be *ten* bolaka fruits for one triplak."

Drusilla smiled down at the mischievous boy. "Do you offer free samples?"

The child looked up at her questioningly. "I do not understand."

"Well, what if I don't like bolaka fruit?"

The boy shrugged. "Then someone else will buy them."

"Good point," she conceded. Handing the boy one of the pebbles, she added, "Just be sure they're ripe."

He grinned at her, his snake's tongue curling over his lower lip. Setting down his pet, he waved his hands in a signal to the animal, which then scampered up a nearby tree. "He will not take long," the boy said.

"What is your name?" Drusilla asked.

"Roger," the boy replied.

"You're kidding me, right?"

"Why? Does my name sound so odd to you?"

"Not really," Drusilla said dryly, "which is why it seems so odd."

"You must come to the market," one of the women prodded. "There you will find anything you need."

"I'm sure I will," Drusilla said, eying the woman's clothing with interest. "How many triplaks for a shirt?"

"Only two," she replied. "But it will look quite lovely on you."

The tiny scrap of fabric the women wore to cover their breasts wouldn't have been much larger than an armband on a Terran; even someone as small as Drusilla would have required two or three of them tied together. "I'll think about it," Drusilla said as she noticed Roger's monkey returning with a bag of fruit.

"Here is your bolaka," Roger said as he retrieved the fruits from his pet. "What is your name?"

"Drusilla," she replied, accepting the bag.

This revelation drew a great many sighs from the native women. "Drusilla," an obviously pregnant female said, drawing the name out as though each syllable had a distinct flavor. "My child will be called Drusilla," she said in a lilting tone as the other women nodded in agreement.

"Better hope it's a girl," Drusilla muttered. Her next thought was to wonder whether the Baradans were mammalian or oviparous, but she wasn't quite sure how to phrase the question, opting, instead, for the time-honored: "And when is your baby due?"

"Not for another month," the woman replied. "This will be my first child, and what to name her has been a great worry of mine."

"Glad I could help," Drusilla said. "How do you know it's a girl—?" Drusilla left the sentence dangling, hoping for a name—and perhaps more information.

"What do you—oh, of course!" the woman said with a musical giggle. "I am called Crystal, and we Baradans always have a female child first. It is not so with your species?"

"Well, no—at least, not naturally," Drusilla admitted. "It can be done, of course, but that's by choice. So, a girl first and then a boy, huh? Do they alternate with subsequent births?"

The woman who had corrected Roger nodded. "Roger is my second son," she said proudly, adding, "I am called Maria."

"You have a fine son, Maria," Drusilla said, hoping she was making the correct reply. Turning to the boy, she went on, "And that's a pretty well-trained monkey you've got there, Roger. How did you teach him to do that?"

Roger stared at her blankly for a moment. "You mean my srakie?" he asked finally and then burst out laughing as he and his chums started off.

"No, really," Drusilla called after them. "That's amazing. How do you do that?"

Roger just waved his hands and ran off into the trees.

"How very odd," she commented.

"We will visit you soon," Crystal said eagerly.

"Or we will see you at the market," Maria added as the others nodded in approval.

Still staring after Roger, Drusilla nodded absently. She had no desire for company just yet—and wasn't sure she needed anything from the market either—but, if nothing else, she could buy some of the local "shirts" to use as handkerchiefs.

As the women dispersed, Drusilla was met by another Baradan male whose job it was to take her to the lake house. He appeared younger than the first one—his orange skin was brighter, less blemished. Wearing nothing but a pair of shorts, and not even sandals on his flat, flipper-like feet, he introduced himself as Lester, which confirmed Drusilla's suspicion that there was a fascination with Terran culture among the Baradans— at least with respect to names—that Ralph had known nothing about. Leading her out to a truck so antiquated as to actually have wheels, he then loaded it with a speed that left Drusilla stunned, and, seeming bent on discovering as many details about Drusilla's life as he could in as little time as possible, he fired six questions at her before she had a chance to reply.

As she climbed into the passenger seat, he was finally quiet long enough for her to answer him: "Yes, I'm female. No, I don't have a mate. No, I don't have any children. Yes, I'm a painter. No, I don't want another cup of fuuslak juice, and, thank you very much, but I don't think I'll be needing a massage."

"Just checking!" Lester said in his rich baritone. "You never know when it comes to offworlders. I might end up stealing someone else's mate or even trying to mate with another male!" He cackled with laughter at the thought of such nonsense and fired up the engine.

Drusilla had been to many different worlds, and though this wasn't the first time she'd been seen as a conquest of sorts—sex with an alien was still an interesting enough concept to gain her all sorts of offers—she'd never been bounced along on such a wild ride through a jungle before. Having left the spaceport, which was little more than an open field near the shore of one of Barada's many oceans, she glanced nervously at the dense jungle undergrowth and wondered again just how much Ralph had known about the planet he'd sent her to. There were no houses on the ground that she could see, only dwellings high in the trees with nets and vines hanging down from them, which had Drusilla trying to imagine what manner of creatures had been nasty enough to drive the Baradans up into the boughs.

Lester noticed her apprehension and said informatively, "There are no dangerous animals here and the house is very secure. You will be quite safe." He hitched his skinny butt uncomfortably on the seat before adding, "But I must tell you that there is an eltran living in the lake."

Drusilla failed to see how a thatched hut could ever be considered "secure" but let that pass for the moment in favor of something that sounded far more disturbing. "An eltran?" she echoed. "What's that? Some sort of man-eating fish?"

"No," Lester replied sadly. "If they were only fish, it would be much easier to control them."

"Control?"

"They are amphibians," he replied. "They live in lakes but can walk through the jungle from lake to lake if needed." He shook his head and let out an exasperated sigh. "They are very… annoying."

"Really?" she said curiously. "How so?"

"You will see," Lester replied mysteriously. "I have no way of knowing how your species will react, but we consider them to be pests. Unfortunately, it is impossible to get them to leave a lake once they've taken up residence."

"If they're such pests, why don't you just kill them?"

Lester drew back in horror and the truck lurched on its wheels, nearly hitting a tree. Wrestling with the wheel, Lester got back on the track before he replied. "They are an intelligent life form," he protested. "To kill one would be a terrible crime!"

"Forgive me," Drusilla said quickly. "I didn't understand."

Though Lester seemed somewhat mollified by this explanation, Drusilla wondered if he was secretly regretting having opened his world to such a callous individual, and his next statement proved it.

"My planet is a very peaceful one, and letting warlike species visit here is sometimes… disturbing."

Drusilla smiled. "The people of Earth have been very war-like in the past, but we're improving." Noting Lester's sidelong glance, she added, "And yes, we look pretty weird too, don't we?"

"You are very odd," Lester agreed. "Your skin is strangely white, and that peculiar growth from your heads looks untidy." Apparently determined to remain diplomatic, he smiled disarmingly and said, "I'm sure we Baradans appear strange to you, as well."

"A little," Drusilla agreed. "Tell me something; if this is such a peaceful planet, why does the house have to be so secure?"

Lester laughed musically. "We did that so visitors would feel safe in coming here. It really wasn't necessary. There is nothing to fear."

"No thieves or murderers?"

"No," Lester said firmly. "And we have no weapons either."

Drusilla nodded. "Yes, I knew about the weapons ban. It's nice to know there aren't any guns here. There aren't many places that can say that."

Lester's smile, though peculiar, was undoubtedly rueful. "It is very sad to think that the inhabitants of so many worlds can't get along with one another."

"But you don't get along with eltrans very well, do you?"

Lester shrugged his shoulders in a jerky gesture—a movement that suggested it wasn't natural for him. "We manage to coexist," he said simply. "They tend to keep to themselves most of the time. It is only when they venture nearer to our homes that we notice them at all. The lakes, which they inhabit, are further inland, and most Baradans prefer to live near the shore, where the fuuslak plants grow." Gesturing toward the tangled path that lay ahead, he added, "This lake house is very remote."

As Drusilla was soon to learn. She probably would have been very tired—not to mention lost—if she'd attempted the journey on foot. There would be no question of making a quick run to the store for anything she might have forgotten. She hoped that the house was well-provisioned because Lester hadn't loaded anything but her own belongings onto his old truck. Looking down at her bag of bolaka, Drusilla wondered if she should have gotten two triplaks' worth. Perhaps she would need to visit the market after all. "Um, what about food?" she ventured.

"The house has a very large stasis unit," he said proudly. "You will have more than enough for your entire stay."

Looking at Lester, who appeared to be little more than skin and bones, Drusilla wondered how much someone like that would consider enough. She was frugal with food, but *still*… "How much is that?"

"We have researched your species," he said with a quick nod and another face-splitting smile. "We Baradans eat only fruit, but we know that you Terrans eat a variety of foods. There is enough stored there to feed four Terrans for six months. You will only be here for three, but if there is anything else you need, there is a comlink. You have only to ask, and it will be brought to you."

And would no doubt be included on the bill with a vengeance. Ralph hadn't told her what all of this would cost, but Drusilla suspected that he planned to make it all back on the paintings he sold. These must be some really spectacular birds, she thought idly.

"What do I do if I get sick or hurt?"

"The Terran trader who delivered the food included medical supplies, which are in the house if you have need of them," Lester said. "There are many healers on Barada, though I do not believe any of them have ever treated anyone from Earth."

"My, how reassuring," Drusilla commented.

Lester went on as though he hadn't heard her, making Drusilla wonder if perhaps sarcasm was as foreign a concept on Barada as war. "We have contact with other worlds, and what our healers don't know, they can always ask. But I will bring this to the attention of the local doctor."

"Well, I'm pretty sure I won't need anything," she said, hoping she wasn't jinxing herself, "but it's nice to know you're prepared."

"It would be very bad for business if our first Terran visitor were to die of some trivial malady or injury during her stay." Eyeing her curiously, he added, "You seem healthy enough, but your skin is so pale."

"Don't worry," she said, laughing. "My pale skin isn't the result of some lingering illness. It's natural."

Lester looked at her doubtfully. "Perhaps our research into your species wasn't as thorough as it should have been."

"I'm sure I'll be fine," Drusilla said, though she couldn't help but wonder if Baradan medicine might kill rather than cure her. She'd been to several different planets over the years—and had never been sick—but none that hadn't been frequented by Terrans for some time. She reassured herself with the knowledge that Ralph would never intentionally put her at risk and he always had her best interests at heart—*nearly* always—but he might not have fully understood the details.

Leaning forward as the truck broke free of the jungle and the house finally came into view, Drusilla sincerely hoped that the birds would make it all worthwhile—Ralph had been quite sure they would, but he'd been wrong before.

Unfortunately, neither of them knew anything about the cats.

Chapter 2

MANX WATCHED WITH A GRIM SMILE AS THE BATTERED OLD truck drove up to the house, undoubtedly bringing another tourist. He hoped this one's stay would be short, but having endured far greater hardships since his escape from slavery, Manx knew he could handle it indefinitely. The house was nice, of course, and though he'd been secretly living there off and on ever since it was built, roughing it came easily to him. He was relatively safe on Barada—he'd never been to a more peaceful world—and probably could have come out of hiding; however, though the natives might not sell him out to the Nedwut bounty hunters, they wouldn't be able to stop them from killing him either.

He wasn't well-armed; Manx's only weapons were his knife and bow, neither of which would be an adequate defense against the Nedwut pulse rifles. His only saving grace had been his highly developed sense of smell—so far, he'd always been able to pick up their peculiar stench quickly enough to keep out of their range.

Still, that last band had nearly had him until he'd stowed away on the ship bound for Barada Seven. Stealth was another of his particular talents; Manx could sneak up on any animal without startling it, and while he had managed to keep himself fed in that manner, it was also quite useful when attempting to board a ship he had no business being on.

Peering around the trunk of a tree, he watched as the visitor got out of the truck, his green, feline eyes widening as he noted the feminine form. His heart nearly stopped as he first thought she might be one of his own kind, but as she turned in his direction, he saw that her eyes were not those of a Zetithian, and his heart sank. In all the years since his planet was destroyed, he'd never seen another Zetithian, but he had never encountered a species like this one either. She was much more interesting than the ugly orange locals, and he watched, spellbound, as she paused to push a stray tendril of dark red hair back from her face. Small and slender, she had an air of fragility about her that instantly made Manx want to protect her from… anything. He was standing upwind from her, so he couldn't judge her by her scent, but he found her appearance pleasing. Perhaps he wouldn't disappear into the jungle just yet.

She smiled at the Baradan, revealing lovely white teeth, but no fangs, and, unlike his, her ears were rounded at the tips. No, she wasn't Zetithian; but there was something about her…

Obviously, she was less fragile than she seemed because she hoisted a heavy bag onto her shoulder with no difficulty whatsoever. The Baradan was insisting that she allow him to carry it, but she seemed capable enough, ignoring his protests as she walked toward the house. *Stubborn*, Manx decided. He liked that in a female. Wetting his lips with his tongue, he wondered how she would taste, and more than that, how she would *smell*. He hadn't breathed in the aroma of a female in several years—not one that aroused him, anyway. It took the scent of feminine desire to arouse a Zetithian male, but Manx was slightly different. He'd forgotten which planet he'd been living on at the time, but he'd learned something then that his brethren never had; he could hold the scent of a woman in his head long enough to maintain his erection and bring himself to climax—whether she was still with him or not. Studying this new visitor carefully, he knew she was physically appealing, but would her aroma be as intoxicating?

Revising his original wish, he hoped her stay there would be a long one. He wanted to learn the answers to those questions before she left.

Moving silently through the trees, Manx headed for the lake, but then stopped short as he remembered Zef. The eltran might give him away—might tell her about him, warn her that he was there in the trees, watching her. Manx was fairly certain that Zef had told no one else of his existence, but Zef was an odd creature; who knew what he might decide to do? And this woman might be one who would betray him to the Nedwuts if they ever came looking for him. Not intentionally, perhaps, but the hairy, snarling beasts could be very intimidating. Would she be able to stand up to them?

Manx knew he couldn't risk it, not for her safety or his own. With a resigned sigh, he melted into the jungle.

———

Drusilla stood in the center of the house, viewing her surroundings with awe. "This is a very nice place you've got here, Lester," she said, turning on her heel as she took it all in. "All I expected was a little cabin in the woods—*nothing* like this!"

"You did not believe the advertisement?" Lester said with surprise. "We included many images."

"I never actually saw it," Drusilla admitted. "Someone else made the arrangements for me." All the comforts and amenities, Ralph had said. "He wasn't kidding when he said it had everything—including canvases. There must be at least fifty of them," she added with a gesture toward the stack just inside the door. Ralph obviously had great expectations for her visit. She wondered what else he'd had delivered.

"We did our best to incorporate things that many species would find necessary," he said. Leaning forward to peer at her through his bulbous eyes, he made a sweeping gesture with a blurry wave of his hands. "Is there anything missing?"

"Just the private landing pad for a starship," Drusilla said absently. "Haven't got a ship, though, so I don't think I'll complain." She gazed up at the soaring, vaulted ceiling, thinking that a much taller humanoid than she would have found it accommodating, and a giraffe would have been tickled pink with it. The living room was palatial, with numerous comfortable-looking sofas and chairs interspersed with a few highly polished tables accented with vases of fresh flowers. The wall facing the lake was transparent and made her feel as if she was right out on the water, rather than the actual thirty meters away. The kitchen contained all of the usual appliances, plus some equipment Drusilla had never seen before, and, as promised, the stasis unit had enough food stored in it for a small army. The huge bathroom was sparkling clean, with beautiful brass fixtures and a tub that would have accommodated a dolphin. There was also a shower that sprayed water into a shallow wading pool, along with a sonic shower for the more hirsute clientele. There were four bedrooms with the largest, softest, most luxurious beds imaginable, complete with ceiling fans. The front windows looked out into the trees and the patio boasted a built-in grill with an elegant table and chairs under a tented roof as well as two capacious hot tubs—one full of water, the other filled with hot, bubbling mud.

Having viewed the interior, Lester led the way through the door to the deck, and from there she looked down on the sparkling lake, complete with a dock and a pontoon boat big enough for a party. There was even a sliding board for jumping into the lake.

"Most everything is voice-activated, and there is a droid and a computer to manage the house, but I will show you how everything operates before I leave," Lester said helpfully. "If you ever have any questions, there are instructions you can read, or you can use the comlink to call me."

Drusilla was still gazing out over the lake as he spoke, and she nodded absently, having just seen a bird skimming the water, searching for fish. She blinked, scarcely believing her eyes as another swooped in to follow the first. *"Oh my God,"* she whispered hoarsely. "They *can't* be real!"

Lester seemed taken aback by her comment and peered at her curiously, tilting his head to one side while his forked tongue flicked in a nervous gesture. "Real? But, of course they are real! Why would you think otherwise?"

"That's the sort of question a person asks when they think they may have just died and gone to heaven, Lester."

The birds were huge—with a two-meter wingspan and legs easily another meter in length—but that wasn't what made them so remarkable. They were every bit as orange as Lester was, with sparkling gold crests like a cockatoo and bills similar to a pelican's, but far more streamlined and graceful. *"Beautiful,"* she whispered.

Lester took a step backward as though determined to distance himself from what might be contagious insanity. "You think you have *died?"*

"Not really, Lester," Drusilla said with a smile. "It's just one of those Terran expressions that no one else seems to understand." She recalled saying something similar on another planet known for its birds, and her driver had taken her directly to a hospital—had her checked in and everything before she realized it wasn't a hotel. Gesturing toward the lake, she added, "It's just that those birds are about the most beautiful I've ever seen—and I've seen quite a few."

"Those birds?" Lester scoffed. "They are not the most beautiful we have here. You should see the warbirds."

"Warbirds?" she echoed. "I suppose that means they can't get along with each other?"

"Sadly, yes," Lester replied. "They fight all the time and make strange noises in the night."

"Sounds like some neighbors of mine," Drusilla murmured.

"What did you say?"

"Nothing," she said with a dismissive wave. "Nothing important, anyway."

Then Lester seemed to think of something else and his fingers began beating the air so rapidly Drusilla thought he might actually take flight. "I must introduce you to Zef."

"Zef?" she echoed. "Is that the name of the house droid?"

"No," Lester replied morosely. "The house droid is called Klog. Zef is the eltran."

His expression of obvious distaste had Drusilla wondering just what kind of disgusting creature could make a Baradan feel such revulsion.

"His name is Zefa'gu," Lester confided. "But everyone calls him Zef."

"Everyone?" she said, glancing around. "Who else comes out here?" Ralph's suggestion that she could swim in the nude was becoming less of a possibility with each passing moment.

"Oh," Lester said with another blurry, fan-like motion of his hands. "You will not be bothered. Perhaps not even by Zef. The last family to stay here never even saw him."

"Maybe he's gone," Drusilla said hopefully. "Moved on to another lake?"

Lester shook his head sadly. "I do not think so."

"Well, then," Drusilla said with an air of resignation, "let's get on with it."

Lester led the way down the stairs to the beach with all the gloom of one going to visit a much despised relative. As he approached the shore, Lester tossed a stone into the water and waited. "Zef will not be long," he said morosely. "He knows me."

Drusilla watched anxiously as the ripples spread across the lake. Nothing happened except that a flock of brightly painted butterflies with wings as big as her hands flew past, one of them deciding that Drusilla's head was a nice perch. Lester waved his hands and it flew off to join the others. "They do not bite," Lester said as he threw another rock.

"How the hell do you expect me to sleep with all that noise?" a raspy voice called out from further down the shore. "Oh… Lester… it's *you.*"

From the sound of it, Zef wasn't terribly happy to see Lester either. "Yes," Lester said with a note of forced cheerfulness. "I have a new tenant for the house. This is Drusilla Chevrault. She is Terran."

Drusilla watched with speechless horror as a lumpy green snake-like creature emerged from the water to stand in the shallows on two big flippers that seemed to be growing out of its tortoise-like head. Its slimy skin had black welts all over it, making it look like a slug with a bad case of poison ivy.

"And I thought the *other* natives were homely," Drusilla said under her breath. Lester didn't catch her comment, but Zef did. Obviously he had ears there somewhere; Drusilla just couldn't tell where they were.

"What'd ya say that for?" Zef demanded. "Homely? *Homely!* I'll show you *homely!* Ever seen the wet, naked backside of a Baradan? Now *that's* homely! And I have to look at it every time one of them swims in my lake. Turn around and drop those pants and show her, Lester!"

Lester, of course, did nothing of the kind. Smiling bleakly, he went on as though neither of the other two had spoken. "Drusilla, this is Zefa'gu, or Zef."

"Go on, you bony little orange—" Zef stopped there, looking up at Drusilla. "Where'd you say you were from?"

"I didn't," Drusilla replied. "But I am from Earth."

"Got any lakes there?"

"Thousands of them," Drusilla reported. "Some of them so big they might as well be oceans."

"Any eltrans?"

"Not that I know of," she said gratefully. She was sure she'd have heard of it if there had been.

Zef's mouth opened, revealing a flat, slobbery tongue and a few broken teeth. "Sounds like a good place for a vacation," he said and then made a loud, crashing, croaking sound that startled Drusilla and made Lester cringe.

Drusilla stared at the open mouth with horror, until she realized he was either laughing, or smiling—or both.

Then her horror intensified. The most stunning birds she'd ever seen and now *this* creature! To paint the birds, she would be setting up her easel by the shore—and have to listen to him yakking at her all the time! She'd been looking forward to a swim too—until now. The thought of swimming in the same lake as this... *thing*... gave her the creeps. She hoped he liked to sleep a lot—preferably during the day.

"Drusilla will be here for three months," Lester went on. "She paints pictures of birds."

"Now *there's* a useless occupation," Zef declared.

"I make plenty of money doing it, though," she defended herself.

"Really?" said Zef. "You get *paid* for doing shit like that?"

"Quite a lot, actually," Drusilla conceded. "Unlike many other artists, I'm not exactly starving."

"Well, you sure as hell look like it," Zef said, eyeing her slender form. "Almost as bad as these scrawny Baradans."

Drusilla considered the comparison insulting but couldn't very well say so without offending Lester. "Well, it was nice to meet you, Zef," Drusilla said, doing her best to seem gracious. "I'm sure we'll be seeing more of each other."

"Well, looking at you will be a damn sight better than looking at the rest of the weird little wankers that live around here!" Zef said grudgingly. "You take a good, long look at Lester's ass and see if you don't agree."

"I need to get back to my village soon," Lester said abruptly, taking Drusilla's arm to steer her back toward the house. "Come, I have more to show you."

As they left the shore, Zef called after them, "That's it, Lester! Go on! Get your bony little butt out of my sight! It's pitiful, I tell you! *Pit-i-ful!*" His hideous laugh followed them.

"Where do they learn to talk like that?" Drusilla asked, fighting the urge to cover her ears.

"From what others have said to them, I'm sure," Lester replied. "His language has grown much more colorful since the first visitors to the lake house." Lester's hands were moving so fast that his fingers seemed as one. "A trio of Arconian sailors on leave," he confided. "They had women with them, and must have had speech with him, but none of the other visitors have liked Zef at all."

"I can't imagine why," Drusilla said dryly. "Must make it a lot harder to rent the house."

Lester's fingers were now all but invisible. "We do not include mention of him in the advertisement," he said.

"I don't blame you a bit," Drusilla said frankly. "Nice lake, beautiful house, fabulous birds… no, I don't think

I'd mention him either." She paused as another thought occurred to her. "Fuuslak juice doesn't work on eltrans, does it?"

"Sadly, no," said Lester. "There are many things that do not 'work' on them."

"Well, I'm sure I'll get used to him," Drusilla said with a shrug. "I mean, after all, how bad could it be?"

Lester looked at her in surprise. "You will stay?"

Once she'd seen the birds, leaving was never an option. "Yes, I'm staying," she said firmly. "I'm sure Zef and I will get along fine… eventually."

"If you do," Lester said ominously, "you will be the first."

Which wasn't true at all. Manx had not only gotten along with Zef, he actually *liked* him. Observing the introductions from the cover of the trees, Manx's sharp ears were able to hear most of the conversation, except when the one called Drusilla spoke quietly to herself. He always got a kick out of watching others meet Zef for the first time, and this was no exception. It was all he could do to keep from laughing out loud.

Manx knew that Zef liked him too, and, for all anyone knew, he might have liked Drusilla, but he certainly didn't care for Lester.

Unlike the Baradans, Manx couldn't afford to be choosy about his companions. He'd seen plenty of animals on this world, but none that were able to talk the way Zef could. Conversation had been one thing Manx missed since landing on Barada, and, so far, Zef was the only one he'd spoken with, even though he'd been there since long before Zef arrived and the house was built.

It was lonely being on the run and never knowing whom you could trust. Manx had made a few mistakes along those lines in the past and had learned to avoid them. The last world he'd been on, he'd led an almost normal life until the Nedwuts showed up. He'd been told that they weren't allowed to land there, but Nedwuts had a tendency to ignore the regulations. The suspicion that they had ignored the rules in order to track him down— and would undoubtedly do so again—haunted Manx. If that was the case, they could also have traced each ship that left the area when he disappeared and might show up on Barada, where his best defense was his ability to vanish into the jungle.

With that in mind, once construction of the house commenced, Manx had intended to move deeper into the jungle, but watching the workers create the beautiful structure intrigued him—aside from the fact that living all alone in the jungle was rather boring. Each night after the men left to return to the village, Manx explored the site, fascinated with the things they had built. As entertainment went, it wouldn't have interested most, but Manx was naturally curious and watched their progress with interest.

When the first visitors came, Manx made the mistake of assuming that they would be there permanently. He didn't like that idea, but Zef was able to enlighten him. Zef had arrived during the construction—much to Lester's dismay—and had been a big surprise to Manx, who had never met an aquatic creature that could speak, let alone pick up new languages so quickly. He'd learned a great deal from talking with the eltran, who had not the slightest fear of conversing with strangers and told him that the tenants of the house were to be temporary. This information both reassured and disturbed Manx; if they were temporary, it would mean that no one would stay long and that the house would be unoccupied at times, but it also meant that the turnover of guests might bring some who would know of the bounty on Zetithians and be inclined to either turn him over to the Nedwuts or pass on the knowledge of his whereabouts. Thus, this new source of social contacts was one Manx decided to avoid.

He had no choice but to interact with Zef, however, since the lake was the only source of water in the vicinity. To avoid Zef, he would have had to relocate, which he could have done in any case, but he had grown accustomed to the area, and it had become home to him.

Zef had come across this particular lake quite by accident, and was delighted to find that a house was being built there. However, it was some time before he became aware of Manx and, having once seen him come to the lake to drink, took to watching for him. The fact that Manx was capable of carving an elegant spear out of a long tree branch with nothing but his knife was fascinating, but even more fascinating was the fact that he could use it to catch fish. The fear that Manx might have speared *him* kept Zef out of range at first, but since Zef was gregarious by nature and had come to the lake looking for conversation, he decided to make the first move.

Manx's furtive behavior was puzzling but eventually led Zef to believe that he was hiding from someone, so he was cautious at first, merely sticking his head up out of the water in mute observation. Being quiet was difficult for any eltran, but he managed it somehow, at least until he finally decided that Manx was an intelligent being, perhaps even capable of speech. One night, he decided to test that theory.

"Like fish?" he said, hoping that Manx would understand.

Manx's head had snapped up in surprise. Narrowing his keen eyes, he scanned the area for the source, remaining silent but on the alert.

"Eat plants, myself," Zef said. "Like fish, though."

Manx said nothing.

"No, you haven't lost your mind," said Zef.

Seeing that Manx was about to run, Zef lost what little patience he possessed and growled, "Aw, come on, you stupid jerk! Answer me!"

This got a laugh from Manx, but nothing else.

"Yeah, you know what I'm saying, don't you, pretty boy?"

"Pretty boy?" Manx echoed. "You're talking to *me?*"

"See any other pretty boys around here?" Zef said. After waiting another moment or two, he asked, "Figured it out yet?"

"Figured what out?" Manx asked cautiously.

"Where I am, you dummy!"

"Uh, no," Manx replied. "I don't believe I have."

"No brains in that pretty head, huh?"

"I wouldn't say that." Manx's eyes scanned the dark surface of the lake until they lit on Zef, who knew he looked more like a rock sticking up out of the water than anything. "Got plenty of brains," he said, aiming his spear at the "rock."

"Ah, so you aren't so dumb after all," Zef said. "Very good."

"What are you?" Manx asked. "A talking rock?"

"Naw, I'm an eltran," Zef replied.

"Never heard of them," Manx said, clearly unenlightened by this revelation. "But then, I haven't lived here very long."

"I can see that," Zef observed. "And you aren't orange like the little skinny-butt natives. Offworlder?"

"Maybe," Manx replied.

"Lost?"

"No."

Zef paused, giving this further thought. "Not lost, not a native. So, what are you?"

"I'd rather not say," Manx said evasively.

"What? You think I'd blab it to the wrong sort?"

"Possibly."

"I can keep a secret," Zef said encouragingly. "Come on, pretty boy. At least tell me your name."

Manx grinned. "If I did, then you'd stop calling me 'pretty boy.'"

"Like that, huh?" Zef said with his odd crunching laugh.

"Been called a lot worse."

"Ah!" said Zef. "Thief? Murderer? Fish killer?"

"No comment."

"Diplomatic too, I see." Zef pondered his options and decided to introduce himself. "I am Zefa'gu," he said. "Come back in the daytime, and you will see why I'd think you were pretty."

"Look that bad, do you?" Manx said affably.

"Perfectly awful," Zef said sadly. "But I can't help it if I'm old and lumpy."

Peering past the surface and into the depths of the lake, Manx said, "I won't hold it against you, though you *are* very ugly."

Zef laughed. "Wondered how you could see well enough to spear fish at night! Good night vision. That's a plus."

"I've always thought so." Manx seemed to make a decision then, and lowered his spear. "My name is Manxarkodrath Panteris."

Zef crunched his jaws again. "Ha! And you think *I'm* ugly! If I had a name like that, I wouldn't tell anyone either."

"Yes, well, I'd appreciate it if you didn't pass on that information."

"I have already forgotten," Zef said genially. "That good enough for you?"

Manx nodded. "Where did you come from?" he asked. "I've never seen any others like you."

"Only one in this lake," Zef replied with a touch of regret. "Saw the house being built and wanted someone to talk to, so I thought I'd stay."

Manx sat down on the shore and began to eat one of the fish he'd speared. "It *is* a nice place," Manx agreed. "Warm climate, plenty to eat, and, best of all, no annoying insects. I've been on other planets where they would practically eat you alive."

"Eaten alive?" Zef echoed. "Sounds horrible."

"Well, they don't *really* eat you alive," Manx said. "It just seems that way. Believe me, you're much better off without them."

Zef watched intently as Manx finished his fish and tossed the remains of the bony carcass into the lake. Zef didn't want to appear greedy—at least, not at first—but he did take note of exactly where it landed. He would get it later, but for now he had a friendship to develop. "Do you like to talk?"

"Sure," Manx replied. "That's the one bad thing about living here."

"I love to talk," Zef said encouragingly. "I'll talk to you as much as you like."

"Well, just don't tell anyone else about me, and we'll get along fine."

"Mum's the word!" Zef declared. "I won't say a thing to anyone unless you ask me to." Peering carefully up at Manx, he said, "So, are we friends now? Might as well be friends now that we've met and all." Zef wasn't about to jeopardize a friendship with someone who could catch fish as easily as Manx, and especially one who didn't seem to care for the bones.

"Sure," said Manx. "I haven't had a friend in a very long time."

"Me either," Zef admitted, trying to remember if he'd *ever* had anyone he thought of as a friend. "So why are you here? Someone chasing you?"

"You could say that," Manx replied. "I've been hiding out for years. Someone set out to exterminate my people. There was a war, and our planet was destroyed. You'd think they could have left it at that, but they seem bent on killing all of us."

"That's terrible!" Zef exclaimed. "D'you know who did it?"

"No, but I know who's been hunting me," Manx said. "If any Nedwuts come around, just try to disappear."

"Nedwuts?" Zef echoed. "Don't believe I know what they are."

"That's probably for the best," said Manx. "You wouldn't like them."

"If they tried to kill my friend," Zef said staunchly, "I wouldn't like them at all."

Manx smiled, seeming to accept the fact that Zef meant what he said. "So, Zef," he began, "you say you like fish?"

"Oh, yes," Zef replied.

"Are you hungry?"

Zef snorted in reply. "I'm always hungry."

"Then hold very still," Manx said.

Zef froze in place as Manx neatly speared a nearby fish and then tossed it to him. At that moment, Zef knew he'd found a friend at last.

Having been given the grand tour and a fair orientation, Drusilla hoped she could remember everything Lester had told her, though she could always call him if she had any problems. Lester hadn't said for sure, but she hoped that Zef would leave her alone unless she threw rocks in the lake—which she would never do, in any case, because it would frighten away the birds. She had no intention of letting Zef run her off. She had to have at least a few paintings to show to Ralph because, while he might act like a little twit at times, he'd forked over plenty of credits to get her there and was undoubtedly expecting a good return on his investment. Drusilla could handle Zef as long as he didn't scare the birds away, and if he did, she'd make a deal with him somehow.

Drusilla considered setting up a blind to sit behind while she painted but hoped she wouldn't have to be quite so secretive. These birds didn't seem to be overly shy and sitting out on the open shore appealed to her. It was hot, but not unbearably so, and she had a big, floppy hat to protect herself from the sun. Taking holographic photos of the birds was another option—with some of the more easily startled species it was a must—but she preferred to paint from life whenever possible. It also helped her to get a better feel for the birds' behaviors, some of which she could capture in her paintings.

It had been said of Drusilla's work that she captured not only the image of the birds she painted, but also something of their inner nature. Some were mischievous, some shy, some cantankerous, and some were down-right belligerent, but they all had an expression of some behavioral trait. This was what had made her paintings so popular and, unlike many an artist, successful during her own lifetime.

Having assured herself that all of her painting supplies had survived the trip, she went to unpack her other belongings, only to discover that the house droid, Klog (an acronym for Keeping the Lid on the Garbage), had already done it for her. Klog was an uninteresting companion, and while he might have been capable of verbal communication, thus far, Drusilla hadn't heard him say very much. Klog would beep when he understood a request and then beep twice when the task was complete. After some time spent with Klog, she speculated that Zef would begin to seem like an old—and very welcome—friend.

While Klog got her settled in, Drusilla did some exploring, culminating with the room on the lower level that opened out onto the beach. Spacious and airy, the room boasted a wet bar complete with a refrigerator and a cabinet filled with snacks, a full bathroom, several cushy chaise lounges, and a couch that reclined. The floor was made of a smooth, slate tile and ceiling fans turned lazily overhead. Drusilla chose a lounge chair that provided the best view of the lake and plopped down on it, gazing out at the tranquil water. It was a peacefully beautiful scene, but, after a bit, staring at all that water made her thirsty. Lester had assured her that Klog could do just about anything, so she decided to give it a try.

"What have I got to lose?" she mused. Aloud, she called: "Klog! Would you bring me a glass of iced tea?" Thinking she should be more specific, she added: "Unsweetened."

From somewhere above stairs, she heard a beep signifying his acknowledgment and lay back to await the outcome. So far, Klog had proven to be capable of sorting clothing, but whether he was any good as a waiter remained to be seen. Some droids had difficulty not only interpreting speech but handling the details of carrying out a task; if nothing else, his choice might be good for a laugh. There were hundreds of different teas on Earth alone, and galaxy-wide, the number of varieties was staggering.

Klog, however, was obviously capable of making at least some of his own decisions—either that or there were no choices, for he hovered down the stairs, bringing her a full glass of perfectly brewed Darjeeling. Beeping twice, Klog then floated off to the beach, where he began picking up fallen twigs and leaves with his many arms and then, lowering his beehive-shaped body to the sand, he smoothed out the surface as he covered every square centimeter between the house and the water's edge. The footprints Drusilla and Lester had left behind were now completely obscured.

"So, do you do that every day?" she asked him as he reentered the house.

Klog replied with a cheerful chirp that could have meant yes or no, or even that he didn't understand. Drusilla knew she should study the operations manual more closely but decided to leave it for later. Having had good luck with the tea order, she moved on to the more complicated matter of what she would like for dinner.

"For dinner tonight, I'd like a grilled steak, medium rare; baked potato with butter, sour cream, and salt; a tossed salad with blue cheese dressing; and, oh, how about a little strawberry cheesecake for dessert?"

Klog beeped promptly and floated upstairs.

"Spooky," was Drusilla's comment. She'd dealt with plenty of droids before, but never one like this. His programming must have been very extensive—not to mention expensive—but how Klog had known she preferred Darjeeling was a mystery. It would be interesting to see what kind of steak she got. She hadn't specified a time either.

But right then, she didn't particularly care. Time wasn't a factor here. She would work through the days and sleep through the nights, relaxing when it suited her without having to conform to anyone's schedule but her own. Taking another sip of her deliciously refreshing tea, she then held her glass aloft and said, "Thanks, Ralph—wherever you are."

—⁓—

Manx was watching from the opposite end of the lake, his keen eyes able to discern Drusilla's reclining figure just inside the house. He hadn't been able to hear her toast, but if he had, he'd have seconded it, for Ralph had sent him the one thing he hadn't had in a very long time—a female whose scent already held traces of womanly desire, even though she could not possibly have known he was there. How she would smell when enticed by a male intrigued him—as much as he knew it would probably overwhelm him.

Inhaling deeply, he tried to single out the sex pheromones, but though there were hints of them, there weren't enough to stimulate an erection. He would have to be closer to her, which was risky—but so was everything in this life. He was beginning to question his earlier assessment that getting closer to her—perhaps even letting her catch a glimpse of him—was too much of a risk. She might be the bait for a very lethal trap, but there were times when instinct outweighed reason, and Manx suspected that this would turn out to be one of those times.

Manx was, in fact, already thinking about throwing caution to the wind and walking right into the house. No doors separated them; all he would have to do would be to circle the lake, and then he could see her up close, inhale her fragrance, and—

And what? Mate with her? Manx knew it wasn't that simple—not even with a woman of his own species. All females had to be tempted, teased, and enticed—and to her, he was not only a stranger, but an alien being. He would have to exert considerable efforts to overcome that obstacle, and though he hadn't had much practice of late, he certainly hadn't forgotten how—that ability was innate among Zetithians.

Manx closed his eyes, trying to remember how such a woman would taste. He'd gotten a better look at her when she'd gone down to the lake to meet Zef and hadn't been disappointed—in any way. Still, looks weren't everything, and he'd been misled before; just because he found a woman attractive didn't necessarily mean she would return the favor.

Manx suspected that if Zef ever got wind of the fact that he was interested in this alien female, he might talk—might tell her about the fugitive who lived in the jungle. And if she reported him to the Baradans, what would happen? Probably nothing. The odor of Nedwuts was one he hadn't picked up in a very long time—and never on this planet—but it was still a possibility. However, if Drusilla had no interest in him, any meeting between them would be a pointless and unnecessary risk. He needed more reassurance before he acted, and so, he resolved to wait.

Until she got up from her chair, walked out to the dock, and, after removing most of her clothing, dove into the lake.

Chapter 3

THE LAKE WAS EVERY BIT AS COOL AND REFRESHING AS IT looked and Drusilla swam lazily across the surface. The water was crystal clear. Zef was nowhere in sight—though now that she was actually in the water, she expected to hear his rasping voice at any moment. Or, what was worse, his slimy tail flicking at her legs.

Still, he seemed harmless enough—if he'd never eaten a "skinny-butt" Baradan, he probably wouldn't eat her either—and this lake was far too wonderful a thing to remain the domain of one, solitary eltran! She didn't care if he was watching her. Sure, he could talk, but he wasn't human and looked more like a big mudskipper than anything. Who cared what a mudskipper saw?

The way her undershirt and panties clung to her, Drusilla might as well have been naked. Next time, she would be, she decided. If she wanted to swim in the nude, she wouldn't let Zef stop her.

But Zef wasn't the only one watching. Manx was exercising considerable self-restraint; if he'd done what his instincts told him, he'd have gone after her—wading out to the depths and then swimming toward her, circling, teasing, perhaps even touching her. If she was receptive, he would take her in his arms and purr in her ear, telling her how she made him want her enough to risk his life for it. But not yet. He'd let Zef take her measure and determine from her interaction with the eltran what kind of woman she was. Would she be kind? Manx certainly hoped so, but knew that it was also possible that she might be mean, vindictive, and delight in his misfortune. She might enjoy watching the Nedwuts hunt him down like a wild animal and then haul him away to be killed.

No, Manx promised himself, she wouldn't be like that. Fate wouldn't be so cruel—wouldn't have left him free for this long only to be betrayed by a woman.

Manx held his breath as Drusilla swam back to the dock and nearly cried out as she climbed the ladder. Her thin clothing clung to her like a second skin as water dripped from her body, her deep red hair plastered to her back. Her rounded hips, the curve of her legs—in fact, the entire backside of her—was perfect in Manx's eyes. If fate had purposely set out to create a woman who could lure him to his death, this was the one. As far as he could tell, her only fault was that she wasn't Zetithian—though that might not turn out to be a fault in the end. No woman could be more difficult to entice than a Zetithian female—which meant that the males of his world had to be the most sexually appealing in the galaxy out of sheer necessity.

Which they were. It was possible that the planet Zetith had been destroyed for that very reason, but that didn't concern Manx at the moment. A Zetithian male's attractiveness to women might have been a curse, perhaps the downfall of his species, but it was also their purpose. There were others he had been able to resist approaching, but not this one. If she stayed long enough, they would meet. He wouldn't be able to stay away. Not now.

Drusilla looked over her shoulder and smiled. Even though Manx knew he was already well hidden, he drew back into the dappled shade of the trees. She couldn't see him, but why was she smiling? Was it because she'd enjoyed her swim, or the fact that Zef had kept quiet? And what was the reason for Zef's silence? Was he as speechless as Manx when confronted with such a vision? Zef didn't like the Baradans in his lake, but he might have enjoyed watching Drusilla swim enough to refrain from chasing her off. Stranger things had happened.

———

Drusilla had smiled for good reason; she had thoroughly enjoyed her swim and also the fact that Zef hadn't touched her, spoken, or even splashed. Perhaps she met with his approval. Either way, the lake was even better than the exotic birds. This could turn out to be more of a vacation than she'd ever dreamed.

Gathering up her clothes, Drusilla walked back to the house, stripping off her wet undergarments as she went. There was something so *liberating* about being naked, and she resolved to spend much of her time in that manner. There was no need to dress for Klog, after all, and Lester had promised to call before making a trip out to the lake if it became necessary—which, he had assured her, it probably wouldn't. Drusilla sighed blissfully. No men—no *people*—no worries; nothing but birds to paint and lakes to swim in. She might get bored eventually, but it would be a good kind of boredom—the sort that comes about when one's mind is truly at rest and there are no concerns other than what to eat for dinner.

Since she was already wet and naked, not to mention slightly chilly, a dip in the hot tub seemed in order. As

Drusilla sank into the bubbling foam, any tension that remained swiftly melted away.

She hadn't been there for more than ten minutes or so when she heard a musical laugh nearby. Her eyes flew open to discover a bevy of Baradan females staring at her from the deck on the opposite side of the tub. Noting that these seemed to be the same women she'd spoken with at the spaceport, she made a mental note that "soon" apparently meant "immediately" to a Baradan.

"We came to visit," Crystal said. "Perhaps this isn't the best time."

"Probably not," Drusilla said with a chuckle. "But since you're already here… Sorry I'm not dressed for company."

"Forgive the intrusion," Crystal said. "I believe you met Maria," she said, indicating Roger's mother, "and these ladies are Aretha and Dolly," she added, pointing to each of the others in turn.

"Why am I not surprised you'd like the name Drusilla?" she said dryly.

"Oh, yes, it is lovely!" Crystal said with enthusiasm. "Terran names have been very popular in this region ever since the first offworlders visited us," she confided. "And as for you not being dressed, that is why we came!" Holding up a strip of colorful fabric, she announced: "We made this especially for you!"

Thanking her lucky stars that she had never been particularly well-endowed in the boob department, Drusilla accepted it graciously, noting that they had apparently been paying attention to her size because it actually looked as though it would fit. "Sorry I don't have any…" Her voice trailed off as Klog hummed through the door to hand Crystal two triplaks.

"We have heard about this device," Aretha said with a gesture toward Klog. "Is it true that it knows what you want without being asked?"

"Seems that way so far," Drusilla replied. "He's pretty handy, but I think it's a little spooky myself."

Aretha laughed merrily, her musical voice making her laughter sound like part of an aria. "If only men could be like that!"

This got a chorus of giggles from all of them, which, again, sounded slightly operatic.

"Yes, but that's not always a good thing," Dolly pointed out. "I like to keep mine guessing."

"And which one would that be?" Aretha prompted.

Dolly stared at her friend in surprise. "There is only one!"

"They are all clamoring for her attention," Maria explained. "Ah, to be so young and lovely!"

Drusilla just smiled back, not daring to get into a discussion about just what made a female Baradan "lovely." She could see that Aretha and Maria appeared to be older than the other two, but the distinctions between lovely and not lovely were lost on her.

Fortunately, Klog provided a diversion by firing up the grill.

"Do you always heat your food before eating it?" Dolly asked curiously as she ventured closer to the grill.

"Her people not only heat it," Aretha said knowledgeably, "but they eat meat too."

Dolly was clearly revolted. "But that means you would have to kill something in order to eat it!"

"Well, yes," Drusilla replied meekly, beginning to wish she was a strict vegetarian, "but usually someone else does that... And not all of our food is cooked—or has to be killed... "

There was a loud sizzle as Klog plopped the thick, juicy steak on the grill. Dolly looked like she was going to be sick, her forked tongue darting in and out of her mouth with nervous rapidity and her hands an orange blur.

"Perhaps we should not have come at a meal time," Maria said diplomatically as she pulled Dolly away from the source of her distress. "These younger ones have not fully grasped the concept of differences between offworld cultures... I hope you understand."

"Of course," Drusilla said with a grin. "I understand completely! I was once on a planet where they ate their food alive—and it was mostly insects—it made me sick every time I—"

This was too much for Dolly, and even Crystal turned a duller shade of orange.

"Sorry!" Drusilla blurted out as the ladies hastily departed, singing their good-byes as they went.

"Well, that certainly went over like a lead balloon," she commented to Klog. "I'm glad you're not squeamish. I mean, I like fruit and all, but—" She paused as he flipped the steak, which was now giving off a mouthwatering aroma. "There's just nothing quite like a good steak!"

Klog chirped in agreement, though Drusilla seriously doubted he had ever eaten anything, much less a steak.

Unknown to Drusilla, Manx's heart had nearly stopped when she pulled off her wet clothes. He had to get close enough to smell her now. He simply had to.

Circling the lake, he approached the house from the opposite direction, watching as she came out onto the patio. Still naked. Still beautiful. His heart racing, he inhaled deeply and caught traces of her scent on the wind. Whatever she was feeling, it must have been sexual in nature because she was now aroused enough to send out a hail to him. As his cock stiffened in response, all he could think of was plunging it into her, using it to toy with her body, driving her wild with pleasure.

But just as he caught a whiff of it, her enticing aroma was stifled once again when she entered the hot tub. Manx managed to control his reaction—something for which he was extremely thankful when, moments later, he saw the Baradan women approaching and, reluctantly, withdrew.

This inadvertent teasing was driving him mad, making him reckless with the need to get closer to her, but he waited until she was alone once again before attempting another look. Moving cautiously, he could see her sitting at the patio table. She had carelessly tied the strip of Baradan clothing around her breasts but was still essentially nude and smelled nearly as good as she had before.

Manx was hungry too, and the aroma of good food coupled with that of hot woman was nearly his undoing. His feet wanted to run to her, his arms ached to hold her, and his penis was taut and dripping with anticipation. He'd never been so painfully, urgently hard before, and it took every ounce of self-control he possessed not to give in to his desires and take her right then and there. *But I have to find out more,* he told himself firmly. *Just because she smells right is no reason to risk everything.*

Manx gripped his stiff shaft and closed his eyes, his teeth clenched tightly to hold back his roar of frustration. Cupping his balls in his other hand, he massaged them while he brought himself quickly to climax, his semen— or snard, as it was called in his native tongue—spewing forth with a force that astounded him, but left him wanting more. He knew what it was; it was *her* pleasure that was missing. He felt empty, perhaps even more so than if he'd remained flaccid. A hard cock was pointless unless there was a wet, willing, and intoxicating female to mate with. He wanted to see her face when she tasted his fluids, when he filled her with his snard and gave her joy.

Manx could still smell her and his dick remained erect even though he'd just come harder than ever before. This was no ordinary female, he decided. How could he possibly resist mating with her another moment? Especially when her body was so enticingly on display? Her breasts may have been covered in the Baradan style, but it did nothing to disguise their shape, and the chair she sat in was open near her hips—he was closer now, and she still looked perfect.

Without thinking, Manx began to purr, but stopped immediately as Drusilla spun around, seeking to discover the source of the sound. Manx froze, his stiff cock still thrust out in front of him as though seeking the source of its arousal. As she turned, Drusilla's knees spread apart and a breeze ruffled her hair, blowing her scent toward him with such a shocking blast that he almost roared again. Never had his senses been bombarded with such force.

———

"Who's there?" Drusilla called out. She paused, listening intently and peering through the trees in the direction of the sound. It had sounded like a purring cat, but a very large and possibly dangerous one. "Klog!" she shouted. "Come here, quick!"

Klog appeared at the door almost instantly.

"Are there any wildcats living around here?" Lester had assured her that there were no dangerous animals, but what would ignore a Baradan might think a Terran looked tasty.

Klog replied with a low-pitched buzz.

"Whatever *that* means," Drusilla muttered, renewing her intention to find out more about him. In the meantime, deciding that it might be best to finish her meal indoors, she gathered up her plate and cup and went inside. "Close the door and lock it," she said firmly. "And don't let the cat in."

What the computer made of that last command, Drusilla didn't know and didn't care. Letting down her guard might have been a mistake—it was bad enough getting caught naked in the hot tub by the local women; what if it had been someone or some*thing* else? She resolved to be more cautious in the future—at least until she received some sort of reassurance from Lester.

Once inside, Drusilla headed toward the kitchen with her plate, but paused for a moment as she noted the slickness between her thighs and her growing ache of arousal.

"That's weird!" she remarked to the droid. "Never thought fear could do *that*." Chuckling softly, she added, "Must be because it sounded like a big, sexy tomcat." Klog, of course, made no comment, and Drusilla decided that it must have simply been some small, innocuous creature that just happened to sound like a purring tiger. "No biting insects, no dangerous animals" had been the key words in what Ralph had told her, and Lester had reinforced that claim. She was beginning to feel silly for having been so spooked, but she kept the door locked anyway. It was getting dark, and Drusilla had no desire to be eaten alive on her first night—or any other, for that matter.

Finishing her dinner, Drusilla told Klog to clean up—though she was fairly certain she didn't need to ask. Returning to the living room, she pulled off the Baradan "bra" and snuggled up on the sofa under a light blanket. The ache had persisted and was, in fact, growing stronger. "Haven't felt this horny in years—maybe ever," she commented aloud. Her nipples tingled and she brushed them lightly with her fingertips, which did nothing to cause the feeling to abate. Having a man around might have helped, but sex had always been so unsatisfying, and Drab Dave had never touched her at all. "Which should have been my first clue," she said morosely, and went on to make a list of the attributes that her perfect man should possess.

Heterosexual was the first requirement, followed by a nice, friendly personality. "Tired of dealing with jerks," she grumbled. "Handsome would be a plus. And a decent-sized cock—one that he'd actually use for sex—and the more often, the better." Sighing deeply, she added, "It'd be nice if he couldn't keep his hands off of me too... dick always hard... good sense of humor... killer smile... cute butt... nice hair."

Laughing out loud as she remembered how that purring sound seemed to have affected her, she concluded that since this was, after all, a fantasy man, he might as well be able to purr too.

Closing her eyes dreamily, Drusilla's fingertips feathered her nipples again while her other hand slid to her clitoris. As her fingers slipped over her moist, sensitive flesh, she lamented the fact that this was happening when she was out in the middle of nowhere where the only men to be had were orange toads and slimy mudskippers! Must be all the fresh air and nudity, she decided. Perhaps if I get dressed it'll go away...

She considered this alternative but then dismissed it as nonsense and rushed boldly on into the arms of erotic fantasy. Sex with her perfect man... one who would kiss her all over, devouring her body with his lips and tongue, driving her insane with desire. She could almost feel his hard, wet cock gliding over her cheeks and lips before he pushed it into her mouth. Drusilla's body contracted in an orgasm that had nothing to do with her clitoris, but she stroked it faster, imagining that she was savoring his delicious cock while she massaged his heavy balls. Her body tightened as she felt her orgasm begin. Picturing his hard cock filling her with hot cream, splashing it in her face, her mouth, and her hair, his imaginary climactic cry became her own.

Her body contracted uncontrollably for several astonishing minutes, after which Drusilla lay dazed and somewhat dumbfounded by what had just transpired. Covered in a light sheen of sweat and blinking hard, Drusilla tried to focus again on her surroundings. She'd never gotten quite so carried away before; had never had such a wild, erotic fantasy—about oral sex, no less!—and all of this from hearing some little kitty purring in the jungle?

The light was still on, and the blanket had slid off of her body. Anyone watching through the window could have seen her—perhaps even the man of her dreams. "Let him see," she chuckled. "Maybe *then* I'll get lucky."

Then she decided that there was no point in making it *too* easy, or to court disaster, so she told the lights to turn off and headed toward the bedroom. The light from the moon lit her way, but as she went, she glanced over at the window that faced the patio. There, near the lower portion of the pane, was a pair of glowing, feline eyes. Letting out an involuntary yelp, she scurried toward the bedroom and closed the door behind her.

Drusilla was badly shaken but managed to inject some degree of logic into the situation. Those eyes had not been those of a Baradan, or an eltran. It was undoubtedly some curious jungle creature that had been drawn to the light. Yes, that was it, she told herself reassuringly. Just a sweet little kitten. There was nothing dangerous out there. Lester promised her—hell, *Ralph* had promised her!—nothing but beautiful birds and no mosquitoes, and so far, it had all been true. And there *had* to be animals living in the jungle; it wouldn't be much of a jungle without them, would it? She had just been surprised and startled at being observed during such a private moment. She climbed into bed and, in spite of her fears, promptly fell asleep.

———

The lights going out so abruptly had caught him unawares, but Manx *had* been watching, and though being separated by glass was quite effective at dousing his ardor—meaning his erection—it didn't do anything to stop his mental reaction. She thought *that* was an orgasm? Manx laughed softly. She wouldn't pleasure herself again if he ever mated with her—wouldn't need to—and neither would he. He'd keep going as long as he could and then do it again, and again, and again. And she would know joy.

Suddenly desperate to fill his head with her scent, Manx circled the house and found the chaise lounge she'd been lying on earlier. He caught a faint whiff of her, but it wasn't enough. Even so, he couldn't bring himself to leave that place, and lying down where she had been, he slept.

Chapter 4

THE NEXT MORNING DRUSILLA AWOKE WONDERING WHAT kind of aphrodisiac Klog had used to spike her tea. "I wasn't even drunk," she grumbled, throwing off her blanket. "Must be that purple sky... some weird form of ultraviolet light that bounces off the retina and triggers all sorts of wild hormones." It wasn't much, but it was as good an explanation as any. She was, after all, reportedly the first Terran to visit Barada—at least, for any length of time—and this might be a side effect no one could have predicted. Nice side effect, she decided—though it was possible that the cheesecake had been responsible.

Yawning, she combed back her disheveled locks as she crossed to the window to gaze out at the lake. The sight before her should have triggered all kinds of spontaneous orgasms because there were now eight incredibly beautiful birds wading in the water. Two of the orange variety she'd already seen, three that were an iridescent teal, and the rest were red with yellow-tipped feathers and looked like they were on fire. "Oh... my... *God,*" she whispered.

Somehow managing to keep a lid on her excitement, Drusilla crept down the stairs, opening the door at the bottom manually to avoid startling the birds. She took one step and waited. Then another... and another. The birds continued to fish without so much as a glance in her direction, and soon, she was walking barefoot in the warm sand. Klog hadn't smoothed it yet, and her footprints from the evening before were still visible—along with another set of prints much larger than her own.

Her gasp of surprise startled the birds, but only three of them actually flew off. The rest remained, seeming to decide that she posed no threat to them, while Drusilla knelt slowly to examine the prints. Although indistinct, they looked surprisingly human. The Baradans all had flipper-like feet, and though it was possible that some other land animal had feet like a Terran primate, she knew it was unlikely. Still, like the purring and the glowing eyes, there had to be a simple, logical explanation for it. Drusilla knew very little about the other life forms that inhabited this world, and, for all she knew, these could have been the bird's footprints—after all, she'd never seen their feet.

—∿∿—

Manx watched from the shelter of the woods and was momentarily delighted that Drusilla hadn't bothered to dress. Then he heard her gasp and, as she knelt down, he realized what she had seen and cursed himself for his carelessness, knowing that he had left a trail of footprints leading to and from the house. He was normally cautious in the extreme and rarely made mistakes that could get him captured or killed, but she had affected him so strongly that habits of half a lifetime had been forgotten.

Manx knew that if Drusilla questioned the Baradans, she would be told that the prints were not those of any indigenous species. She would become suspicious and wary—perhaps not even trusting him if he risked a bare-faced introduction. Zef could help with that—he could at least vouch for Manx's character. Though, upon further reflection, Manx decided that having the eltran vouch for him would be akin to having your worst enemy recommend a good doctor—especially if Drusilla disliked Zef as much as everyone else did.

While Manx was puzzling over the question of introductions, Drusilla had decided that with footprints like that around, she had no desire to be caught without her clothes. Still moving slowly and deliberately to avoid further startling the birds, she went back inside and yelled for Klog. Sniffing the air, she realized he was already fixing breakfast—without an order of any kind—and, better still, was making waffles.

"Are you making those for someone else?" she asked curiously.

Klog buzzed at her and went on with his cooking.

"How do you *do* that?" she demanded. "I love waffles with"—she paused, noting what else he had laid out—"butter pecan syrup and baked apples! How could you *possibly* know?"

Klog ignored this question and, having arranged everything on a plate, topped it with whipped cream, which he squirted out of one of his "fingers."

"Well, that's certainly impressive," Drusilla remarked. "Do you make mixed drinks too?" Since Klog's beehive-shaped "body" was large enough to hold any number of different liquids, she had an idea he could whip up a pretty good margarita if she were to hand him a glass.

Klog once again made a chirping sound.

"I believe I'll take that as a yes," she said, then added firmly, "Tea. Earl Grey. Hot."

Klog beeped once, drifted over to the cabinet for a mug, and then poured the piping hot tea from the tip of another finger.

"Well, I'll be damned!" Drusilla declared as he beeped twice more. "You must have cost a fortune!"

Klog chirped his reply and floated off to clean the waffle iron.

What with strange footprints in the sand and big, purring cats lurking nearby, Drusilla donned her robe before sitting down to breakfast, thinking she probably ought to reconsider her intention to swim in the nude. Then she remembered Zef yammering on about the skinny-butt Baradans and decided against it completely.

She also decided that she should mention to Klog that serving her the kind of meals that stemmed from her deepest, most hedonistic cravings was probably a mistake—unless he wanted to remake all of her clothes in a larger size. Drusilla was petite, but with Klog in charge of the menu, that was likely to change. Still, waffles on her first morning seemed celebratory; she'd wait until later to tell him that a little fresh fruit and toast would be adequate from then on—no matter how much she might want waffles.

With that thought in mind, Drusilla leaned back in her chair to ponder her life. When was the last time she'd done anything just because she wanted to? It took her a long time to come up with an answer for that, and she realized that, prior to diving into the lake on the previous afternoon, she would have to go back at least several months for the last spontaneous fulfillment of her heart's desire. That, of course, was the day she told Drab Dave that he could go to the drag queen convention without her.

Not that she wouldn't have enjoyed it; her refusal was purely a matter of principle. Dave had been chagrined, but not overly cast down, and had gone on to attend the event with his friend Charles, who had no objection to sharing a room—or a bed—with Dave. By the end of the summer, their ensuing love affair had reached legendary proportions.

Drusilla sighed deeply, wondering if it was possible for her to find a love as intense as theirs. Enthusiasm was something that had always been lacking among her suitors. They liked her. She liked them. They got along fine but never felt any overwhelming passion—never even held hands in public, let alone exchanged stolen kisses, and even in intimate moments there was a decided lack of fervor. People in films were always falling into each other's arms, kissing hungrily and ripping clothing in their haste, but Drusilla was convinced that that sort of thing never happened in real life—at least, not to her—and if it ever did, Barada was the last place she could expect it to occur. What made it worse was that she had some inkling of how it *should* feel; she'd always felt a passion for her work, and the discovery of some fabulous new birds always sent her blood racing, but men? Not lately—and possibly not ever.

Until she had taken the time to design her dream man, that is. She'd felt something the night before that was entirely new to her. Passion. Lust. Excitement. Unfortunately, he only existed in her mind…

Manx had begun his day quite early, spearing fish for breakfast and exchanging news with Zef. Manx was understandably curious about the new tenant, and the garrulous eltran had plenty to tell.

"Her name's Drusilla," he said without preamble. "Thought you'd want to know."

Manx didn't bother to deny it—or to admit that he already knew. "How long is she staying?"

"Three months," Zef replied. "She's from Earth—wherever the hell *that* is! I've never heard of it."

"Me either," said Manx. "It must be a long way from here."

"Yeah," Zef agreed. "Lots of lakes there, though—a fuckin' eltran paradise to hear her tell it! Would you believe she's only here to see the birds and paint pictures of them? Ever hear of crap like that before? Stupid thing to do, if you ask me."

Manx grinned. "She didn't ask you, though—did she?"

"Aw, hell! Nobody gives a flying fuck what I think—or what I like," Zef grumbled. "Except you."

"Me?" Manx said with surprise. "I have no idea what you like!"

"You know I like fish, and you *always* throw your fish bones back in the lake," Zef protested. "I *love* fish bones!"

"Never knew that," Manx admitted. "I was just making sure no one would find the bones and wonder what ate the fish."

Zef's pectoral fins wobbled. "You mean you weren't doing it just to be nice?"

Manx shook his head regretfully. "No, Zef. Sorry."

"Well, if that don't beat all!" Zef exclaimed. "Here I thought I'd finally found a friend and you just turn out to be—"

"But I *am* your friend," Manx said reassuringly. "And just to prove it, I'll be sure to tell you when I'm throwing away the bones from now on."

Zef seemed to think this was a perfectly wonderful demonstration of friendship. "And to prove I'm *your* friend," he said, cocking his head to one side, "I might tell Drusilla there's someone else living around here who'd like to meet her."

Manx wanted to say yes more than anything—and if he'd been downwind of Drusilla at the time, he might have responded differently—but since he wasn't, he chose to be cautious. "Why don't you talk to her some more before you tell her about me," Manx suggested. "She might not be as nice as she looks."

Zef was quick to pick up on Manx's double meaning. "Oh, ho! So she looks good to you, does she? Better looking than the Baradans, maybe, but not by much. About like you, I'd say."

Manx laughed. "And you used to call me 'pretty boy'!" Pausing for a moment, he added, "Of course, if you'd be nice to her, we might get a better idea of her personality than we would if you irritate her." Manx eyed Zef unblinkingly. "You *know* how you are."

If Zef felt chastised, it didn't show. "I am what I am," he said staunchly. "Can't change, don't want to change, and refuse to try."

Manx was shrewd enough to know that anyone could change, and also that everyone had their price. "What would it take? More bones?"

Zef laughed. "No," he replied. "Just toss me a whole fish once in a while—preferably one that's already dead. I'm getting too slow to catch them anymore. Had to resort to eating plants just to stay alive." The eltran shifted his weight painfully from one ragged pectoral fin to the other. "Don't ever get old, Manx," Zef advised. "It's pure hell."

"Perhaps," Manx conceded. "But I have no intention of dying young just to avoid it."

"And certainly not before you've met Drusilla," Zef added. "I think you'll like her."

Manx didn't want to admit it to Zef, but if her scent was anything to go by, he had a strong feeling he already did.

"What about you?" Manx inquired. "Did *you* like her?"

The eltran let out a loud bark. "What difference does *that* make?" he demanded. "I don't give a damn—" Zef broke off there as though considering his reply. "Well, maybe it does matter," he admitted grudgingly. "She seemed nice enough—didn't swear at me, anyway. Most of the people staying in that house have told me to get lost, or fuck off. She didn't do that."

"What about that swim in the lake?" Manx went on. "Did you enjoy watching her?"

"Didn't hate it, if that's what you mean," Zef replied. "Like I said before, she's a lot like you." Zef looked up at Manx with a friendly eye. "Never minded you."

"Well, then, do me a favor and try not to scare her off—let her swim without being bothered—unless, of course, you two decide to be friends. Then she probably wouldn't mind." Maybe.

"Rather be swimming with her yourself, wouldn't you?" Zef said shrewdly. "You haven't come right out and said it, but you fancy her, don't you?"

"Fancy?" Manx echoed. "What do you mean by that?"

"Means you like her, numb nuts! Want to mate with her and all that crap!"

Manx's lips curled into a grin. "You wouldn't have said it was crap when you were younger."

"That's another reason never to get old," Zef grumbled. "I got so old and ugly they voted me out of the lake! Imagine that, now—being sent off to live out the rest of your miserable days without any of your own kind!"

Manx just looked at him for a long moment with a slightly raised brow.

"Oh, yeah," Zef said. "Sorry. Forgot! Guess you'd know all about that, wouldn't you?"

"Yes, I would," Manx said. "And if you don't mind my saying so, the 'rest of my days' is going to be a very long time—provided that no one kills me—and I'm thinking I'd like to spend those days with someone like Drusilla." Actually, it wasn't someone *like* Drusilla that Manx had in mind, but Drusilla herself, though he didn't want to get his hopes up too soon. After all, Drusilla wasn't the first potential mate he'd spotted, just the one he found the most appealing.

Manx had come very close to choosing a mate on Serillia, which was where the Nedwuts had caught up with him last. Larita was her name. She was pretty and very nice, but Serillians weren't nearly as much like Zetithians as Drusilla was. They'd become good friends, but Manx wasn't sure he could have mated with Larita; her scent wasn't quite right, and he'd had doubts that they were genetically compatible. Manx was also honest enough to admit that he hadn't truly loved Larita, but he did regret not saying good-bye to her. He had warned her about the threat of capture and hoped she understood why he had to leave so abruptly, but there was no way to be sure.

Zef hadn't thought so when Manx had related the story to him. "Just thought you were making an excuse to run out on her," he'd said. "Not a bad excuse, either."

But Manx didn't want to make excuses anymore, and he was getting tired of being alone. He wasn't that old—just entering the prime of his long life, in fact— and being on the run wasn't much fun, either. There had to be *someplace* where the Nedwuts wouldn't find him. Perhaps this "Earth" that Drusilla was from was just such a place...

Chapter 5

MANX HAD NO WAY OF KNOWING IT AT THE TIME, BUT EARTH was a *very* good place for a Zetithian to seek refuge—and Captain Jacinth "Jack" Tshevnoe of the starship *Jolly Roger* was the reason why. A Terran herself, she'd bought a Zetithian slave whom she'd subsequently freed and then promptly fell in love with. She'd dubbed him "Cat" and, since her marriage to him, had become the champion of the remaining Zetithians throughout the galaxy. Granted, there weren't many of them left, but those she'd found were now well protected—especially by the women who loved them.

Given to shooting Nedwuts on sight, Jack had managed to discourage most Nedwuts from collecting the bounty on her husband, but she had recently discovered that the bounty was not only still being offered, but had, in fact, been raised to five million credits. Someone wanted them exterminated very badly—someone with plenty of money and the ability to remain anonymous.

Nedwuts were hairy, snarling, wolf-like primates who were generally regarded as the worst the galaxy had to offer. Thanks to Cat's visions, it had become known that, while people from several worlds had been engaged in the war on Zetith, it had been the Nedwuts who were responsible for its ultimate destruction. This, coupled with the fact that no one liked them anyway, made Nedwuts *persona non grata* on most civilized worlds.

But with a five million credit bounty on Zetithians, those who had the resources kept looking.

Jack was a trader in legal goods throughout the galaxy but had lately tended to keep to the Terran quadrant, where it was safer for her husband and six children. She and Cat traveled with Leo, another Zetithian, and his wife, Tisana, who was a witch capable of telepathic communication with animals and who also possessed the power to set things on fire with a glance. These were both useful skills when it came to defending her own husband and children, and though Tisana was a peaceful sort of witch, she didn't hesitate to use those powers when she deemed it necessary.

The men had all been taken prisoner at the end of the war on Zetith and had been sold as slaves by an enterprising soul who had seen no point in executing these last few soldiers when he could make a tidy little profit on them. In addition to Cat and Leo, Jack had found Trag, Tychar, and Lynx on her trading runs, and all but Trag had found Terran mates. Trag, who was now a pilot for an arms merchant, was holding out for a Zetithian female, and despite Jack's efforts, thus far she had come up empty-handed. Trag's brother, Tychar, was a galaxy-class rock star—and had women on a host of planets drooling over him, including his wife, Kyra—but he hadn't run across any either. If there were any Zetithian females left, they were keeping their heads down.

Manx had been the only one of them to escape from slavery, but the rest were, as yet, ignorant of his whereabouts, as well as his continued existence. Until now.

When Jack had discovered that a band of Nedwuts were on the trail of another Zetithian, she became determined to get to him first. Jack had once tracked her sister's trail across the galaxy and had managed to find her, and though this trail wasn't as easy to follow, experience had taught her the best methods. The Nedwuts in question had been blabbing about their next kill in some seedy little bar, and the proprietor had been more than willing to share this information with Jack—for a price, of course.

The Nedwuts had reportedly been grumbling about how many planets they'd been searching since they'd lost their quarry on Serillia and how difficult it was to gain information, but Jack had an advantage: People didn't mind talking to her, but they hated dealing with Nedwuts or helping them out in any way. So, Jack was able to avoid searching all of the possible planets that the man could have gone to after eluding capture and instead focus on the one that he *had* landed on.

On Serillia, instead of looking for the Zetithian, Jack had posted a picture of her husband along with the information that he was searching for his lost brother. Jack had no idea if the man they were looking for was Cat's brother or not but decided it was worth a shot, and it paid off.

A woman named Larita had come forward and said that though Cat had black eyes rather than green, he had the same long, curly black hair, pointed ears, and feline eyes as a man she had known who had suddenly disappeared without a trace. In addition to his physical description, she was also able to report that he had an amazingly good sense of smell. The trail was cold— he'd been gone for more than a year—but with this new information, though Jack suspected that Larita could have added a few more sensuous details which would have clinched it for her, Cat was able to identify him.

"It is Manxarkodrath," Cat told Jack after hearing Larita's description.

"Who?" Jack said.

"Manxarkodrath Panteris," he repeated.

"That's his *name?* You've *got* to be kidding!" she began, but added, "No, you're not, are you?"

Cat shook his head. "He had green eyes and black hair and only had to be downwind of a receptive female to—"

"Get it up?"

Cat grinned devilishly and nodded. "He had the best nose of any of us. We called him Manx."

"Manx, huh? Probably should have called him Snuffles," Jack said with a chuckle. "But at least we know who we're looking for now—and have a pretty good idea of when he left. Hope the guys at the spaceport are feeling talkative. Probably have to trade them something for that info," she muttered, mentally reviewing the contents of her ship's cargo bay. "By the way, what did Larita want in exchange for her little tidbit?"

Cat smiled again. "A lock of my hair."

"You guys just *kill* me," Jack grumbled. "Did you give it to her?"

"Yes, I did," Cat replied. "You are angry with me?"

"I'd only be angry if you gave her some of your joy juice," Jack said frankly. "Give away any of that, and we'll have to talk!"

Cat began purring as he took her in his arms. "I would not do that," he said. "That is only for you, my lovely master."

She never could resist Cat once he started purring. He could have gotten anything from her but only wanted her love. "I think we need to get back to the ship," she whispered, "—and soon!"

Inhaling the intoxicating aroma of her desire, Cat smiled mischievously. Pushing a stray lock of hair back from her eyes, he kissed her softly.

"That Larita wasn't pregnant, was she?" Jack asked suddenly.

"I do not believe so," Cat replied. Zetithians were known for their occasional "visions" and Cat's claim to fame was in knowing when the women of his acquaintance were pregnant—especially if another Zetithian was the father.

"God, I hope there's nothing wrong with him! What if he's like Lynx?" Jack shuddered with horror at the thought. Lynx had been a harem slave, and the women there had literally worn him out. This had caused Jack a great deal of concern—a surviving Zetithian who couldn't reproduce was something that she couldn't stand the thought of—and though he had recovered, Jack didn't ever want to go through that again.

"Larita knew he was on the run from the Nedwuts but didn't mention that he'd ever been a slave," Cat said soothingly. "Perhaps he managed to escape that fate."

"I certainly hope so," Jack said roundly. "But if the Nedwuts ever catch up with him, he's dead meat."

"But they have not caught him yet," Cat reminded her. "He could be very elusive and was an excellent hunter himself."

"Yes, but could he smell Nedwuts a kilometer away?"

"Perhaps not so far as that, but he did have an excellent nose."

"Better than yours?"

"Yes," he replied. "If you will recall, when you left me in the slave market, I thought you were gone forever."

"No chance of that," Jack said wryly. She'd seen his cock in full bloom during the pre-auction inspection and wouldn't have left before seeing where he wound up, even if she hadn't bought him herself. Of course, if she hadn't been there, he wouldn't have been sold at all because the level of restraint he seemed to require made him less attractive to other bidders. Jack had been the only one bidding on him, getting him for a paltry five credits. "I know a bargain when I see one."

They arrived back at the *Jolly Roger* and boarded, only to discover that Leo and Tisana had taken all of the children on an outing to the local zoo.

"Cat!" Jack whispered excitedly. "Do you realize this means we have the whole ship to ourselves?"

"It has been a long time since we have had such freedom," Cat agreed. "We should not waste it."

Since Jack was already unbuckling his belt, this encouragement was completely unnecessary. Sliding her hands inside his breeches, she reached down to grab his buns and pull him closer. "My sentiments exactly."

Taking her face in his hands, Cat kissed her, the sensation of heat already beginning to grow inside him. His cock became hard as he inhaled her scent and he reveled in the feel of her hands on his skin. Licking first her neck and then teasing her earlobe, he began purring in her ear.

"Mmm, Kittycat," she said. "I just love it when you do that."

"And I love it when you call me Kittycat," he returned. Purring might be one of a Zetithian male's surest means of enticement, but his lovely Jacinth knew all the ways to entice him as well.

—∿∿—

It was tedious work, but Jack and her friends managed to trace each ship that had left the spaceport within a few days of Manx's disappearance. While several captains had reported possible stowaways, only one mentioned something that the Nedwuts wouldn't have made anything of: the stowaway in question had apparently liked sweets.

"What makes you think that?" Jack asked.

"Nothing ever went missing from the food locker but sweets," the captain declared. "That was the only clue there was anyone aboard. Very good at hiding, he must have been, because we never found any trace of him—and we *did* look."

Now, Jack knew how partial Cat was to sweets and, with Leo as further evidence to support her theory, suspected that all Zetithians had a sweet tooth, which made this the most likely lead to follow.

"Where did you land on that trip?" Jack asked.

"Let me see now," he said, checking his log. "After Serillia, we made the rounds of the neighboring systems. Nurate, Bexal, and Barada Seven—in that order."

Jack had been to all of those worlds before and knew that if she'd stowed away on a ship, Nurate and Bexal were some of the very *last* places she'd want to get off, which left Barada Seven.

"Have the stowaway the whole time?" she asked casually.

"Unless one of my men was lying."

Jack doubted that. "Any of them gain weight on the trip?" she inquired with a mischievous grin.

"Not a gram," he replied. "In fact, most of them *lost* weight."

"Bingo!"

"I beg your pardon?"

"Nothing," Jack replied, but it wasn't nothing; it was a good, solid lead. Manx was as good as found.

But Jack and the Nedwuts weren't the only ones on his trail.

"Did you get it?" Lutira asked her sister as she took her place at the control panel.

"Yes," Tash'dree replied. "They are bound for Barada Seven."

"Good," she said with a gesture toward the other vessel. "They are still preparing to depart, but our ship is secure and ready. Now is not the time to falter when our goal is so near. We must launch." Their ship was small, and the cramped space designed for a far less statuesque race than their own, but it had served them well thus far, being much more powerful than its appearance would suggest.

As the engines began to fire, she turned the disk over in her hand, activating the holoposter once again. The image of a tall man with long dark hair and feline eyes sprang to life from her palm.

"You are certain he is the one?" Tash'dree asked, gazing at the male form.

"Yes, he is the one," Lutira replied. "And where he is,

there will be others of his kind, as this message suggests." Her glowing blue eyes grew fierce with determination. "There are more of them. I am certain of it now."

"Then this quest will not have been in vain."

"It was *never* in vain," Lutira said firmly. "The original bloodline will be preserved in any case, but the addition of another line would be worth all of the sacrifices we sisters have made."

"And if they discover our intent?"

Lutira shrugged, tossing her long dark hair back from her face. "There still may be a chance."

"Why the secrecy then, Lutira?" her sister argued. "I have never understood the need for it! What was given to us before was given freely."

"Perhaps," Lutira said slowly. "But we do not know all of the circumstances, and remember, what we seek is a separate bloodline. It is best to find a different man— unattached if possible—and find him before they do. If he knows of the others, he may not be as willing, or he may suspect our motives."

Tash'dree disagreed. "It is not our way—"

"It has been the way on our world for many generations," Lutira reminded her. "But for that, our world would have been lost."

"Sometimes I think it would have been better if it had been so," Tash'dree said sadly. "The subterfuge, the pitting of one faction against another, the continued ruse… " Shaking her head, she added wonderingly, "Would we have truly been destroyed?"

"We as sisters would not exist if that were not so."

"Perhaps that would have been best—" Tash'dree began, but was cut off by Lutira's steely gaze.

"The sisterhood is what enabled our world to survive long enough to succeed," Lutira said fiercely. "Never forget that."

"Ah, but have we succeeded?" Tash'dree said archly. "Sometimes I wonder."

"Nevertheless, we must reach Barada Seven before they do," Lutira said firmly. "Prepare to launch."

No one took note as the small, insignificant ship rose from the surface with the two beautiful women at the controls—and perhaps least of all, the ship that had just departed.

"It was said that Nedwuts were seeking information as well," Tash'dree said. "There could be trouble."

"We have dealt with their kind before and will undoubtedly do so again." Lutira's tone denied any concern. "They will not be allowed to destroy any more of them."

In the meantime, the Nedwuts were bullying everyone they could find on Bexal, but to no avail. If there was a Zetithian on that planet, nobody was talking. Barada Seven was next.

Chapter 6

AFTER BREAKFAST, DRUSILLA PUSHED ALL THOUGHTS OF WILD jungle cats firmly out of her mind and went out to the lake with the intention of spending the day at her easel. After donning her swimsuit and thongs, she put on her hat and smock and then gathered up her painting gear and carried it down to the lake. The air was cool and pleasant, and a lively breeze played with her silky smock—which was one that Ralph had insisted on giving her when he'd seen the coarse, paint-stained "thing" she had worn for so many years. Ralph considered it an affront to his delicate sensibilities and had given her this one: a flowing, multi-colored, lace-edged garment that deflected the sun nicely and gave her the ethereal, artistic look that Ralph had been aiming for. With that and her hat, she would have made a good subject for a painting herself, but Drusilla liked it for a more practical reason: she could get paint on it without it being noticeable.

Having found a large beach umbrella in the shed by the back door, Drusilla set it up in a spot that provided a clear view of the lake and the surrounding jungle and then sat down beneath it to sketch in the background while she waited for the birds to arrive. She was engaged in the effort to capture the purple hue of the sky when Zef popped up for a visit.

"Hey, Drusilla!" Zef rasped from the shallows. "So, this is what you do, huh? Sit by the water and doodle on that thing?"

"Good morning, Zef," Drusilla said in a pleasant voice. "Yes, this is what I do. And this 'thing' is called a canvas, by the way."

"Canvas," Zef repeated. "Must remember that—can't think why, but I'm sure I'll need to know someday."

Drusilla rolled her eyes and went back to her work. "Just another bit of useless information, is that it?"

"Possibly," Zef cautiously agreed. He was remembering Manx's admonition to be nice, though it went against his nature—and his habits—to do so. "Nice day," he added, which was just about the only nice thing he could think of to say—at least the word "nice" was in there.

"Yes, it is," she agreed. "Does it rain very often?"

"What a stupid question!" Zef exclaimed. "We're surrounded by a fuckin' jungle and you ask—" Zef stopped himself there and paused a moment to regroup. *Be nice*, he reminded himself. "Yes, rains all the time," he said. "I like rain."

Drusilla chuckled. "Just can't keep from speaking your mind, can you?"

"Don't usually see any reason not to," he said.

"Or keep from swearing every other word," she added. "Any thoughts as to what I might do here on rainy days?"

Zef suspected that his friend Manx could keep her endlessly entertained whether it rained or not, but he almost broke a tooth in an effort not to mention that fact. "What's the matter? Don't like rain?" he asked instead.

"Makes it hard to paint," Drusilla explained. "Though this umbrella could probably withstand anything short of a hurricane—which is fortunate because I'm sure Ralph is expecting a whole series of Baradan bird paintings when I get home. He sent enough canvases to keep me busy for years."

"Ralph?" Zef echoed, thinking for one awful moment that Ralph might be her mate—which would spell trouble for Manx. "Who the hell is Ralph?"

"My boss," Drusilla replied. "Well, sort of, anyway. I paint the pictures and he sells them in his gallery. He's paying for this trip, by the way, so I'm sure he wants results."

"You share the profits with him?" Zef thought this was a very bad idea.

"Yes," Drusilla replied. "He gets a commission on every painting he sells."

"Sounds like a filthy parasite to me," Zef observed. "I'd get rid of him if I were you."

Laughing out loud, Drusilla said, "Ralph doesn't see himself as a parasite, but rather as an enabler."

"Enabler?"

"You know, someone who makes it possible for me to paint and not have to worry about the business end of things—a patron of the arts."

"Sounds like a damn crook if you ask me!" Zef declared. "How do you know he's not cheating you?"

"Well, you know, Zef," Drusilla said somberly, "sometimes you just have to take people at their word—though their signature on a contract doesn't hurt."

"Mmm," Zef said. "Trusting, are you?"

"Up to a point," she agreed, "And Ralph hasn't cheated me yet—at least not that I know of."

Zef thought having a woman with a trusting nature would be a good thing for Manx—after all, it wasn't as though she could check his background and be reassured. Zef knew that he couldn't help much in that department since he didn't know a whole lot about Manx's past himself. Yes, trust was good.

"So, Zef, since you've lived here for a while, you should know this, so tell me, are the birds very easily frightened? I mean, will our conversation keep them away?"

"Want me to shut up and go away, don't you?"

"I didn't say that," Drusilla said, "but now that you mention it, it might be better if we tried to be quiet."

Since Zef had seen a bird or two around while he'd been talking to Manx—and also during the noise of construction—he doubted that this would be a problem. "Naw, they won't mind us talking. Just don't scream or throw rocks at them. They don't like that."

"Neither would I," Drusilla said. "I prefer peace and quiet."

"What? Don't get lonely?"

"You can have peace and quiet without loneliness, Zef."

Zef didn't agree. Without someone to talk to, the loneliness threatened to overwhelm him. "Like to talk, myself," he said.

"So I've noticed," Drusilla said mildly.

"Yes, I like to talk," he said. "Used to have lots of eltrans to talk to, but now it's just you and—" He broke off there, knowing that he'd probably said too much already.

"Me and—who?" she prompted.

"And anyone else who stays in the house," Zef finished, grateful for having had a moment of inspiration.

"I thought you might have meant Lester," she said.

Zef snorted, which sounded like a combination of a growl and a fart.

"Don't care for Lester, do you?" she chuckled.

"The filthy little orange wanker!" Zef muttered. "Tried everything he could think of to get me to leave this lake! Even said there were eltran-eating monsters in here. Ha! Knew he was lying. I know a monster when I see one."

"Seen any around here?" Drusilla inquired nervously. "Something that has footprints like mine?"

"Dunno," Zef said, pretending not to know just exactly what she meant. "Let me see your feet."

Drusilla slipped off one of her thongs and stuck out her foot. It was a nice, shapely foot, Zef noted. Smaller than Manx's, but very similar. "Maybe," Zef replied cautiously. "Not a monster, though."

"Not a monster?" she echoed. "Well, I certainly hope our definitions of 'monster' are the same, but whatever it was, it left footprints going to and from the house. Know what it is?"

Zef reflected on the possibilities for a long moment. Tell her too much and she might send someone to get rid of Manx, not tell her enough and it might scare her into doing just that. "Friend of mine," Zef replied at last. "Harmless."

"Ah, so you know a whole lot more than you're telling."

"Don't sell out my friends," Zef said shortly.

Drusilla nodded in agreement. "I wouldn't either. So tell me, does this friend of yours purr by any chance?"

"Purr?" Zef said, tilting his head to one side.

"You know, like a cat?"

"You're not helping me any, Drusilla," Zef said gruffly. "Don't know what purr means or what a cat is."

"A cat is a four-legged animal with claws and sharp fangs, and purring sounds like this," she said, humming.

"Heard something like that a time or two," Zef admitted. "Not sure where it came from, though."

"Uh-huh," she said skeptically.

Zef was sure she didn't believe him, but, thankfully, a trio of birds flew overhead just then and, after circling the lake a few times, settled down in the still waters near the opposite shore.

"Got to get to work now, Zef," Drusilla said quietly. "If you want to talk, it's fine with me, but keep your voice down, please."

Zef had never been asked to be quiet so politely before, and it had the effect of leaving him momentarily speechless. During those moments of silence, he decided that this woman was just nice enough for his friend, Manx. He drew in a breath to call Manx down to the shore from his post in the trees, but decided that such an action went against Drusilla's request to keep his voice down. Then Zef realized that if Manx wanted her as a mate, it might be helpful to know whether or not she already had one.

"Got someone back home waiting for you?" Zef ventured.

Looking at him in surprise, she laughed softly. "Why would you want to know that?" she asked. "Looking for a girlfriend?"

"Oh, not for myself," Zef said hastily. "Too old for that! But my friend might—"

"Zef," Drusilla said gently as she sketched the group of birds on her canvas, "I'm not sure your 'friend' and I would be… compatible."

"You should let me be the judge of that," Zef said firmly. "Besides, I think you'd like him."

"Him?" Drusilla echoed. "Well, at least it's a 'him.' That's a plus."

Zef wasn't quite sure what to make of this comment, but went on doggedly. "He's a... nice fellow."

"They always are," Drusilla sighed. "Now, don't take this the wrong way, Zef, but one of the reasons I came here was to get away from 'nice' fellows. Thanks, but I think I'll pass."

This attitude had Zef considerably perplexed, and he considered hollering for Manx again, but decided that having a conference with him first would be best. "Well," said Zef, "you let me know if you change your mind."

"Sure, Zef," she replied absently. "You'll be the first to know."

Zef backed off and swam into the depths of the lake, heading down to where the shore curved out of sight of the house. If her hearing was any good, she might hear him talking with Manx, but he considered it a risk worth taking.

Manx, however, was watching Drusilla and Zef from the trees and felt no desire to leave his current post to talk with Zef. She had spoken kindly to the eltran, even laughing a few times. The sound of her laughter had sent thrills through Manx. Nothing so far indicated that this woman wouldn't be receptive to him, and the more he watched her, the more perfect she seemed. Having seen his footprints, Manx suspected that she might hole up in the house and never come out again, but her presence on the beach indicated otherwise. She wasn't easily frightened—she'd been startled, perhaps, but not scared enough to leave. That was good.

Then the wind changed subtly, sending her fragrance wafting toward him. No sexual arousal this time, but it was a pleasing aroma, all the same. She smelled of contentment and an absorption in her work, and Manx could see her painting beginning to take shape even from where he stood. Her slender, graceful hands held her brush in a delicate grasp, stroking the canvas almost lovingly.

Manx had no idea how long he stood watching, but he knew that a considerable amount of time must have passed because Klog came out and cleaned the beach and then later on brought out Drusilla's lunch. Manx's stomach grumbled at the mouth-watering aroma. He knew firsthand what a good cook Klog was. The droid—not caring that Manx was, in effect, a trespasser—had prepared meals for Manx before, setting his plate out on the table where Drusilla had enjoyed her dinner the previous evening. *Before I started purring and scared her off,* Manx reminded himself. He wanted to kick himself for that—first purring and then leaving footprints! He knew she'd spotted him watching through the window as well. She was bound to be nervous as a result, and if Klog started fixing dinner for two, her anxiety level was sure to increase.

Manx's mind drifted off as he considered what it would be like to share a meal with her. He could look into her eyes from across a table, see her up close, inhale her scent, and then mate with her. He began purring again without realizing it. She didn't hear him, though; the distance was too great and she was fully occupied.

Manx had never watched an artist at work before and was impressed with Drusilla's dedication. It was a fascinating thing to observe, and he would have enjoyed it even if she hadn't been one to send his mind into erotic locales. Without realizing it, he began to admire her talent and skill along with her appearance. He liked the way she moved, too, along with her occasional mutterings to herself. Drawn to her like a magnet, he gradually moved to the edge of the woods and sat down on a fallen tree to observe.

—~~~—

Drusilla ate her lunch, once again astonished that Klog could somehow read her mind and know that she'd been craving grilled cheese and chicken soup. Calculating how many paintings she'd have to produce and sell to acquire a Klog of her own, she sighed wearily, doubting that she could accomplish enough in her lifetime. She hoped she was wrong about that and made a mental note to ask Lester when she saw him next. All the housekeeping and cook droids she'd ever dealt with had been noisy, irritating, and inept. This one was truly a gem.

After lunch, the birds left the lake, but the butterflies were dancing over the water, so Drusilla decided to add a few of them into the painting. They were huge, with hues even more vivid than those of the birds, and, best of all, they seemed to enjoy landing on her so observing them up close wasn't a problem. The problem was trying to get them to go away.

"Lester was a lot better at this than I am," she muttered. "Beat it!" she shouted, waving her hands furiously as the butterflies landed in droves on her hat and arms, several of them even attempting to kiss her cheeks.

She was still batting at them without success when she heard a quiet giggle behind her. "They like the taste of you."

Turning, she spotted Roger crossing the sand toward her. With a quick wave of his hands, the butterflies left her instantly.

"Neat trick," she commented. "They've just been ignoring me. Don't guess you're going to tell me how you did that, are you?"

The boy merely shook his head and laughed, sitting down in the sand beside her, his srakie perched on his shoulder. "Did you like the bolaka?"

"Yes, I did," she replied. "I had some for a snack this morning. It tastes sort of like a mango."

"My srakie can get you more," he said eagerly, gesturing toward his pet. "Or he can get something different."

"I saw lots of fruit hanging from the trees when Lester drove me here. Are they all edible?"

Roger nodded. "It is why we live in the trees."

"I noticed that too. I heard there were no dangerous animals, so I wondered." Remembering that long, bumpy ride from the village, she asked, "What brings you out this far, Roger? It's a pretty long walk from the spaceport. Is it really worth one triplak to sell me more fruit?"

"My mother sent me," he replied with a broad grin. "She wants to know if it's okay to visit you again." Pointing at her canvas, he said, "She and some of the other mothers want to see what you're doing."

"Art lovers, huh? Well, they can come if they like, but they might want to wait until I've got more to show them."

"It takes a long time to do this?"

Drusilla shrugged. "It depends on what I'm painting. Some take longer than others, but if I have plenty of time and few interruptions, I can get finished much faster."

Roger was nothing if not intuitive. "So, we should not visit?"

"Once in a while is fine, but, like I said, I'm here to work."

Nodding, Roger put down his srakie and it bounded over to the trees and quickly climbed one. "I will let you try some trelas fruit and see if you like it," he said, adding with a grin, "A 'free sample.'"

"You're quite the little entrepreneur, aren't you?" Drusilla said approvingly. "You catch on quickly."

The srakie ran back to Roger, jumped into his arms, and handed over a soft, purple fruit. "I did not think about visitors not knowing what our fruits taste like," he said. "But I will give them a free one from now on."

Drusilla took the trelas from him and bit into it. Her lips went into an immediate pucker and her tongue felt as though all of the moisture had been sucked out of it. "Is it ripe?" she asked in dismay. "Tastes like a green persimmon to me."

"Oh, yes," Roger replied. "But it is more the effect than the taste that our people enjoy."

"Effect, huh?" Drusilla said doubtfully. "You *like* the inside of your mouth feeling like it's full of sour sand?" Reaching for her glass of tea, which was empty, she let out a sob.

"No," said Roger with a shake of his head, "it makes you sleepy."

"Well, maybe so, but I'm not sure I could sleep with this taste in my mouth—even if I could stop drinking long enough to doze off."

Klog came floating out just then with a refill. "Thanks, Klog," she gasped gratefully. "I needed that!"

Roger looked at Klog with awe. "I have heard about this thing," he said. "It does work for you?"

"Yes, and he can read minds too," Drusilla said with a nod. "I just wish I knew how he does it."

Klog beeped once as a small compartment opened near the upper rings of his body, from which Klog removed something that looked suspiciously like a Twinkie and held it out to Roger.

"What is this?" Roger asked after a careful inspection.

"It's a very popular snack food on Earth," Drusilla replied. "Go ahead. Try it."

Roger took one bite and immediately spat it out. "That is not food!"

"That has been a topic of debate for about a thousand years," Drusilla said dryly. "But where I come from, most people love them."

"I believe I will go home now," Roger said, giving the remainder of the Twinkie back to Klog. "I will tell my mother to visit again when you have been here longer."

"Okay," Drusilla said. "Give me a couple of weeks and I'll have more to show them."

As Roger trotted off, Drusilla looked questioningly at Klog, who beeped twice.

"I've never known you to make a mistake like that," she said. "And I know I'd rather not be inundated with visitors. Did you do that to get rid of him?"

Klog chirped and floated off to the house.

Obviously he could be counted on to fulfill more wishes than what she wanted for dinner. Too bad he couldn't pull her "fantasy man" out of a hat.

—ᴍ—

Drusilla couldn't have said if it was the trelas that was responsible, but something was making her feel sleepy, so she pulled a lounge chair closer to the shore and settled down to lie in the sun for a while. It was peaceful and still, with only the sound of the breeze stirring the leaves and the occasional bird call to break the silence. As she lay on the verge of sleep, the calls became more frequent, eventually joining together to form a melody. Hauntingly beautiful, it continued on, gaining strength until she realized it couldn't possibly be a bird song. She'd been to many different worlds and had heard a lot of birds before, but never any who could sing like that.

She knew very little about Baradan culture but had to assume that they had some form of music — nearly every culture did. This was simply someone off in the distance playing a flute — it might even have been Roger, though she hadn't noticed him carrying anything but his srakie. She was trying to imagine the sort of mouthpiece such an instrument would have to have for a wide-mouthed Baradan to play it, when the song ended.

She waited for a time to see if it would begin again, and when it didn't, she considered going for a swim or a ride in the boat. Both sounded good, so she went out to the dock and climbed aboard. The boat was a large pontoon; rectangular in shape with a flat deck surrounded by padded seats on all sides and a safety rail at the outer edge to keep the careless — or intoxicated — from falling overboard. She'd piloted a similar craft in her youth and, knowing that it took very little skill to maneuver, had no qualms about taking it out alone. Rummaging around beneath the pilot's console, she found a visor to shade her eyes from the sun's glare and then gave the engine the command to start. It engaged without as much as a sputter, and, after casting off the mooring lines, she settled herself into the large, contoured pilot's chair, took the wheel, and steered it easily away from the dock and out toward the open water. The lake was relatively narrow near the house—an easy swim from shore to shore—but further to the east, it widened out to a vast expanse of water that seemed to be very deep. After a relaxing cruise of its full length, she returned to the center of the lake, stopped the engine, dropped the anchor, and dove in.

The water was cool and silky on her bare skin and the quiet stillness surrounded her completely. The only sounds were the birds and other jungle creatures—none of which were dangerous, she reminded herself as a snake skimmed along the water's edge. She swam lazily for a while and then lay on her back and floated.

After a bit, she heard the sound of something emerging from the water and wasn't surprised to hear Zef's voice.

"Isn't this just the best damn lake you've ever seen?" Zef said, lolling nearby.

"Sure is," she replied. Somehow, her previous conversation with Zef had removed the aversion she felt toward him, and the idea of swimming in the same lake with him didn't bother her anymore. For such a hideous creature, he moved through the water as gracefully and effortlessly as an otter, and he disturbed her no more than the fish—until he spoke, of course.

"My friend's been watching you," Zef blurted out.

"Is that right?"

"Yeah. Says you're nice to look at."

Memories of the Ionian Impressionist returned. He'd said the same thing, though Drusilla didn't return the sentiment. "Sweet of him to say so."

"Told you he was a nice fellow, didn't I?"

"Yes, you did."

"Don't mind him watching you?"

"Not particularly."

It was obvious that this lack of interest disturbed Zef, for he made another sound like that of an exasperated snort. "Don't feel interested or irritated?"

"No."

"Want to meet him?"

"Not really."

"Sure about that?"

"Yes," Drusilla replied. "No men, no worries."

"He's pretty."

"Pretty what?"

"Just pretty."

"I prefer handsome to pretty," Drusilla sniffed, "but I don't want either one right now." She had her fantasy man, after all, who was much better than any real one could ever be. "Besides, what you would call pretty, I'd probably call..." Momentarily at a loss for the right word, she realized it didn't matter. Nothing did. She was drifting, floating, relaxed, and nothing mattered. "I don't mean to be rude, Zef, but I'd rather not talk about him."

"Later on, perhaps?" suggested Zef.

"No. Not ever," she said firmly. "And Zef?"

"Yeah?"

"I don't want to talk at all right now," she murmured. "I'm sure you'll think it sounds completely boring, but right now, I just want to... *be*."

"Well, all right," he grumbled. "Just promise me you won't drown in my lake."

"I'll try not to."

"Lester would give me hell for letting anyone drown," Zef went on, but then paused for a moment as though struck with a novel thought. "You *could* drown, couldn't you?"

"Well, yes," Drusilla admitted. "I *could*. But I think I'd rather not."

"Well, what if my friend were to rescue you... save you from drowning?"

"I'd be eternally grateful, I'm sure," Drusilla said amiably. "But I'll try not to put him to the trouble."

Meanwhile, hoping her eyes weren't as good as his, Manx had ventured nearer to the shore. He never dreamed he'd ever be jealous of Zef, but he was now. She was wet, practically naked, and floating on the water like the answer to his deepest needs and wildest dreams. All he had to do was pluck her out of the lake...

Drusilla chose that moment to right herself in the water and glance toward the shore. Manx, elusive as ever, was visible for only a second before retreating behind a nearby tree.

It had only been a moment, but the fleeting glimpse of a humanoid male with long, black hair imprinted itself on her mind—a humanoid male even more naked than she was herself. He'd had something around his waist, and what might have been a bow and quiver slung across his back, but that was all. That's *got* to be him, she thought. Hmm. Might not be a bad idea to… No, she wouldn't. She couldn't. It was a *very* bad idea.

Three months, she reminded herself. Three long months painting birds, swimming in the lake—and talking to no one but Zef. For a fleeting moment she thought that Ralph—good old matchmaking Ralph—must have set up this entire scenario to get her to fall for… someone. She wouldn't have put it past him to plant this guy on Barada just for her to find, but she dismissed the idea immediately; even Ralph wouldn't go to the trouble to concoct such an elaborate scheme. No, this had to be a simple coincidence. The way Zef talked, this guy was a friend of his, which meant he'd been there for some time.

Lester must not have known about him or he would have warned her, just as he had warned her about Zef. If Lester had gone to the trouble of introducing her to Zef, whom he obviously disliked, he probably would have made a point of telling her all about the Fugitive of the Jungle as though he was some sort of tourist attraction. No, Lester didn't know about Zef's friend, and as furtive as he was, he didn't seem to want Drusilla to know about him either.

"He might be pretty, but he's pretty shy too," Drusilla told Zef. "How come he doesn't just come right out and talk to me?"

Zef hesitated before answering. "Wants me to find out what you're like first," he said truthfully.

"And?"

"I think he'd like you."

"Maybe, but would I like *him?* I'm going to be here for a long time—and I'm all by myself. I don't want to make any enemies."

"I don't think you would," Zef said nonchalantly. "And especially not him."

She remembered the purring—perhaps it had been done by the man Zef was talking about. He'd seen her out on the patio, enjoying dinner in the nude, and later on had watched her through the window while she'd been engaged in her sexual fantasy—those glowing cat eyes *had* to belong to a guy who could purr! It was safe to say that though she didn't have many secrets from him, he seemed to be hiding something. "Maybe not," she conceded, "but why is he so secretive? What is he—an escaped felon?"

"Felon?" Zef echoed. "Is that a bad thing?"

"Yes," she replied. "A violent criminal."

"No," he said firmly. "He's not... bad."

Drusilla laughed. Here she was, treading water in the middle of a lake beneath a purple sky, talking to an amphibious creature who was trying to fix her up with his buddy. "It could only happen in the Milky Way," she sighed.

Zef didn't respond to that, and during the lull in the conversation, Drusilla gazed across the water to the patch of jungle where she'd last seen her secret admirer. "What's his name?" she asked.

Zef began to reply, but stopped himself. "If I tell you, you have to promise not to tell Lester," he said.

"Lester? Why not?"

"Dunno," Zef admitted. "But my friend always

disappears when anyone else comes around—like he doesn't want to be found."

"Well, he's very good at it," Drusilla commented. "He's almost like a ghost—except for the footprints." She paused as something else came to mind. "Tell me, does he play the flute?"

Ignoring her question, Zef persisted, "Do you promise?"

"Yeah, sure," Drusilla said in an offhand manner. "Lester probably wouldn't care anyway."

"Well, don't tell him," Zef advised. "Manx might stop talking to me otherwise."

Drusilla chuckled. "So, his name is Manx, then?"

"Shouldn't have said that," Zef said morosely and then growled: "You're making me careless!"

Just then a shout from further up the shore put an end to their conversation. Lester was standing on the dock waving at her.

"Rrrggghh!" Zef said with a shudder. "Wouldn't you know it? It's that damn Lester again!"

Drusilla couldn't help but laugh, thinking it odd that Zef should have such an aversion to the Baradan. Granted, Lester wasn't what Drusilla considered to be attractive, but then, neither was Zef.

"Hey, Lester!" Drusilla called back. "What's up?"

"I must speak with you!" Lester shouted. "It is urgent!"

"Better go see what he wants," Zef advised. "Otherwise, he'll swim out here. Rrrgghhh! Can't stand that!"

"Okay, okay," she said to Zef. The absolute last thing Drusilla wanted to do was to stop what she was doing and go talk to Lester, but it seemed there was no alternative. Raising her voice, she yelled out, "I'm coming!" and swam back to the boat.

Upon her arrival at the dock, Drusilla could see that Lester was in a serious state of agitation; his hands were moving so fast they almost seemed to vanish.

"There is danger!" he said dramatically. "I have come to warn you!"

"Yeah, what about?" Drusilla asked, unperturbed.

"There is a vicious creature loose in the jungle! A large wildcat with deadly fangs and claws!"

Drusilla hadn't seen him closely enough to know anything about fangs and claws, but the purring seemed feline, so, while she was fairly certain that Lester was referring to Manx, she was just as certain that he wasn't the least bit dangerous. There had been any number of times thus far that he could have attacked her, but he had always kept his distance. "Is that right?" she said, doing her best to seem properly concerned. "Do you think I should pack up and leave?"

"Oh, no," Lester said quickly. "But you must beware! And I have b-brought you a-a weapon." As he said this last bit, his normally musical voice dropped to a hoarse, stammering whisper.

Since Lester was holding what appeared to be a serviceable pulse pistol, Drusilla gazed at him in surprise. "I thought there were no weapons on this planet," she said finally. "Where did that come from?"

"It was confiscated from some offworlders," Lester said. "It was deemed necessary for you to have it until this creature is killed—or caught and returned to its owners."

"So it's an escaped *pet?*" Drusilla said. "Are you sure it's all that dangerous?"

"Oh, yes!" Lester said emphatically. "It has already attacked another offworlder."

"Another offworlder?" she echoed.

Lester hesitated for a moment, then replied, "There were two females. One was attacked, but the other frightened it away."

"And it only goes after offworlders, huh?" Drusilla mused. "That's pretty convenient, don't you think?"

If anything, Lester seemed even more uncomfortable with this idea. "I am sure it was a coincidence."

"Then why not arm everyone?" she asked. "Seems to me you ought to be more worried about your own people."

"But you are alone and far from the village," Lester reminded her. "You are also our guest. We wish no harm to come to you."

"Mmm, bad for the tourist trade, I suppose," Drusilla remarked. "Attacked a woman, you say? Was she badly hurt?"

"She was injured but will recover," Lester reported. "She would have been killed but for her sister's intervention."

Somehow this didn't sound at all like Manx, who seemed to avoid contact with everyone, including, at least so far, herself. Nevertheless, to satisfy Lester, Drusilla accepted the pistol, promising to keep an eye out, though she had no intention of shooting Manx or anyone else—aside from the fact that she probably wasn't capable of hitting anything much smaller than an elephant.

But Manx might have been. He'd had something hanging from his belt, which could have been a holster, or a sheath for a knife. He'd had a bow too, but neither of those weapons necessarily meant that he would attack anyone, unless it was in self-defense. She considered it unlikely that anyone on Barada would pose a threat to him—unless they'd seen something they shouldn't have. She'd have to ask Zef about that.

Drusilla took a moment to consider. Never having met Manx, she only had Zef's word that Manx wasn't a bad sort, and what kind of recommendation was that? Zef, on the other hand, never bothered to hide his feelings on any subject, which led Drusilla to suspect that lying, for any reason, was something he just plain didn't do.

Assuring Lester that she would be very cautious, she walked back to his truck with him and after some brief instructions on how to fire the weapon, he finally left.

Drusilla examined the pistol and decided that she at least ought to practice with it. Taking aim at a nearby rock, she pulled the trigger. The rock exploded into a million pieces.

"Let's back that off a bit, shall we?" she said to herself. Adjusting the intensity to its lowest setting, she aimed at another rock. This time, it flew off and hit the trunk of a nearby tree with a distinct thud. "Good enough," she said and engaged the safety lock, thankful that the pistol's operation was easy enough not to require an owner's manual. Chuckling to herself, she decided that they had to be pretty simple or your average dim-witted thug wouldn't be able to use one of them.

What she didn't know was that the pistol had originally belonged to a Nedwut—which would prove very important in the days ahead.

Tash'dree wiped the crusts of dried blood from her sister's pale face. She was in a great deal of pain, but was bearing it well.

"The weapons ban on this world was unexpected," Lutira whispered. "But this is a jungle planet, much like our own world. We have an advantage that many others would not."

"You would think that after being attacked they would have given back our rifles," Tash'dree said irritably.

"They did allow us the one pistol," Lutira said. "You must take it and continue the search."

"And leave you here unprotected?" Tash'dree scoffed. "I wasn't sure you would live after what that beast did to you."

Lutira shook her head. "I am weak, but not helpless, and I will be safe aboard the ship."

"Perhaps," Tash'dree admitted, "but I still wish we had brought our own healer with us. We have been lucky thus far, but that Baradan healer was... inefficient."

"All healers do not have the abilities of the Zerkans," Lutira said, "but I will recover in time. If you will not take the one weapon we have, you have your knife and with it you can make a bow—though I doubt that you will need more than your knife against that beast. If we had known of its existence, we would have been prepared and it would have been no match for either of us. You *must* continue the search," she stressed, "for the others will arrive soon. The Baradan mentioned another offworlder—a female— staying in a house near a lake somewhere in this region. Seek her out and discover what you can from her."

Tash'dree was reluctant, but she knew that such a small ship as theirs might not be noticed among the larger ones at the port, though, granted, there were not many. No one knew their true purpose, nor would they suspect it.

While her sister rested, she worked on making a bow from a springy branch and long fibers from the tough vines that dangled from the nearby trees. The arrows took longer, but with her skills, they were straight and would fly true. Thus armed, the danger from the wildcat could be discounted; Tash'dree had begun hunting swergs at a very young age and, pitted against those cunning predators, she had few equals.

Sheathing her knife, she stowed the bow and arrows in a sack slung over her back and, having ensured that all was well with Lutira, set off through the trees.

Chapter 7

AFTER TARGET PRACTICE, DRUSILLA WENT BACK DOWN TO THE lake to collect her paints and easel. Critically observing her canvas, she noted some seemingly stray marks in a blank spot near the outer edge that resembled a smiling face. Being quite certain that she hadn't done it herself, she searched the tree line for Manx but saw nothing. Lester might have done it—he would have passed by on his way to the dock—but she doubted this; Lester was far too anxious to please and it seemed a bit presumptuous of him. Thinking that it was intended as a message of some kind, Drusilla stood silently for a moment, wondering how to reply.

The obvious answer came to her as she surveyed the perfectly smooth, sandy beach. Klog wouldn't perform his beach-keeping duties again until the next day, so, with the end of her paintbrush, she wrote, "Hello, handsome!" in the sand. "No," she decided, erasing it with her foot. "Too suggestive. Sends the wrong message." Being friendly was fine, however, so she simply copied what he had drawn, gathered up her gear, and, with a quick glance over her shoulder hoping to catch another glimpse of him, went back to the house.

Drusilla was still thinking about Manx as she stripped off her bathing suit and stepped under the hot spray of the shower. His similarity to her fantasy man was disturbing. Had he somehow implanted his own image in her mind?

He was not human—she was certain of that—and every alien species had its own set of innate abilities; for all she knew, this was typical of his kind, and the idea intrigued her. She closed her eyes as the hot water sluiced down her bare skin, and the thought of what it would be like to have him there with her hit her with a jolt, leaving her momentarily breathless. One glimpse of him had her all atwitter; one touch would have done her in. Then she remembered that he had gotten more than a glimpse of her through the window the night before—but had he known what she was doing?

"Oh, of course he did, the lecherous weirdo!" she grumbled aloud, momentarily regretting the smiley face in the sand. Perhaps packing a pistol wasn't such a bad idea after all.

—◦◦◦—

It was raining the next morning, so Drusilla worked indoors, touching up a few spots on the painting she'd started and adding in more details. She sat facing the lake, hoping to see more of the birds, but while she worked, her eyes were frequently drawn to that smiling face at the edge of the canvas. She was kidding herself and she knew it. She wasn't on the lookout for the birds; she wanted to catch another glimpse of Manx. The knowledge that the rain had probably washed away her reply—along with any further message he might have left for her—was disappointing, though she hated to admit to her curiosity.

"Don't want to hear back from him," she muttered. "Don't need lecherous aliens hanging around. Zef is bad enough."

As Klog floated by and began dusting the furniture, Drusilla began to understand why it *did* matter. She'd never stayed anywhere quite so secluded before, and while all the peace and quiet had seemed like a wonderful thing at the outset, the lack of human contact was already beginning to make her feel strange. Perhaps she should have encouraged Roger to bring his mother and her friends to visit again. As long as Klog didn't offer them Twinkies or fried chicken, they could have had a long chat over a cup of tea and a bowl of fruit and she would feel normal again. Or maybe she needed to call Ralph and tell him about the birds. No. She didn't want to talk to Ralph—she wasn't *that* desperate—at least, not yet.

She hitched in her chair irritably. No, what she wanted to do was to go look for Manx—or at least check her "mail." The need to go down to the beach was becoming unbearable. It was like sending an email to someone and then constantly hitting the "get mail" button to check for a response. She hadn't seen Klog go out for beach maintenance, but it was raining cats and dogs and there was just no way…

Getting abruptly to her feet, Drusilla knew it didn't matter if she got wet; she wouldn't melt. She could go out on the beach, check the sand and see that there was nothing there, and then she could concentrate on her work again. Having to change clothes or dry her hair was no big deal, after all. Klog had nothing better to do than to clean up after her, and she wasn't getting anything done anyway.

Not even bothering to grab an umbrella, she ran straight down the stairs and out onto the beach. The rain was coming down in buckets, soaking her to the skin in moments. The umbrella she'd been sitting under the day before was leaning to one side and now sheltered the sign she'd drawn.

Except that now there was another symbol next to it. One she didn't recognize and to which she could attach no meaning. Still, it constituted a reply of some kind— but the tone of it was difficult to determine. The best she could do was to write a question mark in the sand, but leaving cryptic messages for someone who probably didn't even speak the same language was a tricky business. Then she remembered Zef. He had been able to converse with her in the Standard Tongue, and he'd obviously done some talking with Manx, so presumably they could understand one another. But what did > ~ < mean? And for that matter, what was the correct response?

Deciding it was at least friendly, she drew another smile and went back to the house, stopping in the beach room to dry off. Taking a towel from the shelf, she began to dry her hair with it, but then noticed something at the back of the shelf that wasn't a towel. Curious, she pulled it down and discovered that it was a man's shirt and trousers, old and worn, but clean and neatly folded.

Under any other circumstances, especially if they'd been dirty and piled in a corner, she would have assumed that the clothing had been left by a previous tenant, but knowing that Manx was nearby made her jump to the conclusion that they probably belonged to him. Klog would have found them and washed them in any case—he was nothing if not thorough—but if Klog *had* found them, he probably would have given them to Lester to return to their owner, unless the owner was still in the vicinity and Klog knew it...

The fact that they were concealed made her even more suspicious. Did Manx have some sort of rapport with Klog, or would Klog do anyone's laundry? Had Manx dropped them off to be washed and not been able to pick them up because she was there? No, she decided, he'd been there the previous night. She'd seen his footprints. He could have retrieved them then—or at any time.

So, he went without clothes by choice. True, the jungle was always warm and clothing wasn't necessary—as Drusilla knew from firsthand experience—but Manx seemed to be keeping them for a special occasion, or because he knew he wouldn't be able to replace them. They were in a place where he could always get to them—that room was open at all times, but...

Was Manx a fugitive of some kind, or was he truly the "pet" that had escaped? He was attempting to communicate with her, first through Zef and now through drawings in the sand, but what was he saying?

Drusilla began to wish she hadn't told Zef she wasn't interested in meeting Manx because as the moments passed, the need to do just that grew exponentially. Her trip out to the beach hadn't helped a bit; in fact, it only made things worse.

Just then, the door from the upstairs opened and Klog floated in. Beeping twice, which Drusilla took to mean that lunch was ready, he then picked up the wet towel that she'd dropped on the floor. Figuring she had nothing to lose by asking, she held out the shirt and asked, "Do these clothes belong to Manx?"

She could have sworn that Klog hesitated a moment before chirping his reply. No doubt about it, the little droid knew something. She'd never cared for the more talkative droids, but just then, she'd have given a lot for Klog to be one of them.

"Does he keep them here all the time?" she went on. When Klog chirped again, she added, "Are these the only clothes he has?"

Klog replied with a sound she hadn't heard as yet, a sort of mumble which she took to mean that he didn't know the answer to that.

Then another thought occurred to her. "Does Manx live in the house when no one else is staying here?"

Klog's chirp seemed more enthusiastic than it had before.

"Do you like Manx?"

Apparently he did because he chirped twice.

Okay, thought Drusilla. Zef likes him. Klog likes him. Lester gave me a pulse pistol to shoot him if necessary—and he's giving me a bad case of the hots! Whose opinion should I believe?

If Manx belonged to someone—was an escaped slave, perhaps—and that person wanted him back—or dead—the rumor that he'd attacked someone would be enough to get him hunted down, or at least shot on sight. Drusilla had no intention of being the one to do that—and she wasn't going to let him starve, either.

"Fix him some dinner tonight, then, and put it out on the patio where he'll be sure to find it, okay?"

Klog beeped once, somehow conveying a feeling of relief with his acknowledgment.

"Don't like letting him go hungry, do you?" Drusilla said with a chuckle.

Klog buzzed emphatically and floated back upstairs.

Drusilla put Manx's clothes back where she found them and then went up to her room to get out of her own wet clothes. Putting on a simple, sleeveless dress which she then covered with her smock, she went back to work, though her mind lingered on a different inhabitant of the jungle than the one she was painting.

Manx was watching, of course. The rain didn't bother him—felt good, in fact. Almost as good as if *she* was touching him. His eyes closed as the thought of the soft touch of her fingertips tantalized him, but that would have to wait. He was anxious to see what she'd written. Go away and leave me alone, perhaps? Or, come on up and see me sometime? The sign he'd scratched into the sand was one from his homeworld, one that a man would send to a woman with whom he wished to mate as the first step toward enticement. He knew she probably wouldn't understand it, but perhaps she didn't need to. It was a gesture—an open invitation—and he hoped she would recognize it as such.

Zef hadn't been very encouraging. He'd told Manx that Drusilla didn't want to meet him, but Manx wasn't so sure about that. Zef had been listening to what Lester had to say and reported that Drusilla was now armed with a pulse pistol and had been warned that there was a dangerous beast lurking in the jungle—a beast with fangs and claws that had attacked someone. Manx knew very well that he hadn't done anything of the sort, though he did have fangs. Once she realized that, she might decide to shoot first and ask questions later, but her response to

Manx's gentle query seemed to indicate that, at least for now, she was receptive.

Manx knew that the females of other species were easier to approach than Zetithians, but, never having tried to entice a Terran female, he had no idea how to go about it in a way that wouldn't offend her. True, he had the time honored patterns of Zetithian mating behavior to aid him, but those behaviors weren't normally conducted from such a distance. Being able to inhale her scent would tell him whether or not he was wasting his time, but to do that, he needed to be a little closer.

"So, what do you think?" Zef asked, popping up unceremoniously at the water's edge.

Manx grinned and threw a sidelong glance at Zef. "I think she likes me," he said with more confidence than he actually felt.

"That's not what she said," Zef disagreed. "Said she didn't want anything to do with you."

"Females don't always say what they mean," Manx said informatively. "And she came out in the rain to see what I wrote in the sand." Manx smiled a very satis- fied smile. He was even beginning to convince himself. "She's curious."

"That's a good thing?" Zef asked.

"Oh, yes," Manx replied. "A *very* good thing."

"You primates have got some damn strange ways!" Zef declared. "Eltrans just mate with whoever happens to be swimming by when our dicks get hard."

"Not very selective, are you?" Manx said with a chuckle.

"Yeah, well, the thing you have to be selective about is where you swim."

"Ah, I see," said Manx. "So it isn't that simple for you either."

"Well, maybe not," Zef admitted reluctantly. "Shouldn't be so hard, but maybe it is."

"When you stop and think about it, it's no wonder females are selective—who could blame them?"

"What d'you mean?" Zef asked with surprise. "The best I can tell, females don't seem to care one way or the other—at least, not about me."

"Zef," Manx said gravely, "we put something of ourselves into a very sensitive place on a female—and they tend to bear young after that. I think I'd be pretty selective if it were me."

"Well, you're not!" Zef argued. "C'mon, Manx! We're guys! We can put our dicks anyplace we want!"

"I'm beginning to understand why you got voted out of your lake."

"Aw, just go fuck her," Zef grumbled. "They all give up and let you do it in the end anyway. Why spend so much time dicking around?"

"Because mating with her one time is not all I have in mind," Manx declared. If he had his way, he would be with Drusilla for years to come—enjoying the endless pleasure of her company.

"Well, then just go show her your pretty face and she'll sigh and fall into your arms and all that crap."

Manx couldn't help but laugh, though he did see the logic in letting her know that he truly was interested. Leaving messages in the sand would only get a guy so far, and hiding out in the jungle when he could be with Drusilla was rapidly losing its appeal. With a firm resolve, he stepped out from the cover of the trees, went down to the lake, and began to swim toward the opposite shore.

"Where the hell are you going?" Zef demanded.

"To show her my pretty face," Manx replied as he swam.

"Not gonna show her your dick?" Zef said with surprise. "That's what I'd do if I were you. I hate to admit it, but that's a damn fine dick you've got there. Better than a pretty face anytime. Might tell her so myself."

"Zef," Manx said.

"What?"

"Be quiet."

"She'll see it anyway," Zef called out as he began to swim after his friend. "You should put some pants on."

"Why? She doesn't wear clothes all the time," Manx said. "I don't think she'd care."

"She's never let me or Lester see her naked," Zef pointed out.

"Well, that makes me special then, doesn't it?"

"You've seen her naked?" Zef said excitedly. "Really?"

"Yes, really," Manx replied as he reached the shallow water and stood up.

"Did it make your dick hard?"

Manx shot a quelling glance at the eltran. "I thought I told you to be quiet."

Zef roared with laughter. "She made your fuckin' dick hard, didn't she?" Then he noticed something very important. "It's not hard now. You're thinking about her, aren't you? What the hell's the matter with you?"

"I have to smell her desire," Manx explained.

"Or you can't get it up?" Zef said in horror. "That's damned inconvenient!"

"Not really," Manx said. "What good is a hard dick without a woman who wants you?"

"Manx," Zef said sadly. "You are *so* fuckin' strange."

"Maybe," Manx said with a marked lack of concern as he knelt to inspect the writing in the sand. "But at least I'm pretty and I have a nice dick."

"Nah, you're not pretty," Zef said. "Now that I've seen Drusilla, I realize I was wrong about that. *She's* pretty. You—well, you're a fuckin' hunk!"

Manx burst out laughing and sat back in the sand, nearly erasing Drusilla's reply with his foot—which, fortunately, wasn't a problem because he'd already seen it. Still beaming, he looked up toward the house.

———

Drusilla had been sitting at her easel but had taken a moment to gaze out at the rain-dappled lake when Manx emerged from the jungle looking like Tarzan himself. She got a quick glimpse of his perfect form and rippling muscles before he sank into the water, and she felt a shock of arousal slice through her like a lightning bolt as he began to swim. His effortless swimming, his body dripping as he emerged from the water, his long hair plastered across his broad chest... Drusilla had seen plenty of men in her time—some of them artist's models who were, quite frankly, to die for—but this, this male *animal* was something she'd never even dreamed of before. She began to rethink the idea that he had planted his image in her mind; Manx made her fantasy man seem pathetic in comparison.

She stood staring at him, open-mouthed with awe, and gasped as he turned his back to her and knelt in the sand. "Oh, my God!" she whispered. Putting a hand to her mouth, it was a moment or two before she realized she was painfully biting her thumb. Then the smile he cast in her direction nearly sent her into orgasm.

Looking closer, she could see that he did, indeed, carry a knife and bow, and also that Zef's head was sticking up out of the water nearby. Manx was still laughing, but his next move dispelled any notion she might have had that he was laughing at her expense. Unbuckling the belt at his waist and laying his bow and quiver in the sand—clearly disarming himself—Manx flipped over, stretching out like a sinuous house cat as he shook his long mane back from his face. She didn't know if he could see her in the window or not, but he was certainly acting as though he could because, very deliberately, he reached out and drew another symbol in the sand large enough to be seen from where she stood. > ~ >

It was slightly different from the other symbol, but she still didn't know what it meant. Then it hit her. She knew them as ∧ and ∨, but the meaning was the same: they were male/female symbols. The ~ was a mystery, but he was asking her to… what? Shake hands? Have sex with him? Marry him?

He was wet, naked, and the most shockingly attractive man Drusilla had ever seen, but now that he was smiling at her, she could also see his fangs and had absolutely no idea what she should do. Run, perhaps? And if so, in what direction?

"Away from the window, you idiot!" she exclaimed to herself. "Now!"

—∽∽∽—

Meanwhile, Zef was giving Manx a few pointers in the fine art of seduction.

"Shake your cock at her," Zef suggested. "Gets 'em every time!"

"That might help with eltrans," Manx said equably, "but I don't think it would work with Drusilla."

"And just what makes you think that?"

"She backed away from the window just now," he said with a nod toward the house. "I think I might have gone too far already."

Rising up on his shaky pectoral fins, Zef crawled past Manx to get some idea of what Drusilla was seeing from her window. Manx didn't look at all frightening to Zef, nor did he appear to have gone too far; in fact, Zef didn't think he'd gone nearly far enough. "She can't see your dick with your leg crossed over like that."

"I'm not trying to show her my dick!" Manx exclaimed. "I'm writing her a message!"

Zef looked at the symbols Manx had drawn with a jaundiced eye. "What the hell does that mean?"

Manx gazed regretfully at the sand. "Well, now that you mention it…"

"What?"

"It's a mating symbol," Manx replied miserably.

"Ha!" Zef exclaimed in triumph. "You're asking her if she wants to fuck, aren't you?"

"Well… maybe," Manx admitted. "Guess I should have used the other one again." Manx erased the female sign and wrote it again in reverse. "This one just means I'd like to talk to her."

"Oh, really?" Zef said. "So now you're telling her, 'No, I don't want to fuck, but I'd like to talk?'"

"You're making me sound like an idiot," Manx said, sounding even more miserable.

"And I'm telling you, you just need to get that willie of yours up so she can see it!" Zef cocked his head, eyeing Manx curiously. "Now, what was it again? You have to smell her?"

Manx nodded. "It worked last night when she was out on the patio eating dinner. She smelled so good it nearly knocked me out."

"Food gets her excited?"

"Well, maybe," Manx conceded. "But she *was* naked. Maybe that's all it takes. Either way, she almost got nailed by a total stranger. Don't think she would have liked that," he added reflectively.

Zef thought it was just possible that it would be the answer to Drusilla's wildest dreams, but women in general were something of an enigma to him. You just never knew how they would react or what they were thinking. "Okay, then," Zef said brightly, "catch her without her clothes, give her something to eat, get your dick hard, and go for it."

Rolling wearily onto his back, Manx let his arms fall onto the wet sand with a loud plop. He stared up at the dark purple sky, not seeming to notice the raindrops that fell in his eyes.

"Zef," Manx said after a moment.

"What?"

"Will you please just shut up?"

Chapter 8

THE RAIN STOPPED BY EARLY AFTERNOON, BUT DRUSILLA didn't leave the house, so Manx and Zef went fishing. Actually, Manx was the one doing the fishing; Zef just ate the fish.

"I would have shared my fish with you more often if I'd known you couldn't catch your own anymore," Manx said as the eltran happily crunched the fish bones. "Why didn't you tell me?"

"Don't like to admit it," Zef said between munches. "Matter of pride, you know."

"Maybe so, but starving to death just because—"

"I'm not starving to death!" Zef protested. "I get plenty to eat—just not what I like."

Manx knew the feeling. "I'm getting tired of fish, myself," he said. "I mean, I like them, but I miss Klog's cooking."

"Hasn't been cooking for you since Drusilla came, has he?"

"He hardly ever does when someone's staying in the house," said Manx, tossing Zef another fish. "I think he's afraid to."

"Well, now that Drusilla knows you're living around here, Klog might decide it's safe to feed you again."

"I certainly hope so," Manx said fervently. "At least then I could have my fish cooked." Manx had been known to use the grill on the patio when the house was unoccupied but had never felt that starting a cooking fire was a good idea for a man who was trying to keep a low profile.

"I'll never understand why you feel the need to cook fish!" Zef exclaimed. "They're perfectly good just the way they are."

Manx didn't bother to reply, since they'd already been through the cooking issue many times before—and his thoughts had already progressed to more important matters. "Maybe I went about it wrong," he said reflectively. "I should give her something."

"Give her something?" Zef echoed. "You mean Drusilla? What for?"

"Women like getting presents," said Manx. "I'd like to give her some rainflowers—they're very pretty—but they don't last very long."

"You could give her some fish!" Zef exclaimed, quick to catch on to the idea. "Then she'll get all hot and bothered and your weasel will work and—"

"Zef," Manx said warningly. "That is *not* the only reason I want to give her a gift!"

Zef ignored this, adding dismally, "Too bad we ate them all."

Manx didn't see this as a problem. "I'll spear some more and take them to Klog and he can grill them for her. Maybe he'll give me some too," Manx added hopefully.

"Oh, joy," Zef groaned. "Grilled fish. Yum."

———

After watching the episode on the beach and trying to make sense of the whole weird mess, Drusilla finally decided that getting plastered was the logical course of action and asked Klog for a margarita. "And make it a strong one," she added.

Klog beeped and came back a few minutes later with a salt-rimmed glass filled with the best margarita Drusilla had ever tasted.

"Is there anything you can't do?"

Klog seemed to think about this for a long moment, but his reply was another one of those mumbles.

"Should have known you'd say that."

Klog went on with his work while Drusilla pondered the situation. What Manx had done was the most blatant come-on she'd ever seen—including the Ionian Impressionist who— "No, don't want to think about that right now," she said with a shudder. Manx's proposition was quite palatable while the Ionian's had been just plain gross. "So, Klog," she began conversationally. "What do you think? Should I have gone down to the beach? Did he want to talk or—? No, he wanted more than that," she said, answering her own question. "Naked men don't smile like that if they're only asking for a donation to charity." She took another sip and thanked heaven for tequila as she felt her muscles begin to relax. She was more tense than she'd realized, though it was silly of her to think she wouldn't have been—not with a hunky Tarzan wannabe out there writing love letters in the sand.

"Love letters, hell," Drusilla muttered. "He doesn't want love. He wants sex."

"And what's so wrong with that?" the tequila asked. "Sex is good!"

"But he's an alien! Hides out in the jungle and talks to amphibians and, and"—blowing out an exasperated breath, she added—"is the sexiest thing I've ever seen in my life! Man, would I like to—"

"What?"

"Nothing."

"Nothing, hell! You'd like to do everything you can think of with him—and you know it!" the tequila said wisely.

"I'd like to do a few things to him that I *haven't* thought of yet," Drusilla admitted. "If only Lester hadn't shown up and told me how dangerous he was!"

"What makes you so sure he was talking about Manx?"

"Oh, he had to be!" Drusilla insisted. "I mean, the guy *purrs,* for heaven's sake!"

"What about the fangs and claws?"

"Well, I don't know about that," Drusilla conceded. "Fangs, yes, but I've never seen Manx close enough to be sure… but even if he *does* have claws, I shouldn't have believed that bit about his being dangerous, should I? Zef knows him better, and *he* never said Manx was dangerous."

"No," the tequila said firmly. "He's just a nice, big, purring kitty who wouldn't hurt a fly. Now, stop worrying and drink up!"

———

Drusilla awoke later that evening resolving never to ask Klog for a "strong one" again. "Never had a margarita talk back to me before," she said with a grimace. Just rolling over on the couch was enough to make her head swim. "Hey, Klog!" she called out, her voice sounding oddly feeble. "What's for dinner? No, wait… you can't answer that. Never mind. Surprise me."

Klog had come in response to her summons and hovered for a moment as though waiting for her to make another request, but then the droid suddenly floated off down the stairs, returning a few minutes later carrying a row of fish hanging from a stick.

"Where'd you get that?" she inquired. "Oh, no, wait. I forgot: yes or no questions only." She paused to rephrase the question. "Did you catch them yourself?" If so, Klog had to be the fastest and most efficient fisherman in the known universe.

Klog buzzed and headed for the kitchen.

It took Drusilla a moment to realize that the droid had scurried off before she could ask him another question—and probably on purpose, too. She got up from her chair and staggered after him, hanging cautiously onto each stick of furniture she passed.

"Did Manx give you those?" she demanded.

Klog chirped and whipped out a knife and began to fillet the fish, prompting Drusilla to back off just in case Klog thought she was asking too many questions and decided to fillet *her*.

"Okay, I'll just leave you to it, then," Drusilla said hastily. "Oh, and don't forget you're supposed to fix him a plate too—oh, wait—you never forget anything, do you?"

Klog didn't bother to answer that.

Drusilla left the kitchen and drifted over to her canvas. On a whim, she sat down and painted in a shadowy figure standing half-concealed by the foliage on the far side of the lake. "He certainly is spectacular," she murmured. As she was adding his long black hair, the urge to run her fingers through it engulfed her like a tidal wave. From there it was a short step to a full-blown fantasy where she was trailing her fingers through all the hair on his body, focusing on the curly nest in his groin. She could almost feel it tickling her cheek as she kissed him all over. Last, but not least, she kissed his cock and then licked it. Then he was doing it to her—kissing her in places she'd never been kissed before, licking her like she was made of candy...

Glancing up at the window, Drusilla was surprised to find that it was now fully dark outside. What had seemed like mere moments of daydreaming had stretched on for at least an hour.

"This has been *such* a weird day!" she sighed. "Hey, Klog! Got those fish ready yet?"

Klog chirped and set her plate out on the table before beeping twice.

Getting to her feet more steadily this time, Drusilla was able to negotiate the distance without difficulty. "Did you feed the cat?" she asked as she seated herself at the table.

With another chirp, Klog gestured toward the patio.

"Mmm, getting more communicative, I see," she said approvingly. "Sign language is good."

Klog responded by squirting tea into her glass.

"I guess I should just accept the fact that you can read minds," she went on, "but it's a little disconcerting. I mean, I know you're not magical, but it's uncanny the things you seem to know. They must've programmed you so you couldn't spill the beans on how that works, huh?"

Klog chirped.

"Thought so." Then something else occurred to her. "Did you call Manx for dinner, or did you just let him find it on his own?"

Klog chirped and then buzzed.

"Yes to the first, no to the second." The fish was very tasty, but the thought of kissing Manx all over was making her crave something sweet. "Is there any of that cheesecake left?"

Klog pulled a plate out of his "belly" and set it on the table. Drusilla stared at the creamy confection smothered in strawberries and imagined Manx tasting it for the first time. "Stuff's downright orgasmic," she muttered. "Don't give any of that to Manx," she said told Klog. "I want to do it." The fact that she wanted to feed it to Manx while sitting on his cock was a bit strange—she couldn't remember ever having wanted to do something like that with a guy she'd never even spoken to. Must be the tequila, she decided. If that was the case… Giggling, she said, "Hey, Klog, how about another drink?"

Klog hesitated as though trying to decide whether or not he should cut her off.

"No, don't," she said. "I might actually go out and talk to him if you did. Don't believe I've ever tried to strike up a conversation with a naked cat-man before," she said thoughtfully. "Not sure what I should say. What are your thoughts, Klog?"

Klog merely mumbled.

"Yeah," Drusilla said shortly. "You're right. But it looks like I'll have to if I'm ever going to have a conversation with someone besides Zef. Talking with Roger and the local women was okay, of course, but I—" Remembering that Klog had set a plate out for him, she jumped up from the table so quickly her chair fell over as she darted to the door for a peek.

The table on the patio was empty. Manx had already been there and gone. "Well, I guess all that smiling and sand writing was just to get dinner, then." Disappointed, she went back to her own lonely meal, thinking that > ~ < must have meant, "I'll supply the fish if you'll cook them."

"Not very romantic," she grumbled, but her expression brightened as she realized that it *had* been a dinner invitation—of a sort.

After dinner Drusilla went out on the deck and leaned against the railing to gaze out at the lake. The rising moon was reflected clearly on the rippling surface, while the dark, dense jungle crowded close to the shore. A lively breeze picked up the hem of her dress and played around her legs. It was the perfect setting for a romantic tryst, complete with longing gazes and desperate kisses. Sighing, Drusilla realized that the only romance she was likely to get on this trip would be the kind that took place in her own mind—unless she could get up the nerve to actually talk to Manx.

A few stork-like birds waded quietly in the shallow water, searching for fish. Mesmerized by their beauty, Drusilla was so focused on them that she didn't notice the dark shape entering the water further along the shore until it cut across her line of vision, swimming steadily through the still water.

For a moment, Drusilla suspected it was Zef and crouched behind the railing to avoid being seen. She was in no mood for a shouted conversation with him, which would not only spoil the mood, but would also undoubtedly frighten away the birds.

She waited impatiently, hoping he would move on, but something about the way it swam made her realize that this was not the eltran out for an evening swim. It was Manx.

———

Manx loved swimming at night. The air was still, the water smooth and silky, caressing his skin like a lover. Of all the places he'd been while on the run, he liked this one the best. It was peaceful and quiet—unless Zef was around—and though he enjoyed the serenity of Barada, he was beginning to crave conversation with Drusilla. He didn't even care what they talked about. He just wanted to hear her voice while he looked into her eyes, perhaps touching her hair, or the warmth of her hand.

Observing her wasn't enough anymore—if, indeed, it ever had been—and though peering through the window made him feel like he was invading her privacy, it did have its rewards. He'd seen that she'd added him into her painting; she must have felt something for him, or she wouldn't have done that.

Manx swam on toward the dock, bypassing the boat as it rocked gently at its moorings, his mind still on Drusilla. She had looked so lovely that afternoon. Those little scraps of dark green fabric she had tied around her chest and hips hadn't hidden very much, and his arms were beginning to ache with the need to hold her. Diving deeply, he swam beneath the surface until he passed the dock, only emerging from the water when he reached the middle of the lake.

———

Peering through the railing, Drusilla watched breathlessly as Manx swam lazily by, apparently oblivious to the fact that he was being observed. As his arms cut through the water, his hair trailed out behind him, and the wake of his passing sparkled in the moonlight. He was so dream-like that she feared if she moved or said a word, he was sure to disappear.

The thin cotton of her gown was all that stood between her and the night breeze that slid between her thighs, teasing her sensitive skin, forcing her to imagine his hot, wet body sliding into hers. She bit her lip in an effort to keep from calling out to him, but was completely unaware that her body was already shouting at him in a language he understood better than any.

She saw him pause, his head going up like a predator catching the scent of its prey before laying back in the water to gaze up at the house as he took long strokes in the opposite direction. Fully exposed to her now, she could see the moonlight shining on his chest, could clearly see the trail of hair growing down from his chest, across his belly to his groin. She hadn't been imagining the size and shape of him; his long, thick cock was right there for her to see. The sight of him lit a fire in her and she wanted to touch him, kiss him, and lick him all over, starting right *there*…

As if he could hear her thoughts, Manx suddenly reversed his direction and swam back toward the house. Reaching the shallows, he stood, revealing his stunningly male body as he waded to the water's edge, gazing unerringly in her direction.

Instinctively, Drusilla began to draw back even further out of sight, but then realized that she was hidden in the shadows cast by the moon. She was sure he couldn't see her there — and just as sure that he *would* see her if she moved.

Drusilla shivered as the breeze touched her again, sending thrills coursing along her bare arms as Manx stretched upward, his head dropping back as his cock began to rise. She stared at it unblinkingly, and though she tried to tear her eyes away, they were drawn back. She'd never seen anyone so unabashedly aroused... so totally and completely *male*...

As his hands reached down to grip his stiff shaft, Drusilla became envious. He could do that any time he liked, while she was beginning to believe she would never get the chance. If only he wasn't so elusive—but perhaps his reticence was her fault. She made herself a promise to tell Zef that she'd changed her mind—though she knew she'd been lying from the start. But perhaps the eltran already suspected the truth—that, despite her protest, she was dying to meet Manx face-to-face, to see his smile up close, to feel his heat...

Spellbound, Drusilla held her breath to better hear his soft groans of pleasure, wanting nothing more than to caress him and make him moan. She wanted to spread her legs and let him impale her with that luscious dick while he licked nipples that were already tight and tingling with anticipation. Her clitoris began to swell with desire and she ached for him, her own creamy wetness spilling down her legs.

As she watched, he turned his profile toward her, enabling her to see his actions more clearly. His attraction was potent and intoxicating; she'd been aroused the previous evening just from hearing him purr and now her entire body tensed in anticipation of his release. His rising passion was mirrored in Drusilla's body—so much so that when his semen finally burst from him, it set off her own climax, and she had to bite her lip to keep from crying out. Then the thought that he might have been doing the same thing the night before sent another wave of ecstasy rippling through her—and another, and another…

When she looked down at him again, their eyes seemed to meet and Manx smiled. But why? She knew he couldn't possibly have seen her, and she hadn't made a sound. Was it from sexual satisfaction or was there some other reason?

Or *could* he see her? His feline eyes seemed to glow in the darkness; perhaps his night vision was keener than hers. Cats were known for that ability—at least those on Earth were. Drusilla knew nothing of Manx's origins but was already longing to visit that world.

Just how he knew she was watching him was a mystery, but the sound of his purr and the sensuous swipe of his tongue across his lips made her absolutely certain. She waited anxiously for him to speak, but he didn't say a word as he disappeared beneath the shadow of the house.

Chapter 9

As soon as he was out of sight, Drusilla sought refuge inside the house, her mind in turmoil. Where had he gone? The beach room, perhaps? And if he had, would he then try to come up the back stairs? Did the house recognize him as friendly? Was he only remaining outside as a courtesy to her? Drusilla was torn between the desire to invite him in or bar the doors. She had the choice to believe Klog and Zef's assessment of his character, or what Lester had said about him being a dangerous beast. She was beginning to wish she didn't have a choice, that he would come inside without being asked—even forcing his way in if necessary—then she wouldn't have to make that decision.

"I need another drink," she muttered. "At least the tequila was willing to give me some advice." She glanced around at Klog who was now tidying up the living room. "Can Manx be trusted?" she asked. "I mean, he's trespassing—and even though you're handing it out, he's essentially stealing food from the house. That's not very honest behavior."

Klog didn't reply. Perhaps he didn't like the idea of being suspected of aiding and abetting a criminal.

"That wasn't a rhetorical question, Klog," Drusilla said irritably. "I want an answer. Can I trust him?"

Klog chirped as he straightened a cushion on the sofa. Drusilla thought there was a certain studied nonchalance in the way he did it.

"You aren't just saying that because you like him, are you?" she went on. Then the absurdity of her questions struck her forcibly. "Oh, God! Here I am, asking the damn house droid if the cat-man of the jungle is trustworthy! I must be losing my mind."

Addressing the house computer, she said, "Don't let anyone in unless I tell you to. Is that clear?"

"Yes," the computer replied. Having given only direct orders prior to this, Drusilla had yet to hear it speak, but it sounded musical and masculine—very much like the Baradan male voices. "No admittance to unfriendly species."

"That's *not* what I said," Drusilla said, sorely tempted to lose her temper completely. Telling off a computer might provide her with a satisfying outlet for her frustration, but she also knew from experience that they didn't always listen. Some of them developed minds of their own, just as Klog seemed to have done, and when that happened, they could become dangerous. Whether this was true or not, what had apparently happened was that the computer and the droid had both become accustomed to Manx's presence and accepted him as "friendly."

Drusilla considered this for a moment. Manx had obviously been around long enough to have ingratiated himself with the computer, the droid, and Zef. Lester talked as though this wild beast of his had only recently been sighted.

"Doesn't add up, does it?" she said to no one in particular. Besides, Manx had never made a move to harm her—and he could have. He wasn't attacking, he was… what *was* he doing, anyway? Was this cat and mouse game a courtship ritual? Or was it just his way of getting fed regularly?

No, that demonstration of his manly attributes out there on the beach just now had *not* been a request for a late-night snack! He wanted a lot more than food.

"Why doesn't he just knock on the door and introduce himself? For that matter, why doesn't Zef introduce us? This is just too weird!"

None of those questions registered with Klog as anything he could answer, but the computer chimed in. "Are you addressing me?"

"Not unless you know the answer to those questions," Drusilla replied.

"The behavior of sentients does not follow any set pattern," the computer replied.

"I suppose not," Drusilla agreed, then suddenly realizing that she *did* have someone to talk to after all, she asked, "Do you have a name?"

"I am Dwell-Com Ten," the computer replied. "And thank you for asking."

"Sorry I haven't asked before now," Drusilla said, somewhat taken aback. This computer had more personality than most—or perhaps it had simply been programmed with knowledge of etiquette. "You must have been very expensive too."

"Possibly," Dwell-Com replied. "When installed, I was state-of-the-art, but I am already obsolete."

"I feel that way sometimes myself," Drusilla said with a sigh. "So, Dwell—is it okay if I call you that? Sounds better than calling you 'Computer.'"

"Yes, you may call me Dwell," the computer replied. "It is the name I prefer."

"Okay then, Dwell, tell me what you know about Manx."

Dwell apparently knew him by name because the response was immediate. "Male humanoid, planet of origin: Zetith."

"Zetith," Drusilla repeated. "Where's that?"

"It was very remote and no longer exists," Dwell replied. "Zetith was destroyed approximately twenty-five solar cycles in the past."

"You seem to know a lot," Drusilla observed. "Why is he here?"

"He is a fugitive."

"From what?"

"Persecution."

"Not a dangerous criminal?"

"No."

"Is that what he told you?"

Dwell seemed to hesitate. "This information is contained in my database."

"But he had to have told you some of it!" Drusilla protested.

"The information is in my database," Dwell repeated.

"And you don't know who put it there, do you?"

The computer seemed to consider this for a moment before replying: "No."

Was Manx capable of programming a computer? If he had simply *told* the computer about himself, Dwell would have remembered it. But why would Manx have done that? Wouldn't it be better not to tell the computer anything if he was, indeed, a fugitive? Perhaps Manx told Dwell about his past in order to gain his support, and then instructed him not to reveal the source of his information.

"Why are you telling me this? Shouldn't it be kept a secret?"

"You are not an unfriendly species," Dwell said promptly. "Nor are you one who will report his presence."

"Perhaps, but how do you know that?"

Drusilla could have sworn the computer snickered. This was obviously true, if for no other reason than the fact that she hadn't already done so.

"Okay, you're right," she admitted. "I won't rat on him." Klog seemed to know what she liked to eat, and it was just possible that he'd already sized her up as trustworthy and had communicated this to the computer. It was also possible that Dwell hadn't volunteered any information regarding Manx until it was deemed safe to tell her. Then it occurred to her that Manx could be down there in the beach room right now, talking to Dwell and telling him what to say.

"Did Manx tell you it was safe to talk to me about him?"

"Yes."

"What else can you tell me about him?"

As long as it took him to reply, Drusilla was now convinced that Manx was downstairs exchanging views with the computer.

"He likes you," Dwell said at last.

"He's never said a word to me!" Drusilla said. "How could he possibly know whether he likes me or not?"

Again, the computer hesitated. "He likes the way you smell."

It was Drusilla's turn to snicker. "Anyone could smell like me if they used the same soap!"

"It isn't the soap," Dwell said after a moment. "It's the scent of *you*."

Drusilla swallowed hard. He could smell her! *That* was how he'd known she'd been watching him! "He must have a very sensitive nose," she commented, trying to keep her tone light and casual—when she was feeling *anything* but calm. Her mind was racing and the ache between her thighs was nagging at her like a toothache, despite the orgasm she'd just experienced.

Drusilla took a deep breath and a moment to consider her options. If he was like most other males, the fact that Manx had just ejaculated would rule out the possibility of having any sort of intimate relations anytime soon, so it would be safe—at least from a sexual standpoint—to go downstairs and talk with him without having to use the computer as a go-between. She was already getting tired of hearing everything secondhand and wasn't entirely sure she wanted to be "safe" from him anyway.

But did she want to talk with him right now? After all, she'd just seen him out on the sand, completely naked, fully aroused, and playing with his dick! She'd watched him jacking off, for heaven's sake—and he knew it! It would be embarrassing to talk with him now. Then she found herself wishing that she hadn't been watching him from a distance—that she'd been closer to him, as naked as he was himself, so she could have at least touched him. The ache deep inside her increased as she pictured herself on her knees in the sand, his cock at point-blank range, watching as it shot her right in the face, his cum dripping down onto her tits, then coming closer to rub his dick in his own cream, to spread it all over her body…

These thoughts—which, if she'd only known it, were similar to those Manx had been having—sent another gush of her own fluids running down between her legs. Then it hit her: *That* was the smell he liked! It wasn't just her own, natural scent—one that could be altered by perfumes and such; he could actually smell her sexual arousal—had gotten himself off while breathing it in! *Oh, my God…*

Suddenly, it was too much. "Tell Manx he can talk to me face-to-face from now on," she said decisively. "But right now, I'm going to bed!"

With that, Drusilla marched purposefully into her bedroom, but as soon as her nightgown-clad body hit the sheets, she felt an overwhelming need to strip naked and tell Dwell to let Manx in and have his wicked way with her. That cock of his looked like the answer to every woman's dream—and the rest of him might have been created from her own fantasies. The symbol he'd drawn in the sand hadn't been an invitation to dinner, either; it meant just exactly what she'd thought it meant in the first place: *The man wants to fuck me*.

Drusilla tried to stop it, but those words kept repeating like a catchy tune stuck in her head. She sought relief the way she had done the night before, but though teasing her nipples and clitoris brought her to climax, she still could not get Manx out of her mind. She wanted to feel him plunging deeply inside her, filling her with ecstasy. Her fingers itched to tangle themselves in his hair—to pull him down hard and then drown in his kisses, his love, his *essence…*

But, Drusilla told herself reasonably, no man was ever as good as her own imagination could make him. She'd been attracted to men before, and had expected great things, but men were never that perfect. They never said the right words, never did the right things, or even smelled the right way.

"I expect too much," she muttered, punching her pillow in frustration—but then she remembered Dave. She hadn't expected much of him at all. Perhaps she'd given up on being choosy before he came along—which might explain why she'd been dating a homosexual without realizing it. He was a nice man, but she hadn't been all that taken with him; he was more of an escort, or an occasional dinner companion, rather than someone to fall in love with. If he'd said he only wanted to be friends, it wouldn't have bothered her at all. If only he'd been honest. If only she hadn't felt quite so *used*...

One thing she could be certain of with respect to Manx, he might want to use her, but not for the same reasons because he *definitely* seemed to like women.

———

"What did she say?" Manx asked the computer.

"You will have to speak with her yourself," Dwell replied.

"That's what you're telling me, or what she told you to tell me?" Manx asked, but, deciding it didn't matter, went on: "Never mind that, what's she doing now?"

"She is lying down on her bed."

Manx grinned. "Doing what?"

"She is not asleep."

"Imagine that," Manx muttered sardonically. "I'm not sure I'll be able to sleep either." Manx chewed thoughtfully on his lower lip. Without her scent, he'd lost his erection, but he knew one whiff of her would bring it right back. "Don't suppose you'd let me in, would you?"

"I was given orders not to let *anyone* in."

"Including me?"

"Especially you."

Manx flopped down on a lounge chair. "I went too far and scared her, didn't I?

"Perhaps."

"You're a big help," Manx grumbled. "Any other suggestions?"

The computer hesitated a long moment. "Would it be difficult for you to speak with her directly from now on?"

"It might be if you won't let me in and she doesn't come out," Manx argued. "Might *never* come out now."

Dwell considered this problem. "She would leave the house if there was a fire."

"I'm sure she would," Manx agreed. "But don't start one."

"That goes against my programming," the computer said, clearly affronted.

"I'm not surprised."

"You could knock on the door," Dwell suggested. "It is what anyone else would do."

It sounded far too simple to Manx, and not very promising. Drusilla might let him in, but it was just as likely that she might open the door only to slam it in his face. Or she might sic Klog on him.

"Try it," Dwell suggested. "She is not yet asleep."

It was, of course, what Manx should have done from the very beginning. Unfortunately, he'd made so many blunders already that where she once might have opened her door with a smile and welcomed him inside, it was just as likely that she would whip out her pistol and blast him.

—∿∿—

"Oh, I don't believe it!" Drusilla exclaimed, throwing the sheets aside as she heard the firm knock at the door. "Dwell! Who is it?"

"Friendly species," Dwell intoned. "Interaction advised."

"You mean Lester, or one of the other Baradans?" Drusilla asked. "Now?"

"Interaction advised."

For some reason, Dwell was being deliberately evasive, but if he was hoping she wouldn't notice, he'd missed the mark.

Drusilla snatched up her robe and was pulling it on as she emerged from the bedroom. Peering through the window, she didn't see anyone at the door. "Are you sure there's someone out there?"

"Interaction advised."

"Oh, quit playing the archaic computer and tell me who's out there!" Drusilla snapped. She'd been in the middle of a lovely fantasy involving Manx and whipped cream when she'd been disturbed, and she wasn't very happy about it. "Is it someone you know?"

"Affirmative."

"Dwell," she said warningly. "Cut that out and talk to me!"

Dwell didn't reply, but Drusilla heard the door unlocking and rushed forward to stop it from opening. But then curiosity got the better of her. "One little peek…"

But there was no one there. She stepped out onto the

patio as her eyes swept the surrounding area. The moon was now directly overhead, and she could see quite well. Venturing further from the door, she listened closely.

"Lester?" she said quietly. Then she realized that if it had been Lester, she would have heard his truck coming long before he arrived. It could only be… "Manx?"

———~~~———

Manx stepped out of the shadow of a nearby tree when she called his name. He'd knocked as Dwell had suggested but thought it unlikely that she would open the door if he was standing there. He hoped he was wrong. Hoped she would have let him in; hoped she'd been lying in her bed thinking about doing that very thing.

He began purring and smiled as he saw her take another step closer.

"Manx?" she said again. "Are you out there?"

Before he could reply, Manx heard a growl as another shadow streaked out from the trees and with a flash of sharp teeth and a snarl, launched itself at Drusilla.

Manx had his knife in his hand and was already running toward her as the wildcat pounced and sank its claws into the soft flesh of her shoulder.

The blade flashed in the moonlight as Drusilla screamed in agony and terror. The cat's mouth opened wide for a killing bite and Manx heard the fabric ripping as blood began flowing down her side.

Manx stabbed at the twisting, snarling beast, but the blade hit bone and turned before it could reach a vital organ. The wildcat had gone for what it deemed the weaker prey, but now it released Drusilla and turned on Manx, raking its claws across his bare chest. Doing his best to ignore the pain, Manx struck again, this time slipping past bone and flesh to reach the heart of the beast. Killed instantly, it fell in a bloody heap at Manx's feet.

———

The pain that flooded through Drusilla's side robbed her of speech and for a moment she stared blankly at Manx, at the blood running down his chest, and at the fire in his eyes, before it all faded to black.

Chapter 10

MANX GATHERED DRUSILLA UP IN HIS ARMS AND HEADED FOR the door.

"Dwell!" he shouted. "Turn on the lights! She's hurt!"

"What did you do to her?" Dwell demanded.

"Nothing! There's a big cat out here; it attacked her."

"There are no dangerous animals living on this planet," Dwell said firmly. "There isn't anything dangerous on the entire world of Barada Seven. I have been programmed with that information. It is irrefutable."

"I don't belong here either," Manx rebutted, carrying Drusilla over the threshold, "but that doesn't mean I don't exist. Shut the door in case there are any more of them out there. Zef told me that Drusilla had been warned about some dangerous creature with fangs and claws." He smiled grimly, adding, "She thought he was talking about me."

"You are not dangerous," Dwell insisted.

"I am if I need to be," Manx said evenly. Lying Drusilla gently on the kitchen table, he called for Klog. The droid appeared promptly, hovering at Manx's side. "Get the medical kit," he said tersely, "and something to use for bandages."

Klog beeped in acknowledgment and floated off. Manx snatched up a towel and soaked it in cold water before applying it to her forehead. Even unconscious, she was beautiful.

The cold towel on Drusilla's face had the desired effect, and her eyelids began to flutter as she came to her senses.

"This is what happens when a man starts thinking with his dick instead of his head," Manx was muttering to himself as he began ripping her gown away to expose the wounds. "Luring her outside in the middle of the night..."

Despite her discomfort, Drusilla couldn't help but feel a twinge of amusement. She toyed with the idea of remaining silent just to hear what else he would say, but decided it might be best to put him out of his misery. However, upon opening her eyes to take a peek, Drusilla was met with the startling vision of Manx up close. His eyes were the color of emeralds with luminescent vertical pupils, and his eyebrows slanted upward toward his temples. His cheeks were smooth—not the slightest trace of stubble—and his long, black hair was swept behind ears that curved upward to a point. If angry, his fierce, feline countenance would have sent even the most determined foe into headlong flight, but his full, sensuous lips promised delights beyond her wildest imaginings.

"I'm okay," Drusilla murmured, finding her voice at last. "It was seeing you all covered in blood that made me faint. Did you kill it?"

"Yes," Manx replied, his brisk tone drawing her attention back to the matter at hand. "I wish I'd killed it before this. Zef told me you'd been warned about an animal that had attacked someone. You should have listened to Lester and gotten out of here."

"I thought he meant you," she said. "It wasn't until a little while ago that I realized it couldn't have been you."

"Because I'm such a nice, friendly fellow who would never hurt anyone?" The wide grin accompanying this remark revealed fangs which could have been deadly, but now only served to intensify his appeal.

"No, because you'd been here too long," Drusilla replied, unable to suppress a smile. "I mean, Zef seems to know you pretty well, and so do Dwell and Klog. You had to have been living around here for a long time to have made friends with all of them, and Lester talked like that cat only turned up recently."

"Oh," said Manx, clearly disappointed. He stared at her—her beautiful green eyes were twinkling up at him despite the gravity of her condition—and for a moment there, he completely forgot what he was doing.

"Ouch!" Drusilla exclaimed as Manx inadvertently touched a sore spot.

"You aren't hurt as badly as I thought you'd be," he said, tearing his eyes away from her entrancing face. "Some of these claw marks are deep, but nothing the medical kit can't fix."

"What about you?" she asked. "You're a bloody mess."

"Most of the blood isn't mine," he assured her. "Wish I could say the same for you. That thing clawed all the way down your side with its hind feet."

"No nooky tonight, then."

"Nooky?"

Drusilla could almost hear his smile when he spoke, and it warmed the cockles of her heart. *Oh, yes, he's perfect...* "What you were, um, wanting from me," she replied. Frowning slightly, she added, "At least I *think* that was what you wanted."

Manx took a deep breath. "Sorry about that. I couldn't help myself. You... *do* something to me."

"No need to apologize," Drusilla said. "You do *something* to me too."

"I noticed that," he said with a wry smile. "My name is Manx."

"Nice to meet you, Manx," Drusilla replied. "I'm Drusilla—which I'm sure Zef has already told you." Sighing wistfully, she added, "Sure wish you'd been standing at the door when I got there."

"Stupid of me, wasn't it?"

"Asinine, actually," she corrected him. "Totally *asinine.*"

"Never heard that one," he said conversationally as he wiped the blood from her shoulder and began holding pressure at the site of one of the deeper wounds. "You can explain it to me later."

Klog arrived with the medical kit and a ripped-up sheet and beeped twice.

"Thanks, Klog," Manx said. "Get some ice to put on this, will you?—or, better yet, just spray her off." Manx grabbed another dish towel and tucked it underneath Drusilla's torn side. Klog beeped questioningly. "Cold water," Manx replied. "Cold as you've got."

Drusilla yelped as the icy stream hit her damaged skin. "*Whoa, momma!*" she exclaimed.

"Sorry, Drusilla," Manx said soothingly. "It'll be better in a minute. I've used this stuff in the kit before. It's great at healing up anything short of an—"

"An—what?" she prompted.

"Amputation," he replied. "Shouldn't say that, though. It sounds too horrible."

"It's okay," Drusilla said. "No amputations. The cold water just surprised me, that's all."

"You must be tougher than you look," he said, scrutinizing her closely. "I've known plenty of women who wouldn't have taken it nearly as well. I'm pleased to see that you aren't one of them."

"I'm glad you approve," Drusilla said. Looking up at him, she decided that she approved of him too. "Lots of guys wouldn't have reacted as quickly as you did," she added. "I'm glad you aren't one of them either."

Klog finished hosing off the blood and Manx took a closer look. "This looks worse than it really is," he said reassuringly. "You should heal up just fine in a few days."

"What about you?" Drusilla asked, still concerned that more of the blood that covered him was his than he was willing to admit. *Men,* she thought with amusement, *never willing to admit weakness…*

"I'll be fine too," he said. "Then there will be plenty of—what did you call it?"

"Nooky," Drusilla replied. "Sorry I don't feel much like it now. You should have been here sooner—you would've gotten as much as you could take."

"That much, huh?" Manx said. "You might be surprised at how much I can take. I think it'll be more a matter of how much *you* can take."

"Promises, promises," Drusilla murmured jokingly. She didn't want to admit it aloud, but she had an idea he wasn't overstating the matter. He looked capable of satisfying *dozens* of women—dozens of highly *insatiable* women.

Manx dried her with a clean towel and bound a firm pad against the worst cuts after slathering them with ointment. Drusilla felt immediate relief and relaxed, closing her eyes. It was so nice to be taken care of by someone who knew how…

"Do you have something else to put on?" he asked.

"Sure," Drusilla replied. "Just help me sit up."

Manx did as she asked, and though Drusilla's head swam slightly, after a few deep breaths, she felt less like fainting—until she got a better look at Manx, that is. He'd looked pretty darn good from a distance, but up close he was perfect. Tall and lean with long black hair, a light dusting of body hair in the usual places, a broad, muscular chest, strong arms, and the biggest, thickest dick she'd ever seen—hell, even his testicles looked fabulous!—but, unfortunately, he was also liberally doused with blood.

"I'm sorry," he said, obviously noting her round-eyed expression. "I guess I should have—"

"Put your pants on?" Drusilla supplied for him. "No need on my account. Like I said before, it's all the blood that's got me bugged."

"I'll wash up as soon as I've put you to bed," Manx said quickly.

He might have already been naked, but the sudden thought of Manx in the shower—hot, wet, and devastatingly handsome—shook Drusilla to the core. Then she pictured lathering him up herself and almost keeled over. "I'm okay!" she assured him, noting his expression of concern. "Just give me a second to adjust."

"*Please*, try not to do that again," Manx said beseechingly. "I feel bad enough as it is."

"Well, you certainly don't look it," Drusilla muttered.

"You look, well, I—I think I'd better leave it at that," she added hastily.

Taking her by the hand, Manx helped her up from the table, and though Drusilla felt steady enough on her feet, she was sorely tempted to wobble just so he would carry her. He'd obviously done it once before, but this time she wanted to be awake to enjoy the experience. Just the thought of being held in his strong arms made her head spin, but since Manx had seemed pleased that she was tougher than she looked, instead of a show of frailty, she merely allowed him to take her by her undamaged arm and walk her to her room.

"I'll be all right now," she said as he released her, though the loss of his support left her feeling oddly bereft.

As he made a move toward the door, the thought of him even leaving the room struck Drusilla with a sudden and marked anxiety. "You're—you're not leaving me here alone tonight—are you?"

"Not a chance," he said firmly. "I'll be right back."

His smile reassured her completely, and the pain of her injuries and the horror of being attacked faded swiftly as they were replaced with the comforting prospect of being able to sleep in Manx's arms. The odd thing was that even though they hadn't actually met until tonight, he didn't seem like a stranger. Now if she could just get the nerve to ask Klog for that whipped cream…

———

Manx stood under the hot spray of the shower, wincing as the water hit the scratches on his chest. The bleeding had already stopped and, as he'd suspected, most of the blood that covered him had, indeed, belonged to the wildcat.

His mind jumped from his injuries back to Drusilla without missing a beat. She was everything he could want in a woman: warm and completely accepting of his apology. She hadn't ranted at him for nearly getting her killed—was more concerned for him than she was for herself—and she was even more beautiful than he'd realized. When he'd taken her by the hand, it was all he could do not to gasp out loud because even her *hand* felt right to him. He'd never met a more perfect woman; it was as if she had been created just for him.

Not that Manx had ever believed in such things. Never one to rely on anything but his own wits to remain alive and free, he had always believed that a man's life is what he makes of it himself, and waiting for some preordained destiny to come to his rescue was foolish. If fate had been standing by to lend a hand, it would have been pointless to escape from slavery and then work to keep one jump ahead of the Nedwuts who pursued him. But when he considered the astronomical odds against the likelihood that he and Drusilla would ever meet, he had to accept the possibility that some higher power might be responsible for her visit to Barada Seven.

And if this *was* part of a greater scheme, he was certainly pleased with how it was turning out. That wildcat might have ruined Manx's plans for the evening, but neither of them had been seriously injured and Drusilla wasn't going to make him leave—at least not yet. He could smell her reactions to him, and though he could sense strong elements of pure sexual attraction, he knew there was more to it than that. There were traces of love in her scent—she might not be saying it out loud, but he could almost feel the warm tendrils of her affection surrounding him. He'd never inhaled such an intoxicating aroma in his life.

Some of her feelings toward him might have been influenced by gratitude for saving her life—she might have felt the same way toward anyone in that situation— but Manx had been the recipient of gratitude before and knew that this was different. He truly had found his mate at last; he was sure of it.

<hr>

Alone again, reality struck. "I just met him a few minutes ago, and now I'm going to sleep with him?" Drusilla mused. "I've never done such a thing in my life."

Even though she'd spoken the words aloud, she didn't really expect a reply, but Dwell answered her promptly. "Should I lock the door?" he asked.

"Probably," she replied. "He *is* awfully sweet though. Zef was right. I do like him—a lot. But I hate to seem too easy."

"Easy?"

"The kind of girl who jumps in bed with every guy she meets," she said. "I'm not like that—never really had the chance to be, but that's beside the point." Gingerly stripping off her tattered robe and gown, she dropped them in a pile on the windowsill. "Guess Klog might be able to fix those. He seems to be able to do everything else."

"Yes, Klog is quite capable," said Dwell.

Drusilla stood in front of the mirror, surveying the damage. "That looks even worse than it feels," she said.

"Though that ointment he put on it is pretty good stuff. Wonder where it came from?"

"It was brought by the Terran trader who supplied the food for your stay," Dwell said. "Its origin is unknown to me."

"Mm-hm," Drusilla replied absently. "I'll have to ask Lester about it." Crossing to her dresser, she pulled open a drawer and took out a fresh nightgown. Unfortunately, the fact that she was completely unable to raise her right arm made it impossible to put it on. She figured she could do it with Manx's assistance, but since he was in the shower, she decided to wait. Crawling into bed, she did her best to remain awake but eventually drifted off to sleep.

———

After his shower, Manx dried himself thoroughly and then slid into bed beside Drusilla—and let out a groan as he was instantly aroused by her provocative scent.

"Are you okay?" she murmured sleepily. "You're hurt worse than you're admitting, aren't you?"

"I'm just fine," he replied. While this was true in a sense, it didn't take into account the fact that his balls felt like they were about to rupture.

Drusilla tried to stifle her yawn—but failed miserably. "I don't want you to think I'm bored or anything, but even though I'm feeling much better, I'm pretty tired. It's been an interesting day."

This was putting it so mildly that Manx couldn't help but grin. "That's all it was? Just 'interesting'?"

"It was only the *day* that was interesting," she replied. "Now, you, you're—" Drusilla paused, letting out a deep sigh. "*Fascinating.*"

"I'm glad you think so," Manx purred.

"Hmmm," she murmured. "Mystery men are so intriguing."

"Not really," said Manx.

"Oh, don't spoil it," she begged. "Let me enjoy my fantasy before you tell me you just got lost on the way to the market."

Manx chuckled softly. "That's not exactly how it happened, but it isn't far off. I got lost on my way home."

"I know," Drusilla said. "Dwell told me about your planet being destroyed. Are you the only one left?"

"Maybe," Manx replied. "A group of us were to be sold as slaves, but the Nedwut bounty hunters have been after me ever since I escaped. They've nearly caught me several times, and I've got a better nose than most. I have no way of knowing if any of the others are still alive."

"I hope they are," Drusilla said. "It would be hard to be the only one left. Maybe you'll find them someday."

"Maybe," Manx said again. "The odds are against it, though. It's a very big galaxy and even if they *are* alive, they could be anywhere."

Drusilla turned over to lie with her head on his chest, but stopped suddenly. "You got scratched up pretty badly; I'm not hurting you, am I?"

"No," Manx lied. She wasn't hurting his chest, but his dick was killing him. He shifted onto his side so that he was facing her with her head resting on his arm, but it didn't help at all, and might have made things worse.

"You didn't dry off very well," Drusilla remarked.

Manx knew exactly what she was referring to because he could feel it too. "Um, it's not that," Manx said, not quite sure how to tell Drusilla that she was not only making his cock hard as a rock, but dripping wet as well. "It's something I really can't control—well, actually, I *can*, but... "

Drusilla giggled. "You mean you wet the bed?"

"It's not *that* kind of control," he said dryly. Manx picked up the movement from her laughter, not only with his arms, but the head of his cock, which, of course, made it drool even more. He fought the urge to slide it over her soft skin, seeking all manner of wonderful places to hide it in. He knew he ought to back off a little, but he had an idea that doing so just might be the death of him.

"Ah," Drusilla said archly. "*I* understand. Your dick is dripping. Is that it?"

"Yes, it is," Manx replied. "And if you don't mind my saying so, it's all your fault."

"Mmmmm, nice," Drusilla said, shifting closer to him. "I haven't done that to anyone in a long time."

"Then you must have spent a lot of time in the company of fools," Manx said roundly. "And, believe me, I am *not* a fool."

"Hmm," she said, smiling. "Where's Klog and his whipped cream when I need him?"

"Whipped cream?"

"You know, to make you taste better."

Manx nearly came unglued but managed to gasp, "I should taste good without any help from Klog."

"Really?"

"So I've been told."

"Mmmmm, I should probably start with your lips, you know."

"You can taste any part of me you like," Manx said. "On one condition."

"What's that?"

"That I can taste any part of *you* I like." Manx's purring intensified and he couldn't help it; he leaned over and kissed her. It might have had more to do with scent than actual flavor, but she tasted like love.

"Oh, Manx," Drusilla sighed against his lips. "Where have you been all my life?"

"Not where I should have been, obviously." Manx trailed kisses from her lips to her cheek and down her neck. Then he froze as he realized something he should have known from the first moment he lay down beside her. "You're not wearing anything."

"Didn't want you to feel under-dressed," Drusilla explained. "Which means that with you around, I may never get dressed again." Laughing softly, she added, "No, actually I couldn't raise my arm well enough to put my gown on."

The fact that she was naked made it even more difficult for Manx to keep from mating with her right then, but the thought of hurting her stopped him cold. He was fairly certain that he could do it without touching her injured side, and even if he did, it wouldn't hurt for long since she'd probably forget the pain in the next heartbeat.

This wasn't just wishful thinking or cocky self-assurance, either; he knew the effect that Zetithian males had on women. As a boy, he'd learned that it was part of the female nature to remain aloof and Zetithian females were highly selective; getting close enough to one of them to mate was extremely difficult. However, he also knew that even the most resistant females could be won over completely, and once they mated, it was for life.

But Drusilla seemed to be different in that respect.

She hadn't treated him like someone to be avoided; in fact, she'd made him promise to stay with her. But did she know what that meant?

"If I promise not to touch your right side," Manx began, "d'you think we could…?"

"Oh, *yeah,*" Drusilla sighed.

Manx felt a thrill shoot through him that momentarily robbed him not only of speech, but also the necessary brainpower to move.

"If you *can,* that is," Drusilla went on smoothly. "You already did it once tonight. I've heard that excuse before."

Manx searched his memory, trying to sort out what she could possibly mean by that and finally gave up. "What?"

"It hasn't been that long ago," she reminded him. "How much recovery time do you need?"

"Recovery time?" Manx was completely bewildered.

"Oh, you know—before you can, um, ejaculate again."

Frowning slightly, Manx said, "Well, I haven't done it for a while, but I don't remember there ever being a time when I *couldn't*—that is, if the woman still wanted me."

"Oh, *wow,*" Drusilla breathed. "You mean I can have all I want? I've *never* gotten all I wanted—of anything."

"Just tell me when to stop," Manx replied, suddenly feeling much more cheerful.

"Ohhhh," Drusilla breathed. "This is going to be *so* wonderful… "

Manx purred loudly and dipped his head down to nibble on the soft, downy skin of her breast, not sure he could hold off from mating with her much longer. His nose told him otherwise, but his head told him that she might not be ready for him yet. He had to take his time;

not rush her or force her. Nothing to make this anything less than perfect for her… just for *her*…

Drusilla took the opportunity to thread her fingers through Manx's long, wavy hair. "I love your hair," she murmured. "It's funny, but before yesterday, I'd have said that long hair on a man wasn't a requirement, but *now*…"

"I'm becoming very fond of *red* hair, myself," Manx said agreeably. "Never thought that was a requirement either." He could have added every other detail, however minute, about Drusilla to that list. From her sparkling green eyes to her sweet smile with that one, slightly crooked front tooth…

Every part of her tasted like love. His lips roamed lower on her chest, and though he knew the ointment would heal her wounds more quickly than his own saliva, he wanted to lick them anyway—anything to let her know just how much he cared for her welfare, and just how badly he felt for letting her be injured in the first place. The gentle touch of her hands led him to believe she didn't hold a grudge, but even so, he wished her nothing but bliss.

And Manx knew he could give it to her, perhaps better than anyone else she would ever meet. Zetithian males had made other men murderously envious because of that ability—but he wasn't thinking about that; he was thinking about here and now, and this woman who stirred him in ways that no other had done—the one who made him want to cherish her and fill her with delight until the end of his days. Just why a virtual stranger would evoke such a desire in him, Manx couldn't explain, and he didn't really want to at the time; he simply knew that she was the one he'd been looking for, had been waiting for all his life, and this was the moment to bind her to him forever.

There was an easy way to do that; he could simply take her now and let his body do what it did best, delving inside a woman and filling her with the cream from his cock, letting it work its orgasmic magic on her. That method was swift and sure, but Manx took his time, lingering over her, giving her the chance to want him enough to plead with him to give her more. Then, and only then, would he give her all he had. Still kissing her lovely skin, he reached the curls at the apex of her thighs and allowed himself one taste of her—but that one taste was nearly his undoing.

His purr was deep and resonant, and as soft sighs escaped her, Manx licked his way back up to her lovely breasts, taking his time and lazily suckling her hard nipples. His hands began a gentle massage and it pleased him to feel her body relaxing completely; he liked the idea that she trusted him and was comfortable with his touch. His mouth drifted on toward her neck, her cheek, and then back to her earlobe; he was purring as he went, delighting in the taste and feel of her. Her breathing became slow and deep, and when he reached her lips at last, they were completely still. She was asleep.

"Well, she did say she was tired," he muttered. "Guess that's what I get for taking things slowly."

Manx toyed with the idea of waking her, but decided against it. She'd been badly injured and he should have known better than to try it so soon—but she'd said yes, and she smelled like heaven. She wouldn't change her mind. He could wait—just not forever. Besides, he needed sleep himself. It would help to heal his wounds, and hers would be better in the morning too.

Sighing with regret, he turned away from her to avoid

her scent so his erection would diminish, but still, it was a very long night.

———

The band of Nedwut bounty hunters who had released the wildcat on Barada Seven might have had some pithy comments to make about Manx's plans for the future if they'd known anything about them, for, in their minds, he was already as good as dead. They'd used the same ploy many times before when tracking someone—send a vicious animal down in an escape pod and then offer to hunt it down, for a price. Of course, the cat wasn't the only thing they hunted—though it *did* provide them with good sport—and they'd collected several bounties in that manner but had never managed to bag a Zetithian. The one they were now seeking was far more cunning and elusive than their usual quarry—and they'd gone to a great deal of trouble trying to catch him. If it weren't for the higher bounty, they might have given it up, but the prospect of collecting five million credits made the chase worthwhile.

Their leader, Klarkunk, knew that they only had to give the wildcat a little more time to wreak havoc on the pitiful locals, and then, when they made their offer, the weak, defenseless Baradans would welcome them with open arms. They would make a big show of hunting it down, all the while searching for their primary target. Klarkunk was sure they would find him this time. The Baradans had no weapons to stop them, and the Zetithian would be theirs for the taking.

———

While en route to Barada Seven, Jack and her shipmates were trying to decide on the best methods of locating one man on a planet covered largely by dense rainforest. Thus far, they had come up with very few workable ideas and even had the children in on the brainstorming.

"Scanners," Tisana suggested. "We could just scan the planet for him and pick him up."

Jack smiled grimly. "There are two problems with that. One, the *Jolly Roger* isn't equipped with scanners, and two, a retrofit would take too long. The Nedwuts are looking for him too, and you know they aren't wasting any time."

"How about putting up a sign again," Jack's son, Larry, suggested. "It worked before."

It sounded like a good idea, but Jack shook her head. "Remember what Barada is like. There are no large, industrial cities, only small villages where the natives live a very simple life. They don't have the technology to send out a planet-wide bulletin like we did on Serillia."

"And Manx was not the one we were trying to find there," said Leo. "We were looking for information only. He would have seen the advertisement as a trap."

"As I recall from our last visit, Barada has only one spaceport," said Cat. "He is likely to be living nearby."

Leo shook his head. "He's also had a year to move on," he pointed out. "And Manx would be able to provide for himself in the jungle."

"No weapons allowed, either," Jack muttered. "I really hate that."

"Puts us all on an even footing, though," Tisana said helpfully.

"Yeah, everyone but you," Jack said. "With your powers, they might not even let you land."

"Well, as long as nobody goes blabbing to the authorities," Tisana shot back, "they won't know about them, will they?"

Jack felt momentarily chastened, knowing that while Tisana preferred to keep her abilities quiet, Jack, unfortunately, had a tendency to brag about the witch's powers to the wrong people.

"Speaking of authorities," Tisana went on, "why don't we just ask them if they know anything about Manx?"

"We can try it, but Manx tried to live a normal life on Serillia, and the Nedwuts found him," Cat said. "He has probably gone into hiding."

"So do we hunt for him, then?" Larry said eagerly.

"It's a big planet," Jack reminded her son. "And like Leo said, he's had a year to disappear. He could be anywhere."

"We should still search the area near the spaceport," Larry insisted. "A ten kilometer radius, at least."

"Yes, but that takes time, and searching a jungle is even harder than it sounds," said Jack. "He could be two meters away and you'd never see him."

"He's also elusive and very stealthy," Leo said. "He was the best man for getting close to the enemy, plus, he had the best aim with a pulse pistol of anyone I've ever seen."

"Whew!" Jack exclaimed. "This guy is going to be tougher to corral than I thought!"

"What about luring him, then?" Larry suggested. "You know, use something for bait. Something he wouldn't think was a trap."

"Too bad we don't have a Zetithian female," Jack chuckled. "—aside from your daughter, Althea, of course," she said to Tisana. *"That* would get him."

"Hmm," Tisana said, her eyes narrowing. "Good nose you say?"

"Amazingly good," Cat replied.

Tisana smiled secretively. "I *might* have an idea…"

Chapter 11

WHEN DRUSILLA AWOKE THE NEXT MORNING, STIFF AND SORE, it took her a moment to remember why she felt that way. Then the events of the previous night came flooding back, helped along by the warm, solid presence of Manx in bed beside her. No, it hadn't been a dream, he was still there. She could hear him breathing.

Sitting up, she tried to remember what had happened. Manx had been kissing her, and she blushed furiously as she recalled some of the places he'd kissed. But then, nothing. Did sex with a Zetithian give you amnesia? Was it so good—or so bad—that it rendered a woman senseless? Had her mind blocked it out as something she'd prefer to forget? As she gazed at his sleeping form, she knew that making love with Manx was something she didn't ever want to forget.

He was lying on his stomach with his arms wrapped around his pillow and his hair lying in tangled spirals down his back. The sheet was draped across him, stopping just below his waist, and the soft morning light cast shadows in the deep contours of his body. As her eyes drank in the sheer masculine beauty of him, Drusilla was reminded of an old fairy tale about a lonely maiden who went to sleep with a frog and awakened to find a prince lying with her.

Except that Manx had never remotely resembled a frog—a cat, perhaps, but certainly not a frog. With her luck, she wouldn't have been a bit surprised to find that, rather than remaining the stunningly sexy man that he was, he'd turned into a toad while she slept.

Slept? Drusilla let out a tortured groan as she realized that no, he hadn't knocked her out with his sexual prowess; she'd simply fallen asleep on him. Other than a flat-out refusal, she couldn't imagine a worse insult to the male ego than conking out while he was doing his best to arouse her deeper passions, unless it was laughing at him. "Must have been all the purring making me sleepy," she muttered. "And I did tell him I was tired." Actually, exhausted might have been a better word. That she'd stayed awake during their brief conversation was surprising enough, but he'd gotten her so relaxed afterwards, anyone could have predicted the end result.

Still, it was embarrassing. Glancing around, she noted that Klog, bless his heart, had already washed and repaired her robe, which now hung from the bedpost. Moving carefully so as not to awaken Manx, Drusilla pushed back the covers and began inching her way to the edge of the bed.

Manx's hand shot out and immediately began searching the place where she'd been.

"Sorry," she said softly. "I was trying not to wake you."

"Don't worry about me," he said. "How did you sleep?"

"Like a rock," she replied, cautiously slipping her right arm into her robe. Clearing her throat self-consciously, she added, "I'm sorry about that too."

As Manx sat up and combed back his hair with his fingers, Drusilla nearly had an orgasm just from watching him. "Don't be," he said. "I knew you were tired, I just couldn't resist." Looking up at her with his glowing green eyes, he added, "I feel as though I've been trying to get close to you for years, rather than days. I should have waited."

Drusilla smiled. "Did you hear anyone telling you to stop? I might have said I was tired, but, believe me, I was just as much to blame as you were."

Something in what she'd said must have disturbed him because his gaze dropped from hers to become suddenly fascinated with the sheet.

"Not that I'm blaming you," she said quickly. "It's just that… I mean, I'd only just met you and—"

Manx held up a hand. "I know what you're going to say. You don't know me at all. I'm just some strange man who's been lurking in the jungle, making you nervous, and watching you through windows."

"I wasn't going to say that," she said. "I just don't want you to think I'm the kind of woman who doesn't take these things seriously, because I do." She paused there as she remembered some of the men she'd dated. Some she'd slept with right away; with others, she'd put it off—mainly because she knew it would be disappointing. If the previous night was any indication, making love with Manx would be anything but disappointing—and it was also something she wanted to engage in when she felt more up to it. It seemed more important than it ever had before, as if she knew it would be the start of something momentous and life-altering, and she wanted everything to be perfect. "I was in bed, fantasizing about you, when you knocked on the door. Then that horrid beast—" She broke off for a moment, shuddering at the memory. "Having it attack me was bad enough, but when it went after you, I—" Drusilla broke off there as her eyes filled with tears.

Manx was out of the bed and holding her in his arms even before the first teardrop fell. Her sobs were muffled against his chest, but he said no words to stop her from crying. Most men couldn't stand a woman's tears, but they didn't seem to bother Manx a bit. He just held her, stroking her back while he purred.

Drusilla could feel the vibrations in his chest and thought it was the most soothing, comforting thing she'd ever experienced—almost hypnotic in its effect on her mind. There was something so solid and safe about him, as though nothing bad could ever happen if he was holding her. She stopped crying long before she expected to and smiled as Manx wiped away her tears.

"That's a pretty neat trick," she said. "All you have to do is purr for a while and the tears just stop."

Manx grinned sheepishly and shrugged. "Something my father taught me," he said. "Works every time."

"Comfort women a lot, do you?"

"Not lately," he admitted. "And not all that often, either."

"You must be terrific at getting women on the rebound," Drusilla said with a wry grin.

"What's that supposed to mean?"

"Oh, you know, a couple breaks up, the girl is crying on your shoulder, and you start purring, which leads to something else entirely, and suddenly you've got yourself a new girlfriend."

"It's not that simple," Manx disagreed. "At least, it hasn't been for me, but then, my situation is unusual. I'm usually the one who has to leave."

"Left a trail of broken hearts behind you?"

"I don't know about that—I mean, I've *tried* not to hurt anyone—but I never know when I'll have to disappear again, so I haven't gotten close to many women."

"Not that they didn't want you to, I'm sure," Drusilla said, knowing full well just how strong his attraction would be to other women. "I'll bet you've broken more hearts than you realize." Feeling a pang in the vicinity of her own heart, she added, "I'm pretty sure you're gonna break mine to bits."

"Well, if I do, it's your fault," he said. "*I'm* not the one who stripped off her clothes and jumped in the lake."

"Saw that, did you?" she said, smiling sheepishly. "Guess I should have known better, but it seemed like the thing to do at the time."

"Oh, I'm not complaining," he assured her. "But when you climbed up that ladder, I almost came after you."

Drusilla was pleased to hear this, but remained slightly skeptical. "You've clearly been alone in the jungle too long," she said firmly. "It's affected your mind."

"I don't know," he said, shaking his head. "I think that would have gotten to me no matter where I'd been—or who I'd been with." Grinning unabashedly at her now, he added, "You've got the most beautiful backside I've ever seen."

"Oh, *please,*" Drusilla begged, rolling her eyes. "Compared to the rest of me, it's huge!"

"If you say so," Manx said with a shrug, "but I thought it was perfect." Drawing in a shaky breath, he added, "I've been wanting to get my hands on it ever since."

"You poor dear," she said solicitously. "I wouldn't want you to feel deprived."

Manx's smile grew devious. "I haven't been deprived."

"What?" she demanded. "Have you been groping my ass while I slept?"

"Well, you turned over," he said defensively. "It was right there in front of me. I was wide awake and I just had to. Besides, I didn't think you'd mind after what I'd already been doing."

Drusilla considered this for a moment and came to the conclusion that, while she liked the idea, she also wished she'd been awake to enjoy it. Grinning evilly, she said, "How do you know I didn't do the same thing to you?"

"Because I wouldn't have slept through that," he said with conviction. "It doesn't take much to wake me up."

"So I've noticed," she remarked. "Just wish I'd been awake enough to try it." Manx had the most awesomely pinchable, squeezable—even kissable—buns she'd ever seen. Then she realized that, standing as close as they were, all she had to do was put her arms around his hips and she could play with them all she liked.

Manx apparently had the same idea. "You're awake now," he said, moving closer.

Not needing any further encouragement, she began with the small of his back, and slid her hands downward, delighting in the outward curve and the firmness of his muscles.

Manx leaned in to nuzzle the side of her neck, inhaling deeply. He was purring again, and Drusilla felt something else, but this time, it was poking her in the belly. All the erection jokes she'd ever heard passed through her mind just then, but she didn't share them with Manx—she didn't want anything to spoil the mood this time.

"Mmm," she said, feeling suddenly dreamy. "You feel *so* good."

"So do you." Pulling up the back of her robe, he soon had his warm, strong hands on her and began a deep, sensuous massage. Drusilla couldn't decide which part felt better—her hands on him, or his hands on her—but she was quite willing to continue for as long as it took to form an opinion.

Klog floated in and beeped twice, the aroma of pancakes wafting in behind him.

Gasping in surprise as she jumped backwards out of Manx's reach, Drusilla stammered, "I—I guess breakfast is ready. Are you hungry?"

Manx was standing there, completely naked with his erection pointing right at her. Swallowing with apparent difficulty, he replied, "Yeah, starving to death."

After one look at him, Drusilla found herself staring at his penis with round-eyed fascination. "It's got a—a ruffle on it."

Manx looked at her blankly. "A what?"

"Your dick," she said, pointing her finger. "It's—I've never seen one like it."

"Standard Zetithian equipment," he said with a swift, downward glance. "Your males don't have that serrated edge around the head?"

"No," Drusilla replied faintly. "And they generally aren't that big, either."

"It's not *that* big," Manx protested.

"I guess it depends on what you consider big," Drusilla said. "And on Earth, trust me, that would be a big one."

"Not *too* big, is it?"

"I certainly hope not." Drusilla knew she was being impolite, but she couldn't keep from moving closer and bending down to inspect it. It had been impressive enough when flaccid, but fully erect it was quite remarkable. It was thick and long with a head much wider than that of a typical human's and as she watched, a clear, viscous fluid began to ooze from the scalloped points of the coronal ruffle. "*Holy Toledo,*" she whispered in awe. "I *definitely* need to have breakfast before tackling *that.*"

"I was afraid you'd say that," Manx mourned. "Thanks a lot, Klog."

Ignoring the sarcasm, Klog merely chirped and led the way to the dining room.

As Drusilla took a seat at the table, she couldn't help noticing that there was whipped cream on the pancakes—mounds of it. "Klog must have been reading my mind again," she observed.

"This is what you wanted for breakfast?" Manx asked, sitting down in the chair opposite her.

"Sort of," she replied. Drusilla took one bite of her pancakes and just as the cream began to melt on her tongue, she nearly choked as the mental image of Manx feeding her whipped cream with his fancy dick popped into her head. "Hope Klog didn't see *that* one," she murmured.

Apparently he had, because the droid beeped once, raised his whipped cream "finger," and hovered toward Manx.

"Didn't mean that, Klog," she said hastily. "I think he's already got plenty."

Klog beeped twice but continued to hover nearby.

"Need anything, Manx?" Drusilla asked, curious

as to why Klog wasn't leaving to go clean the beach or something.

"A cold shower, maybe," Manx replied. "But not now," he added, as Klog raised another arm. "Maybe I'll just go for a swim."

Drusilla looked down at her plate to hide her smile. It would probably take more than a cold shower to get *that* raging hard-on to back down. "So, how do you like the pancakes?" she asked, changing the subject.

"They're very good," Manx replied. "I've never eaten anything like this before."

"I don't eat them very often," she confided, "but sometimes they're just exactly what I want."

As Manx watched a forkful of pancakes and whipped cream disappear into Drusilla's mouth, he knew exactly what he wanted too—and it had *nothing* to do with food.

———

After breakfast, Drusilla wanted nothing more than to spend the day discovering the secrets of Zetithian male anatomy, but she found it extremely difficult to say so. She was leaving those sorts of suggestions up to Manx, but he was obviously having second thoughts as well.

"I—I think I'll go for that swim now," he said awkwardly.

"Sure, whatever," she said, trying to sound nonchalant. "I'll just take a shower—and maybe put some more of that ointment on these cuts—you should too."

"I will," he said. He seemed to hesitate for a moment, looking as uncomfortable as she felt. Giving her a quick nod, he left the table and headed down the stairs to the beach.

Drusilla remained at the table, staring off into space. What would he say when he came back—*if* he came back? "Thanks, ma'am, but this was a mistake. I'll let myself out," or, "It's been fun, but my wife is expecting me home for dinner"? She'd taken everything he'd told her as the gospel truth. But was it? He'd seemed sincere, but what did she really know about him, anyway? It had all seemed so different the night before. He'd saved her life and she owed him a debt of gratitude she could never repay.

Or could she? If Manx was on the run from Nedwuts, Barada Seven, with its peaceful natives and lack of weapons, hardly seemed the best place for him to live. Earth would be much safer, and taking him there would certainly constitute a reward. The trick would be to get him there.

———

"So," said Zef as Manx swam past him, "Did she like your willie?"

"I think it scares her, actually," Manx said ruefully. "She looked at it like she was afraid to touch it."

"That's odd," Zef remarked. "Nice big dick like that shouldn't scare anybody. She'll get used to it."

"You think?" Manx said. He'd never been overly concerned about how big his cock was before, but just then, he was wishing he could downsize it.

"Did she like you?"

"I think so," Manx replied. "Seemed that way—at least, she smelled like she did."

"Then she'll get used to it," Zef said firmly. "Maybe she'll take you back to Earth with her."

"I'm not so sure about that," he said. "We started off—oh, I was forgetting, you didn't know. A wildcat attacked her when she came out of the house after I knocked on the door."

"You mean the beast that idiot Lester was telling her about? It was real?"

"Oh, yeah, it was real," Manx replied, swimming lazy circles around Zef. "It nearly killed her." His expression became chagrined as he added, "And if it had, it would've been my fault. I knocked on the door and then hid in the trees to see if she'd come out."

"Well, that was pretty fuckin' stupid," Zef observed. "What'd you do a fool thing like that for?"

"I didn't think she'd open the door if I was standing there."

"You dumb butt! You should have just stood there in front of the door with that big weasel hanging out—"

"It *was* hanging out, which is why I backed off," Manx said. "I should have put my clothes on before I knocked on her door." At this point he was regretting that omission even more.

"But you saved her from the beast?"

"Well, yes, but—"

"She owes you one, then."

"One what?"

"Nice big willie like that and you can't figure out what to do with it," Zef said disgustedly. "She owes you a fuck."

"Not if it kills her," Manx pointed out.

"It won't kill her, you big idiot," Zef argued. "Most females like the big ones. You just have to be careful how you use it."

"That's another thing," said Manx. "She got hurt

pretty badly by that cat. She seemed better this morning, but I don't want to push it."

"You don't know a damn thing about women, do you?" Zef said bluntly. "You saved her life. She's probably up there at the house thinking of all the things she can do to thank you."

"Well, she did want me to stay with her last night," Manx admitted. "She acted like she wanted to—and we almost did it—but she fell asleep."

Zef began laughing uncontrollably. "Fell asleep?" he echoed. "Are you *that* boring?"

Manx glared at his friend. "She wasn't bored, she was tired."

"Oh, big difference there," Zef said, his voice dripping with sarcasm. "But with the same end result."

"I got to spend the night with her, though," Manx said defensively. "We even had breakfast together. It was probably the best breakfast I've ever had in my life, too. Ever hear of something called pancakes?"

"Nope," Zef replied. "Taste anything like fish?"

"Not at all," said Manx. "They're sweet and fluffy and—"

"Are you talking about the food, or Drusilla?" Zef interrupted.

"The food."

"Ha! Well, I'm sure it was tasty, but the damned menu can wait. Tell me more about Drusilla, and why you're down here swimming when you could be up at the house fucking her." Eyeing Manx suspiciously, he asked. "She didn't throw you out, did she?"

"No, what makes you think that?

"You said she didn't like your dick."

"She didn't really say she didn't like it," Manx said. "It was just the way she looked at it. Made me feel weird."

"You know, when it comes to sex, we eltrans are much less inhibited," Zef said frankly. "Tell me this: has any other woman ever *not* liked it?"

Manx grinned. "No, to be honest, they've all liked it pretty well."

"Cocky bastard!" Zef said approvingly. "You see? That's the spirit! Give 'em plenty of dick and they won't ever—"

"Ever what?" Manx prompted when Zef stopped.

"Get you voted out of the lake," Zef mourned.

"So it wasn't just because you were old and ugly?"

Zef looked at Manx as though he'd like to bite him for saying that but agreed anyway. "Nope. Weasel doesn't work very well anymore," he said, clearly doing his best to make it seem less of a tragedy than it truly was. "Happens when you get old."

Since Manx's "weasel" hadn't worked at all until Drusilla showed up, he could relate to that problem better than Zef realized. Manx had been wondering if his dick would ever get hard again—which was another thing to be thankful for. Imagine if Drusilla had arrived and her scent hadn't aroused him! Manx stopped that thought cold; it was too depressing to consider. "Aren't there any older females who wouldn't mind if it didn't work?"

"If there were, they got out-voted," Zef replied.

"But what about the other males?" Manx asked. "Don't tell me they voted against you too!"

"Don't have a say in it," Zef muttered.

"What was that?"

"The males can't vote," Zef said, raising his voice slightly. "If the women don't want you, you're out."

Manx considered this for a moment. "What about getting together with other males?"

"I think there was one in this lake a while back," he said. "But he died." Zef looked up at Manx with a sad look in his bulbous eyes. "We don't last long without anyone to talk to—and the fish bones have helped keep me going."

"So, are you saying that if I'm not here anymore, you'll die?"

"Oh, I'll die anyway," Zef said staunchly. "But maybe sooner rather than later."

Manx didn't want to be responsible for that. "Well, I'm still here for now," he said after a moment's reflection. "You never know what might happen."

"Enough about that," Zef said briskly. "Don't want to think about it right now. I'd rather hear more about Drusilla! So, you liked each other?"

Manx gazed off into the distance. "I think so—I liked her, at least, and she seemed to like me pretty well—once I finally talked to her."

"See, that wasn't so difficult, was it?" Zef said, his jaws crunching with amusement. "You just need to go back up there and do your stuff. She'll like it. I know she will."

"Maybe I should," Manx said pensively.

"Yeah, but before you go, mind doing some fishing?"

"Hungry?" Manx said with a grin.

"A little," Zef said. "Actually, I want fish badly enough to try to catch them myself, and though I hate to admit it, I probably wouldn't catch any." Looking at Manx hopefully, he said, "So, fishing first?"

"Fishing first," Manx agreed. "How many do you want?"

"How many can you catch?"

"Zef," Manx said warningly. "I haven't got all day."

"Used to be, you did," Zef said. "You've already got me longing for the good old days when no one lived in the house and you and I could do as we pleased. I'm gonna miss that."

"You'll survive," Manx assured him. "I'll just tell Klog to start feeding you pancakes. You'll probably live forever."

"I dunno," Zef said skeptically. "Sweet and fluffy? I like things that crunch."

"You don't know what you're missing," Manx said. "But I'll catch a few fish for you anyway."

It didn't take Manx long to catch Zef's breakfast, and as the eltran happily crunched on the fish, Manx knew he couldn't put it off any longer, and Zef seemed to agree.

"You're a good friend, Manx," he said with a heavy sigh. "I'm gonna miss you."

Manx grinned. "I'm not going anywhere yet—and maybe I'll never leave."

"Well, if you pass up the chance to spend a lifetime with Drusilla just to hang out with me, you're even dumber than I thought."

"All right! I'll go talk to her."

"That's the spirit!" Zef called after him. "And be sure to wave your cock at her. She'll love it!"

Manx went back to the house but stalled a bit by taking a shower before he went upstairs. He toyed with the idea of putting on his shirt and pants before he went inside, then decided it was too late for that now. Dwell let him in without comment and he found Drusilla by the window, painting.

"So how's Zef this morning?" she asked pleasantly. "I saw you two out there swimming."

"Fine," Manx replied. "I caught some fish for him, so he's happy."

"That's nice," said Drusilla. "He's quite a character, isn't he?"

"Yes, he is." Manx just stood there after that, not knowing what to say to her.

"Is there something you wanted to say?" she prompted after a bit.

"Do you—"

"Do I what?"

Manx sniffed the air in her direction. "No, I guess not."

"What are you talking about?"

"Well, you said you wanted to have breakfast first, and then you took a shower, I just wondered if you —I mean, before Klog interrupted us, we were about to—"

"Ah, yes, the nooky." Glancing down at his groin, she added, "You don't seem to be feeling as much enthusiasm as you were earlier."

"Oh, I feel it," he assured her. "But you don't."

"How do you know that?

"Your scent," he replied. "If you don't want me, I can't do it."

"What?"

"Your scent," he said again. "If I can't smell your desire—"

"Your dick doesn't work?"

"That's right."

"Guess I shouldn't have taken a shower, huh?"

"Water does wash away some of it," he admitted. "But I'd still know if it was there."

"Well, I wouldn't worry too much about it if I were you. I'm sure it'll come back at some point." She focused on her work again before adding, "It's just that I tend to get very absorbed when I'm working—I don't think about much else."

"That's very good," he said, coming closer to peer over her shoulder. "That's me hiding there in the jungle, isn't it?"

"Yeah," she said. "Not a very good likeness, but then I'd only caught a glimpse of you when I painted it." After a brief pause, she continued, "So tell me, Manx, what does a guy like you do out in the jungle all day?"

"Mostly hunt for food," he replied. "And I swim with Zef a lot too. We've kept each other company for a while now."

Nodding, she went on with her painting. "And how long is a while?"

"A year or so," he replied. "It's hard to tell here. The seasons don't change."

"So it's always like this?"

"Pretty much."

"Must get boring after a while," she observed. "So, where were you before you came to Barada?"

"Serillia," he replied. "I worked in a restaurant there."

"Was that your usual line of work?"

"Oh, no," he said. "I've done all kinds of things. When I first get to a planet, I usually earn a little money as a street musician, and then I—"

"So, that *was* you playing the flute," she interjected. "I thought so."

Nodding, he reached into the pouch that hung from his belt and pulled out a small instrument made of different sized tubes lashed together with strips of bark. "I can make them too," he added. "I sold lots of them on Serillia."

Taking it from him, Drusilla examined it closely. "I saw a man playing one of these at an art fair once—it's a very ancient type of instrument," she said. "They call it a pan flute where I come from."

"They've been played on Zetith since ancient times too," he said. "My mother taught me—she tried to teach my brothers and sisters, but they weren't interested."

"And all that beautiful music is lost now," Drusilla said wistfully. "That and everything else, except for you and what you remember." She paused as she gave him back his flute. "That must make you feel very lonely."

"Sometimes," he admitted. "I try not to think about it too much."

"I'm sorry," she said gently. "I didn't mean to bring up things you might prefer to forget. I just wanted to know more about you."

"I understand," Manx said. "I'd like to know more about you too. Zef told me all he knew, which wasn't much aside from you being a painter."

Drusilla snickered. "Did he also tell you what he thought of that as an occupation?"

"Yes, he did," said Manx. "Art doesn't mean very much to him, but fortunately I don't share his opinion."

"Well, that's a relief," said Drusilla. "Tons of people think art is a waste of time." She smiled as she remembered all the snide comments she used to get about her bird paintings from passersby. "I remember setting up my paintings at art fairs back when I was a struggling

young artist. I'd sit there with the other artists all day
in the sweltering heat or freezing cold while crowds of
people passed us by—no one buying much of anything,
of course—and if you ever did sell something, any
profits you made were spent on lunch."

Manx laughed. "Sounds like my flutes and I would
fit right in."

"You certainly would," she agreed. "I can see us
now: me with my paintings set out under a big, shady
tree, and you playing the flute, drawing in all sorts of
potential buyers—mostly women, of course. I'd imagine
you sold lots of flutes just because the ladies wanted an
excuse to talk to you."

"Not all species find Zetithians attractive," he
pointed out. "In some places I was more of an oddity
than an attraction."

"Not on Earth," Drusilla said with conviction. "On
Earth, you'd draw women like a lemonade stand draws
yellow jackets."

"Not sure what that means," said Manx.

"You'll understand what I mean if you ever go to a
late summer picnic," Drusilla said. "Yellow jackets are
a real pain." The full impact of their conversation hit
her then; if she didn't take him with her to Earth, there
would be no art fairs or late summer picnics, at least not
with Manx, and the thought of that had her eyes filling
with tears.

"What's wrong?"

"I don't know," she said slowly. "This is so strange.
Here I am already thinking about you living on Earth—
and us doing all sorts of things together—and we barely
know each other. I don't understand it."

"Neither do I," he said. "Maybe it's best not to think too hard."

"Take it on faith?"

"Something like that."

Drusilla closed her eyes, trying to remember the last time she'd done such a thing—really taken a leap of faith about anything—and came to the conclusion that she never had, until now.

"It was you," she said softly, raising her eyes to his in wonder. *"You* were my leap of faith. I should have realized it."

"Me?"

"Yes, you. When Lester warned me about the vicious beast loose in the jungle, even though so many things pointed to you, I didn't believe it. Somehow I just knew it wasn't true." She paused again, gazing up at him. "What in the world am I waiting for?"

Manx smiled grimly. "We haven't waited," he said. "We've been interrupted."

With that, Drusilla called out for Klog, who promptly emerged from the kitchen. "No lunch or dinner or any interruptions for the rest of the day, unless I specifically ask you for something. Okay?"

Klog beeped once and floated off.

"Well, that was easy enough," Drusilla muttered. "Should have thought of that before." After putting down her brush and wiping the paint from her fingers, she then stood and said, "Okay, Manx. You now have my undivided attention."

Grinning wickedly, Manx sprang into action. Scooping her up in his arms, he made a beeline for the bedroom.

"Are you sure you're okay?" he asked along the way.

"What?" she said, momentarily puzzled. "Oh, you mean the cat scratches. They're not too bad; that ointment is amazing," she said. "At least I got my shirt on with no trouble."

"That's the reason I asked," he said. "Because I'm about to take it off."

"Oh, well then, go for it."

Manx set her on her feet and then pulled her top off so gently she never felt a thing. Then his belt, which was his only garment, hit the floor, and he skimmed off her shorts. Having accomplished all of that, he sighed, "That's much better."

"Yeah, you look so much better without that nasty belt."

Manx burst out laughing and landed on the bed with Drusilla in his arms. Taking her face in his hands, he looked at her and grinned. "I can't stop smiling," he said. "All I have to do is look at you and I feel... different, better, happier somehow. I can't explain it."

"Then don't try," she said. "I know what you mean, anyway."

Drusilla leaned forward and as their lips touched, she melted into his warm embrace. His hair was soft and thick, and as her fingers delved into it, all she could think of was getting lost in it forever. Manx deepened the kiss, and she could feel him tasting her, heard him inhaling deeply as he gorged himself on her scent.

As their tongues entwined, Manx thrust his fingers through her hair, pulling her to him. "Pull me in and drown me," he groaned helplessly.

But Drusilla was already drowning herself. His

fangs were probably dangerous, but she braved the kisses anyway; they were soft, then hard, sweet, then ferociously feral, bringing out the animal inside her. She couldn't seem to get enough of the feel of him in her hands; they wouldn't open wide enough to feel all she wanted to feel. Hands, arms, and lips weren't enough. She was aching for him; he had to come inside.

And she took him in.

Nothing in her life could have prepared Drusilla for what happened next. Manx pulled her on top of him and pushed her down on his cock, which slid effortlessly into her core. He was so big he should have hurt her, but instead it stretched her until they fit perfectly, her snug warmth wrapped tightly around his thick shaft.

He was hot; Drusilla couldn't remember ever being with a man who could actually warm her from the inside out. But then he began twirling that rod and suddenly her entire being took on a different perspective. She would have been in a perfect position—the one, in fact, that she had imagined—to feed him delicious bites of cheesecake, but she didn't think she would have had enough coordination to do it.

Then their eyes met. Manx forgot to purr. Drusilla forgot to *breathe*.

She could feel him moving, but the warning signal her body sent out was even stronger. Something was about to happen, something that would forever change her. It began deep inside her, near where the head of his amazing cock was sweeping back and forth, and sent a stream of fire out to all corners of her being. Letting out a guttural cry as her orgasm detonated, Drusilla fell forward helplessly onto Manx's chest.

Capturing her in his arms, Manx held her tightly before cupping her cheeks in his hands and pulling her up to face him, watching her expression as the realization struck. He kept moving, gently rocking into her, feeling her warmth sheathing him as he tried to disappear inside her completely.

As another orgasm burst from her, and then another, and another, Drusilla gasped in astonishment. "Does it ever stop?"

Manx grinned delightedly. "Eventually," he replied. "But it takes a while." Taking note of her dreamy eyes and her equally dreamy smile, he asked, "Good?"

Drusilla nodded, still smiling. "Better than strawberry cheesecake."

Manx laughed.

"You don't know what that is, do you?" Drusilla asked.

"No, but from the look on your face, I'd have to assume it's something *very* good."

"It's one of the best things I can think of," she said, "but I think I'll have to put what you're doing at the top of my list from now on."

"I can keep it up for as long as you like—or I can stop any time," he said. "You just tell me when you've had enough."

Shuddering as yet another wave of ecstasy swept through her, Drusilla couldn't imagine *ever* wanting him to stop, but thought she could probably stand a break once in a while. Manx sat her up then, altering the angle slightly and as her mind tilted sideways, Drusilla decided that if other men were comparable to strawberry cheesecake, Manx was *chocolate* cheesecake with strawberries, whipped cream, chocolate curls—and maybe even some pecans. "Ohmygod," she sighed. "How are you *doing* that?"

"It's a Zetithian secret," Manx replied in a conspiratorial whisper. "Don't tell anyone."

He wasn't even moving much and she was still feeling the fireworks. "You haven't even told *me*," she gasped. "How could I possibly tell anyone else?"

"You're pretty smart," he said with a knowing nod. "You'll figure it out."

"Mmm, don't want to," she murmured. "Besides, I think it's magic."

"No, Drusilla," Manx said. *"You're* the magic." Gazing up at her, Manx longed to hold her, giving her joy forever—but he knew he could do better. "Think it would hurt your shoulder if I laid you on your back?"

"My darling Manx," Drusilla whispered. "Right now, you could probably rip my arm off and I wouldn't feel it."

Grinning broadly, Manx flipped over with Drusilla still impaled on his cock, her beautiful hair spilling out across the sheets. "How was that?"

"Impressive," Drusilla replied. "But then, everything about you is impressive."

"Put your arms around my neck," he said, sounding pleased. "And hold on tight."

Drusilla was looking up at him, but just then her eyes lost focus as he *really* began to move.

Manx gave it to her every way he could think of—in and out, back and forth, up, down, and sideways. Undulating his spine and curling his hips forward, Manx plunged in deeply, drowning in her, never, ever, wanting to come up for air again. Drusilla was moaning with every move he made, but when he started doing figure eights inside her, she screamed, and Manx lost all control. Letting out a growl, he gave up trying to be creative and simply fucked her as hard and fast as he could until his balls spewed forth their sweet, intoxicating cream. The sweeping motion of his corona soon followed, and he delighted in the delirious sensation of fulfillment.

"I can feel… *something,*" Drusilla gasped. "I feel…" Momentarily speechless, Drusilla's eyes widened as she felt a warm glow begin in the small of her back, felt it grow and spread as it fanned out to the tips of her fingers and toes. Then, suddenly, her entire body seemed to burst into bloom.

As Manx gazed into Drusilla's lovely eyes, he saw the sight he'd been craving ever since catching that first glimpse of her. "Joy," he whispered, "unlike any you have ever known?"

"Oh, yeah, that's it," Drusilla sighed, pulling him down for a poignant kiss which lasted until sleep overcame her.

Manx laid her down gently and cradled her in his arms, purring contentedly until late in the afternoon. He would gladly die to protect her now, and if he ever lost her, he'd simply give up and let the bounty hunters take him, knowing that, without her, he'd probably die anyway.

Drusilla awoke to the most deliriously beautiful morning of her life. Outside her window the sky was a brilliant purple hue, the green leaves of the jungle were glossy after a day of rain, and the lake sparkled invitingly.

There were no dangerous animals afoot, and Manx was still beside her, right where he belonged. Birds were singing, and a whole flock of what looked like aquamarine flamingos were wading in the shallows.

"Dwell," Drusilla said quietly. "Do the windows open?"

In reply, a soft breeze blew in from the lake, touching her hair and caressing her skin. She stretched, finding it remarkable that there was hardly a twinge of discomfort from the wounds on her shoulder and side. Among other things, Manx seemed to be a pretty good doctor—though his skill as a healer was *nothing* compared with his ability as a lover! She'd been with other men—had heard other women's descriptions of their own experiences—but Manx was so far beyond the rest that you couldn't even call it sex; it was more like… well, she couldn't even come up with a word that described it.

She felt absolutely perfect. The only thing she might be missing was—

"Thank you, Klog," she whispered as the droid hovered beside the bed with a cup of tea. She took the cup and inhaled the sweet fragrance of white tea flavored with peach and mango. "Perfect."

If only Manx would be as perfect when he awoke. Drusilla sighed, taking a sip of her tea. Men were *never* perfect. *Women* were never perfect. It was too much to ask of anyone, but Manx seemed to come awfully close…

She gazed at him, her eyes drinking in the steady rise and fall of his chest, his thick mass of curls, his deeply tanned skin. He was lying on his side, facing away from her, almost on his stomach and she wanted nothing more than to spoon up behind him, let her hands glide over his back and shoulders, down his arms… If the way she felt wasn't love, it was definitely something very special—and Manx was the reason for it.

Drusilla hadn't taken more than a few sips of her tea before she simply had to put it down and nestle up next to Manx, resting her hand on his hip, laying her cheek against his back while his hair tickled her face. She could feel him breathing, hear his heart beating as she closed her eyes and inhaled his essence, hoping that nothing would ever disrupt the way she felt right then. She wanted to remember this moment forever—never to forget how much her life and her whole world had been changed by this one, remarkable being.

But Manx had been awake even before Drusilla and was just as afraid to do anything to disrupt his feeling of *laetralant* bliss. Was she having second thoughts? If he rolled over and took her in his arms, would he be repulsed, or would she be as warm and welcoming the morning after as she had been the day before? Then she touched him; he felt the warmth of her body against his own and knew he couldn't feign sleep any longer—and began to purr.

Drusilla smiled, her eyes filling with tears of joy. No, he wasn't going to spoil it. It would go on as it began.

Chapter 12

BREAKFAST IN BED WITH YOUR LOVER WAS TRULY A JOY, Drusilla decided—especially when neither of you had to get up to fix it. Klog was the perfect solution to the lack of privacy associated with a real, live cook; you didn't have to worry about being caught in a compromising position by a droid.

Klog might not have had any feelings on the subject, but Drusilla suspected that he approved, somehow. She couldn't explain why—at least, no more than she could explain why Klog had been so pleased to be able to fix dinner for Manx again—but she definitely got that impression. It might have had something to do with his programming—an overall desire to serve, perhaps—but it seemed to go beyond that.

However he felt about the situation, Klog outdid himself with a breakfast of biscuits and gravy with bacon and eggs, something Manx remarked upon.

"Klog never made anything like this for me before," he said, digging into a mound of scrambled eggs and cheese. "This is *really* good."

"He must be making up for the fact that we missed dinner last night," Drusilla said. "Though this *is* a traditional Earth breakfast, at least, in the region I'm from. Might not be typical in China." Scrutinizing Manx out of the corner of her eye, Drusilla decided he didn't look at all malnourished, so he must have been eating something, even when Klog was trying to remain discreet. "What do you usually have for breakfast?"

"Since I've been here? Fish, mostly, and, I'm sorry to say, the occasional bird," Manx replied.

"You can catch the birds?" Drusilla said incredulously. "Really?"

Manx nodded. "Other animals too," he said. "Some of them I can catch by hand, but for others I use my bow or spear. I don't go hungry when I'm living out in the wild."

Drusilla laughed at this. "Klog must have thought you were starving."

"Maybe," Manx conceded. "But I wasn't. He *is* a good cook, though."

"Any idea why he always seems to know what you want even before you ask him for it?"

Manx shrugged. "No."

Drusilla frowned as she considered the matter. "Maybe he can sense your body chemistry and know what you're craving that way." Then she laughed as she thought of something else entirely.

"What?" Manx prompted. Her laughter was infectious, and Manx found himself chuckling along with her without even knowing why.

"I've been craving *you*," she explained between giggles. "I'm surprised he didn't drag you in here sooner."

"He didn't *drag* me in here," Manx protested. "Actually, Dwell and Zef had more to do with it," he added reflectively. "They helped me find out more about you." With an apologetic smile, he added, "You have to understand, I've been hiding out—I don't normally have breakfast with just anyone."

Drusilla smiled. "So, I'm special?"

"You are so much more than special," Manx assured her, leaning over to steal a kiss. "In fact, you may be my destiny—though I never believed in that sort of thing before now."

Drusilla was already feeling quite warm and fuzzy about the entire scenario, but bringing destiny into the equation made it seem even more romantic, and she snuggled closer to him. "You mean we were destined to meet?"

"Seems like it to me," he said. "After all, neither of us belongs on this planet, and yet, here we are."

"Yeah," she said thoughtfully. "What were the odds?" Slim to none, as the saying went. "And the really strange thing is that it feels surprisingly comfortable, like we've known each other for years."

"I know exactly what you mean," he said. "I feel the same way." Taking a sip from his cup, he asked, "What did you say this was?"

"Tea," she replied. "Like it?"

Manx nodded. "I'm not used to drinking hot fluids, but yeah, I like it. Warms you up on the inside."

This description took Drusilla back to the night before when Manx had done the same thing to her—but with his hot cock, rather than a cup of tea—and the warm, fuzzy feeling intensified. "There's another thing I don't understand. I've never felt quite like this before. It's an afterglow sort of thing, but more... I don't know, I—"

"It's called *laetralance* in my language," Manx said. "And you don't just feel it after mating, either. It's a—a state of mind that comes when you're at peace and—"

"Everything's right with the world?"

"Yes, but it's got something to do with your soul, too."

"Well, whatever it is, you must be the reason I'm feeling this way," Drusilla said warmly, leaning up against him. "And it feels really good. Thanks for sharing it with me."

Manx smiled. "You're not the only one who's feeling grateful. Not every woman would have responded to me the way you did. Here I am, hiding out in the jungle like a wanted criminal—between your leap of faith and my sense of destiny… it's a pretty strong combination."

Klog floated in and took their empty plates, leaving Drusilla curled up in Manx's arms while he purred. It was nice, cozy moment, but one that quickly progressed to something more… feral. Drusilla's fingers toyed with the hair trailing down to his groin, reaching ever lower, becoming more sensuous, until finally she was teasing his cock. Stroking upward from base to tip, she reached the head and then froze. Pushing back the sheets to get a look at what her fingers were telling her, she gasped in astonishment. She'd already seen the ruffled corona, and fluid was pouring from the star-like points, but it was what he was able to do with it that had her completely amazed. "No wonder you had me going nuts last night!" Mesmerized, she watched as it pulsed, sending more fluid cascading down the shaft before it shifted to point right at her lips. "You can move it?"

"Mm-hm," Manx replied. "In any direction." To demonstrate, he drew circles and squares in the air with the head.

"Holy Toledo!" Drusilla exclaimed. "How come no woman has you tied to her bed?"

Manx grinned. "That's been tried—well, sort of. I was a slave, remember?"

"But you escaped?"

"Before I was ever sold, actually, so technically I wasn't ever a slave, come to think of it," he added reflectively. "Came damn close, though."

"No women since then?"

"Yes," Manx replied, "but none that were *anything* like you." The look in his eyes was enough to assure her that he meant that from the bottom of his heart.

"I could say the same for the men in my life," Drusilla agreed. Since her lovers had all been human, this wasn't surprising. Experimentally, she pushed his cock sideways and it stood right back up again like a punching bag. "And you have to smell my desire for it to get hard?"

"Yes," Manx replied. "And believe me, you smell better than anything I've ever *dreamed* of."

"It was plenty hard that night when you were out on the beach," she pointed out. "Are you saying you could smell me from that distance?"

"Mm-hm," Manx purred. "It was fabulous."

She was still gazing longingly at his groin, thinking about the way it had felt inside her— "But what about the orgasms? It wouldn't do that to me just because of the shape, would it?" If that was the case, there would have been dildos made in a similar form long ago, and while Drusilla hadn't made a study of such things, she knew she'd never seen one quite like it.

"The shape has less to do with it than you might think," he said. He pulsed it again, causing more fluid to flow from the head. "Taste it."

"Yeah, *right,*" Drusilla said witheringly. "Most guys will say anything to get a girl to suck their dick."

"No, really," Manx protested. "You don't have to suck it. Just taste it."

Cocking her head to eye him suspiciously, Drusilla grumbled, "Well, okay. Just one taste."

Drusilla leaned down to lick the clear fluid from his cock, and then backed off. It was essentially tasteless, she noted, other than being slightly salty—which was just like that of a human male's but— "Oh, wow!" she exclaimed as the fluid took effect, triggering the kind of orgasm that normally took quite a bit of time and effort to achieve—though upon further reflection, Drusilla decided that this was even better than the usual sort.

Manx laughed out loud. "And you thought I was lying!"

"Not really," she managed to gasp. "I just thought it would take more than that."

"Oh, well, if you really *want* to do more than just taste it, be my guest," he said amiably. "I won't try to stop you. Just the feel of your tongue on me nearly sent me over the edge, and watching you suck me would… well… "

Gazing at the most spectacular male animal she'd ever beheld lying cock up on her bed stirred the beast in Drusilla once more and she pounced on him, sucking that big, hard cock like it was made of candy—which it seemed to be, except that his fluids had a more potent effect than any chocolate she'd ever tasted.

Manx was passive at first, but then, to Drusilla's delight, groaned and thrust his hips up, sending his cock even deeper into her mouth. Growling, she wrapped her fingers around his balls, reaching underneath him to encourage him to do even more. Then she got up on her knees to get at him better, and Manx took the opportunity to pull her on top of him with her sweet center right in his face.

She smelled as if she was on fire, and Manx fought to hold back his own climax. *Not yet*, he told himself fiercely. *Not until I'm done with her*. He tried to ignore her lips on his cock while he plunged his tongue into the source of her desire, the taste of which drove him wilder still. With a buttock gripped in each hand, he held her while he circled her clitoris with the tip of his tongue and sucked it the way she was sucking his cock. At last he got what he'd been waiting for: the scream erupting from her throat and the pulsation of her clitoris in his mouth. Then he let himself come, feeling the ecstasy of release as he filled her with his creamy snard and then waited for her to realize what else Zetithians were noted for.

Drusilla's body was still contracting spasmodically in the longest orgasm of her life when Manx spurted in her mouth. His semen was amazingly sweet, and she savored it on her tongue before letting go of him to swallow it. Seconds later, she felt that same euphoric warmth suffuse her entire being. Unable even to hold herself up any longer, she sighed deeply, relaxing on him with her head pillowed on his inner thigh. His testicles were well within range of her tongue and, as his soft hair tickled her cheek, she licked his nuts lazily, engulfed in a cloud of bliss even more profound than it had been the first time. Manx's cock lay stretched out across his stomach and she watched as it relaxed, the points of the corona seeming to shrink before the head disappeared inside his foreskin.

Who was this man that could come into her life and change it so completely? She'd never lain on top of a man and nibbled his nuts in her entire life—had never even *thought* of doing it before—but now, it seemed like the most fulfilling pastime she could imagine, unless it was actually fucking him. He was like one of those drugs that hook you with the first high, only he wasn't a drug; he was a living, breathing man whom Drusilla suspected she now wouldn't be able to live without. She would put up with damn near anything for the distinct honor and privilege of sucking his dick. How *very* odd…

But with Manx, she didn't see that she'd have anything bad to put up with at all—unless it was continuous sex. He was pure gold, manna from heaven, and love itself. And she'd found him here, out in the middle of nowhere on a planet so remote that she'd never even heard of it before. Manx was right; it was destiny. It had to be. And she vowed to let nothing come between her and that destiny. Being with Manx was an awakening of the spirit, a new lease on life; just breathing in the air that surrounded him made her feel more alive and joyous. If only she could capture that feeling on canvas, she could truly call herself an artist.

Art. That was why she was on Barada Seven. She had to paint—it was what Ralph had sent her there for. But how was she ever going to get any work done with a distraction like Manx around?

Simple, she told herself. I'll just paint *him*.

Of course, Drusilla's next thought had her laughing uncontrollably.

"What's so funny?" Manx murmured. She was lying on top of him, licking his balls with her ass in his face.

He didn't think there was anything funny about that at all—although he *did* like the way it felt to have her laughing when she was in that position.

It was a moment before Drusilla could refrain from giggling long enough to reply. "I was just thinking about doing some paintings of you—starting with a close-up view of *this*," she said, giving his cock a squeeze.

"If you were that close, I don't think you'd feel much like painting," Manx pointed out. "At least, I *hope* you wouldn't."

Drusilla nodded. "I'd have to take a picture of it and do the painting from that," she agreed. "Though I don't like to paint from photographs, as a rule. I get too technical, and they don't turn out as well as when I paint from life. It's something about the setting and the movement—an impression I get from being near something to study it and learn its ways… that sort of thing."

"You need to experience it," said Manx. "It's like the way I feel about you. A picture of you wouldn't have the same effect. It's your entire *being* that's attractive, not just your appearance."

Drusilla smiled at this sentiment but knew there were other things to attend to. "Yes, and I need to be *experiencing* more of the birds around here, or Ralph is gonna kill me. In fact, there were some humdingers out there in the lake when I woke up this morning, which I should be out there painting right now. I've never seen birds that color before in my life—and trust me, I've seen a lot of birds!"

"You mean the blue ones?"

"Maybe, but these were actually more of an aqua— well, I guess there *are* some parrots that are close to being that color, but not quite. They were absolutely beautiful."

Drusilla sighed, thinking how she'd always had such a passion for birds—a passion that now seemed to have been transferred to Manx. She wasn't sure she could do him justice, however. She was a competent portrait artist but had never really cared for it—perhaps because the birds didn't distract her with attempts at conversation. People tended to do that—out of boredom, perhaps—while Manx, on the other hand, would distract her without ever saying a word. She might have to paint him from memory in order to get anything accomplished.

Memorizing every last bit of Manx would certainly be an enjoyable pastime. Gazing at his eyes would be a source of endless pleasure—her own eyes might have been compared to jade, but his reminded her of glowing emeralds—and she even considered his feet to be worthy of artistic interpretation.

Manx lay quietly, wondering if there was anything he could do to help her out. He'd seen many birds deep in the jungle that didn't come to the lake. Perhaps he could catch some of them for her—alive, of course, for Drusilla probably wouldn't enjoy painting pictures of dead birds—*and* make a cage for them. He was going over the cage design in his mind when he suddenly realized that there wasn't anything he wouldn't do for her. It was a different way of thinking for him—not that he'd ever been particularly selfish—it was simply due to the fact that he'd had only himself to look after for such a long time. The more he reflected upon it, the more he liked the idea. It made him feel useful and needed—which was another thing your average fugitive didn't get to experience on a regular basis.

And useful was something Manx felt he needed to be for Drusilla—if he ever expected her to take him with her when she left Barada Seven. Sexual attraction might not be enough. She needed to truly love him, and he needed to become not merely appealing, but indispensable to her.

Of course, Zetithian males excelled at that. Their own women were highly independent and largely indifferent to males—until they were enticed to the point of desire. Then, and only then, could a man make his move, binding her to him for life.

Being bound to Drusilla for life appealed to Manx—which was a good thing since it had probably already occurred—so he knew he'd best be getting some birds for her.

Since this decision prompted him to get out of bed while Drusilla was lying there trying to commit every square centimeter of him to memory, Drusilla, understandably, couldn't follow his logic.

"Where do you think you're going?"

Manx looked at her blankly. "To build a cage and catch some birds," he replied. "Where did you think I was going?"

"Right now?"

"Well, why not?"

"I was memorizing you," she replied. "So I can do a painting of you."

"I thought you needed to paint birds," he said. "There are some in the jungle you've never seen. They're very hard to catch, too. Might take me a while."

Drusilla just sat up, gaping at him. Men were so strange—and the alien ones were often even more inexplicable than human males. "Whatever made you think I wanted you to run out and catch birds for me?"

Manx shrugged. "I just want to help."

Drusilla shook her head slowly. Nonstop romance would have been nice for a while—whether she ever finished any paintings or not. She could handle Ralph— maybe. "You can help me more by—" She paused there, having been about to tell him to get back in bed and they'd make love all day and into the night. He'd said she could have all she wanted, but perhaps he was right: she *did* need to paint, aside from the fact that there was no need to wear out his dick on their second day together. "Never mind. I appreciate any help you can give me. I'll just get my paints and easel and head on down to the lake. Hopefully I won't scare away those flamingos—or whatever they're called." She looked up at him; he was so… Manx-like, standing there, like a big, black panther. Closing her eyes, she could still see him. Yes, she could already paint him from memory—and it would be fabulous.

Manx seemed puzzled by her sudden turnaround. "What were you going to say?"

Drusilla's expression was grim. "That I'd like to have some more of you. You said I could have all I wanted."

"And I'll give you more, but I don't want to keep you from getting your work done."

"But—"

"Drusilla," Manx said gently. "I'll be back. I'm not leaving; I won't run off into the jungle and never come back, unless the Nedwuts are chasing me. Is that what you're afraid of?"

"Maybe," Drusilla conceded, though a bit grudgingly. "It's just that I've never had a feeling like this before, and I don't want to lose it."

Manx smiled broadly. "You won't," he assured her. "I could have left any time and you wouldn't have been able to stop me. But I didn't, and I *will* come back." He paused briefly on the threshold, adding with a meaningful smile, "And that feeling of *laetralance* is something I can give you for the rest of your life—that is, if you want me to."

"Like I'd ever turn *that* down," Drusilla muttered. "Okay, okay," she grumbled, getting out of bed. "You can catch birds and I'll paint them. We'll be quite a team that way."

Manx grinned. "That's the plan."

———

Meanwhile, back at the lake, Zef was feeling so left out of the loop he considered crawling across the beach and banging on the door to discover what had been going on. He'd kept quiet long enough, in his opinion, and thought it was high time for an update. Having done his best to encourage Manx to persist in his courtship of Drusilla, he was quite certain that Manx would succeed, but he still wanted to hear the details. Zef chuckled to himself, hoping that, in the end, Manx had done exactly what he'd suggested and waved his cock at Drusilla. Zef had known all along that it would be the best way of getting her attention, and while he tried to avoid feeling envious of Manx, he also knew that with a dick like that, he would *never* have been kicked out of his old lake!

Still, the prospect of dragging his tired, old body out of the water didn't appeal to Zef in the slightest, so he dove down to nibble on some of those rubbery plants that grew a little ways out from the shore. They weren't nearly as tasty as fish bones, but until Manx went fishing again, he knew he wouldn't be getting anything else.

As he grazed on the lake bottom, Zef was reminded that introducing Manx and Drusilla might not have been one of his better moves. If Drusilla really liked Manx, she might take him with her when she left Barada, which would leave Zef with no one for company—no one friendly enough to toss him fish bones, that is. He would miss Manx terribly, but he also knew that an excellent fellow like Manx deserved much more out of life than he'd had so far. Zef was happy for Manx and was determined to be philosophical about it, but the prospect of having to live out the rest of his days without his friend was rather bleak.

———

When Manx stepped out on the beach, the whole world seemed so much brighter than it had before. He not only had a woman he was crazy about, but he had also come up with a way to be more than just her lover. Not that a lover's role wasn't important—and he was astute enough to realize that most men were quite capable of giving women joy if they bothered to take the time— but Manx had always felt that to be a good pair, you had to complement one another; what one needed, the other could provide. He knew that he could help her find birds to paint, but what she could give to him took him a while to realize. What he wanted was a mate to have his children.

Perhaps that was what all men wanted, but Manx felt it more strongly than most. It was entirely possible that he was the last of his kind, and he did not want the Zetithian race to die out completely just because he'd failed to reproduce. He wanted a woman to love him and care for him, of course, but the need for sex was something that went even deeper. "Survive and reproduce," he said to himself. "That's all we have to do, and I've only done half of it so far." He couldn't be certain that it was possible for them to mate and produce children, but if the way she smelled and fit together with him was any indication, they would have dozens of them.

Calling out for Zef as he approached the shore, Manx waded in and swam out to deeper water. Drusilla should have been with him, he decided. He was looking forward to swimming with her—for that matter, he was looking forward to doing *everything* with her. He couldn't think of a single activity that wouldn't be improved by having her there to share it with him. "It must be love," he sighed.

Zef heard this comment as he surfaced nearby and responded with his coarse, crunching laughter. "Have a good time?"

Manx grinned at him. "Yes, I did."

"Waved your dick at her, didn't you?"

Manx thought for a moment. He knew there was much more to it than that, but he also knew that Zef didn't want to hear about destiny and leaps of faith. "Well, yes, I suppose I did," he replied.

"Told you it would work," Zef said smugly. "Whatcha gonna do now?"

"Catch some birds for her."

"You're fuckin' kidding me, right?"

"No, she paints birds, so I'm going to catch some for her."

"Ought to be up there fucking her," Zef advised. "She'd like that better."

"Maybe," Manx admitted. "But everyone has to take a break sometime, and she's here to paint, so I'm going to help her."

"I'll never understand primates," Zef said. "You go to so much trouble doing useless shit like that, when all you really have to do is find food and fuck."

Since this sentiment was very similar to what Manx had been thinking earlier, he couldn't argue the point. "Yes, but this is Drusilla's way of finding food," he said. "Indirectly, anyway. It's how she earns a living."

"Still think it's stupid," Zef said. "Things were much simpler before. You'd catch fish and throw me the bones, we'd swim a little, sleep, catch fish, eat, sleep. It was a wonderful life—no fucking, of course, but—"

Manx held up a hand for silence. "I'll spear some fish for you, Zef, but then I'm going bird hunting."

"Ha! And *then* you'll fuck."

"If she wants to," Manx said. "It's her choice."

"That's even dumber, if you ask me," said Zef. "But I guess you primates are all a bit stuffy."

"Trust me, Drusilla is not the least bit stuffy," Manx said. "She—well I guess I shouldn't tell you *everything*."

"Yep, *definitely* stuffy," said Zef.

———

Drusilla gathered up her painting gear and headed out, only to find that there wasn't a bird in sight. However, since Manx was standing in the shallow water holding a handmade spear poised to strike, Drusilla knew she wouldn't have to look any further for an interesting subject to paint. Manx was far more worthy of being immortalized on canvas than any bird she had ever seen—aquamarine flamingos included.

It surprised her that he would be fishing so soon after breakfast, but then she saw Zef nearby. Manx speared a fish and immediately tossed it to Zef. Then he did it again. Drusilla was impressed not only with his ability, but with his kindness to the irascible old eltran. You could open a thousand oysters and never find one, she thought in wonderment, but Manx was a pearl.

The sky might have been purple, the lake might have sparkled like a million diamonds, but Manx was the one who had drawn her eye, and she sat on her stool, sketching his outline before reaching for her paints, nearly breathless with excitement. There was something mesmerizing about the way his hand held the spear, the way the breeze stirred his hair, and the perfection of his form. He was mysterious, dangerous, and sensuous all at the same time. Drusilla wasn't sure she could capture all of that completely, but she painted as she had never done before; the stroke of her brush swift and sure, the colors seeming to blend perfectly all by themselves, while the whole world grew hushed and still as though trying to hold that pose.

Intent on her work, Drusilla suddenly realized that Manx was no longer there—which didn't matter because she had moved on to the background by then—but the light was also nearly gone. Somehow, Klog must have known not to disturb her, with the result that her stomach was now grumbling in protest. Pausing for a moment to study her work, she realized that it wasn't just a picture of a man holding a spear, it was a portrait of a hunter: perfect in symmetry, breathtaking with raw, undiluted power, and alive with cunning. It was as if, seeing that depiction of him, you knew he would not miss; his aim would be true, his quarry as good as caught.

Drusilla shivered as she gazed at it, knowing that no painting she'd ever done could even begin to compare. The odd thing was, she could scarcely remember doing it; it was as if someone else had taken on the task, working through her, using only her hands to create it. She was looking at a work of art far beyond her own capabilities—something that only a great master could have accomplished—and yet, she knew she had done it herself.

Hearing a footstep behind her, Drusilla realized that not only had Klog left her undisturbed for an entire day, but Zef and Manx had too. Her shoulder was nearly frozen in place and her fingers felt cramped and numb.

"I caught some birds for you," Manx said proudly. "Real pretty ones."

"Thank you," Drusilla said faintly. "But I don't think I'll need them."

"What do you mean?" Manx demanded. He'd worked very hard at his self-appointed task and felt a twinge of resentment that she wouldn't appreciate his efforts on her behalf.

"Look," she said, pointing to the canvas.

Manx was no art critic, but even so, what he saw astonished him. The painting was by no means finished, but the impact was complete. "It's me," he said softly. "Is that really how you see me?"

"It's the way you *are,*" she replied.

"Really?" Manx would never have thought that any painting of himself would hit him in the gut quite so hard. It was like looking into his own soul.

Drusilla nodded slowly. "Manx," she said quietly. "I've just been inspired to create my masterpiece. I don't need birds anymore. I only need you."

Chapter 13

WHILE MANX APPRECIATED THE SENTIMENT, HE WASN'T SURE that being an artist's model qualified as a real job. "I... aren't you even going to look at them?"

"What? Oh—yeah, right. Birds," Drusilla said, her voice still a faint whisper. Tearing her eyes away from the image of Manx on the hunt, she gazed up at the real Manx standing beside her and became even more convinced that she never needed to look at another bird again.

His hair was snarled with bits of twigs and leaves and he was dirty, sweaty, and so utterly masculine he took away what little breath Drusilla had left. The knife hanging from his belt and the bow slung over his back, along with the claw marks across his chest, only added to his mystique. The fact that he was holding a crudely constructed bird cage containing a trio of dove-like birds, each one more vividly colored than the next, was insignificant. For sheer animal magnetism, he had no equal.

Swallowing hard, Drusilla forced herself to examine the birds. "They're b-beautiful," she stammered. "I don't think I've ever seen colors like that."

"These are just the easiest ones to catch," Manx said informatively. "But I've always thought they were real pretty. I can get others tomorrow."

Drusilla didn't want Manx to do anything but lie on the beach while she painted another portrait of him, but she nodded anyway. Then the image of Manx killing the wildcat flashed through her memory, and she knew she could paint him whether he was there in front of her or out hunting birds. Clearing her throat with an effort, she said, "Well, it looks like I'm going to be busy!" Smiling up at him, she felt another jolt of electricity when he smiled back, which momentarily paralyzed her.

Manx didn't seem to notice—or so she thought. "Is it me, or the birds?" he asked with a wry grin.

Drusilla stared at him in bewilderment.

With a swift, downward gesture, he drew her eyes to his groin, where his thick penis was beginning to rise.

"You," she whispered hoarsely. "Like I said, I don't think I need birds anymore."

His grin grew wider. "Want to go inside?"

"Not really," she whispered.

"I'm all dirty," Manx said. "Maybe we should go for a swim first."

Drusilla shook her head. "Don't want to do that either."

Glancing at the sky, Manx saw that the sun was just beginning to set behind the trees and his mind was assailed with the image of Drusilla in the moonlight. Making love on the beach with her...

Manx set down the birdcage and pulled Drusilla into his arms. "I've wanted to kiss you all day." Sighing as his lips found hers, he gradually deepened the kiss, delighting in her flavor and becoming even more intoxicated with her scent. She tasted like nothing he'd ever dreamed of and smelled like the fragrance of rainflowers on the wind. As he pushed her loose clothing aside, he felt Drusilla's knees nearly give way beneath her and the sight of her pearly skin immediately had him purring with wild anticipation. His cock was so hard it shone and the fluid coursing from the tips of the head ran down her legs as he held her closely to him. "I didn't get a good look at you before," he purred. "You make me wish I was a painter."

"And you make me very glad that I am one." Drusilla's knees did give way then, and she landed on her discarded clothing, pulling him down with her.

Manx captured her lips once more. He couldn't seem to stop kissing her—didn't want to, either. Once again he was consumed with the desire to get lost inside her, and, nudging her legs apart, he did just that. Burying his cock to the hilt, he gazed into her misty eyes, watching her reactions to the feel of him inside her. That was one of his favorite moments—those moments when her eyes filled with desire just from him, rather than his orgasmic fluids. It didn't take long for the first one to hit, but until it did, his cock danced inside her, making her eyes roll back with exquisite pleasure. When she came, he felt her hot inner muscles grip his shaft, pulling him in deeper and sucking him dry. There was a regular rhythm to her climaxes, and he savored those moments in between the peaks even more than the heights.

Manx took up a slow, steady rhythm, rocking her as gently as the waves in the nearby lake. He knew he could keep going long enough for the chemical effect to dampen—or he could stop the flow of it altogether—but to do either of those things, he had to pace himself. It was difficult with Drusilla. He wanted to take his time and show her all he could give her, but at the same time he longed to reach one pinnacle just so he could leap on to the next. But he did it anyway. Most women couldn't take that much and let him keep going, but Drusilla was different—and not nearly as delicate as she appeared to be. Her contractions became less powerful, less frequent around his cock. And suddenly, he felt the change in her; the total relaxation.

"Now it's just me," he whispered. "This is the best part."

Drusilla's eyes had drifted lazily shut, but they flew open as Manx shifted into another gear. His hot meat pulsed, pushing gently against her sweet spot until he was almost drumming his cock inside her.

"Do you like that, Drusilla?" he purred.

"Mmm."

Manx laughed. "I was hoping you'd say that." Scooping her legs up in his arms, he pushed them forward and leaned into her, hoping to keep going indefinitely, but his body had other plans. He gazed down at her. The moon was up and his beautiful Drusilla gleamed in the soft light like a glowing pearl. He couldn't stop now, the sight, feel, and scent of her was too much; the tension tightened in him like a wire, driving him on until it snapped.

In his mind, a million brightly colored lights suddenly burst into being, obscuring his vision and triggering his release. Manx pumped his snard into Drusilla with a force that astonished him, and he remained high on the pinnacle of ecstasy longer than he ever had before. The lights in his mind pulsed and expanded before subsiding into nothingness. When he could see again, he was looking down into her eyes and saw the same lights reflected there. She appeared sated, but the emotions she evoked overwhelmed him with the need to give her even more.

Manx knew what he needed to do, but it was with the utmost reluctance that he withdrew, and the loss of his warmth made Drusilla groan in protest. But she would know only one moment of regret because Manx didn't just lay his head on her stomach to relax, or roll away from her. No, he buried his face in her creamy wet heat, licking her gently before latching onto her clitoris. Her eyes widened, then rolled before taking on a dreamy expression of pure bliss.

"I've always wanted someone to do that."

Manx paused for a moment to smile at her. "I know."

Dipping back down to suck on her hard clit, Manx drank in her scent and felt his cock stiffen in response. He waited for her rapturous scream, and then plunged into her once more.

As she gazed up at his face, Manx could almost feel her eyes caressing him. "I wish you could see what you look like right now," she whispered. "The stars are shining all around you; the moon is beginning to rise, casting shadows on your face… your hair glistening in the starlight… your glowing eyes… absolutely beautiful."

Manx smiled but shook his head in denial. "You're the beautiful one."

"Guess we could argue about that all night."

"There are much better things to do than argue," Manx purred. "Boat rides, moonlight swims—there are all kinds of things we could do."

"Mmmm, those both sound wonderful," she said dreamily. He could have suggested almost anything and she would have agreed—being with him would have made any activity special.

Getting to his feet, Manx took her hand and led her to the water's edge. "Just stay there for a second," he said before quickly wading out to the deeper water.

The water swirled around him like shining silk as he pushed off the bottom to propel himself away from the shore. "Now it's my turn to look at you," he said. "You look like some magical lake sprite standing there sparkling in the moonlight. I've never seen anyone before who could actually *shine*."

"And I've never met anyone whose eyes could actually *glow*," Drusilla countered. "Maybe that's why I seem to shine."

"Never happened with anyone else," Manx declared. "It must just be you." Beckoning to her, he said, "Come on, let's go for that swim."

As she waded into the still water, Manx pulled her into his arms and kissed her. As his kiss deepened, Drusilla wound her arms around his neck, pressing the full length of her body against his before wrapping her legs around his hips. He moved off then, and she let him swim for both of them, not wanting to let go, his shoulders solid and strong beneath her hands, his lips warm and inviting.

"Hold on," he said, turning in her embrace.

Grasping his shoulders, Drusilla circled his waist with her legs as Manx cut through the water with powerful strokes. After a few moments, she stretched her arms up toward the sky, riding him like a dolphin as he swam. Never had she felt so free, so joyous, so *alive*.

Swimming toward the dock, Manx grasped the ladder and then gestured for her to climb up ahead of him. She did so, and was reaching for a towel when Manx seized her from behind and spun her in his arms to capture her lips for another fiery kiss. Gripping her hips, he pulled her up against him, parting her thighs and settling her down on his cock. As his slick cockhead penetrated her heat, Drusilla groaned, a groan that was drowned by Manx's deep, rumbling purr.

"The last time I saw you climbing a ladder, your clothes were clinging to you like a second skin, but this time, watching the water dripping down on me from your naked body... " He paused, taking a deep, ragged breath. "I knew I had to mate with you again or die."

"I certainly wouldn't want you to die," Drusilla said with a smile. "What exactly would it take to save you?"

"I want to see you," he said as he eased himself down on the dock, stretching out beneath her. "The way your wet skin shines in the moonlight, the way you move... I can't take my eyes off of you."

With her arms above her head, Drusilla danced on him, flexing her spine, plunging him in deeply and enjoying him to the fullest. As she moved, he moved, tightening his butt to offer his cock up for her enjoyment. Having Manx laid out before her in the moonlight was a feast for the eyes and a treat for the soul. Drusilla could feel his cock moving inside her with a steady drumbeat; his purring she could both hear and feel in the depths of her core; his eyes glowed, his black curls spread out on the dock, his pearly fangs gleaming as he smiled up at her.

I've got to paint that, Drusilla told herself—*his tanned, muscular chest, spectacular hair, and that incredible face... just like this...* Closing her eyes, she tried to imprint his image on her mind, never wanting to forget it, whether the distance between them was nonexistent or vast.

Drusilla came again and again, her body constricting around his cock as it became even more engorged. Then his nuts tightened and the dam burst, flooding her with his creamy snard. The slickness oozing out over his balls drove Drusilla onward; Manx was going crazy beneath her, and yet she couldn't seem to stop, couldn't get enough of him until the euphoria took her in hand, washing through her being like a soothing balm and filling her with joy.

"I've always wanted to do it by a lake in the moonlight," Drusilla said, settling down on him with a sigh. "How did you know?"

"I didn't," Manx replied. "But it's something I've always wanted to do too."

"Was it all you thought it would be?" Drusilla asked coyly.

"Not even close," Manx replied. "Being with you makes it so much better than anything I've ever dreamed of—you have no idea."

"I might," she said, laughing at the thought that his pleasure might be greater than hers. In her mind, it couldn't possibly compare. "Though I must admit, I never imagined that I'd be doing it with someone quite like you. This goes way beyond fantasy." Gazing down at him in wonder, she added, "Somewhere along the line, I must have done something *very* good to deserve you."

Manx shook his head. "I still think it's destiny… of the very best kind."

It had a nice ring to it, so Drusilla didn't argue. If destiny was responsible, then so be it; she would take all that destiny had to give.

———

Drusilla reveled in the feel of the wind in her hair as she sat on Manx's lap while he steered the boat across the still lake beneath a starry sky. Moonlight flowed across the water like a river of pearls and she breathed in the cool night air, closing her eyes, trying to memorize yet another cherished moment with Manx. There were so many already, things she never wanted to forget. Someday, she told herself, I may want to revisit this memory as one of the very best of my life.

But didn't everyone feel that way when they first fell in love? Drusilla tried to remember how she'd felt with other men in her life and knew that nothing could compare with the way she felt now. Manx truly was the man of her dreams—dreams she couldn't even remember having, but they had come true, nonetheless. She felt excited but content at the same time, and even ordinary activities seemed extraordinary just because Manx was there to share them with her.

Drusilla could have stayed out on the boat with Manx all night, until she suddenly remembered her canvas still sitting on its easel at the water's edge. Her masterpiece had been left on the beach like a forgotten sandal.

"We need to go back and put my paints away," she said. "Then we can come back if you like."

"Actually, going back wouldn't be a problem," Manx said. He'd been thinking about turning back anyway. Her warm bottom on his lap was making him think of other things besides boat rides. "I'm thinking I'd like a nice, hot shower with a beautiful woman and then maybe curl up in bed with her."

Drusilla didn't have to see his dick to know it was raring to go again; she was sitting on it. "Mmm, a shower sounds wonderful," she said dreamily. "That master bath is big enough for two."

Manx grinned delightedly. "I know."

Looking into his eyes in the moonlight sent shivers up and down Drusilla's spine. Manx was like a sweet, intoxicating drink, one she knew she would never tire of. "You *will* come with me when I leave here, won't you?"

"Just try to stop me," he replied. "I know you come from Earth, and if you leave me behind, I'll get there and find you if it's the last thing I do."

Drusilla had no difficulty believing that he would somehow manage to do just that, but she saw no need. "I won't leave you behind, though it may be tricky. We'll figure something out."

"How do you mean?"

"A way to get you there alive," she said solemnly. "You might have to wear a cloak with a hood. Maybe a veil over your face. I could say you were my brother and you had an accident and don't like to show your face."

"Might work," he conceded. "But I don't think anyone will believe I'm your brother."

"Okay, then," she said agreeably. "You'll just have to be my slave."

Manx's glowing eyes brightened suddenly. "I think I would *enjoy* being your slave," he said. "You could make me do all kinds of interesting things."

"Like washing my clothes or combing my hair?" she teased.

"More like taking *off* your clothes and running my fingers *through* your hair," Manx countered. Then he paused for a moment before adding, "*All* of your hair."

"And then you'll wash me?" she suggested with a mischievous smile.

"Only if I can do it with my tongue," he said silkily. "I'd like to lick you all over."

Drusilla's mouth went dry and she felt all the moisture in her body settle right where his cock was, bathing it in her own sweet nectar. "I—if you like," she stuttered.

"I would like that very much," he said. His eyebrows lifted suggestively. "You could do it to me too."

"Lick my slave?" Drusilla drew back in mock dismay. "I don't think most masters do that."

"Ah, but if I'm your *love* slave it would be expected of you," he said. "Of course, if you would sit just a little further this way," he added, shifting her weight slightly, "I could be a live chair for you to enjoy."

"A very *erotic* chair," she corrected him. "A nice, warm chair complete with a cock to sit on. Mmm, sounds fabulous. You wouldn't mind being used as a chair?"

"To tell you the truth, I wouldn't mind if that was the *only* thing you used me for," Manx admitted. "I mean, being used like that could grow on a guy."

"Not boring?" Drusilla asked and then gasped as his hard, slick meat penetrated her heat.

"Never that," he assured her. "I could sit here twirling my cock inside you for a *very* long time."

"Um, shouldn't you be watching where you're going?" she suggested. "We don't want to run aground."

"No danger of that," he assured her. "I could cruise this lake blindfolded."

Taking her chin in his hand, he raised her face to his and kissed her deeply as his dick began its sinuous dance. When his tongue slipped past her lips, Drusilla captured it, sucking it the way she would suck his dick, and the feel of it in her mouth sent another wave of sexual heat crashing through her, pooling in her center to wash down over his thick rod.

Manx must have felt it too, because he began purring softly. "You're so hot," he whispered. "You could keep me warm even on the coldest world."

"Ever been anywhere like that?" Drusilla murmured. "It's cold where I come from, but only part of the time." Then she thought what a pity it would be for Manx to ever have to put on even a stitch of clothing. "Maybe we could live in South America. The Amazon jungle is hot all year round, and they have some fabulous birds there. The natives don't wear very much, even now that the jungle plants have made them quite wealthy, so you'd fit right in."

"You like me naked, don't you?" Manx purred.

"To be quite honest, I can't even begin to imagine you with clothes on," Drusilla replied. "Don't think I want to, either," she added reflectively. "I like you this way. Always ready for love."

"I'll always be ready to love you, whether I'm dressed or not," Manx declared. As he let go of the controls, the boat slowed to a stop, gently rocking on its own wake, and Manx ran his hands down the sides of her body, cupping her hips on his palms. "I'm already thinking about what I'll do to you the next time."

"Something kinky?" Drusilla suggested with a sultry giggle.

"Kinky?" Manx echoed. "You mean something… unusual?"

"Yeah," she replied, grinding her slick pussy on his cock.

"You mean like bending you over the side of the boat and fucking your ass?"

An involuntary shout of laughter escaped her lips. "Where did you hear that one?"

"From Zef," he replied. "Those Arconian sailors were a wild bunch—and they had women with them."

"Did you watch?"

Manx nodded. "They did some things out there on the beach I'd never even *thought* of! Even the men were fucking each other." Pausing to focus on the silky feel of Drusilla on his cock, he added, "Don't believe I'd care for that."

"I hope not!" Drusilla said gratefully. "If I have to fight off women *and* men to keep you, I'll never have any peace!"

"You won't have to fight," Manx said solemnly. "I am yours to keep for as long as you want me."

"Forever, then," Drusilla sighed.

"Even if I do something kinky?" he said with a smile.

"Especially if you do something kinky," she assured him.

"Let's do kinky then," he said, getting to his feet with Drusilla still impaled on his prick. "I want to make love to your beautiful ass."

"It'll probably kill me," Drusilla giggled. "You're huge!"

"I'll take it slow," Manx promised as lowered her to her feet.

Drusilla felt like a siren, the kind of woman who summoned men to their deaths with their beauty as she danced to the side of the boat. She'd never let anyone do that to her before, and now, here she was, beckoning a man with a dick big enough to rip her in two. She didn't care. She wanted him in every possible way. She wished her tits were big enough for him to bury his meat in and then have him come all over her chest, neck, and face. She wanted to lie on her back with him straddling her while he jacked off and covered her with cum. With thoughts like those in mind, wiggling her tush at him caused her no embarrassment whatsoever. Bending at the hips, she reached out and grasped the safety rail with both hands as she placed one knee on the padded bench seat that ran the full length of the boat. Then, arching her back, she offered herself to him.

———

Manx's eyes crossed as she reached for the rail, her beautiful backside gleaming in the moonlight, driving him to a frenzy of desire. He vowed to take her slowly, though he wasn't sure he could; already his balls were tightening as they threatened to fire. He closed his eyes for a moment in an attempt to regain control, lest he dive into her with one plunge—a plunge he knew would have her screaming in pain. And he didn't want her to feel pain—only pleasure.

His cock was so hard it shone like glass; the thick syrup dripped from the shaft as he let it slide between her buttocks, coating her with his orgasmic elixir. The blunt head soon found her entrance and teased it, rocking the boat gently as he pushed against her. A powerful orgasm gripped her as he penetrated ever deeper until she thrust backward suddenly, driving him in to the hilt.

Manx stole a glance downward as his cock disappeared inside her and he gritted his teeth in an effort to maintain control, but the sight of her was too much, and he emptied his balls into her.

His own creamy snard enveloped his cock as he plunged into her anyway. It was impossible for him to stop, even after his own climax. He kept his eyes on that fabulous ass and kept right on fucking as Drusilla backed into him, pushing against the rail to brace herself for his thrusts. Her cries of ecstasy told him what she was feeling—the euphoria from his snard, the heat of his body, the grinding motion of his cock.

"I never dreamed anything could feel so good," she gasped as tears poured down her cheeks.

She was making sounds unlike any he'd ever heard before. Though Manx knew he was stretching her to the limit, she couldn't seem to stop—twisting her hips and riding his cock relentlessly while his scrotum teased her slit.

Manx was fairly certain he wouldn't lose his erection with a vision such as that, but he reached down and coated his fingers with her essence and, bringing it up, he smeared it on his face, inhaling deeply as he felt his cock tighten in response. Then he went back for more, this time licking her juices from his fingers. With her scent in his head and his climax so recent, Manx knew he could go as long as he needed to; could fuck her until she'd had enough, and enjoying the view enormously, he hoped she wanted it for a long, long time.

His balls were bouncing against her wet, swollen pussy as Manx reached for her breasts, teasing her precious nipples with his fingertips. He felt another ejaculation building and marveled that he had anything left when he felt his snard spurt into her, filling her with his sweet cream once more. The added lubrication seemed to drive Drusilla mad with lust, and as she ground her butt into his groin, Manx's purr became more of a growl—similar to the deep-throated guttural sound issuing from Drusilla. Manx came again, and knew it was his last, just as the boat bumped into the dock, loosening Drusilla's grip on the rail and sending her sprawling sideways onto the bench.

Manx's abrupt departure had Drusilla screaming in ecstasy; as though just pulling out set off a kind of fireworks she'd never imagined. Gasping and writhing as every cell in her body seemed to climax, she lay shuddering as Manx dropped to his knees and gathered her up in his arms.

While Manx's kisses rained down on her face, her paroxysms slowly subsided and her eyes regained focus as she gazed up at him. "I think that's something we should save for special occasions," she murmured. "Don't think I could take that very often."

"Good, though, wasn't it?" Manx purred.

"The best ever," she replied. "Who'd have thought I'd ever find a kinky cat in this jungle?"

Manx shrugged. "I found a kinky bird painter. Like I said before, it has to be destiny."

But what they didn't know was that destiny held all the cards and was about to play one that neither of them expected.

Chapter 14

DRUSILLA SAT AT HER EASEL WITH MANX BESIDE HER WHILE she painted. She couldn't remember a more perfect day. The sun was warm, the sky a crystalline purple, the clouds were puffs of lavender cotton candy, the birds were cooperating, and even the butterflies were being less persistent than usual. Zef was sunning himself in the shallows, sound asleep and quiet for once in his life. Manx had wanted to go bird hunting again, but she'd overruled him. "I want to spend this whole day with you," she said after breakfast, "never letting you out of my sight."

"Going to paint another picture of me?" Manx teased. "Or do you want to do something else?"

"Doesn't matter," she replied. "We could be crawling around in the sand digging for worms and it would be fun as long as we were doing it together. Do you know what I'm saying?"

"Yeah," he replied. "I'm feeling it too."

He hadn't been with her the entire day, of course. He had played his flute for a time, the melodies echoing across the lake, but after a bit, he had walked along the shore, finally disappearing from view. When he returned with a large, gnarled chunk of driftwood, she was diverted from her painting for a time as he began carving it with his knife. At first, she thought he was just idly whittling on it to pass the time, but after a bit, something seemed to be taking shape.

"What *is* that?" she asked finally.

Drusilla's heart nearly stopped as he flashed a mischievous grin at her. "You'll see," he replied.

It took her a moment to recover, but she did her best. "Ah, a man of mystery," she said knowingly. "I like that."

"Not sure I do," he said. "Did you ever meet someone and you wanted to know everything there was to know about them, down to the most insignificant event of their life?"

"You mean before now?" Drusilla asked. "No, I never have."

"Me either," he said, carving off another long strip of wood. "But right now, I want to hear everything. What you think, how you feel, what you want, what you've done… Everything."

"Hmm, that might take a while."

Manx grinned at her again, stealing even more of her breath. "Got anywhere you need to be?"

"Nope," Drusilla replied. "Start talking."

"No, you first."

"Manx, my life up until now has been completely boring!" Drusilla insisted. "I'm sure you've had a much more interesting life."

"Well, maybe," he admitted. "I mean, I don't know that much about your life to be able to judge, but I've been lots of places."

"And had a girl in every port, I'll bet."

"Some," he said hesitantly. "The trouble was, I knew I might have to go on the run again at any time. It didn't make for a very lasting relationship."

"Knowing what I do now, I'm surprised they aren't chasing you all across the galaxy." The vision of an army of his ex-lovers banding together to track him down popped into her head and Drusilla began giggling uncontrollably.

"Well, believe it or not, I've tried to prevent that," he said, trying to remain serious in spite of her infectious laughter. "I didn't go around chasing women on every planet. They had to come after me, and I had to like them really well—but all the same, there were some things I just couldn't do in good conscience."

"Such as?"

"Well, I haven't left a trail of children behind me," he replied. "That would have been the worst, but I also haven't let many of them have… you know," he paused and Drusilla could have sworn he was blushing, "the, um, full effect."

"The joy juice?"

"Yes," he said with a nod, seeming relieved that she understood him. "I learned how to stop it. Believe me, it's not easy—and I always used a condom so they wouldn't get the snard effect either. No one ever complained—they didn't know about it, so how could they?—and under the circumstances, it seemed best."

Having felt the "full effect" and the resultant attachment to Manx, Drusilla realized just how kind it had been not to get a woman hooked on him, knowing he had to leave. "That was very thoughtful of you, but you didn't do that with me," she said. "Mind telling me why?"

"Because you're different," he replied. "I just couldn't hold back with you." He flashed a sly grin at her. "That, and the fact that I don't have any condoms."

"So, I'm either very special or just incredibly lucky," she said dryly. "Any idea which?"

Manx laughed. "Very special," he replied. Sheathing his knife, he pulled another tool out of his pouch and began carving holes in the wood.

"Still not gonna tell me what you're making there?" she prompted.

"Nope," he replied. "It's still a surprise."

Chuckling softly, she reached down and rummaged in her box for a smaller brush. "I like surprises," she said.

"Do you?"

"Only the good ones," she stipulated. "I've had a number of surprises that weren't so hot."

"Tell me about them," he urged.

"The most recent was having a homosexual boyfriend."

"Ouch!" Manx said. "That hurts."

"No kidding," she agreed. "The worst part of it was that I was too busy painting and promoting my work to notice."

"You've *definitely* been working too hard," Manx said forcefully. "You need me around to make sure that doesn't happen again."

"With you around, I doubt I'll ever go looking for another boyfriend, so that's a moot point, but it's nice to know you'll be there to watch out for me."

Manx's eyes narrowed as he leaned over to study her canvas. "You're painting me again, Drusilla," he pointed out. "You're supposed to be painting birds."

"Sorry," she said sheepishly. "Can't help it."

"There are some perfectly good birds over there," he said with a gesture toward the lake. "Paint them."

"Oh, all right," she grumbled, reaching down for a rag to wipe the canvas. With a gesture toward the driftwood sculpture, she asked, "Where'd you learn to do that?"

"I was always pretty handy with a knife," he said with a shrug. "I used to make toys for my sisters, and I made other things too."

"Such as?"

"Spoons, boxes, bowls… things like that—along with the flutes."

She watched him working; his strong, capable hands coaxed the shape from the wood with a level of skill that made it look easy. "With a full set of tools, you could make some pretty nice stuff," she commented. "Hand-carved items always sell well—on Earth, anyway." The pleasant vision of being with him at art fairs came back to her then. He was just the kind of man she wanted—a gentler sort of man, an artist or a musician who would be content to create beautiful but practical things rather than going off to pursue some high-powered career.

As they continued to work in companionable silence, she stole glances at him from time to time, realizing there was something about being near him that simply made her feel complete; a serenity she had never felt with anyone else. She closed her eyes and could almost see the rest of their lives stretching out before her: endless blissful days and long, passionate nights.

The sound of Manx clearing his throat brought her out of her reverie, and Drusilla began dutifully painting the birds again, becoming so absorbed in her work that she didn't notice when he finished his project. However, she *did* notice when he began gathering up her painting gear.

Glancing up at the sky, she said, "What's the matter? Is it going to rain or something?"

"Nope," Manx replied. "I'm just putting this stuff where it belongs."

"It doesn't *belong* anywhere," she said. "I just set it wherever I—" She broke off as she saw what he was doing. His piece of driftwood now had a place for her palette, holes for her brushes, a compartment for her cleaning fluid, a shelf for her box, and a hook for the cleaning rags. It even had a cup holder for her tea.

"Oh, Manx," she began, but the lump in her throat and the tears welling up in her eyes slowed her down. "I—I don't know what to say—I—"

"You don't have to *say* anything," Manx said with a lopsided grin, "but if you'd like to kiss me, you go right ahead."

"That's worth a whole lot more than a kiss!" she protested.

"Not to me, it isn't," he replied, pulling her to her feet and into his arms.

With the first taste of his lips, she felt her bones turning to jelly, and the erotic warmth of his tongue stroking hers soon had her body clamoring for more. His skin was hot from the sun, but as her hands gripped his shoulders, the thought of the mess she was making distracted her. "I'm getting paint all over you."

"I don't mind," he murmured against her lips before renewing the kiss. "It won't hurt me."

"It *is* non-toxic paint," she agreed, "but I should probably clean it off."

"That sounds interesting," he admitted, "but you can do that later. Right now, I don't care if you get paint all over my whole body."

The thought of painting designs directly onto his hot, nude skin set off an explosion inside Drusilla not unlike one of the orgasms his joy juice elicited. "Oh, Manx," she sighed, melting into his arms. "You say the most amazing things..."

Her mind took flight, and before long, he was lying spread-eagle in the sand while she painted emerald green wings on his arms and swirling masses of tail feathers across his hips and thighs. She'd seen body paintings before but had never done any herself—wouldn't have wanted to until now—but at the moment, it seemed like the best idea she'd ever had in her life.

She was engaged in painting his scrotum when his cock began to ooze its fluid. Wiping it dry with her hand, she said teasingly, "Do you think you could stop that? It's messing up the paint."

"I'll try," Manx gasped, "but I'm not sure I can do it right now. You're driving me insane here."

Drusilla smiled seductively. "That's the idea."

As she painted nearer and nearer to his stiff cock, his entire body quivered with anticipation. "Suck me," Manx begged.

"Nope," she replied, shaking her head. "I'm not finished yet."

Gritting his teeth, Manx let out a long, tortured groan. "How much longer?"

"You can't rush these things," she said, moving around to kneel between his outstretched legs. Lifting his testicles by the softly curling scrotal hair, she began painting the underside.

Manx's back arched as his fingers dug into the sand. "I'm gonna come right in your face in a minute!"

"Promises, promises," she chided.

"No, really, I mean it," he said earnestly.

"Really, really?"

"Really, really," he replied.

The points of his corona were tightly engorged and every vein was standing up on the shaft when, without warning, she went down on him, sucking his hot meat into her mouth. Manx's sigh of relief was soon replaced with moans of pleasure as she slid her lips and tongue up and down the length of him. She did her best to reach the base, but it was too long; backing off, she wiped the paint from her fingers and gripped it near the root.

"No joy juice," she reminded him as she took him in her mouth once again.

Manx wished he'd never told her he was capable of that as he watched her sucking him. Before she'd begun, she'd removed her swimsuit, and that ethereal smock was all she had on. It may have protected her back from the sun, but it hung open in the front, revealing her luscious breasts, soft stomach, and the enticing patch of auburn hair between her thighs. That image alone should have made him climax, but the effort it took to hold back the coronal fluid also had the effect of increasing his stamina. Not that he particularly wanted more stamina at this point, but something told him that following her instructions was the best plan. The stroke of her brush teased him; her gaze focused intensely on every square inch of him enthralled him—and her scent! It had always been strong before, but this was unbelievable! He'd never dreamed that a woman could be capable of such passionate desire.

Drusilla was reveling in the power. Without his fluid to trigger orgasms, she was able to savor his cock like never before: hot, pulsating, and as strong and hard as a tree trunk. She licked the scalloped edge, teasing each point as though daring it to drool. She knew the incredible amount of concentration it was taking him to hold back; could see it in his face, hear it in his tight, labored breaths as he fought for control.

Finally, though not completely sated by any means, she decided the time had come to reward him. "Let it go now," she whispered.

Manx's growl was deep and guttural as rivers of fluid poured from each point of his cockhead. Drusilla bathed her hands in it and then grasped his hard penis, sliding her hands from base to head and back again in a slow, firm movement.

"Go ahead, Manx," she said fiercely. "Come in my face."

In three excruciatingly slow strokes, he came, his snard spewing from his cock as though fired from a cannon. Catching her across the mouth, it ran down between her naked breasts, but on the second round, she aimed it away from her, splattering a jet of creamy semen across his freshly painted chest.

"The finishing touch," she whispered with awe. *"Absolutely fabulous…"*

Her erotic painting might have been finished, but Manx certainly wasn't. He rose up off the sand and pushed her onto her back, thrusting his still-spewing cock into her with one swift stroke. As he hung poised above her, the full effect of snard, cock, and coronal fluid hit her in one exquisite moment as her climax meshed with his. She gazed up at him in wonder until he began to move, and then lay helplessly beneath him as he unleashed the wild fury of his passion.

Manx drove in deeply, shutting off the coronal flow once again, determined to let her have it for as long as he possibly could. As he rocked into her, her eyes were barely open and her every breath a moan. When at last he felt her relax her grip on him, he went on, bringing her to climax again and again; she was his, and he would give her all he had.

When he ejaculated the second time, he kept right on going, his cock slick with his own snard until he pulled out and buried his face in her creamy heat, sucking her clit until she screamed and her body convulsed around him.

Then, his cock still rock hard, he plunged into her again.

The sun was barely peeking past the horizon as Lester faced the band of Nedwuts that had reluctantly been allowed to land on Barada Seven. Most of the time, the authorities disarmed them and sent them back to their ships with a warning never to attempt to land on their world again, but this time, they had actually been invited as hunters to track down the wildcat that was prowling the jungle. Lester thought it was a very bad idea, himself; the cat wouldn't live forever and hopefully was male and wouldn't reproduce. At least the cat only had claws and fangs. These snarling beasts had pulse rifles.

"And you say you have not heard from this Terran

female in several days?" the lead Nedwut, Klarkunk, asked when Drusilla was mentioned.

"Yes," Lester said, his hands displaying his anxiety. "I have been concerned about her. She did not answer when I called yesterday, though it's possible that she may have been out all day—on the boat, perhaps."

"Why have you not gone to check on her?" Klarkunk demanded. "Are you such a weak coward?"

Being a peaceful soul, Lester didn't consider himself to be particularly brave; on his planet, bravery wasn't necessary most of the time, but neither did he consider himself a coward. "I had intended to visit her today."

"Don't bother," Klarkunk said. "Just tell us the way."

The thought of sending these horrid Nedwuts to check on the lovely Terran had Lester's hands flying in all directions at once. "No!" he asserted. "I will go with you. She knows me and has no reason to trust you. You may frighten her. She is our guest, and we will not have her treated in such a fashion."

"As you wish," Klarkunk said with a sneer. "You can be bait for the cat."

Lester turned a slightly paler shade of orange as the other Nedwuts all laughed aloud at Klarkunk's jest, but Lester had an idea he wasn't joking. "I will go to see that our guest is not harmed. You will not approach her, or the house, without me."

Klarkunk knew he could do just as he pleased, whenever he pleased, and Lester wouldn't be able to stop him, so he agreed with only a passing show of reluctance. The thought that they might not only bag a Zetithian, but also be able to take a Terran female captive, appealed to Klarkunk. Females of all species could be sold as slaves on the right worlds, but Terrans were highly prized on several, and would bring a better price than most. Not nearly as much as the bounty on a Zetithian, but enough to make it worthwhile. He sincerely hoped that the cat hadn't done its job too well.

Jack bolted upright in bed. "I know where he'll be!" she announced to her startled husband. "A Terran was going to be staying on Barada Seven. That's why we delivered all of that food, and I'm pretty sure they said their visitor was a female, traveling alone. If your Manx has as good a nose as you say, I'll bet he's sniffed her out by now."

"Jacinth," Cat whispered. "They could each be on opposite sides of the planet. Even Manx's nose isn't *that* good."

"Still, it's the best hunch I've had yet," Jack insisted as she twisted around to face him. At her thought, the glowstone at the bedside illuminated, revealing him and setting off a wave of fond desire that coursed its way through her entire being. One look at Cat was just about all it took, and the sound of his voice or the touch of his hand intensified the effect. Purring sent her over the edge. "Wonder if Nedwuts know how drawn you guys are to Earth women."

"Possibly," Cat replied. "The fact that you keep killing them to protect me could have gotten back to others."

"I doubt it," Jack said candidly. "I hardly ever let any of them live once they've seen you."

"I have noticed this," Cat said dryly, "but other witnesses may have spread the word."

"Maybe," Jack conceded, "But nobody else likes Nedwuts much. Can't see anyone ratting on us—not even for money."

"I do not agree," said Cat. "I have seen too many horrific things done for money; free men bought and sold like animals and then tortured for sport. Selling information to Nedwuts is minor compared to the many atrocities I have witnessed in my lifetime. If they do know of our affinity for Terran females, we must be quick to reach this woman before the Nedwuts do. She will be in danger from them as well."

With her own sister's kidnapping and Jack's subsequent six-year quest to find her still fresh in her memory, Jack didn't need to be reminded. "All the more reason to check up on her first," she said firmly. "As soon as we get there, that's where we're going. What was that little guy's name? You know, the orange one?"

"They are *all* orange," Cat reminded her. "But you mean Lester, I believe."

"Yeah, that's the one," Jack said. "He's the agent for several properties near the spaceport, and one of them is that house by the lake. I'll bet that's where she is, and I'll bet Manx is with her."

"It is unlikely that they are together," Cat reiterated, though he was probably wasting his breath.

"Just as unlikely as it was that I found you and then we found your other friends," Jack pointed out. "I think we've got God or fate or *something* on our side! The Zetithians were dealt a bad hand. It's up to us to make sure they don't lose the game."

Cat shook his head and leveled a questioning look at her.

"Don't know what that means, do you?"

"Does that surprise you?" he countered.

"Well, no, actually, I enjoy coming up with figures of speech you won't understand. I like that exasperated look you get. Makes you look sexy."

Cat chuckled. "You think everything makes me look sexy."

While this was true, there were some things that affected her more than others. "Don't suppose your dick's hard, is it?" she inquired.

"Do bees be? Do bears bear?"

"Ha! Finally figured that one out, have you?"

"Not really." he admitted. "But this is the correct context for its use, I believe."

"Sure is!" Jack declared. Gazing at her beloved husband with all of her desire for him written plainly on her face, she added with conviction, "Manx and that woman *have* found each other, Cat. I just know it. And she won't give him up without a fight. Those Nedwuts had better look out."

~~~

The next morning, Drusilla was startled awake by the sound of the doorbell. She had barely had time to register what the intrusion was before Dwell's voice chimed in.

"Untrusted species," he said urgently. "Interaction NOT advised."

"What?"

"Untrusted species," he repeated. "Avoid interaction."

Throwing off the blanket, she noted that Manx was already up before she pulled on her robe and headed for the door to see just what Dwell considered to be "untrusted."

Pushing the view button on the doorjamb, she saw what he was talking about and was very glad she hadn't opened the door. Five hideous beasts armed with pulse rifles stood on the patio, along with a very agitated Lester.

"Let me hear what they're saying, Dwell," she whispered. "But don't let them hear me."

"As you wish," said Dwell as he activated the link.

"She is our guest," Lester was saying. "I had not intended to disturb her so early."

"The wildcat may already have killed and eaten her," one of the hairy, wolf-like creatures snarled. "Do you not wish to make certain that she is safe?"

"I—I gave her a pulse pistol," Lester stammered, his hands an orange haze in front of his chest. "And she promised to be careful."

The wolf-man barked out a laugh. "Those cats are masters at taking their prey unawares."

"You... *know* of them?" Lester's musical voice had taken on a suspicious edge. "But... how?"

"The owners reported to us," the Nedwut said. "We are expert hunters and know about all manner of prey— and predators."

The way his lips curled back from his cruel fangs led Drusilla to believe that these horrid creatures would prey on just about anything. Though she'd never seen their sort before, her mind made the jump to the obvious conclusion. "They're Nedwuts!" she exclaimed. "And they aren't here to hunt for that cat! They're after Manx!"

Spinning on her heel, she ran through the house looking for him, but Manx was nowhere to be found.

Scrambling down the back stairs, she checked the towel cabinet and found that even his clothes were missing.

A rage unlike anything she'd ever felt before in her life welled up within her, and Drusilla stormed back up the stairs and ran to the door. There, on a nearby table, was the pistol Lester had given her. She never thought she would need it after Manx killed the wildcat, but apparently she did. Twisting the setting to kill, she shouted for Dwell to open the door.

"Interaction not advised," Dwell said.

"I heard you the first time!" Drusilla shouted. "Now open the door or I'll blast it down!"

Drusilla thought she heard a sigh of resignation from the house computer, but the beep from Klog startled her as the door unlatched and began to swing open. Glancing over her shoulder, she saw that the house droid was armed with a large butcher knife and an ice pick. "Good boy, Klog," she said approvingly. "I feel a lot better knowing you've got my back."

Klog beeped twice and moved in behind her.

Drusilla had never met up with any Nedwuts before, but it was easy to read the expression of evil delight in their eyes when they got their first look at her. Then they saw the pistol in her hand and seemed much less delighted.

Lester looked both terrified and relieved at the same time. "You are well, then?" he said anxiously. "They are here to hunt for the cat."

Drusilla knew better. She understood their ploy now, but knew she couldn't let them have any inkling that Manx was involved, or that she knew anything about him.

"I killed it," she said bluntly. "Sorry I forgot to tell you that, Lester, but I've been busy."

"Busy?" the Nedwut asked. "Doing what?"

"Painting," she replied. "Birds. It's what I do and why I'm here." She pinned Lester with a pointed glare. "I was told that I wouldn't be disturbed. This is twice you've been here now."

"But only to ensure your safety," Lester hastened to explain. "We normally would have no need, knowing you would be quite safe, but this cat has caused a great deal of unrest."

"Well, the cat is dead, so you will have no further need to visit." Drusilla's voice was taut with barely suppressed disgust for these horrid Nedwuts, especially knowing what she did about their role in the pursuit of surviving Zetithians. One of the beasts toward the rear of the pack was drooling and licking his chops as though he'd like to eat her. If Lester hadn't been there to witness it, she would have been tempted to shoot them down where they stood.

The Nedwut's eyes narrowed as he gazed past her. "We will not trouble you any further, then," he said.

Drusilla hoped that seeing the well-armed Klog behind her had made them think twice about doing anything to harm her, but Drusilla didn't believe she'd seen the last of them—especially when she turned around once the door was closed. Her masterful painting of Manx was sitting across the room on her easel in plain sight.

"Oh, my God," she whispered.

Drusilla sat down heavily on the sofa, still holding the pistol in her trembling fingers. What hope did she have of ever seeing Manx again? These evil monsters would hunt him down and kill him—possibly kill or take her too—and there was no one on Barada Seven capable of stopping them unless there were more of those confiscated pistols lying about. She had Klog as an ally, but he was all she had.

Manx must have known they were coming—had smelled their scent or something. There was no other explanation for his disappearance. "You could have at least said good-bye," she whispered, dissolving into tears.

Klog handed her a tissue and made an odd, whirring sound that Drusilla had never heard from him before. Perhaps he was crying too.

Drusilla had no illusions that the Nedwuts would leave Barada and never return. They might seem to do so, but she was certain they would land somewhere in the wilderness and then hunt Manx down without mercy. She wished with all her heart that he had taken the pistol with him; at least then he would have had a chance. As matters stood, all he had were his knife and his bow, which were no match for the Nedwut weapons.

Still, he had eluded them for this long, perhaps he would come back to her. A little voice inside her head warned her that this was only wishful thinking. He wouldn't risk his life to come back. He would, hopefully, elude his hunters, but he would never risk coming back to the lake house. Zef would miss him too.

She sighed, wondering if it wouldn't be best for her to return to Earth as soon as possible. The Nedwuts had seemed pleased enough with her to want to capture her as well. She was in as much danger as Manx, and perhaps it was only her show of force that had prevented it. Lester's presence she discounted. These creeps would have no qualms about killing Lester and taking her. It was a wonder they had bothered to bring Lester with them at all. The house would have been easy enough to find if one only followed the track through the jungle, or, since they'd obviously come on a spaceship of some kind, it was possible that they would have all manner of sensors to scan the area looking for a likely spot for tourists.

Drusilla knew that searching for Manx would only lead the Nedwuts to him—if she ever found him, that is. She wanted to leave but at the same time thought she should stay right where she was forever, just in case he decided it was safe to come back. Not knowing which path she should follow, she did what she always did when confronted by an untenable situation; she painted.

First one canvas, and then another, on into the night and until the glimmer of lavender dawn the next morning. Klog brought her food that went largely untouched, she slept for brief periods only to awaken and pick up her brushes again.

In the lake, on the beach, in her bed, in her arms, and in the jungle surrounded by birds, she painted Manx in every pose she could imagine, desperate in her attempt to capture his image before she forgot it. Crying when she realized how little she knew about him, how she would never learn anything more. Never feel his touch or hear his voice again. She painted for an entire week, never once leaving the house even to talk to Zef. She wasn't ready for that yet. Perhaps in time she could, but the fact that Manx had not come knocking on her door made her all the more certain that she had seen the last of him. Her dear, sweet Manx might even be dead by now.

The idea horrified her and she knew she had to do something to get it all out of her mind. She finally decided to send her finished paintings to Ralph. She felt the need for his input, but was quite sure he would recognize them for what they were. Reluctantly, she called Lester on the comlink.

"I need to ship some paintings back to Earth," she said. "Have those awful *things* gone?"

Lester didn't need to ask who she was talking about. "You had killed the cat," he said. "There was no reason for them to stay any longer, so their landing rights were revoked."

"You kicked them off the planet?" Drusilla said with surprise. Somehow she couldn't see the timid little Lester standing up to anyone.

"Force was not necessary," Lester said. "I am very sorry they frightened you."

"Yeah, well, I'm not so sure they won't be back," she said. "Mind if I hang onto the pistol until I leave?"

Lester's hands flew in all directions in a frank display of his distress. "No one here would want it," he assured her. "It is an abomination to even have it on our world."

"How *do* you manage to keep creeps like that from landing if you don't have any weapons?"

Lester seemed completely taken aback by this question. "If anyone lands without permission, we tell them to go and they go."

Drusilla snickered her skepticism. "You guys are so naïve," she remarked. "Those thugs don't look like the types to do anything they don't want to do unless you threaten to blast them into space dust."

"Most others respect our customs," Lester insisted. "You did not bring any weapons with you, and though it is rare among our other visitors, some do land who seem bent on wrongdoing, but they are easily disarmed."

"Lester," she said gently, "that's because the only thing you have to offer here is peace, quiet, scenery, and a little fuuslak juice. If you had something they valued, they would take it, whether you liked it or not."

Lester's wide grin seemed a bit forced to Drusilla. "How fortunate that we have nothing here of any value."

"Klog's probably worth a bundle," she said, remembering that he had been standing behind her when she was facing down the Nedwuts. Perhaps they hadn't seen Manx's portrait after all. It was further away, and that side of the room had been fairly dark; Klog might have been all they were looking at.

"Yes, he is," Lester agreed. "But those droids can't function much beyond the house they are designed to serve. They self-destruct if they are forcibly removed."

"I wonder if they know that," she muttered.

"Who?"

"Those creeps who were here last week." Deciding to feign ignorance to gain more information, she added, "What were they, anyway? I've never seen their kind before."

"I have," Lester said grimly. "They are called Nedwuts. We found several of them on Barada illegally a few years ago. That pistol you have was taken from one of them."

"I still don't understand how you get them to cooperate," Drusilla said with a wag of her head. "They don't strike me as the type to follow anyone's rules."

Lester hands looked like someone twiddling his thumbs, albeit very quickly. "They have always followed our laws once they have been explained," he said stiffly. "Everyone does."

"Well, I'm glad to hear that," she said wearily, even though she didn't believe it. "But would you come out and get some paintings and ship them back to Earth for me? I'd really like to get some feedback from Ralph on them. I mean, if he doesn't like them, I'll need to work on some more."

"That will be no problem," Lester said. "I will come for them tomorrow." He eyed her hesitantly. "You do not mind if I come there?"

"No, I don't," Drusilla said. "Come anytime you like—just don't bring any more Nedwuts!" This directive was more automatic than heartfelt; if truth be told, she didn't think she would mind if the Nedwuts showed up and killed her on the spot. There was a sense of hopelessness without Manx, one she'd tried to keep at bay by painting, but now that she had stopped, she realized that it was the only reason for her to go on living. Painting Manx would be her life's work—she could see that now. It would be the one thing that kept her alive. It would keep her love for him alive too. Possibly inflated out of all recognition, but alive, nonetheless. Aside from that, she felt like an empty shell. There was a void in her that no other man could ever fill. She knew that now. No matter where she looked, she would never find a cure for the loss of him.

It didn't matter, she told herself as she drifted away from the comlink, leaving a rather befuddled Lester to wonder why she was behaving so peculiarly. Perhaps he would chalk it up to the visit from the Nedwuts, which was undoubtedly the reason Manx had left so unceremoniously. Manx had taken everything but her creative drive with him when he disappeared, leaving her heart and soul as barren as a desert. She would survive, but she would never again feel truly alive.

—⁓—

Lester came the next day in his old rattletrap of a truck and hauled away her paintings. She had crated them up before he arrived, not wanting him or anyone else within a score of light years to see what they were. Ralph would know what to do with them. She'd put a note inside, warning him never to divulge what planet they originated from. If Manx was still free, she wouldn't endanger him in that manner. His whereabouts would go with her to her grave.

Chapter 15

ARRIVING AT BARADA SEVEN IN GOOD TIME, THE *JOLLY ROGER* was given permission to land in a large, grassy area near the village. As always, the ship was greeted by a contingent of Baradans to confiscate any weapons. Even knowing that it would be returned prior to their departure, it killed Jack's soul to hand over her favorite pistol, "Tex," but she did it in spite of her best intentions.

As before, Lester was part of the welcoming party. "You will not require weapons during your stay," he said to Jack, who appeared to need consoling. "Barada is, as you know, a very peaceful world."

"Hmph," Jack snorted. "Tell that to the Nedwuts. Haven't seen any of them lately, have you?"

"As it happens, there was a group here not long ago hunting for a wildcat," Lester reported. "However, the cat had already been killed by an offworlder, and they departed peacefully."

Upon hearing this news, each one of the *Jolly Roger's* crew exchanged horrified glances.

"Tell me more about this cat," Jack said. "What did it look like?"

"It was a vicious predator with sharp teeth and claws," he replied. "It attacked another visitor—it was very dangerous! It was later killed by the Terran female who is staying at the lake house. She is a painter, here to paint pictures of our birds."

"Let me get this straight," Jack said. "She's an *artist?* And she killed a wildcat?" Jack paused, shaking her head. "Doesn't that sound a little *unlikely* to you?"

Lester took a deep breath, his hands waving gently and his expression of regret clearly displayed in his bulbous eyes. "She was given a weapon," he said, his musical voice suddenly sounding coarse and strained. "It was deemed necessary for her safety."

"Then this world is not as safe as you would have us believe," said Cat. "Perhaps you should return our weapons."

"Oh, no," said Lester. "The beast has been killed. The threat no longer exists."

"Did you take back the weapon you gave her?" Cat went on.

"No," Lester replied. "She was afraid that the Nedwuts might come back for her. It seemed best to let her keep it for the duration of her stay."

"Well, that was wise," Jack said dryly. "Did you know that Nedwuts have been known to kidnap Terran women and sell them as slaves?"

"No, I did not." Lester was clearly becoming more agitated by the moment.

"Well, they do," Jack said firmly. "Trust me on that one." Pausing for a moment, she added, "Maybe we should go talk to her—just to make sure she's all right."

"I do not think she likes visitors," Lester said. "She was very angry when the Nedwuts came looking for the cat."

"I'll just bet she was," Jack said shrewdly. "Don't think I'd appreciate a visit from a pack of them either." Choosing her words with care, she went on, "Tell me something else, Lester. Did you actually *see* the body of this cat?"

Lester blinked rapidly. "No, I did not," he replied.

"Then how do you know it's dead?"

"Drusilla said she killed it," Lester said firmly. "I have no reason not to believe her."

"Yeah, well, I've got a bridge in Brooklyn you might be interested in too," Jack said with a chuckle. "Do me a favor, Lester. If any Nedwuts ask permission to land, would you let me know?"

Lester nodded in reply and departed.

"Bet he's wishing they'd never opened this planet to offworlders," Jack commented after he left. "Don't blame him for that, either. A few Nedwuts are enough to have anybody putting up force fields."

As it happened, Jack was right about that. Lester would be very glad when these strange offworlders left Barada completely. If it had been left up to him, he doubted they would be there at all.

———

Manx had gathered up what little he possessed and disappeared into the jungle. He had always feared the Nedwuts would find him eventually, but he was hoping that just this once they would lose his trail and never find it again. There might have been other options, but endangering Drusilla was not worth any of them. He could elude the Nedwuts—he had a much better sense of smell than they did and the stench they gave off ran on ahead of them for a long ways, but even after three days he could still smell them and knew they were there somewhere.

He sniffed the air again, trying to convince himself that the scent was getting weaker, but cast that notion aside as wishful thinking. As long as it didn't get stronger, he was probably safe, but he kept moving anyway.

Further from Drusilla. He'd had to leave other women in the past, but none that he felt as bonded to as she. She was his mate, and it was ripping him apart.

He kept on, pausing only briefly to rest or when he spotted an unwary animal in range of his bow. He knew his best bet was to find another spaceport, if there was one, and stow away on an outbound ship. Perhaps he could even find one bound for Earth if he was lucky. At least he had a destination in mind this time; before, his goal had always been simply to go as far and as fast as he could. Unfortunately, what little he'd learned from Zef led him to believe there was only the one port, but living as isolated as he did, even Zef didn't know every-thing. He considered checking out other lakes for eltrans to obtain more information, but not knowing if he could trust them kept him wary.

It rained in the night, waking him from a light slumber. Manx caught water by funneling it from leaf to leaf and into the small bottle he carried in the pouch with his flute. Together with his knife and bow, these items had kept him going for a very long time and would do so again. He tried to convince himself that it was no different than it had ever been, but he knew he was lying to himself. It *was* different, and it took every scrap of his will to keep going with the image of Drusilla etched in his mind. Would he still remember her years from now, or would she fade from his memory as so many others had done? The sad truth was that he'd *have* to forget her if he intended to remain alive. Thinking about her would make him weak and distracted, and weak, distracted prey usually got caught. Gritting his teeth, he went on, passing through the jungle as silently as a shade.

Morning came and with it, Manx discovered that he was nearing a village. Even knowing it was unlikely, he kept to the outskirts as he circled it to see if there might be a port of some kind. A small Baradan boy ventured into the jungle just as Manx was passing, but he never saw the Zetithian. It was rare that anyone did, as practiced as he was at stealth and concealment. Drusilla had seen him, but only because he had been so fascinated by her that he forgot to be wary.

Drusilla. She kept running in and out of his thoughts no matter how hard he tried to banish her. Someday he could afford the luxury of setting his mind adrift on his memories of her, but not yet. Not while he could still smell Nedwuts.

Days passed and still he moved on, hunting for food and catching snatches of sleep whenever he could. Manx had a good sense of direction, but deep in the jungle it wasn't always clear where he was headed. The scent was very faint now, which either meant that he was further from its source, or that the Nedwuts truly were gone and he was only catching lingering traces of them.

That being the case, Manx allowed himself one full night's sleep and with the dawn, he discovered a lake nearby. After scouting the area and deciding it was safe to approach, he drank his fill quickly, refilled his bottle, and then left as swiftly and silently as he had come. He hadn't gone far when his head went up in alarm—not for

Nedwuts, but for something else. Something he'd never dreamed he would ever experience again.

Somewhere on this jungle planet was another Zetithian.

It was a trap set by the Nedwuts, Manx decided. It had to be. As determined as those hunters were, it was unlikely that there could be any of his kind left. He raised his head to inhale deeply and held it for a long moment, letting the pheromones sift through his senses until he was certain. Males. Two of them. Perhaps the Nedwuts had other captives and were using them as bait. Then he realized something else. The odor of Nedwuts was missing entirely.

He had a choice to make. Should he continue onward, or circle back around to investigate the source of the scent? He had aimed toward the east when he left, enabling the prevailing winds to blow the Nedwut scent his way and to allow his own to pass on ahead of him. But what if the Nedwuts had somehow gotten upwind of him? He could be headed right into a trap.

He did have one other option, and that was to remain where he was, but the scent was persistent and compelling, and suddenly, it seemed he had no choice but to follow his nose.

———

The comlink shattered the silence, screeching its summons with a relentless clamor.

"Dwell!" Drusilla called out from her easel. "Shut that thing off, will you?"

"I think you should answer it," Dwell advised. "It is a deep space link, not Lester."

"Ralph, then," she sighed. "He must have gotten those paintings. He's probably calling to yell at me."

Getting up stiffly from her stool in front of yet another portrait of Manx, she went to the comstation and activated the link. "Hey, Ralph," she said. "What's the matter? Not enough birds for you?"

"Drusilla, darling," Ralph began. "Who *is* this *dreamy* creature you've painted? I've never seen a more *virile* male in my life!"

"Getting you hot and bothered, is he?" Drusilla said, unable to suppress her first smile since Manx's disappearance.

"Oh, absolutely!" Ralph replied. He peered at her through the viewscreen. "Could it be that you have found love at long last?"

"More like *lost* love," Drusilla said grimly. "It's a long story. I'll tell you more when I get home."

"You *are* coming back, aren't you?" Ralph said, sounding a bit worried. "When these paintings arrived without you, I began to have serious doubts. Not that I'd ever want to leave him myself, but—"

"Don't worry, I'll be home just as we planned," Drusilla said. "He's—" Not wanting to hear herself say it aloud, she hesitated for a moment, biting her lip before adding, "Already gone."

"Oh, my dear, dear girl!" Ralph said sadly. "How perfectly awful for you!"

"Yes, it was," Drusilla replied. "But I'll get over it." She was lying through her teeth, of course, but refused to explain to Ralph that Manx would not only never be hers, but had also ruined her for anyone else. Ralph would continue to introduce her to men she would never love and life would go on as it had always done.

"How are the other natives, then?" Ralph prompted. "Friendly?"

Drusilla had to smile again, thinking of Zef. "They're all very nice," she said. "There were some disreputable sorts here briefly, but they're gone now." At least she hoped they were. She hadn't gone out since that last visit and had no desire to. Still, Zef would want news of Manx. Then it dawned on her. If Manx had left a message for her with *anyone* before he left, it would have been Zef.

"Well, I don't have to tell you this," Ralph said candidly, "but the paintings are priceless—even the ones of the birds." This last comment was completely unnecessary; Drusilla knew a good painting when she saw one, and the wildfowl studies were nothing in comparison to those she'd done of Manx. "We're all just *dying* to have you back so we can have a showing at the gallery! Gerard is already experimenting with the lighting and the frames will cost an absolute *fortune*, but these will go for the highest prices of anything you've ever done." Ralph beamed at her warmly. "Well *done,* my dear! You've got several weeks left before you come home, and I'm sure anything you bring back with you will be equally fabulous—or feel free to ship them on ahead so we can drool over them," he added with a titter.

"Yeah, I'll do that," Drusilla said, suddenly uninterested in anything to do with gallery events or the mindless drivel of people with far more money than anyone needed. Manx, who had nothing but a few meager possessions, had meant so much more to her than any of the rich and famous she'd ever met. Terminating the link, she took one last, longing look at her most recent painting of Manx and headed out to the lake.

The sky was a brilliant purple and the sparkling water looked just as it had on the day he left, but there weren't even any footprints in the sand to prove Manx had ever been there. Klog had gone on with his beach cleaning duties and it looked as pristine as ever. A flock of birds flew overhead, babbling to themselves like wild geese before settling in the treetops beyond the shore. As Drusilla gazed out across the lake, she was struck by a sudden fear that the old eltran might have died of starvation without Manx to feed him fish bones.

Calling out for him, she tossed several stones into the depths and waited anxiously for Zef to surface. Several butterflies landed on her shoulders, but she ignored them completely.

"About time you came out of your little love nest," Zef grumbled from further down the shore. "Where the devil is Manx? I haven't had any fish for days and days! He comes out here one morning, catches a few fish, and then goes off into the jungle. I should have known I wouldn't be seeing him again anytime soon—though after that last bit on the beach, I'm surprised I've seen him at all."

"Yeah, well, me too," Drusilla said morosely, choosing to ignore the fact that Zef had obviously been spying.

"D'you mean to say he didn't come back?" Zef said, apparently very much surprised. "I just thought he was off to catch more birds for you. Where d'you suppose he went?"

Drusilla winced. So, Manx hadn't told Zef anything either. "I was hoping you knew," she said, plopping down in the sand. The startled butterflies fluttered briefly about her head before resuming their positions. "You were my last hope. Just wish I'd thought of it sooner." Peering at the eltran, she thought he looked the same, but he was so ragged it was hard to tell. "Are you okay—getting enough to eat, I mean?"

"I eat the stinkin' plants when I can't get fish," Zef said gruffly. "I'm doing just fine—but you look like fuckin' shit."

"Gee, thanks, Zef," Drusilla said with an involuntary giggle. "That makes me feel *so* much better."

"So he's run off, has he?" Zef said. "Wouldn't have thought it of him. Seemed pretty well taken with you."

"I don't think it had anything to do with me," she said quietly. "Some Nedwuts showed up the day he disappeared. I'm pretty sure they didn't catch him, but I haven't seen him since."

Zef made an odd, grunting sound which Drusilla took to mean he understood. "Been in there moping all this time?"

Drusilla shook her head and began drawing idly in the sand. "Painting, actually," she replied. "I can't seem to stop. Every time I think I can paint birds again, I wind up painting another portrait of Manx."

"You should come out here to paint," Zef said kindly. "It might help."

There were some stunning swan-like birds gliding across the water near the opposite shore, their iridescent feathers an eye-catching blend of chartreuse and lemon, but Drusilla barely took note of them, shrugging indifferently. "I don't really care anymore, Zef. It might run its course eventually, and then I'll be able to paint birds again, but even if it doesn't, Ralph assures me that I'll make enough money on Manx's portraits to last the rest of my life. But, like I said, it really doesn't matter."

"Trust me, I know how you feel," Zef said. "It's the way I felt before I met Manx." Letting out a weary sigh, he added, "Don't suppose you're any good at fishing, are you?"

"Never tried it," she replied. "I don't think I could spear them like Manx does—did—can." With that, Drusilla's tears began to fall. "Zef, I miss him so much! I—I know *why* he left, but couldn't he have taken me with him?"

"Now, if he was in danger, he couldn't very well take you with him," Zef said reasonably. "You might get yourself killed. Think how he would feel if that happened!"

"I don't really care," Drusilla said frankly. "At least I would have been with him until the end."

"Yes, but having you along might have gotten *him* killed," Zef pointed out. "Ever think of that?"

Wiping away her tears, Drusilla shot Zef a withering look. "How come you're so damned sensible?" she grumbled. "Of course I wouldn't want him to get killed, but Lester gave me a perfectly good pulse pistol. Couldn't he at least have taken it with him?"

"Must've thought you needed it more," Zef said promptly.

"You men!" Drusilla growled. "You're all the same. You think nothing of dying to protect women who would rather die themselves if it means living without you. You think the only real hero is a dead hero, and that's a bunch of bunk!"

"Must not be the same with eltrans," Zef disagreed. "I don't think dying is very heroic. Damned silly if you ask me—but I know Manx, and that's probably exactly what he was thinking."

Eyeing Zef curiously, Drusilla had to wonder if Zef knew more than he was telling her. "If you know so much, do you think he'll ever come back? I've still got a few weeks left here. That's plenty of time for him to decide it's safe and come back, but what if he shows up after I'm gone? Will you tell him where to find me?"

Not answering right away, Zef scratched the sand with his worn pectoral fins. "Yes, I'd tell him," he said at last, though he sounded a bit grudging about it. "Where will you be?"

"Earth," Drusilla replied sadly. "Too far away—no, wait. He could use the comlink in the house! It must be a darn good one if Ralph can call me here. I'll get the code and tell you before I leave." Gazing doubtfully at the old eltran, Drusilla was quite certain he could remember every curse word he'd ever heard, but a link number? Calling home from Barada must require a dozen different codes. "Think you could remember it?"

"Might ought to write it down," Zef said. "Somewhere Manx would find it if he came back and I was gone."

"Gone?" Drusilla echoed. "Where would you—"

"If I was dead, I mean," Zef said gruffly. "I'm old. I won't live forever, you know."

"Leaving the code wouldn't make any difference anyway," Drusilla sighed. "He's probably on another planet by now." Dropping her head, she added, "And I never even got to fool around in the hot tub with him—or feed him strawberry cheesecake. Rats!"

"Rats?"

"Yeah, rats!" she replied. "Nasty furry little rodents that everyone hates."

Zef was still puzzled.

"It's a mild curse word, Zef," she explained. "Nicer than saying fuck."

"Got it!" Zef said brightly. "Rats it is!"

"You know something, Zef?" Drusilla chuckled. "I'll miss you too. You're one of a kind."

Zef knew he would feel the same. Drusilla was one of the few females that had been nice to him since his dick quit working. Come to think of it, she was the *only* one.

～～～

Tash'dree had followed many paths through the jungle but found no sign of any offworlders—nor had she encountered the wildcat. Tired and dispirited, she marched on, moving through the jungle like a ghost, leaving a trail behind her that very few could have followed. Having lived in a jungle all her life, she knew how to plot her course through the trees and avoid becoming lost, but with no clear destination, all she could do was divide the region into sectors and explore each one.

She was startled when a young Baradan crossed her path, moving even more silently through the trees than she.

"Who are you?" the boy asked curiously.

"I am Tash'dree," she replied. "And you?"

"Roger," the boy replied. Cocking his orange head to one side, "Are you lost?"

Tash'dree considered her options and decided she had nothing to lose by telling the truth. "I am looking for a house by a lake where an offworlder is staying. Do you know of it?"

Roger appeared to consider her as well. "I do," he said after a moment. His voice was as soft as a whisper, but with a distinct melodic quality to it. "I will show you the way, but you must pay me one triplak."

Tash'dree agreed without hesitation, realizing it was what she should have done at the outset. Handing the boy a small pebble from the pack slung on her back, she gestured for him to lead the way.

Now that she no longer had to concentrate on her search, Tash'dree began to consider how to approach her quarry. The woman she discounted, but what she would say to *him* when she found him—*if* she found him—had her puzzled. It was an odd request, to be sure, and one she didn't feel entirely comfortable making. Lutira had been the one driven to fulfill this goal; no doubt she had her persuasive speech all prepared, but she hadn't related it to Tash'dree.

The journey took longer than she expected, but at last, the trees began to thin out and she caught glimpses of the lake. Glancing at the sky, she realized that this was in the next sector she would have searched, and though she didn't grudge the boy his payment, she would have preferred that there be no witnesses to her visit.

As Roger walked on ahead, Tash'dree saw the woman sitting out on the beach, but she appeared to be alone. It wouldn't do to bungle this part, she realized, and considered leaving her weapons behind, but decided against it. They were, after all, concealed…

———

Drusilla sat at her easel and was doing her best to paint the warbird that was trolling the shallows on the opposite shore, but knew she couldn't do the bird justice, neither from her current vantage point, nor in her present state of mind.

"Here I am, out here at least *trying* to paint the damn birds, and they won't cooperate!" she grumbled aloud, as another butterfly settled on her arm.

"You could always paint me," Zef suggested. Turning to the left, he added, "This is my good side."

"I'm sure it is," she said dryly, "but Ralph wants birds, so birds are what I have to paint."

"I still think that Ralph character is some kind of parasite," Zef said. "Fuck him, I say!"

"I don't think he'd like that," Drusilla said, chuckling. "He's gay."

"What?" Zef said, raising his head questioningly. "Oh, right. Forgot! Means he likes men. Never understood that."

Drusilla shrugged. "It's not a question of understanding, Zef. It's just the way some people are—it's not something they choose."

"Not eltrans, though," Zef said with conviction. "Never heard of such a thing until those sailors showed up here."

"Well, it's not something either of us needs to worry about right now, so I don't think—" She broke off there as Zef's attention was obviously caught by something behind her.

"It's not—?" she began, as she whirled around.

"No, it's not him," Zef said quietly. "But it's pretty fuckin' interesting."

Drusilla looked up to see Roger approaching, accompanied by a tall woman with long dark hair and the most stunning figure Drusilla had ever seen. Dressed in furry animal skins that only covered the important parts and gazing out of deep blue eyes that seemed to be lit from within, she was incredibly beautiful by anyone's standards. Though at first glance she appeared to be human, Drusilla noticed that her nose was slightly flat and she had an extra finger on each hand. She greeted Drusilla with a smile that would have made even Ralph reconsider his sexual preference.

"Wave at her," Zef said, keeping his voice down.

"Why?"

"Because I want to see her wave *back*," Zef said. "That's—she's—*wow!*"

Drusilla rolled her eyes and giggled. "Thought you didn't care for us two-legged types," she said, but waved anyway.

"Normally I don't, but—"

Zef got his wish as she raised her hand in greeting. "I wish you good day," the woman said. "I am called Tash'dree."

Zef choked and had to submerge himself for a moment to get his gills re-situated.

Drusilla returned the greeting and introduced herself, but was wary. After the visit from the Nedwuts, she was suspicious of anyone, whether Roger was with them or not, and was thanking her lucky stars that she'd chosen to paint the warbirds that day instead of another portrait of Manx.

"She was looking for you," Roger explained, "and since I was coming to see you, I brought her along."

Drusilla's suspicions increased. "Looking for me?" she echoed. "Why?"

"I heard there was an offworlder staying here and was curious to meet you," Tash'dree replied.

This sounded pretty flimsy to Drusilla, but, having traveled extensively, she was well aware that different worlds often had widely divergent customs, some of them downright bizarre. For all she knew, this could be no more than a form of common courtesy, or it could have been obligatory. Nodding noncommittally, Drusilla said, "And what did Roger charge you for this visit?"

"One triplak," Tash'dree replied, "though I would have found you eventually, even without his help."

"And he was already on his way here," Drusilla said, shaking her head at the boy. "You're really something else, aren't you, Roger?"

Roger merely grinned in reply and waved away the butterflies that were accumulating on Drusilla.

"Don't bother," she said. "I'm starting to like them. Their tongues sort of tickle."

"I do not like the tickle," Roger said as he began to subject her painting to careful scrutiny. "You are painting the warbirds," he said after a moment. "The eyes are not right."

"Well, if I could get them to come a little closer, I might have done better," Drusilla said with a touch of asperity. "They get upset and look away every time I try to use my binoculars and then they start squabbling with each other."

"They are very shy," Roger said. "I will help."

"And just how many triplaks will that cost me?" Drusilla inquired.

Roger grinned and waved his hands in protest. "I'll do it for nothing."

"Look," said Tash'dree. "They are already coming closer."

The elusive birds were now wading through the water toward the shore, stopping near the water's edge as though posing for their portrait. "Hmm, well, I see what you mean about the eyes, Roger," Drusilla said as she got a better view of them. "So why are they coming over here now? I've been sitting out here, quiet as a mouse for hours—even Zef has been asleep half the time. Do they like being part of a crowd, or what?"

Roger grinned again. "I asked them."

"Oh, really? Talk to birds, do you?" said Drusilla. "That's a neat trick."

"Are there any other offworlders with you?" Tash'dree asked suddenly.

"No," Drusilla replied shortly, her suspicions aroused once more.

"I have seen—" Roger began, but Drusilla cut him off.

"The only other offworlders I've seen were Nedwuts, and trust me, you wouldn't want to visit them."

"But that is not—" Roger protested.

Darting a quelling glance at him, Drusilla hoped Roger would get the message and keep quiet. She had no idea whether he knew anything about Manx or not, but she wasn't taking any chances. Zef, at least, was silent; he knew better than to discuss Manx with strangers—though it was quite possible that Tash'dree's presence had rendered him speechless. "Are you here alone too?" Drusilla asked Tash'dree.

"No," she replied. "My sister is here as well, but she was attacked by a wild animal and was injured."

"Not badly, I hope," Drusilla said quickly.

"She is recovering," Tash'dree replied. "I am hunting the beast."

"The wildcat? You needn't bother," Drusilla said, breathing a sigh of relief. "It came after me and I killed it."

"I am very pleased to hear that," Tash'dree said with another dazzling smile.

Drusilla just sat there for a moment, gaping at her with awe. If this gorgeous creature had been hunting Manx instead of the cat, a passably attractive woman like herself wouldn't stand a chance. "I wonder why it only attacked offworlders?" she mused, and then with a pointed look at Roger she added, "Must prefer the taste of tourists over that of the locals."

Roger's hands went up in dismay, sending the butterflies fluttering. "I do not know," he said. "There has never been such a creature on our world before."

"Well, I guess that's what happens when you let offworlders visit," Drusilla reflected. "You pick up all sorts of 'contaminants' that way."

Drusilla thought Tash'dree's interest was piqued by the mention of "contaminants" but decided not to pursue it. "So, where are you from?" she asked her instead.

"Statzeel," Tash'dree replied. "It is located on the outer edge of the Andromeda Quadrant."

"Which is probably why I've never heard of it," Drusilla remarked. "I've never been outside the Terran Quadrant, myself." Brushing a butterfly away from her face, she added, "What brings you to Barada Seven?"

"Political business," Tash'dree replied after a brief hesitation.

The evasive nature of Tash'dree's reply wasn't lost on Drusilla. For her own part, she couldn't imagine any kind of business—political or otherwise—that would bring anyone from the next quadrant all the way to Barada, unless it was to lay in a supply of fuuslak juice, which, in Drusilla's opinion, was highly overrated. Still, it was as good a reason as any. "Need some fuuslak juice to make everyone back home get along better?" she suggested.

"Perhaps," Tash'dree replied. Gazing out at the lake, she added, "The males on my world are very belligerent."

"Can't imagine why that would be," Zef said gruffly. "Not with beautiful women like you around. But maybe that's why you left."

"Finally found your tongue, did you, Zef?" Drusilla chuckled.

Tash'dree and Roger both looked down at Zef with utter disdain, but it was Tash'dree who spoke. "Your pet can speak?"

"Strictly speaking, Zef is not my pet," Drusilla replied. "He's my friend. Tash'dree, meet Zef. He's what they call an eltran around here."

Tash'dree gave a quick nod in Zef's direction before dismissing him with a flick of her brow. "This fuuslak juice you mention. I had a sample of it when I arrived here. It has a calming effect?"

"Well, they *say* it does," Drusilla admitted, "but maybe you have to drink a steady supply of it. It was very refreshing, but aside from that, I couldn't tell that it did much for me."

"I think it's because you're nice enough without it," Zef put in. "Always been nice to me, anyway."

Tash'dree glanced at Zef as though a slug had been speaking to her and then addressed Drusilla. "Perhaps it would be useful to transplant these fuuslak plants to my world. The climate and vegetation here are similar to that of Statzeel."

"I'm sure Roger would be happy to dig some up for you," Drusilla said, laughing. "Might be illegal to export them, but—"

"We can ask Lester," Roger said eagerly, taking Tash'dree's hand, his other hand a flurry of excitement. "Come, I will take you."

Tash'dree said good-bye to Drusilla and went off with Roger, who was gesticulating madly as he spoke, extolling the virtues of the fuuslak plant and its juice.

"Well, that was weird," Drusilla commented to Zef. "Did she strike you as odd?"

"Maybe," Zef admitted, "but fuckin' beautiful, just the same."

Chapter 16

"ARE YOU SURE THIS WILL WORK?" JACK ASKED. "I KNOW Manx has a great sense of smell, but this pot's been on the boil for two days now, and—"

"I haven't made a concoction like this in a very long time," Tisana said equably, "but if you've got any better ideas, I'd love to hear them." As an accomplished witch, Tisana was capable of a great many remarkable things, but distilling the scent of Zetithian male was trickier than most. She was glad she'd brought her books along when she and Leo had left her homeworld of Utopia to travel with Jack and Cat, otherwise she would have had to wing it—with uncertain results.

"Well, we've had you talking to all the animals around, and none of them have seen him, or if they have, they haven't lived to tell about it. Cat says Manx was a darn good hunter. He might have killed all the witnesses."

Tisana rolled her eyes. "He hasn't killed them all," she said with a chuckle. "If he's even here."

"You heard what Lester said," Jack countered. "There were Nedwuts here looking for a cat. Now, if you believe it was a real cat and not Manx, you're not as smart as I took you for."

"Lester also said that the woman at the lake house killed it," Tisana reminded her friend. "You don't think she'd kill Manx, do you?"

"Not for a minute," Jack said staunchly, "which is why I think she's either seen him, or knows him, and is protecting him. I'd also be willing to bet those Nedwuts are just biding their time before they come back looking for him again. We had pretty good evidence he was here, and they must have too, or they wouldn't have come to begin with."

"Do we really know they *didn't* find him?"

"Lester said they left peaceably—"

"Which should be your first clue not to trust them," Tisana warned.

"*And* weren't ever out of his sight! If they'd captured Manx, Lester would have known. Since they didn't find him and knew they couldn't use the, 'We're here to hunt down the nasty cat' line again, they had to retreat and think of something else."

Tisana shook her head in wonder. "I can't imagine Nedwuts giving anything that much thought, can you?"

"For five million credits?" Jack scoffed.

"You have a point."

Just then, Leo emerged from the ship and came across the clearing to peer into the boiling cauldron with his golden eyes. "Need anything else?"

Even after marriage and children, the vision of her husband's feline grace mixed with raw leonine power could still take Tisana's breath away. "No," she replied after taking a brief moment to regain her composure. "We've got sweat, hair, semen, urine, and a few skin cells from each of you again today—I think that should do it. I just hope his nose is as good as you say it is."

Cat broke off from a rousing game of tag with his sons to add, "We should include aroused Terran female scent in that potion. Manx would find it irresistible."

Jack smiled at this, but remained doubtful. "Won't he just smell this stuff and think someone's boiling Zetithians alive?"

Tisana shook her head as she swept a lock of dusky curls back from her damp brow. "No, he won't," she said firmly. "I made sure of that."

"How?" Jack inquired.

"I put something in it to make sure it didn't smell that way," Tisana replied. Her tone was nonchalant, but her green eyes sparkled with mischief.

"Oh, yeah?" Jack said, still eyeing the cauldron curiously. "What?"

"Just a little something I picked up on Terra Minor," Tisana replied. "You really don't want to know the details."

Jack looked at Leo who shrugged his shoulders and then at Cat who merely shook his head.

"I know what's in it," Tisana's daughter, Althea, piped up from her seat on a nearby tree stump. She was engaged in directing the local butterflies to dance in unison to the delight of her two brothers as she spoke, an ability which only hinted at the extent of her powers. "But I promised not to tell."

"You witches and your odd little secrets just kill me," Jack muttered. "I ask a simple question, and all I get is the runaround."

Tisana smiled approvingly at her tiny daughter. With her mother's dark hair and her father's Zetithian features, she would be a beauty—as well as the most talented witch in centuries.

"Had any luck talking with the birds?" Leo asked his wife.

Tisana's eyes narrowed. "You *know* how it is with birds," she said witheringly.

"On this planet too?" Jack knew that most birds were short on brains, but she was hoping it wouldn't be true on Barada Seven.

"So far, I've talked with warbirds, something that looks like a long-legged silver duck, and a little purple dove," Tisana said wearily, "but none of them seem to be able to comprehend that I'm looking for someone who just *looks* like Cat, and not Cat himself. They've pointed him out to me several times already—along with your boys."

Jack glanced over at her three eldest sons playing nearby. They all looked very much like Cat too. "And those little pig things that live in the jungle haven't seen him, either?"

Tisana shook her head. "Nor have the... well, I'm not sure what you'd call them—you know, the ones that hop like a rabbit, but look like long-legged salamanders?— they aren't any smarter than the birds and don't seem to pay much attention to the locals, either. They barely paid attention to me when I was trying to talk to them. I don't think they'd have noticed Manx."

"Those little pet rat-monkeys the kids all seem to have might know," Jack went on. "What about them?"

"The srakies?" Tisana said. "They're pretty smart, actually—smart enough to keep a secret if they need to. If any of them know anything, they aren't talking."

"I still think we should go talk to that woman at the lake," said Jack. "What did Lester say her name was?"

"Drusilla," Cat replied.

"Yeah, and she paints birds," Jack commented. "You know, sitting out there by the lake, painting birds, a person would be bound to notice something like Manx hanging around."

"But Lester said she was alone," Cat reminded her. "And that she did not appreciate having company."

"I still don't believe it," Jack said stubbornly. "If I'd been her and had hooked up with Manx, I wouldn't want any visitors either—especially if they brought along a band of Nedwuts!" She peered into the bubbling cauldron and shook her head. "I still don't think he's just gonna smell that and come running." Pausing to look questioningly at Leo, she went on, "You're the best tracker we've got, Leo. Don't you think we should be looking for him, and not just waiting for him to come to us?"

"But I have no scent to follow," Leo pointed out.

"Bet we could find one if we went to that lake house," Jack declared.

"It might be dangerous," Tisana said. "If that woman killed a wildcat, she might take a few potshots at you."

Jack waved a hand dismissively. "If she didn't fire on a band of Nedwuts, she won't shoot at me." Grinning at Cat, she added, "Especially if I bring someone along who could pass for Manx's brother!"

"Lester said not to," Tisana reminded her again. "You don't want to get us in trouble, do you?"

"I've been in more trouble on more planets than you can count," Jack said dismissively. "I always manage to get through it."

"Which never ceases to amaze me," Tisana said. "But there's a first time for everything. This could be it."

"What Lester doesn't know won't hurt him," Jack said roundly. "And if what I suspect is true, I think Drusilla will be very glad to see us." Turning to her boys, she said, "Now you guys hold the fort until we get back. Don't let anything happen to Tisana or that potion!"

"Don't worry," Larry said bravely, indicating himself and his two litter mates. "And we'll protect the babies too."

"We are *not* babies!" Aidan insisted, looking away from the butterfly dance.

"I wasn't talking about you," Larry said. "But you *are* younger."

Tisana chuckled. "I can look after myself," she said. "And I've got Max around to sound the alarm if he smells a Nedwut, but I'm glad you boys take your responsibilities seriously."

Tisana looked over at her dog, Max, and Jack suspected there was a telepathic exchange of thoughts going on between them because a moment later, Max raced off into the jungle.

"Where's he going?" Jack asked as she watched the black hound's sudden departure.

"Reconnaissance," Tisana replied, giving her potion another stir.

"Ah," said Jack. "I still wish you could recruit a bird."

"Don't even go there," Tisana warned.

"Yeah, right. Bird brains." Jack took a deep breath. "So—Cat, Leo? How about we take a little speeder tour through the jungle? See what's out there. After all, we're tourists, aren't we?"

"You look like a commando even without your gun hanging from your hip," Tisana remarked. "No one would ever mistake you for a tourist."

"You don't look like a witch either, but you are one," Jack countered.

"And here I've been trying so hard to look the part,"

Tisana said glumly. Twirling around so that her shimmering green skirt clung to her hips, she added, "Doesn't this dress make me look like a sorceress?"

"Um, don't do that right now," Jack said with a nod toward Leo. "You're getting your hubby all hot and bothered, and right now I need him."

"You know, Jack," Tisana said wearily, "sometimes you're tougher than the soles of a Darconian's feet."

Cat and Tisana exchanged a speaking glance. "You *know* how she is when she is on the hunt," he said.

"Hey, finding Zetithians might be my passion," said Jack, "but kicking a little Nedwut ass in the process is the icing on the cake. Just let me at 'em!"

"I will get the speeder out of the hold," Cat said. "And we will see what is 'out there.'"

Jack grinned. "Thanks, Kittycat!" As Cat turned to go to the ship, Jack looked at Leo. "Nose all clear and ready?"

Leo laughed. "Your eyes are very sharp and your nose is nearly as good as mine," he said. "Between us, if Manx is anywhere about, we should be able to find him."

"I'm sure we will," said Jack. "I just hope we aren't too late."

The trip to the lake house might have been accomplished much more comfortably than taking the journey in Lester's truck, but Lester had the advantage of knowing where he was going. It took them far longer to find it than Jack had anticipated, but at last they found the track and the clearing.

"So, do we just knock on the door first, or take a look around?" Leo asked.

"I don't know," said Jack. "That depends. I'm not really picking up a scent, what about you?"

Leo shook his head. "Nothing," he replied. "But I haven't seen Manx in a long time—and I must admit, I never paid much attention to his scent back then."

Not the least bit surprised to hear that, Jack grinned and motioned them onward.

Approaching the house, Jack let out an appreciative whistle. "Man, this place is fabulous! Wouldn't mind spending a little time here myself. We could all use a break."

Cat took one look at the lake and the boat and began purring.

"Down, boy," Jack admonished him, knowing exactly what he had in mind. "Plenty of time for that later."

"Yes, there will be," said Cat.

Jack paused for a moment, weighing the situation carefully. If this woman had met Manx, she would be interested in seeing Cat and Leo, but if she hadn't, the sight of two big cats on her doorstep might not be the best opener. Jack, on the other hand, was Terran, so Drusilla should see her as a common Earthling and be more willing to talk. "Why don't you two head down to the lake and see if you can find out anything there while I talk to the painter."

Jack knew this woman had supposedly killed the wildcat and was armed with what was probably the only weapon on the planet, but if she was feeling any qualms, they didn't show as she strode up to the door and pushed the bell. Inside the house, she heard a voice intone. "Known species. Interaction deemed benign."

Ordinarily it might have ruffled Jack's feathers a bit to be considered "benign," but in this case, it was justified. She felt naked without Tex strapped to her thigh, and hoped she looked friendly enough that the woman would at least open the door. Jack mulled over what she should say to her, but as the door opened, her anxious expression told the whole story. Manx had been there, but just as surely was now gone.

"Hello, there!" Jack began heartily. "Thought I'd come out here and see how you were doing." Offering a hand, Jack went on, "I'm Captain Jack Tshevnoe—you know, the one who brought supplies for the house? Tell me, did you like the cheesecake?"

Drusilla had nearly knocked over her easel in her haste to reach the door, all the while praying it was Manx. Her disappointment at finding this woman on her doorstep was reflected in her pathetic smile and weak handshake. "I'm Drusilla Chevrault," she said, "and the cheesecake was quite delicious."

"Knew you'd like it," Jack said, beaming a smile at her that nearly took Drusilla's breath. "It came from a deli in Indianapolis. Best cheesecake in the universe!"

Drusilla gazed past her odd visitor, praying there weren't any Nedwuts with her. She certainly seemed honest enough, and couldn't have known about the cheesecake unless her story was true, but in light of recent events, Drusilla knew that Barada wasn't quite as safe a place to visit as she'd been led to believe. "So, are you here all by yourself?"

"No, the guys are down checking out the lake—and the boat," Jack replied. "You know how men are about boats. Actually, we were thinking of renting the house sometime. Mind if we take a look around?"

Out of the corner of her eye, Drusilla could see Klog hovering nearby. He had a wire whisk in one of his hands, but she knew he could whip out a knife in the blink of an eye if he sensed danger—and his senses had been spot-on thus far. Then she remembered a pertinent detail. "Is Lester with you?"

"No, he seemed to think you didn't want company, but I knew an Earth girl this far from home was bound to be lonely. Actually, I wasn't even sure where the house was. We just sort of stumbled on it while we were cruising around the jungle in my speeder."

"You have your own speeder here?" This sounded like a great thing to Drusilla. Perhaps they might be able to use it to find Manx, if they were willing to look for him, that is—or if she even dared to mention him.

"Oh, yeah. I wouldn't ride around in that old rattle-trap of Lester's if you paid me," Jack said frankly. "Bet you had a bumpy ride out here."

"I'm surprised I didn't lose any teeth," Drusilla said, unable to suppress a smile.

"I hear you're a painter?" Jack said, returning her smile. "Would I have heard of you?"

Drusilla shook her head. "Not unless you like birds," she replied. "They have some positively stunning birds here, so my agent booked the house for me. I've sent most of them back to him already but—" Drusilla broke off there, realizing that she didn't have a single finished painting in the house that was not of Manx; the bird paintings she *did* have weren't done; and she suspected they never would be.

"But?" Jack prompted.

"I—I haven't got any ready to show you," she stuttered. "If that's what you're looking for."

Jack shook her head slowly. "No, birds are not what

I'm looking for," she replied. "I'm looking for something far more exotic than birds." Cocking her head to one side, Jack eyed her speculatively. "Seen anything interesting?"

"Um, well… there's an eltran living in the lake," Drusilla said, grasping at straws—anything to divert attention from one portrait of Manx that was, unfortunately, sitting right out in plain sight. She made a mental note to put it in her bedroom at her earliest convenience, but just then, she couldn't risk drawing attention to it.

"An eltran, huh? What's that?"

"His name is Zef," Drusilla replied, barely able to mask her sigh of relief, "and he's quite a character."

"Is that right?" Jack said, displaying a mild interest. "Well, you'll have to introduce us, then."

"Sure," Drusilla said briskly. "I'll just go down to the lake with you."

Jack stepped aside as Drusilla hurried out, closing the door manually, rather than waiting for Dwell to do it.

Leading the way, Drusilla took the stone path that curled around the house and on down to the lake.

"Hey, guys!" Jack called out. "This is Drusilla. She's going to show us the house."

Drusilla cringed inwardly, because that was not her intent at all. She was hoping they'd find Zef so offensive that they would leave without ever setting foot inside the house; however, as the two men turned to face her, all thoughts of Zef fled from her mind.

For one heart-stopping moment, Drusilla thought one of them was Manx, but there was no recognition in his eyes—eyes that were a glittering obsidian rather than Manx's sparkling green, plus he had a deep scar on his cheek. Both men were tall and lean with long, curly hair—one black and the other a tawny gold—and both were dressed in loose tunics over boots and breeches. They were both amazingly attractive, but what made her gasp was the fact that they were obviously Zetithian.

Jack was watching Drusilla intently and didn't miss one jot of her reaction. "Cool, aren't they?" Jack said easily. "The black-haired one is my husband." Sighing, she added, "Ever seen anything like them?"

"N—no," Drusilla stammered. "I—I haven't."

"You sure about that?" Jack prompted. "We got word there was a friend of theirs hiding out on Barada and that a pack of Nedwuts were hunting him. Sure you don't know anything about that—haven't seen anything *strange* while you were out exploring the jungle?"

Drusilla was torn between wanting to trust these people and the certainty that it was another trap being set for Manx. "I don't think so," she said slowly. "I just paint the birds that come to the lake. I haven't been exploring much."

"Uh-*huh,*" said Jack. "Well, Cat, guess we'll have to look elsewhere for Manx. Funny, I was so sure he was here."

"You looking for Manx?" Zef's raspy voice called out from the lake.

Drusilla's eyes squeezed shut in frustration as the garrulous eltran made an appearance.

"I've been wondering what happened to him too," Zef went on. "He was a good friend of mine. Be fuckin' fantastic if you could find him. Used to give me fish bones all the time," Zef added reflectively. "Miss that."

"Um, this is Zef," Drusilla said. "Meet Jack and—I don't know the men's names."

"This gorgeous hunk is Cat," Jack said, pointing to her husband, "and that other handsome devil is Leo."

"Do you know our friend Manx?" Cat asked Zef.

"Sure do!" Zef said. "Hasn't Drusilla told you?"

"About what?" Cat inquired.

Zef looked up at her questioningly, but Drusilla gave her head a quick shake, trying desperately to get him to shut up. "About fuckin' Manx!" Zef said with a snort.

"Um, about *Manx,* or about *fucking* Manx?" Jack put in.

Drusilla ignored the innuendo and hissed at Zef, "Zef, will you *please* be quiet?"

"Ah," said Jack. "So you *do* know him?"

Drusilla shook her head again. "I don't know what you're talking about."

"Look," Jack said evenly. "The Nedwuts have nearly exterminated the Zetithian species. These guys are among the few that are left. You can trust us, Drusilla. We're here to protect Manx, not hunt him down."

"She kills Nedwuts on sight," Leo said with a gesture toward Jack. "And so does my wife."

"Wish *I* had," Drusilla muttered ruefully.

"What was that?" Jack asked.

Drusilla let out a pent up breath. "Guess I might as well tell you everything."

"Yeah, why don't you do that?" said Jack. "If he's missing, we might be able to help you find him." Gazing at Drusilla with a speculative eye, she added, "You *do* want him back, don't you?"

Drusilla's hand flew to her mouth in an attempt to stifle her sob, but her tears were unstoppable.

Jack put a consoling arm around Drusilla's trembling shoulders and nodded at Cat. "I think we can take that as a yes." She gave it a few moments and then asked, "When's the last time you saw him?"

"I don't know," Drusilla whispered. "I—I've lost track of the time." Running a fretful hand through her disheveled locks, she added, "I've been painting ever since he left. I just woke up one morning to find Manx gone and a band of Nedwuts on my doorstep."

"I can tell you exactly when he left," Zef said. "He came out very early one morning to fish, caught a few and tossed them to me. Then he went back to the house in something of a hurry. I saw him head off into the jungle after that—fully dressed, by the way—which is something I'd never seen before. Kinda caught my eye, you might say."

"He's Zetithian, all right," Jack said with a smile. "They don't like to wear clothes unless they have to."

Cat rolled his eyes. "That is not true," he insisted. "We wear clothes all the time."

Jack gazed at him with a knowing eye. "Yeah, right," she said with a sardonic chuckle. "But not by choice."

"Well, no," Leo agreed. "Clothing is so *restrictive*."

Drusilla was fairly certain that everyone else knew exactly what Leo was referring to, but Zef chose to eluci-date. "No room for your dick when it gets hard, is there?"

"Oh, you're a lot of fun, aren't you?" Jack observed with a quick grin at Zef. "We'll have to talk later. In the meantime, which way did Manx go?"

"That way," Zef replied with a nod toward the east.

Leo nodded. "The winds here blow from west to east. That would make his scent trail very difficult to follow."

"For Nedwuts as well as us," Jack agreed. "Well, then, east it is. Maybe we can pick up a trail of some kind."

Cat was skeptical. "If Manx does not wish it, it is unlikely that we will find him."

Jack exhaled sharply. "That good, is he?"

"He was always very elusive," Leo said. "And after so many years as a fugitive, he will have become even more skilled."

"Damn!" Jack exclaimed. "That means we have to rely on Tisana's potion, then."

"Potion?" Drusilla said curiously. "How can a potion bring him back?"

"One that smells like these two," Jack said with a gesture toward the two men. "It's the best plan we could come up with. We've never actually gone looking for another Zetithian. So far, we've just stumbled onto them, but Manx is cagey enough to think this is a trap."

"Wish you could trap those awful Nedwuts," Drusilla said with a shudder. "I had the oddest feeling that they didn't believe a word I said. I—I think they'll be back. They seemed very persistent."

Jack snorted derisively. "For five million credits? I should think they would be."

"Who would pay that much?" Drusilla wondered aloud. "And why?"

Jack shook her head. "That's something I'd like to know myself," she said. "I have my own suspicions as to why, but the 'who' is a mystery." She paused for a moment as though something else had just occurred to her. "You know, maybe we've been going about this all wrong," she said biting her lip thoughtfully. "We've been gunning down bounty hunters all over the quadrant, but others always pop up to replace them. What if we could stop this madness at the source?"

"The *who*?" Drusilla suggested.

"Yeah, and when we know that," Jack said with a firm nod, "we'll understand the why."

"But how?" Leo asked.

Jack thought for a long moment and then her lips stretched into a diabolical grin. "I think I need to call in a favor," she said. "Hell, it might even work." Looking rather pleased with herself, she patted Drusilla on the shoulder before giving her a quick squeeze and releasing her. "Got another idea, too. I think we need to add a little something to Tisana's potion."

"What's that?" Leo asked.

"Essence of Drusilla," Jack replied. "Manx won't be able to resist it." Eyeing Drusilla, she added. "Think it could be an *aroused* Drusilla? That would make it even more irresistible."

"I don't know," Drusilla said doubtfully. "Without Manx, I'm not sure…"

"What if I loaned you Cat?" Jack suggested. "Just let him hold you and purr for a while. If you close your eyes, you'd never know the difference."

Cat appeared indignant, but it was Leo who made the offer. "We will take her back with us to the ship," he said. "Tisana will be able to help."

Jack's eyes narrowed in suspicion. "Do you mean to tell me that she really *can* whip up a love potion? I tried for months to get her to brew one up for Lynx a while back and she said she couldn't." In an aside to Drusilla, she added, "Lynx is another Zetithian who was having some, ah, sexual difficulties for a while, but he's better now. Got a wife and kids and everything."

Leo raised one golden eyebrow and smiled. "Just because she refused to do it does not mean that she is incapable."

"Shit! I knew it!" exclaimed Jack. "She got all huffy and noble when I asked about it before. I should have known she was fibbing." Turning to Drusilla, she said, "So, what about it Drusilla? Feel like taking a ride into town?"

Drusilla's lips were set in a thin line of determination. "I'll do whatever it takes to find him. Then I'm taking him back to Earth with me and never letting him out of my sight again as long as I live."

"Good girl!" Jack said approvingly. "That's the spirit!"

⸻

The ride into town was much more comfortable than Drusilla's previous journey and was accomplished in far less time. As they approached the open area where the *Jolly Roger* sat, Drusilla was immediately struck by the sight of children out playing with their dog. In the center of the clearing, a lovely dark-haired woman in a shimmering green gown stood by a huge cauldron stirring the contents with a long wooden spoon. As she watched, the woman bent down and shot fire from her eyes, encouraging the fire beneath the pot to flame up and curl around the edges.

"That's Leo's wife, Tisana," Jack said informatively. "She's nice enough, but witches can be very dangerous. Don't piss her off."

"I'll be careful," Drusilla said, heeding the warning, though at the sight of Tisana's smile and friendly wave, she doubted there would be any problems.

Jack jumped out of the speeder the moment it shut down. "How's it going?"

"I'm not sure how well this is carrying through the jungle," Tisana said ruefully. "I can't control the weather the way some witches can, so all we have to rely on is the wind, and there's not much of it at the moment."

"Well, we found a little something to add to the brew," Jack said. "This is Drusilla." With a broad grin, she added, "Manx's girlfriend."

"Ah," said Tisana. "Nice to meet you, Drusilla."

"According to her, Manx was here, but he took off when some Nedwuts showed up, and she'd really like to get him back. Adding her scent to the potion would help, but it would be even better if you could cook up something to make her smell more like a lover," Jack said cautiously. "We want this potion to be as irresistible to Manx as possible."

Tisana's simmering gaze lit on her husband, who was doing his best to appear innocent. "Leo, what did you tell her?"

"Nothing she didn't already suspect," Leo replied evenly. "And in this case, I believe you could use that forbidden potion of yours without remorse."

Tisana sighed deeply. "I suppose so," she said. "But don't make a habit of asking me for it, Jack. Don't know why you think any Zetithian would need that kind of potion, anyway. Your boys may only be six years old, but they're already attracting women like flies. I even saw some Baradan girls hanging around a while ago."

"Aw, they were just looking at the ship," Jack said with a careless wave.

"I don't know," Drusilla chimed in. "Those boys are pretty darn cute. Wouldn't mind having some like that myself." Then she realized that while they weren't identical, they seemed to be the same age. "Triplets?"

Cat chuckled. "Our Zetithian females always had three, and so far, Terran women seem to do the same."

"Not sure why that is, either," Jack commented. "Not enough time to study it, but Vladen—he's a doctor on Terra Minor—thinks that Zetithian semen causes Terran women to ovulate at a higher rate than normal—sort of like a fertility drug."

"Just what I need," Drusilla muttered.

"Oh, now, having triplets isn't as hard as you'd think," Jack said in a hearty tone. "I've done it twice."

The fact that Drusilla was much smaller than Jack made her doubtful that she'd have it as easy, but Leo was quick to put in his observation. "You may be small, but your hips are—"

"Leo!" Tisana said warningly. "Don't say it!"

To everyone's surprise, Drusilla laughed. "Deceptively huge, don't you think? No one ever believes me when I tell them that, but it's true."

Leo appeared relieved, but Tisana's expression was grim. "You shouldn't be looking at her hips, Leo."

"She sat in front of me in the speeder," Leo said blithely. "I'm not *blind.*"

"Yeah, well, that's probably my fault for wearing shorts," Drusilla said, remembering that Manx had been particularly fond of that part of her too. "I probably should have dressed up a little, but you caught me at a bad time."

"You look just fine to me," one of the boys piped up.

Drusilla looked over at the dark-haired Zetithian boy who was smiling unabashedly at her. Judging from his expression, he liked her tight shorts and tank top very much, indeed. "They start young, don't they?" she observed.

Jack rolled her eyes. "You don't know the half of it," she said darkly. "They may only be kids, but they don't miss much—especially when it comes to pretty women. Won't be long before they've got girls crawling all over them." Motioning to the kids, she added, "Guess I should introduce you. The big guys are mine: Larry, Moe, and Curly, and the next batch are Tisana's: Aldrik, Aidan, and Althea. My other babies are asleep."

Following Jack's gesture, Drusilla noticed three sleeping forms in the shade of a large tree. "What are their names?" she asked.

Jack's expression went from smiling to disgruntled in the space of a heartbeat. "We haven't named them yet," Jack said, casting a glowering look at Cat.

Cat threw up his hands in innocence. "I am not the one who has been putting it off."

"No, you just want to give them horrendous names," Jack grumbled. "Perfectly cute little boys and you want to name them something I can't even pronounce."

"I have agreed to Kirk, Spock, and Bones," Cat reminded her.

"Yes, but the Zetithian versions are horrible!" Jack exclaimed. "And I don't *like* the name Bones—it sounds creepy! What's wrong with Groucho, Chico, and Harpo, anyway?"

"I do not want sons with those names," Cat said,

folding his arms in a stubborn manner. "Nor will I agree to Huey, Dewey, and Louie."

Drusilla was understandably mystified and looked to Tisana for enlightenment.

"They have to do with characters in ancient Earth culture," Tisana explained.

"Yes, but I'm from Earth and I've never heard of them," Drusilla declared. "Must be really obscure."

"Hobby of mine," Jack said with a casual wave of her hand, but her eyes never wavered from Cat's glittering orbs.

"You got away with Larry, Moe, and Curly," Cat reminded her. "I was not aware of the origin then, but I am now."

Drusilla put up a tentative hand. "Um, do they have to be named after someone?"

"What?" Cat and Jack said in unison.

"Can't they just be names you like?" Drusilla inquired.

"There has to be a theme," Jack explained. "Tisana and Leo are going alphabetically, and Cat and I are going with famous trios."

"Famous?" Drusilla echoed.

"Well, they were at one time," Jack argued. "I know there are some that are more recent, but—"

"What about Kang, Kor, and Kolath?" said Drusilla.

Jack stared at her blankly. "Who?"

"They're painters," Drusilla replied. "from Dellera. I think their names are really old," she added reflectively. "But I'm not certain of their origin."

For some reason those names sounded vaguely familiar to Jack, though she was having a hard time placing them. "Hmm, not bad," Jack said, looking to

Cat for approval. Then it hit her. "No, wait! I've got it! Michelangelo, Donatello, and Raphael!"

"Yes, they're painters too," Drusilla agreed. "Pretty ancient, but—"

"*And* Teenage Mutant Ninja Turtles!"

"Uh, there were *four* Ninja Turtles," Cat pointed out.

"Yes, but the fourth was Leonardo, and we've already got a Leo," Jack said. "Why didn't I ever think of them before?"

"Because there were four of them?" Cat suggested.

"You aren't going to call Raphael 'Rafe,' are you?" Tisana said with a grimace.

"Ooo, hadn't thought of that," Jack said. "Rafe was Tisana's ex-boyfriend and Leo's last owner," she told Drusilla. "Bad idea to name a kid that." Jack looked at Cat. "So, did you like those?"

"Which ones?"

"Drusilla's."

"Kang, Kor, and Kolath?"

"Yeah, not bad, are they?"

"I like them fine," Cat said.

"You mean we actually agree?"

"I believe so," Cat replied.

Jack looked at Drusilla gratefully. "Now all we have to do is decide which one is which."

"Birth order?" suggested Drusilla.

"Well," Jack said slowly, "we do have them numbered."

"You're kidding me, right?"

"No, take a look."

Drusilla walked over to where the babies lay sleeping. Each one of them had a bracelet on with a number. "Okay, one is Kang, two is Kor, and three is Kolath."

Tisana looked up at the sky and murmured something Drusilla didn't catch.

"Thanking the gods, aren't you?" Jack teased.

"And anyone else responsible, especially Drusilla," Tisana replied, reaching out to give her a hug. "You have no idea what it's been like referring to those boys by number!"

"Glad I could help," Drusilla said as Tisana squeezed her so hard she could barely speak. "Now, if you'll just help me find Manx…"

"Oh, no problem," Tisana said promptly. "One love potion coming right up—although, strictly speaking, it's an aphrodisiac, not a love potion. You might want to stay away from Cat and Leo, though," she cautioned. "Not sure they'll be able to resist your scent once you've had a taste of it."

"I have a pulse pistol," Drusilla said helpfully. "Lester gave it to me. I could stun them if necessary."

Cat and Leo looked at one another and shook their heads, but Jack's eyes began to glow with excitement. "Oh, that's right!" she exclaimed. "Where is it?" Jack didn't wait for a reply, but smacked her forehead as though she'd just remembered something else. "I'll be right back. Gotta go send out a deep space hail."

Drusilla took a deep breath as Jack took off running toward the ship. "Is she always like that?"

"Most of the time," Tisana replied. "But don't worry. You'll get used to her."

"No you won't," Larry said. "No one ever does."

The baby whose name was now Kolath began to cry and Curly went over and picked him up. "Mine is named what?" he asked.

"Kolath," Larry said. "And mine is Kang. Moe's is Kor."

Drusilla was astonished. "You each have one to take care of?"

"They are old enough to care for babies," said Cat. "This is the way it was done on Zetith. Can you think of a better method?"

Drusilla was forced to admit that she couldn't. It was taking care of that first litter that had her worried. Of course, that would be a moot point unless she found Manx again. Then there was always the possibility that he didn't want to be found. Drusilla didn't want to think about that.

Chapter 17

IT MIGHT HAVE TAKEN DAYS OF CAREFUL PREPARATION, BUT Drusilla had never partaken of what was surely toxic waste before, and she saw no reason to start now. "I have to *drink* this?" she asked Tisana.

"Yes, and don't you dare tell Jack what it looks, tastes, or smells like or she'll be trying to brew it up herself."

"Can't think why she'd need it," said Drusilla. "She seems to have no problems in that department."

"Oh, it wouldn't be for her, it would be for some other poor, unsuspecting soul, and that goes against every rule in the book." Tisana shook her head as a weary sigh escaped her. "I've kept the recipe for that potion in my head for as long as I've known her. I tore the page out of my potions book and burned it not long after we came aboard. Didn't trust her."

"You could have just called it something else," suggested Drusilla, still eyeing the evil-smelling potion with distaste. "All you'd have to do is list it under 'Things no one in their right mind would ever touch' or 'Rodent Repellent' and I'm sure it would be safe. You could even write it on a blank page in one of your books that way."

"Yes, I suppose I could do that," Tisana admitted, "but I still wouldn't trust her not to go looking for it—especially now that she knows it exists."

"I see your point," Drusilla said. Then another

possibility occurred to her. "You're sure you remember how to make this correctly?"

"Yes, I'm sure," Tisana said gloomily. "It was one of those forbidden potions my mother warned me about, which was why I was so interested in it as a child. Can't think why she didn't rip the page out herself," she added reflectively.

"Or substitute the ingredients for a really good laxative," Drusilla suggested with a giggle.

Tisana appeared momentarily struck by this idea, but her arrested expression made Drusilla even more nervous.

"You, um, *have* made this before, haven't you?" Drusilla asked. "You're sure it works?"

"What?" Tisana said absently. "Oh—the potion? Yes, it works. I was just thinking."

"Don't do it," Drusilla warned.

"Do what?" Tisana asked innocently.

"I've seen that look before," Drusilla said knowingly. "I may paint mostly birds, but I watch people too. You're not really going to—"

"If Jack was going to use the potion on herself I might consider it, but since other unsuspecting people would be her targets, I have no intention of making them suffer unnecessarily." Tisana motioned for her to drink up. "It won't hurt you, even if it doesn't affect you."

"Now she tells me," Drusilla murmured. "As bad as it smells, it *better* work."

It smelled like something on fire that should *never* be burned, tasted even worse, and went down like lava. It occurred to Drusilla that Tisana might be attempting to murder her, but then the fire seemed to spread, reaching throughout her body to stimulate every erogenous zone she possessed. Her nipples tingled as they and her clitoris became engorged to the point of being uncomfortable and then an ache began between her thighs that rapidly became unbearable. All Drusilla could think of was getting someone—or something—inside her to ease the feeling of complete and utter emptiness.

"Is there an antidote to this?" Drusilla gasped.

"Unfortunately, no," Tisana said, with sympathetic smile. "At least, not unless Manx shows up." Reaching for a pair of scissors, she went on, "We should take some of your hair too, I think. Just a little will do." Snipping off a small portion, she dropped it into a jar.

Drusilla didn't even notice what Tisana was doing. She was too focused on the clamoring of her body as all the moisture in her mouth seemed to dry up and head south. "Can I have something else to drink?"

"Oh, yes, I suppose you would like something to wash that down with. Nothing completely cuts the effect, but wine helps the burn."

"Great, now I'll be horny *and* drunk," Drusilla grumbled. "I feel terrible."

"Wouldn't feel a bit bad if Manx was around," Tisana said reassuringly. "In the state you're in, a good hard cock is the only thing you need."

Drusilla knew she was right, but, as Tisana had so helpfully pointed out, Manx was nowhere near. "I sure hope we can find him!" she gasped. "I was anxious to find him before, but now I really *need* him!"

"You'll be all right—eventually. Drink this down and then get me a sample of every body fluid you can think of," she said, handing Drusilla a small glass of wine and doing her best to sound firm. Pointing toward a doorway, she added. "Then you can go lie down until it wears off."

"How long does it take?"

"Not long," Tisana replied. "About three or four hours at the most."

"Not long?" Drusilla squeaked. *"Not long?* If you felt like this you'd—"

"I'd go find Leo and hope he could keep up with me," Tisana said equably. "Don't worry, Drusilla. With any luck, Manx will be here soon."

"But he's been gone for days and days," Drusilla lamented. "It could take him even longer to return."

"Let's hope not," Tisana said. "He's probably already getting a whiff of the original signal brew and is on his way back as we speak. This is just to make him hurry."

"I hope it puts wings on his feet," Drusilla declared. "I already felt bad enough, but now I feel like I'll die without him." Drusilla hated to admit this, even to herself, but just then, any man would have done. "Or somebody," she added lamely.

"That's the reason I don't like to use this potion," Tisana said. "It's not very specific."

"Yeah," Drusilla agreed. "It just makes you want to fuck so bad you'll do it with anyone."

"My point exactly," Tisana said. "But Jack will never listen to reason."

Drusilla supplied Tisana with the samples she required and then shut the door.

Once the door was closed, Drusilla stripped off her clothing and reached between her legs to stroke her engorged clit. She hadn't felt this wild even when she had been watching Manx out on the beach that first night. Her entire pelvic region ached, and she couldn't keep her legs together. Her clitoris climaxed from the stimulation she gave it, but it wasn't enough; in fact, she suspected that even a whole army of men couldn't have satisfied her. She wondered briefly what this potion would do to a male and decided that if Manx had drunk any of it, she wouldn't have needed an army; he would have been able to fuck for hours.

Not that he couldn't do that anyway. Aside from being the most inherently likable and lovable man she'd ever met, he could probably outperform just about any other man in existence. This thought and the added effects from the potion made her consider dashing out into the jungle in search of him, but she retained enough rational thought to realize that she had absolutely no idea where to look.

Sighing, she lay back on the bed. It was going to be a very long four hours.

Tisana considered throwing out the remainder of the aphrodisian brew, but on the outside chance that it might be needed again, she poured it into a glass vial and set it up on the shelf along with her store of medicinal herbs. Then, on second thought, she tucked it behind several other containers. No point in leaving it out in plain sight where anyone could find it—especially Jack.

Adding Drusilla's sample to the cauldron had a side effect Tisana didn't expect; Cat and Leo were nearly incapacitated by the scent. Leo was purring all over his wife and licking her neck while she stirred her potion.

Cat opted to sit down under a tree and pull Jack backwards onto his lap.

"This isn't very comfortable," Jack complained. "It's like sitting on a rock."

"With an aroma such as that in the air, it is hard for me to be anything *but* a rock," Cat purred.

"Guess it would make a great perfume ingredient," Jack observed. "For Zetithians, anyway." She paused a moment to settle herself more comfortably on Cat's rigid cock. "You sure this isn't hurting you?" she asked.

"Not at all," replied Cat. "But if you would like to do something *different*, I would not complain." Cat was ready to carry Jacinth off into the jungle and get wild when she twisted around to face him, her expression decidedly pugnacious.

"Hey, I thought you married guys wouldn't get all hot and bothered by another woman's scent," Jack argued. "What gives?"

"Ordinarily it would not affect us," Cat replied, "but there is something different about this potion of Tisana's that renders it extremely stimulating."

"Well, Manx is sure to like it, then," Jack said with a sigh of relief. "I just hope the wind is blowing in the right direction. In the meantime, we need to get you and Leo upwind of it before the kids see something they might wish they hadn't." Then something else occurred to her. "Hey, the boys wouldn't be affected, would they?"

"I believe not," Cat replied. "But they *are* half human. It might be different for them."

"Ha!" Jack scoffed. "Which half? They don't seem to be *human* at all."

"In appearance, perhaps," Cat agreed, "but no one knows what differences there might be with respect to their physiology."

"Don't get technical with me, Kittycat," Jack warned, getting to her feet and calling to her children. "Come on, boys, we need to go to town or something. Or inside. Anywhere away from the steam."

"You're right, Mom," said Moe, wrinkling his nose. "It stinks."

"You see?" said Cat. "No problem."

"I certainly hope you're right," Jack said with relief. "That's something I'm just not quite ready to deal with."

At Tisana's insistence, Leo had also retreated to the ship to avoid a very public display of lust with his wife. He wanted nothing more than to lie down on his bed and wait for her, but the door to his and Tisana's room was firmly closed. Correctly assuming that Drusilla was in there resting, he sat down at the table in the galley. His cock was beginning to assume more normal proportions when he noticed something odd.

Tisana was very exacting about how she arranged her store of herbs, and it was somehow comforting to Leo that they were always lined up in the same fashion, but something had changed. Upon closer examination, he discovered a tall, slim vial with a crystalline stopper. Taking it down from its perch, he pulled out the stopper and sniffed it. It might have smelled horrible, but the scent alone was enough to send desire coursing through his body like a flood. Even so, without Tisana's scent to fully arouse him, his cock remained as it was.

Smiling, he replaced the stopper and put the vial back where he found it. He knew what it was and where it was. He would make use of this information at a more opportune time.

———

Coordet was the third planet in a neighboring star system and one of the few in the region that didn't require adhering to endless regulations for permission to land. It might not have been a pretty world—it was more rocky than green—but it did have the virtue of being warm. Despite their hairy bodies, Nedwuts were intolerant of cold, but, fortunately, Zetithians didn't seem to care for it much either; Klarkunk had yet to find one on any of the frozen planets he'd reluctantly visited while on the hunt.

"You won't believe what I saw on Barada Seven," Veluka said quietly. The noise in the crowded barroom was enough to keep anyone from overhearing, but it didn't pay to take chances.

Klarkunk knew what was coming next. He'd left Barada completely against his will, and still couldn't understand how it happened. He'd about decided there weren't any Zetithians left that were unaccounted for when he'd stumbled onto the trail of this latest one. Barada Seven had been his last, best hope, and having to leave the planet without having captured his prey had left him seething with resentment. He hadn't gone far before Veluka had contacted him for a meeting. He didn't completely trust Veluka—and doubted that anyone else did either—but he'd been the source of useful information in the past, so Klarkunk had nothing to lose by listening to him. "Let me guess," he said. "A Zetithian?"

"Oh, not just one," Veluka said eagerly. "A whole fuckin' band of them. Kids, too."

"How many?" Klarkunk tried to control his reaction, but his beady eyes widened with greed—a reaction not missed by the scaly native of Nerik who sat opposite him.

The expression on Veluka's face was so smug Klarkunk had to fight the urge to smash it in with his fist. "Two adult males, five boys, and one girl," Veluka reported. "There were some babies too, but I don't know if they're male or female."

"A female?" Klarkunk said with a contemptuous snarl. "They aren't worth shit, but the males are worth five million apiece."

"Females are worthless?" Veluka's large pupils dilated briefly, which was very noticeable against the total white of his almond-shaped eyes.

"No bounty on them anymore," Klarkunk replied. "I've heard it's because without a male of their own kind, they won't reproduce, so they aren't a threat to anyone."

"I've never understood the threat," Veluka said with a shrug, "but I do know the value of thirty-five million credits."

"Make that *forty* million credits," Klarkunk amended. "There's another one somewhere on that cursed planet. We tracked him there and then turned a wildcat loose so we had an excuse to land, but some Terran woman claimed to have killed it, so we had no choice but to withdraw. She had one of our weapons, so she could have done it, but I'm betting on the Zetithian." The Nedwut made a rude gesture to demonstrate his contempt for Drusilla's claim. "She was no hunter, and she'd painted a fuckin' picture of him! I just couldn't find him before the Baradans revoked our landing permit."

"Wouldn't think that would be much of a problem for you," Veluka said. "You Nedwuts tend to ignore everyone's rules."

"There was no point in remaining," Klarkunk said, but he knew he was lying just to save face.

Veluka, however, seemed sympathetic. "Funny thing about Barada," he said with a nod. "I've gone there plenty of times intending to cheat those weird little natives out of every credit they've got, but something always happens to stop me. Can't figure it out."

Klarkunk had no answers. He'd had a similar experience himself, but for that many credits, he was quite willing to go back and try his luck again. "Where are they?" he asked.

"Got a ship berthed just north of the spaceport. Quite a little encampment—kids out playing like they're on holiday; they've even got a dog. The ship belongs to a trader—Jack Tshevnoe. Ever hear of her?"

"Yes," Klarkunk said shortly. Captain Jack's record against his kind was enough to have her on every Nedwut hit list in existence. "She kills every Nedwut she lays eyes on."

Veluka laughed. "A lot of people do that these days, but you can't really blame her for not wanting you guys hauling her husband in for the bounty," he said smugly. "She's pretty tough, I grant you, but someone who was *not* a Nedwut might be able to get close enough to bag one of them."

"Meaning you, I suppose?" Klarkunk growled.

"Meaning me," Veluka said. "For a price."

The idea had merit, but Klarkunk was as greedy as the next Nedwut. He might use Veluka, but he had no intention of sharing the bounty with him.

"Up front," Veluka said, correctly assessing Klarkunk's intent.

Klarkunk's anger flared. "I don't need a fuckin' Nerik to help me," he snarled. "Now that I know where they are, I'll land illegally if I have to. Wouldn't be the first time. I know some spots that even the Baradans don't go."

"You do, do you?" Veluka said with a chuckle. The sharply pointed black scales covering his body rose as he laughed, lifting the fabric of his tunic and making his broad shoulders seem even wider. His laughter was disarming, but intimidating at the same time. "Better keep that to yourself, then."

"Your problem is you don't know how to redeem the bounty," Klarkunk said with a sneer. "That's something only *we* know, and it'll stay that way until they're all gone."

"You know, you should leave this band alone," Veluka suggested. "The way they're multiplying, in a few years, you could have a *real* fortune."

"Forty million *is* a real fortune—for anyone."

Veluka laughed again. "If you don't get yourself killed in the process."

"If I take out Jack Tshevnoe first, the rest will fall."

"The witch who travels with her is more dangerous," Veluka cautioned. "And the Zetithians are trained warriors. You just watch yourself."

"I don't need advice from you," Klarkunk growled. "But I will pay you for the information." Shoving back his chair, he stood up and tossed a credit on the table. "There, buy yourself a drink. On me." Barking out a laugh, he rounded up his cohorts and headed for the door. None of the other customers even looked up.

Veluka stared at the credit lying on the table in front of him, his scales now flattened with anger. Raising his eyes, he watched as the Nedwuts left, Klarkunk pushing another customer roughly aside as he passed through the open door.

Then he smiled.

The journey through the jungle was difficult, but Manx followed the scent as if he would draw strength from it—especially since it seemed to be drawing him back to Drusilla.

In his mind he had never left her side. When he slept, he dreamed of her, and when he awoke, he tried to shove the memory of those dreams aside, but failed miserably. He should never have run, but fear that Drusilla would have been killed or captured along with him had driven him onward.

But now a similar fear was driving him back. The Nedwuts might have taken her anyway. True, she had the weapon Lester had given her, and she did know how to use it, but unless she'd had it on her when confronted by the Nedwuts, he couldn't count on it being of much use. He knew he should have remained to fight, but running had become second nature to him, and he'd never doubted that those he left behind would be much safer without him. But this time, he wasn't so sure. The thought of his delicate Drusilla at the mercy of those beasts had haunted him from the beginning. It was time to stop, once and for all. He should have known that already, should have known he couldn't abandon her, and not knowing her fate quickened his pace.

Then he noted a change in the air and his cock stiffened in response. Not only did the wind now carry Drusilla's scent, but that of an *aroused* Drusilla.

For a moment, anger flared in his mind. If she was *that* aroused, there must be another male responsible. Another *Zetithian* male. Desperate to know the truth, he started running, not caring if it *was* a trap.

—∾∾—

Veluka waited until the Nedwuts were out of sight and then set off toward his ship, the *Okeoula*. Never let it be said that he didn't plan ahead. He knew exactly where the Nedwut ship was berthed and just how much it had cost them to leave it there.

Klarkunk was a fool. It was much cheaper where Veluka had docked his own vessel and no one asked any nosy questions—or let any unauthorized persons anywhere near it. He waited until he saw the Nedwut ship blast off.

With a smile so wide that his scaly face made a cracking sound, Veluka fired up the *Okeoula's* engine. Already knowing where they were headed, he decided to wait until later to activate the homing beacon. After that, it would be easy to find them—especially since the beacon was on Klarkunk.

—∾∾—

Following the direction of the scent, Manx arrived at the lake house only to find it deserted. Drusilla's things were still there, though, and Dwell let him in without question.

"Where is she?" he demanded. "Did the Nedwuts take her?"

"No, another of her kind came to visit," Dwell reported. "They left together."

"How long ago?"

"Three days," Dwell reported. "She has not returned."

"Any idea where they went?"

"She did not say, but they had a speeder."

"They?"

"A Terran female and two males of your kind."

"So, I haven't been imagining it!" Manx exclaimed. "Though how their scent could be so strong—and Drusilla's, too." He shook his head, still not understanding how it was possible. "You didn't see any Nedwuts, did you?"

"Five of them visited with Lester after you left," said Dwell. "They said they were hunting the wildcat, but left after Drusilla told them that she had killed it." Dwell's voice became softer as he added, "I did not explain that it was you who killed it, rather than she."

Manx laughed out loud. "Thanks, Dwell. I appreciate that."

"I did not like the Nedwuts," Dwell said frankly. "Klog said they were evil, and Klog is always correct."

"Did Drusilla take that weapon with her?"

"No, she did not."

Manx heard a soft beep just behind him. Turning, he saw Klog holding it out to him, handle first. "Thanks, Klog," he said, checking the controls before pocketing the pistol. "I wish you could come with me, but I guess I'll have to go it alone from here."

"What will you do?" Dwell asked as the house droid floated toward the kitchen.

"I don't know," Manx replied, "but I'm sick of running. I want to find Drusilla and go back to Earth with her. That is, if she'll still have me after taking off and leaving her like that."

"She has been very distraught since you left," said Dwell. "She has done many paintings since then. Nearly all of them were of you."

Manx knew that he'd done the same thing himself, except the pictures he painted of Drusilla were etched in his mind. He would not have forgotten her easily.

"Well, she wouldn't have left all of her things here if she was going back to Earth," Manx decided. "And she didn't appear to have been taken by force?"

"No," Dwell replied. "But if you wish more information, I believe they talked with the eltran."

"I'll bet that was interesting," Manx said with a wry smile.

Klog hummed in from the kitchen and beeped twice before handing Manx a sandwich and a glass of juice.

"Klog believes you are hungry," Dwell reported.

"He's right about that," Manx declared. "I've been trying to get here so fast I haven't stopped to eat much other than a little fruit I found along the way." Taking the food, he then headed down to the lake, knowing that someone else was probably hungry too.

Calling out for the eltran, Manx waited by the shore, chewing thoughtfully on his sandwich. If Drusilla had gone willingly, but hadn't taken her belongings, then that must mean she intended to return. In that case, Manx could just sit tight and wait for her, but the scent that still hung in the air was very compelling. It had to be there for a reason.

"Well, look who decided to come back," Zef taunted.

"Don't start, Zef," Manx warned. "You know very well why I had to leave. I always told you if I ever got a whiff of Nedwut, it would be the last you saw of me."

"Yeah, you did say that," said Zef. "I just didn't think you'd do it. 'Specially with Drusilla around."

Manx's eyes narrowed. "You know exactly why I left."

"Yeah, Drusilla pretty much figured it out too. Said you were being noble and heroic. Load of weddle crap if you ask me."

"Really? She said that?"

Zef rolled his eyes. "Can you *really* hear her saying shit like that?"

"Well, no, but—"

"She said there was nothing heroic about a dead hero and she didn't really want to live without you."

"Now *that* I can believe," said Manx. "So who was here? Dwell said it was a Terran woman and two Zetithian men."

"Yeah. Jack, Cat, and Leo," Zef replied. "The one called Cat looks a lot like you."

Manx knew there was at least one possible survivor who resembled him. "What color were his eyes?"

"Black," Zef replied. "That was what threw me off. That and the scar on his cheek."

Zef had never seen Manx smile with such delight. "Cark!" he exclaimed. "It has to be him!"

"Well, they did say they were looking for a friend of theirs," Zef said gruffly. "Wasn't sure I believed them, but you say you know each other?"

"Haven't seen him since we were captured," said Manx, "but if it's Cark, yeah, I know him. The other one was who?"

"Leo," Zef replied. "Had long, golden-brown hair and gold eyes." Zef looked mischievously up at his friend. "Lot better looking than you."

Not bothering to rise to the bait, Manx said firmly, "It must be Leccarian." Taking a deep breath, he added, "I've got to get going, Zef. If they take Drusilla and leave this planet without me…"

"Now hold on a minute," Zef said. "She had a visit from someone else while you were gone. Pretty woman with the most incredible tits—"

"I'm sure she was lovely, but—"

"Lovely?" Zef echoed. "Hell's bells! She was the most gorgeous thing I've ever seen! Glowing blue eyes, long dark hair, wearing nothing but a few animal skins, and, well, no offense, Manx—I mean, I know you like her and all—but she made Drusilla look fuckin' plain!"

"I'm really not interested—" Manx began.

"Oh, no?" Zef cackled. "Well, I think she might have been interested in *you*. Drusilla acted like she didn't want to tell her anything, and she was out here for a pretty stupid reason. That Baradan kid, Roger, brought her, but she was already looking for the place; said she was curious to meet the other offworlder. Now, that sounded pretty flimsy to me, and Drusilla thought so too. Then she said her sister had been attacked by that wildcat and she was hunting it—but she only said that later. Now, she looked like she could probably take it on and win the fight, but she also asked if Drusilla knew of any other offworlders even after Drusilla told her the wildcat was dead."

"You mean you think she was looking for me?"

"Yeah, I think she was looking for you, and Roger seemed to know something about you too. I know you've tried to avoid them, but have any of the Baradans ever seen you?"

"Once," Manx admitted. "Right after I first arrived. I wasn't sure he spotted me, but obviously he did."

"Well, Drusilla shut him up pretty quick, but then they got to talking about fuuslak juice and Roger took her off to see about getting some plants to take back to her homeworld."

Manx just shook his head and thought for a moment, still trying to remember a woman in his past that fit that description, and couldn't come up with one. "Did she say where she was from?"

"Statzeel," Zef replied.

"Never heard of it," Manx said. "And I *know* I've never been there."

"She didn't say much about it except that the men were really nasty and most of the planet was jungle, like this one."

"But why would she be looking for me?"

"Damned if I know," Zef said gruffly, "but when Drusilla left here with those friends of yours, I spotted her up there in the trees," he said with a nod toward the house. "She was right behind them. You be careful."

"I will," said Manx.

Zef was nothing if not a realist. Manx might have returned to the lake, but Zef knew their friendship was drawing to an end. "No time to fish?"

"No time to fish."

"Damn. I knew you'd say that."

"If all goes well, I'll be back soon and I'll catch as many as you can eat."

"Don't believe it," said Zef.

"What, you don't think I can catch them?"

"No," said Zef. "Aren't that many fish in the whole fuckin' lake."

Manx grinned and began to turn toward the house, but movement on the far side of the lake caught his eye. Manx should have smelled their stench long before he could see them, but his senses were filled with Drusilla's scent and the wind was against him this time. He was standing on the open beach as a band of Nedwuts emerged from the jungle on the opposite shore.

It took Veluka two days to reach Barada Seven, but considerably less time to locate his quarry.

"Veluka, you scaly old rascal!" Jack exclaimed as he approached. "How'd it go?"

"Perfectly," Veluka replied. "They have landed in a clearing deep in the jungle and are headed this way. They should be here any time now. Here's the tracking module for the homing beacon."

Jack stowed the device in a zippered compartment in her flight suit before tossing Veluka a bag of credits. "I put a few extra in there to keep you quiet."

"Quiet?" Veluka said with a blank expression on his angular face. His pupils had constricted to pinpoint size, making his eyes seem completely white. "Me? Quiet? Never!"

Jack scowled at him. "You can tell anyone else you like, just don't tell Cat. I don't think he likes it when I set them up."

"Nedwuts, you mean?"

"Of course I mean Nedwuts! Although, this time I'll be leaving some of them alive to question. Hell, maybe I'll leave *all* of them alive if it'll get them to talk. I want to find out who's offering the bounty and put an end to this crap once and for all."

"Good luck," Veluka said. "But I don't think they'll tell you."

"They already know I shoot Nedwuts on sight," Jack pointed out. "Shouldn't be too hard to convince, especially if I blast their ship and strand them here. The Baradans don't seem to care for them. Might ship them back to their own scuzzy little planet if we're lucky."

"You would have made some serious enemies."

"I've *already* made some serious enemies," Jack retorted.

"Good thing I'm not one of them," Veluka said with a grin that revealed nearly all of his pointed black teeth.

"That's only because no one's ever made it worth your while."

Veluka chuckled softly, ruffling his scales. He had no intention of ever crossing Jack Tshevnoe. Getting on her bad side might not get you killed, but it was guaranteed to make life difficult. Jack had some form of clout on just about every planet in the quadrant, and aside from that, she always paid for information—good information, that is. Selling her bad information was tantamount to committing financial suicide. "Just don't let Klarkunk find out I had anything to do with tagging a beacon on him and there'll be no danger of that."

Jack grinned. "You know I never reveal my sources."

"Don't start now." The wily Nerik peered at her closely. "So, Jack, what will you do with yourself when you no longer have a reason to hunt Nedwuts?"

"Hunt them?" Jack echoed. "Since when have I ever had to hunt them? They swarm around Zetithians like fruit flies on a rotten banana! I could just sit here and wait for the whole stinkin' lot of them to come after us and then pick them off one by one, but that would cramp my style too much."

"Can't have that, now, can we?" Veluka said. "Your 'style' has earned me quite a number of credits."

"You scratch my back and I'll scratch yours?" Jack ventured.

Veluka had never heard the expression before, but its meaning was clear. "Now you owe me one," he said with a nod.

"Uh, no, I think we're square," Jack said affably. "Just count those credits if you don't believe me."

"Oh, I will," Veluka said smoothly. "You may be certain of that."

"Count them *now*," said Jack.

There was no mistaking her tone. Jack was not one to be jerked around. Veluka sighed and tried to appear innocent, which was difficult for a being as inherently disreputable-looking as a Nerik. "You don't trust me?"

"I trust you to come back in a few months telling me I'd shorted you and asking for another favor," Jack said with a snort. "It never ceases to amaze me the way you insist on taking one simple deal and milking it forever."

"Very well," said Veluka. He poured the credits into his hand. All the agreement called for were present, plus an extra twenty. "Okay, Jack," he said sadly. "We're square."

"Good, now get going before the Nedwuts see you."

"I am already gone," Veluka said with a bow. "Until our paths cross once again."

"See ya," said Jack.

Veluka went back to his ship knowing that Jack had somehow managed to get the best of him once again. He wouldn't mention this to his cronies; after all, he needed to keep his reputation intact. Unfortunately, he kept forgetting that Jack had her own reputation to protect as well.

Chapter 18

REALIZING THEY'D BEEN SEEN, THE NEDWUT PACK FIRED several shots, but all of them fell short. Manx whipped out his pistol and fired a wide stun beam in their direction as he sprinted across the sand to the cover of the house. Once inside the beach room, he weighed his options briefly. He knew he could hold off against them for a while, but not forever.

"Dwell!" Manx whispered urgently. "Can you call out on that comlink?"

"Yes," replied Dwell. "I am capable of that."

"Then do it! I don't care who you tell, but let someone know the Nedwuts are back and they've got weapons!"

"I will inform Lester," Dwell said.

Though Manx had never actually met Lester, he'd seen him around often enough to feel as though he had, and somehow he didn't strike Manx as the best person to notify. He knew from talking to Zef that weapons were virtually unheard of on Barada, which meant that the Nedwuts had to be flouting some kind of law. Manx couldn't begin to imagine what the gentle Baradans could do against something as ruthless as a band of Nedwuts, but there weren't many other options. "Don't know how he'll stop them, but maybe he's got backup or can at least tell Cark and Lec."

Peering around the corner, Manx saw that his shot had scattered the Nedwuts, who were now hurrying to circle the lake. The lake wasn't as wide at that point, so Manx tried a narrower beam, which actually hit one of them. Fortunately, it was the one in the lead and as he fell into a crumpled heap on the beach, two of the others tripped and fell over him. Manx got off a few more shots as the remaining thugs scrambled to their feet and made for the cover of the trees.

―――

Drusilla simply couldn't stand it anymore. She pulled on her shorts and top and ran right past the men sitting around the table in the galley and left the ship, fully intending to run all the way back to the lake house, when Jack pulled her up short as she burst out of the open hatch.

"Whoa there, girl! Where do you think you're going?"

Drusilla's breath was short, as though she'd already run all the way to the house. "Got to find Manx!" she panted.

"You see now why I won't let you use that potion on anyone?" Tisana blurted out. "It makes people absolutely sex-crazed!"

"Maybe you gave her too much," suggested Jack.

"I did not," Tisana said. Her tone was ominous, and her fiery green eyes sparkled with indignation.

"Whoa, now!" Jack said soothingly, holding up a placating hand. "No need to get your panties in a wad and start shooting fireballs at me. You can save them for the Nedwuts."

"Nedwuts?" Tisana echoed, her eyes swiftly scanning the perimeter of the clearing. "Where?"

"Uh, anywhere," Jack replied, trying not to sound too evasive. "You know how they always seem to show up wherever we go."

Tisana wasn't fooled for a moment. "Are you saying some of them are here?"

"I'm afraid so," Jack began. "They didn't get Manx when they were here legally, and I just got word that they've landed on the northeast side of the lake. There's a clearing there just big enough for their ship. I was really hoping Manx would get here before they did, but they were a lot quicker than I thought they'd be."

"We've got to find Manx!" Drusilla shouted as she tried to wrestle away from Jack. "I can't let them get him!"

"Now hold your horses," said Jack. "You shouldn't be facing them on your own. I've got everything under control. We'll go after him *and* the Nedwuts."

"With what?" Tisana demanded. "It's against the law to carry a weapon on this planet, and you know it."

"Yeah, I know, and it always gripes my cookies to have to turn them over whenever we land. I'd steal Tex back right now if I knew where to look. I should be able to—"

The men and boys had followed Drusilla's mad dash and were now grouped just outside the ship. "You're gonna get us all thrown in the slammer, Mom," Larry said darkly.

"What?" demanded Jack, momentarily diverted.

"Thrown in the slammer," Larry repeated. "You know: the pen, the big house, sent up the river—"

"What *have* you been teaching that boy?" Tisana asked in dismay.

"Everything he needs to know to survive," Jack shot back. "Okay then, if I can't carry a weapon, Drusilla can. Lester gave her a pistol, remember? That gives her some kind of license to kill, doesn't it?"

"That's putting a very broad interpretation on the matter," Tisana said mildly.

"Oh, for the love of Mike!" said Jack. "What was I thinking? You're the best weapon we've got, Tisana, and nobody can confiscate *you*."

Leo and Cat nodded in agreement.

Tisana knew they were right. "Okay, but where do we look?"

"The lake house," Drusilla said, doing her best to control her wild, sexual urges and growing panic. "It's where he would go if he came back."

"Yeah, you're probably right," said Jack. "We should have been cooking up the potion there at the house. Would have made more sense—though we didn't know he'd been living there when we started. It just seemed like the easiest—"

"Does it matter?" Drusilla said desperately, interrupting Jack's explanation. "We've got to find him!"

"Okay," said Cat. "But the children must wait aboard the ship." Turning to Larry, he placed a hand on his son's shoulder. "As eldest, you will see to the safety of the others. Close the hatch and let no one in."

"Not even you guys?" Larry asked.

"Not even us," said Cat.

"We can palm open the hatch ourselves," Jack reminded her son. "You just make sure those Nedwuts don't get aboard."

Larry stood up taller. "I will protect the others," he said staunchly. "If they try to take us, we'll blast them!"

Tisana's eyes narrowed in suspicion. "Do you mean to tell me that those boys know how to fire the ship's weapons?"

"Well, maybe," said Jack.

Tisana began to protest, even though she knew that where Jack and Cat's boys were concerned, she had no say, but it still seemed wrong to her.

"They have to stay alive," Jack reminded her friend. "Whether we survive or not."

"Yeah, right," said Tisana with a reluctant nod. "Let's go."

"We'll need the other speeder," Jack said. "Cat and I will get it and follow you."

"Wow," said Drusilla. "You have more than one?"

"With all of this lot to haul around?" said Jack. "We ought to have a frickin' bus!"

In the meantime, there was some unrest in the Nedwut ranks, especially once Klarkunk let slip just who it was they were up against.

"There are three adult males!" Klarkunk said exultantly. "We will take them all and then search for the children."

Betlefat viewed his captain with a skeptical eye. "Are you sure about that?" he said doubtfully. "That's Jack Tshevnoe you're talking about. You didn't tell me we'd be going up against her gang. They've killed more of us than the Scorillian plague."

"Fool!" Klarkunk spat contemptuously at his lieutenant. "We will defeat them and then we will collect the bounty."

"Yeah, and live long and prosper for the rest of our lives," Xentondu said.

"You always were an ass-licker," Betlefat said,

dismissing Xentondu with an obscene gesture. "We've got to be *alive* to prosper. Think ignatz here is planning to leave us alive to share?"

Klarkunk growled menacingly. "You doubt my word?"

"Yeah, I doubt your word," said Betlefat, squaring up to face his opponent. "Don't know why I've believed it this long."

"You would falter now that our prize is within our grasp?"

"Don't give me that crap," Betlefat said. "One *unarmed* Zetithian alone was what we were hunting originally, now we're going up against the likes of—"

"All the more sweet our victory," Klarkunk insisted, cutting him off. "Our people will hail our triumph over such a pestilence."

Betlefat had seen quite enough hardship in his life thus far and was getting sick of it. He was ready to go back to their homeworld and do nothing but relax, fuck, eat well, and grow old. "They wouldn't kill us if we'd quit hunting them."

"For five million credits apiece?" Klarkunk scoffed. "They will be hunted until they are too tired to fight and will give themselves up."

"I don't think so," said Betlefat. "If they get tired they'll just retreat to Earth, and you know we have no hope of ever getting them there."

"But you forget the Baradan ban on weapons. They will all be unarmed."

"How do you disarm that witch?" Betlefat countered. "Answer me that?"

"We simply kill her first."

Betlefat shook his head. "That's been tried too."

"But never on a weaponless world," Klarkunk said. "We may never get such a chance again."

"How do you know they haven't smuggled in weapons just as we have?"

"They are fools and respect the law. Besides, they do not know we are coming for them." Klarkunk was growing weary of the argument and was sorely tempted to blast his lieutenant without further discussion. "You will fight with us, or you will die right now," said Klarkunk. "It is your choice."

Betlefat had an idea that his death was in the near future either way, but opted to postpone it for as long as possible. He held up his rifle in a gesture of solidarity.

"A wise choice," said Klarkunk, clapping him on the back. "We will be victorious."

The band of brigands cheered, but Betlefat wasn't sure there was anything to cheer about—at least, not yet.

—⁓—

Abandoning the speeders a little ways south of the house, Jack and her cohorts moved down the path through the jungle. The wind had shifted slightly, coming out of the northwest. Leo's head went up and he sniffed the air. "I smell them. They are there," he said, pointing into the wind.

"I smell them too," said Jack. "How many do you think there are?"

Leo shook his head. "Not sure, but there are several."

"Shit, and all we've got to fight with is Tisana!" Ordinarily, this would be plenty, but if she was taken out by a pulse beam, it was all over. Jack hated being without her trusty Tex. Somehow the situation just didn't call for obeying the law—anyone's laws—unless it was the law of survival. She still didn't understand how she'd let the others talk her out of it. Still, she had the beacon Veluka had given her; Leo's assessment only confirmed what she already knew, but it wasn't doing her a bit of good because she knew that the beacon was only on the leader, Klarkunk. If they split up, it could still result in an ambush.

Jack hated feeling so defenseless. When she'd said she had everything under control, it hadn't been completely accurate. Things could still go terribly wrong.

The house was just barely visible through the trees ahead, but though Leo and the homing beacon insisted the Nedwuts were there, nothing stirred but the birds singing in the jungle canopy.

Cat raised a hand and halted. "We should stop here for now," he said.

"Drusilla," Jack said suddenly. "Where did you say that pistol was?"

"Just inside the house," Drusilla replied. "Want me to go get it? Klog and Dwell can help us too."

Jack wasn't sure just how, but she wasn't about to refuse help in any form. "We know the Nedwuts are here, and while they might have an idea we're coming, I seriously doubt they can see us as they seem to have retreated into the jungle. Tisana can cover you while you go get it. Don't dawdle, either; come right straight back. Do you understand? Straight back, no matter what."

Drusilla nodded. She had to do something constructive because otherwise she knew she was going to come completely unglued and start screaming for Manx. The speeder ride through the forest had been a torment, but at least she hoped she was moving closer to him then. She gave Jack a tight smile and sprang from the shelter of the jungle to dart across the clearing to the door, hoping that Dwell had had sense enough not to let anyone else inside.

The door opened promptly and then closed firmly shut behind her. "Thanks, Dwell," she said gratefully. "Anything happening here?"

"Yes," Dwell replied. "There have been some new developments."

Drusilla gasped in horror as she saw that the pistol was missing from the sideboard where she'd left it. "Where's the gun?" she asked in dismay.

"Manx has it," Dwell replied. "He is in the downstairs room. The Nedwuts have returned, but I have summoned help."

Momentarily heartened by at least part of this information, she couldn't keep from commenting. "Help, huh? By that you mean Lester, I suppose?"

"Of course," Dwell replied. "Who else would I call?"

"Oh, I don't know," Drusilla muttered. "The Mounties, maybe, or the Marines?"

"I do not understand."

"You wouldn't," Drusilla said ruefully. "Manx is okay?"

"Yes, and he is armed, but he is trapped in there. He has managed to hold them off for a time, but if they rush the room in force, they may be able to take him."

"Damn Nedwuts," Drusilla growled, sounding more like Jack than she could possibly have known. "Where are they?"

"There has been weapons fire from across the lake,"

Dwell reported, "but Manx thinks they have moved to the western edge."

"Closing in, huh?"

"Yes."

"Well, I've got to get to him," she said roundly. "Somehow!"

"No," Dwell said. "He cautions you not to come to the beach room, or to that side of the house. Stay inside."

"I'd like to, and I know I should," Drusilla replied, "but if I don't get my hands on him soon, I'm going to explode or something."

"Explode?" Dwell echoed. "Why would you explode?"

"Some potion the witch, Tisana, gave me," Drusilla said, running a nervous hand through her hair. "I—I can hardly even think clearly."

—⁓—

Manx was in the room beneath her, desperate that Drusilla should not expose herself to danger. "Open a link, Dwell," he said urgently. "Let me talk to her."

"Link is open," said Dwell. "You may proceed."

"Drusilla?" Manx called out, trying to keep his voice steady. "Don't come down here. Do you hear me? Don't do it!"

"I—I have to," she said, though the sound of his voice helped to soothe her frazzled nerves.

"No you don't!" he said with more urgency in his tone. *"Stay there!"*

"Can you come up here?"

"No," Manx replied. "I'll get shot at if I make for the stairs, and you will too, if you come down them."

"You could cover me," she said desperately.

"And have two of us trapped down here?" he scoffed. "I don't think so. Is anyone else with you?"

"Yes," she replied. "Some friends of yours from the old country. They're in the jungle not far from the house." Drusilla felt a maddening urge to laugh hysterically at the irony of their predicament, but she somehow managed to hold it in check. "Funny you finally coming back and I can't get to you."

"We'll be together soon," Manx promised. "If Zef was right and they're who I think they are, there's hope. Cark and Leccarian are both good fighters."

"There'd be more hope if they had some weapons," Drusilla said with a brittle laugh. "They have a witch with them who can start fires or something, but that's all we've got besides the weapon you have."

Manx's hopes for survival diminished slightly with this news, but he wasn't completely disheartened. "Guess they weren't expecting the Nedwuts to be here."

"Yes they were," admitted Drusilla. "At least they figured the Nedwuts would come back for you eventually. Guess we should have come after the pistol sooner, but if we had, you wouldn't—" Her voice cracked as she realized that without it, Manx would be dead now. Swallowing the bile that rose in her throat, she went on, "The plan was to lure you in, but the bad guys got here a little too quickly."

"Lure me in?"

"With the scent potion," Drusilla explained. "Tisana—that's the witch—made it smell like the other two men and… well… me—only an *aroused* me—which is why I'm in the state I'm in."

"Is that what it was?" he said admiringly. "I'll have to say, the witch makes a mean brew. It worked. My dick stiffened up like you were standing right in front of me. I can still smell it." He cleared his throat with difficulty and took a moment to squeeze his cock in an effort to ease the discomfort. "So, they knew there might be Nedwuts here and they *still* came without weapons? That was risky."

"Yeah, I know," Drusilla agreed. "But you know how the Baradans feel about violence."

"Guess the natives should have thought of that before they let offworlders visit their peaceful little planet," Manx said grimly. "But I'm glad they did or I never would have met you."

"I know," Drusilla said. "I can't stand the thought of going on without you."

"I had to leave," he said. "You know why that was."

"Yes, I'm sure I was in no danger as long as you weren't around," she said, her irritation with the whole situation rising rapidly. "But, let me tell you something, big guy, I don't believe that crap. The Baradans could have helped if we'd just told them about you."

"Yeah, and then turned me over to the Nedwuts," he scoffed. "Listen, I've trusted the locals on other planets before, and believe me, between bribes and Nedwut intimidation, they usually crumble pretty fast."

"I didn't," Drusilla reminded him.

"Yes, but you love me," he said, surprised that he could say it so easily and with such conviction. "There's a difference."

"Yeah, I do," she sighed. "Hey, I've got to get back. Jack told me not to dawdle, but I can't go back without something." She began to form a thought in her mind, and shouted, "Klog! — oh, there you are. Don't guess there's any reason to tell you," she said as Klog suddenly appeared at her side and handed over a bundle of knives of all shapes and sizes. They might have been intended for cooking, but perhaps the guys could throw them at the Nedwuts if nothing else. "Thanks, Klog," she said gratefully. "You're a prince."

"See you soon, Manx," she called out. "I love you. Don't forget that."

"I won't. Be careful."

"You too."

Hustling across the patio to the shelter of the trees with her bundle, Drusilla fell in with her cohorts. "Manx is here, but they've got him trapped downstairs. He's got my pistol, but I brought these. Are any of you good with knives?"

Leo chuckled. "You could say that," he replied.

"He once threw a sword a good thirty meters and killed a guy galloping *away* from him on horseback," said Tisana, knowing that Leo would never say it. "I'm pretty sure he could take out some Nedwuts with these."

"He was about to run you down, Tisana," Leo said. "I think that had something to do with my aim."

"Why didn't we think of that?" demanded Jack, smacking her temple with the heel of her hand. "We've got knives in the galley."

"We don't have any like these," Leo said, holding up a blade that was surely intended for skewering a wild boar. "Unless you count our swords, and they were confiscated."

"Obviously we should have more cooks on our side," Jack said dryly. "Damn, that's a helluva knife."

Leo tested the edge with his thumb. "Sharp, too," he

remarked. "I can throw the smaller ones, but this one would be better for close combat."

"Against a pulse rifle?" Tisana scoffed. "Surely you don't mean that."

Cat grinned. "We know a great many defenses against such weapons," he assured her. "You have not seen all that we are capable of."

"Okay, enough with the testosterone fest," Jack said, waving her hand for emphasis. "What we need is a plan."

"We could circle around and come up behind them," suggested Leo. "If I could get a clear aim, I could throw the knives."

"Yes, but in a jungle you won't get a clear shot."

"Plenty of natural cover, though."

"Yes, but there's plenty of stuff to step on and trip over too," Jack pointed out. "You'd have to be really stealthy."

Cat rolled his eyes and looked at her witheringly. "We are cats, remember?"

"You are, but we aren't," Jack said, indicating the other women. "What are we supposed to do? Draw their fire?"

"That's actually a good idea," Tisana said. "With my powers, we aren't completely defenseless. I could—"

Just then Max the dog came bounding up out of the depths of the jungle.

"I thought I'd never find you guys!" he complained, panting heavily. *"I know where the Nedwuts are!"*

"Are they all together?" Tisana asked her pet.

"Sort of," Max reported. *"They're spread out through the trees by the lake."*

"And we already know which direction they're coming from," Tisana mused. *"How many are there?"*

"Nine," Max replied. *"But one of them seems to be hurt."*

"I guess Manx must have gotten one," she reflected. *"So, they outnumber us."*

"What's he saying?" Leo asked.

Tisana gave them Max's reconnaissance report. "We need a diversion," she said, "something to draw their attention away from the rear so you guys can sneak up behind them."

"That shouldn't be too hard," Drusilla said without hesitation. "I'm supposed to be living here, remember? All I have to do is walk across the beach."

"You might be captured," Leo pointed out.

"I don't care if they do capture me if it will save Manx," Drusilla declared.

Jack grinned. "Spoken like a woman in love with a Zetithian."

"Don't worry, we'll cover you," Tisana said. "Here, you'll want one of these," she added, handing Drusilla a small green stone mounted on a clip.

"Jewelry? At a time like this? What am I supposed to do with it? Use it as a bribe?"

"No, it's a comstone," Tisana replied, laughing. "No one ever suspects what it is, so they don't know we can communicate with it. Just tap it and call out the name of whoever you want to talk to."

"It's just a rock, isn't it?" Drusilla said, marveling at the simplicity. "How on earth does it work?"

Tisana shrugged. "No one knows. We bought them on Darconia. They come in real handy sometimes."

"I'll bet they do," Drusilla said, clipping the stone to her shirt. She just wished there was one of them on Manx.

Chapter 19

ARMED WITH KNIVES, LEO AND CAT CIRCLED AROUND TO THE west to come up behind the Nedwut position, making more noise than Manx would have, perhaps, but with considerably more stealth than a Nedwut. At last their quarry was in sight. The Nedwuts were ranged along the edge of the jungle that faced the western shore of the lake, with the house in full view.

Meanwhile, the three women had moved further to the west to try and spot the Nedwuts from the front. Jack's eyesight was keen and she was able to locate some of them holding their position among the trees.

"Do you see them, Tisana?" Jack asked quietly.

"Not really," Tisana whispered back. "My eyes aren't as good as yours."

"There are two of them standing beside that big tree," she went on, pointing them out.

Tisana followed Jack's line of sight, seeing nothing but the trees. "I still don't see them," she said, shaking her head.

"Drop a tree limb on them and you'll see them quick enough," Jack suggested.

Focusing her gaze on a low, heavy limb, Tisana burned through it within mere moments and it fell, crashing down on the two unsuspecting Nedwuts standing beneath it.

"Bingo!" Jack remarked. "You're getting better at that, Tisana."

"Practice makes perfect," Tisana said with a smile. "Plus, I seem to be getting better with age."

"Ha! Aren't we all?" Hoping that the Nedwuts might assume that the tree falling on them was a natural occurrence, Jack pointed out another foe further on up the tree line.

"They'll get suspicious if I do it again, don't you think?" said Tisana.

"Probably," Jack admitted. "Get ready, Drusilla. As soon as the guys are in position, I want you to stroll casually around the house and head down toward the lake."

"And then what?" Drusilla asked.

"I don't know," said Jack. "I'm making this up as I go along." Noting Drusilla's horrified expression, she added, "Okay, then, just head for the dock like you don't know there's anything to worry about. You can always take off in the boat if they start shooting at you, but I really don't think they will."

"Wish I shared your optimism," Drusilla said. "If they've been shooting at Manx, how will they ever believe I don't know they're there?"

"Good point," said Tisana. "She wouldn't be that stupid."

Jack rolled her eyes. "This is a *diversion,* Tisana. It doesn't have to make sense."

"Well, that's a relief, because it doesn't."

"Trust me, it'll work." Jack wasn't sure how it would play out, but it would certainly get the Nedwut's attention.

Leo and Cat moved in to collect the Nedwut rifles while their owners struggled to free themselves from the tangle of vines and branches. "Not bad, Tisana," Leo said over his comstone. "You got two of them."

It was a useful addition to their arsenal, but it also served to alert the Nedwuts to their presence. "They have taken our—"

The Nedwut's cry of alarm was cut off by a heavy stun beam. "That should keep them quiet for a while," Leo said.

"I am wondering what they were waiting for," said Cat.

"Us?" Leo suggested.

"But how could that be if they did not know we were here?"

Leo shrugged. "Well, they do now."

"Jacinth," Cat said, tapping his comstone. "You have not told us everything, have you?"

Jack took a deep breath. "Okay, okay, *okay!* I sent Veluka out to tell them we were here so we could trap them. I don't know about you, but I'm getting sick and tired of having to kill every Nedwut on sight. I want to find out who's paying the bounty and put an end to this. I doubt that it could be a Nedwut; they don't have that kind of money—their planet is notoriously poor, which is why they're such thieving, trouble-making bastards, and why they do a fair amount of bounty hunting. There's got to be someone else holding a grudge against Zetith and I want to find out who it is."

"There were several worlds making war on my planet," Cat said grimly. "It was not just one person or entity."

"Which ones?"

"We never knew, but there were different ships and different beings in the war."

"And you'd never seen a Nedwut outside of the vision you had that they destroyed the planet."

"Yes, but—"

"Didn't you think that was strange?"

"Perhaps."

"Did it ever occur to any of you that you were being attacked not by many different worlds, but by different bands of mercenaries that someone hired?"

"That would explain some things," he admitted, "but not why."

"I already know *why*, or at least suspect it," Jack said. "This wasn't a war to gain wealth or territory; it was an extermination, otherwise why destroy the whole planet? They tried attacking you on the ground and from the air, right?"

"Yes," Cat said, not quite sure what she was getting at.

"But you guys put up such a stiff fight, they had to do something more decisive to kill all of you, so they came up with a way to obliterate the planet. Then they put a bounty on the survivors to make sure your kind was completely eradicated. I just want to find out who that exterminator was."

Leo's head jerked up as he heard a movement in the underbrush. "They are moving this way."

"Let them come," said Cat. "We have weapons now, and Jacinth is right. This needs to end."

Crouching behind a fallen tree, the two Zetithians waited until the sounds moved closer. The Nedwuts were stealthy, but the jungle footing was against them. A twig snapped nearby and, with a quick, mutual nod of agreement, Cat and Leo sprang up and fired.

Three Nedwuts dropped in a dusty, smelly heap.

"These are good rifles," Cat remarked, thoughtfully examining his weapon. "I believe I would like to keep one."

"If the Baradans don't confiscate it," said Leo, "it's all yours."

Cat grinned. "We do not have to tell them *everything*."

"Larry was right. You and Jack probably *will* end up in the slammer."

"They have to catch us first," said Cat. Tapping his comstone, he called for his wife.

"How many did you get?" Jack asked eagerly.

"Three," Cat reported. "That's five down and four to go and we have plenty of weapons now."

"Better odds than we had before," said Jack. "Okay, Drusilla is going to create a diversion. Get ready to shoot anything that moves."

When Xentondu saw Drusilla walking blithely toward the beach, he recognized her immediately as their best leverage against one particular opponent who had eluded them for a very long time. Taking advantage of the natural cover, he moved closer and then began to sprint across the sand.

"Holy shit!" Jack exclaimed as she watched the bold move begin. "Get him, Tisana!"

Leveling her gaze, Tisana shot a ball of fire from her eyes that exploded in the sand just ahead of the Nedwut bounty hunter, who, though momentarily shaken, began running a zigzag pattern. Pulse beams from Cat and Leo's weapons sprayed the area, one singeing the Nedwut's arm, but none of them stopped him.

Drusilla made a dash for the corner of the house in hopes that she might make it to the shelter of the beach room and, therefore, Manx's arms, but Xentondu was too quick for her and she was grabbed roughly from behind just as she turned the corner. The stench of his breath was sickening and his hairy arms gripped her like a vise. Then the barrel of his pistol smacked up against the side of her head, causing her to see stars.

"Surrender your weapons," he roared, "or the female dies!"

Cat and Leo held their fire, fearing to harm Drusilla, but had no intention of surrendering just yet.

Manx heard the scuffle and saw Drusilla with the Nedwut weapon pointed at her head and knew that if Drusilla died, there would be no reason for him to live. Stepping out onto the beach, he took careful aim.

"Let her go," Manx growled.

As Xentondu spun around, the pulse beam from Manx's pistol heading right for his nose was the last thing the Nedwut saw. Xentondu dropped in his tracks and Manx seized Drusilla, pulling her to safety as the other Nedwuts sprayed the area with pulse beams.

"I told you not to come down here!" Manx said, trying to sound angry, but failing miserably.

Drusilla made a muffled, inarticulate noise against his chest.

"What?" he said, reluctantly releasing his tight grip on her.

"I can't breathe!"

"I feel as if I haven't been breathing since I left you," said Manx as he leaned in for a kiss. He drank in her scent as he tasted her lips and was immediately lost in a maelstrom of delight as the effects of Tisana's potion bombarded his senses. Spearing his fingers through her hair, he pulled her even closer to him, vowing never to let her go again.

With his kiss, the fiery passion that Drusilla had somehow managed to bank down suddenly erupted into an inferno and she wrapped her arms around his neck and her legs around his waist, wanting nothing more than to have the whole world stop while they fulfilled their mutual desire.

"Drusilla!" Jack's voice sounded over the comstone. "Are you all right?"

Drusilla reluctantly tapped her own stone. "Just fine," she murmured against Manx's lips. "Manx saved me."

"Of course he did. That was a stupid question for me to ask, wasn't it?" Jack said smugly. "Say, do you think you two could come back up through the house if Tisana lays down a few fireballs to give you some cover?"

"Sure don't want to," Drusilla muttered. "But I guess we can."

"Okay then, get ready to run."

"Dwell!" Drusilla called out. "Open the door to the upstairs… now!" As Tisana's fireballs began exploding all along the tree line, Manx and Drusilla made a run for the stairs. Even with the diversion, pulse beams were hitting the walls, spraying the two lovers with bits of stone and mortar as they raced to safety.

Unfortunately, the Nedwuts weren't completely stupid. Tisana's fireballs gave away their position and she and Jack came under fire. "We've got to move!" Jack shouted, pulling Tisana along with her as Manx and Drusilla came bursting out the front door.

Scrambling through the underbrush, the four of them retreated further into the jungle. Drusilla's clothing was totally inadequate; branches and thorny vines ripped at her exposed skin, but she kept running, holding on to Manx's hand for dear life.

Jack led them on a straight path for several meters and then veered to the west. "We need to meet up with Cat and Leo," she said as they paused to regroup.

Tisana's dress was torn in several places; Drusilla had a rip in her arm that looked rather nasty. She put her thumb on the spot and held pressure, unsure if it would stop bleeding without further intervention. Manx looked a bit scuffed up compared to when Drusilla had last seen him; the dog took the opportunity to sit down, panting hard, but Jack wasn't even winded. "Nice to meet you, Manx," she said pleasantly. "I'm Jack Tshevnoe, and this is Tisana."

"Nice to meet you too."

"You know, you really do look a lot like Cat," she remarked. "Not as handsome, of course, but—"

"You have to forgive her, Manx," said Tisana as she fought the urge to put a hand over Jack's mouth to shut her up. "She's like this with all the new ones."

"You don't hear me complaining, do you?" Manx asked, shaking Jack's hand. "And yes, Cark was always better looking."

"That's a matter of opinion," Drusilla protested.

"You seem to have lost your accent," Jack observed. "Leo has too, but Cat's hanging onto his. It's really sexy, you know."

"I've worked hard at losing it," Manx said, smiling at Jack. "I tried to blend in wherever I was at the time."

"Probably wise, but I still say that Zetithian accent is really hot, though perhaps Drusilla doesn't mind."

"Um, I'd never even *heard* the accent before Cat showed up," Drusilla said. "I like the way Manx talks just fine."

Jack sighed. "No accounting for taste, I suppose. Hey, let's see that pistol you've got there, Manx." As he held it out, Jack let out a low whistle. "Well, would you take a look at that? It's a Nedwut pistol—about the only kind that can actually stun one of them. Most others have to be set to kill to even slow them down." Looking at Drusilla, she added, "And you said *Lester* gave this to you?"

"Yes," Drusilla replied. "He said it had been confiscated from an offworlder."

"A Baradan getting a Nedwut to give up a weapon," Jack said with a mixture of awe and disbelief. "Now *that* I'd like to see."

"Speaking of Cat," Tisana said. "Shouldn't we be telling them we've got Manx?"

"Oh, yeah, right," said Jack. Tapping her comstone, Jack whispered, "Hey Cat, we've got them both safe. Want to retreat, or keep going?"

"We have accounted for five of them," said Cat, "and Manx got one, so there are only three of them left. We have taken their weapons, but—"

"Wish you could have gotten that slimeball's gun, Drusilla," Jack lamented, cutting off Cat's reply. "Would have been a big help about now."

"Sorry," Drusilla said, then added under her breath, "Not the most important thing on my mind at the time."

"I didn't catch that," Jack prompted.

"You heard her," Tisana said darkly. "And I'm surprised she didn't slap you upside the head when she said it."

Jack rolled her eyes. "Oh, now, don't get all bent out of shape—"

"Hey, I'm not the one who paid someone to tell the Nedwuts where we were," Tisana said indignantly. "I swear by all the gods there are that if any of us get killed because of this, I'm gonna fix you a potion you'll never forget!"

"Speaking of potions, I think you need a little fuuslak juice, Tisana," Jack said. "Might make you a little less crabby."

Manx gave Drusilla a nudge. "Are they like this all the time?"

"Seems like it," Drusilla replied. "I'm thinking we should have just stayed in the house and let Klog handle the Nedwuts."

Manx looked down at her arm and gasped. "You're bleeding!"

"Like a stuck pig," Drusilla agreed. "Think we could stay here and let the others come back to us?"

"I'd like to," said Jack as she consulted her tracking module, "but the Nedwuts are headed this way—one of them is, anyway."

Tisana shook her head in disbelief. "You've got a *beacon* on one of them? How?"

"Veluka did it," Jack said absently as she adjusted the settings. "Went to a lot of trouble to tag Klarkunk for me."

"Veluka!" Tisana exclaimed. "You mean that Nerik who tried to cheat you blind?"

"Uh-huh," Jack replied. "He owed me one."

"And you *trusted* him?"

"I paid him," Jack argued. "We're even now."

While the other two were wrangling, Manx took the opportunity to cut a strip of fabric from his shirttail and began to bind up Drusilla's arm. "What am I going to do with you?" he said. "Every time you stick your nose out, you wind up getting hurt."

"Not every time," Drusilla said, "but you do seem to spend an awful lot of time patching me up."

"Mmhm," said Manx. "I'd prefer you stayed in one piece from now on."

"I'll try—and Manx?"

"Yeah?"

"Thanks for coming home."

Manx grinned. "Coming home? I like the sound of that."

"Okay," said Jack, after conferring with Cat. "Cat and Leo are headed back this way, and Klarkunk, at least, is following them. I think it might be best if they were leading the hairy bastard into a trap, don't you?"

Chapter 20

JACK CONSULTED HER TRACKING MODULE AND THEN TAPPED her comstone. "Cat, you two need to pick up the pace a little. Klarkunk is gaining on you."

"How the devil do you know that?" Tisana demanded. "Let me see that thing." To her surprise, there were three labeled dots moving on a grid. "Three of them?"

"You didn't think I'd let Cat and Leo go down there if I didn't know exactly where they were, did you? I might know exactly where Cat is all the time just by his scent trail, but where he is in relation to Klarkunk was more important this time."

Tisana shook her head in wonder. "I should have known. How are they tagged?"

"Nanobots," Jack replied. "They burrow under the skin and are completely undetectable by any scan—if you believe Veluka, that is—and they're so tiny the tagged person can't feel them, either. Not sure how long they remain functional, but we'll see."

"This means you could track Klarkunk anywhere, doesn't it?" Manx said.

"Yeah," said Jack. "Nice thought, isn't it? If we can't get any information out of him, we can follow his big, hairy ass all over the quadrant."

Manx leaned in to look at the viewscreen. "What's the range?"

"Don't know that, either," Jack replied, "but it must be pretty far or Veluka couldn't have tracked them in space. 'Course, he knew where they were headed, but—"

"How much did you have to pay for that?" Tisana asked.

"On the legit market, it's probably worth a fortune, but—"

"—since Veluka undoubtedly stole it, you got it cheap," Tisana finished up, shaking her head.

"Something like that," Jack said with a grin.

"You're completely incorrigible, you know."

"That's why you all hang around," returned Jack. "I keep you guessing."

"I'd settle for being kept alive," commented Drusilla. "Shouldn't we be, you know, *doing* something?"

"Oh, yeah, right," said Jack. "Let's do this on the road, I think. Open space, easy to defend, lots of cover, etcetera."

"You make it sound so simple," Drusilla said.

"The best plans always are."

Unfortunately, to get back to the road required traipsing through more of the dense jungle. This time, however, it was Manx who led the way, and the going seemed much easier to Drusilla. Her arm had finally stopped bleeding, and she had no desire to rip it open again. Somehow having Manx with her again made her feel that there was no way they could fail. Tisana's potion was already wearing off, so her libido was back to normal, and she hoped she was no longer having a detrimentally distracting effect on Manx.

Manx threaded his way through the jungle with ease; this was his territory and he knew it very well, better than most Baradans, and certainly better than any Nedwut. He was still having a hard time believing he'd actually come face-to-face with one of them and escaped. He'd begun to see them as relentless hunters, not even mortal because there always seemed to be more of them coming after him. If he could just make it through this episode, he might never have to fear that they would come hunting him again. Drusilla had told him he would be safe on Earth, and he hoped it was true, but first, he had to get there. It might be easier to believe when he saw Cark and Leccarian again. He still couldn't quite believe that they were actually alive and well. It had been so many years since he'd fought alongside them, and thus far, they'd only been moving dots on Jack's tracking module—not real men at all.

Jack had been talking with Cark over her comstone. Manx heard his voice, and it was undoubtedly his old friend and comrade, but it still didn't seem possible. There would be many things to catch up on, and even more things to discuss with Drusilla—a thousand details to be worked out, but first, he had to earn the right to be her mate. He'd deserted her, which was one of the worst offenses a Zetithian male was capable of. He had known the circumstances warranted it, but he still felt that he'd failed her, and even saving her from the Nedwut hadn't completely absolved him of the guilt. He'd caused her pain, and even though he'd brought pain upon himself, he knew he had a long way to go to make it up to her.

Manx looked back at Drusilla and smiled encouragingly. She had kissed him as though she truly understood and forgave him. He hoped nothing would happen to change that.

The sound of weapons fire in the distance brought him up short, but Jack waved him on. "That's just Cat and Leo slowing them down," she said. "They're going to head for the house, and then if they can break out from the cover of the jungle without the Nedwuts seeing them, they'll run on up the road to us. That'll give us a little time to get our ambush ready."

"There's a place up ahead where the road curves," Manx said. "Just beyond that would be a good place to set up. There are some trees there that are easy to climb."

Jack nodded. "Sounds great. I'm glad we've got you with us. We fiddle-farted all over this jungle trying to find this place the first time, but I don't remember a whole helluva lot about it. The jungle all looks the same to me."

Drusilla dropped her head to hide her smile. She would have been willing to bet that Manx knew every single tree and branch even better than Jack knew her star charts. She started to brag about how he could catch birds with his bare hands and spear live fish with uncanny accuracy, but decided against it. There would be time for that later.

The funny thing was, she'd never had a boyfriend she'd ever felt like bragging about before. Manx was so different from any of the others, and it was more than just being from another planet. She was proud of him. Somehow she knew that this was a feeling that both Jack and Tisana would understand; comparing notes would certainly be interesting. In the meantime, just being able to see him there ahead of her was comforting.

Manx led them unerringly to the precise location he'd mentioned. He helped Drusilla climb up on a tree limb, and then stood at the base of the tree, hidden from the road by the wide trunk. Tisana and Jack took up positions on the opposite side of the road with Tisana perched in a tree and Jack waiting nearby.

"You know, we couldn't be far from where we left the speeders," Drusilla mused. "Seems like a better idea to just go get them and then go back to pick up Cat and Leo."

"It might be if escape was the only plan," Manx said. "I'll have to agree with Jack on this one. I'd love to know who was responsible for the destruction of my planet, and I'd like to make sure that any remaining Zetithians would be safe from them."

Drusilla sighed. "Yeah, you're right. It's just that it seems foolhardy to sit and wait for them to come."

"It's a lot different from what I'm used to," Manx admitted. "I never thought I'd see the day when *I'd* be trying to capture *them*."

"It does seem odd," she agreed. "Apparently Jack's never done it either."

Drusilla was watching Jack as she consulted her tracking device. Her eyes lit up and she waved to the others, motioning for quiet.

Cat and Leo barely made a sound as they rounded the bend in the road at a swift pace. If Drusilla hadn't been so scared, she would have enjoyed taking the time to marvel at the fluidity with which they ran. However, just as quickly as they appeared, Jack threw out a branch to get their attention and they both veered off the road in opposite directions and immediately disappeared into the jungle. Leo slipped in beside Manx and tossed a pistol to Drusilla. Suddenly, everything was as quiet as if they had never been there at all.

Then the Nedwuts came running around the curve. Some of them must have recovered from being stunned because there were now five of them, Drusilla noted, and she found herself wishing that they had used more than the stun setting on them while they had the chance. It was unlike her to feel quite so murderous, but remembering the pistol held to her head made her feel less forgiving; she had no doubt that it had been set to kill. She held her breath as Cat, Leo, Jack, and Manx fell in behind them just as Tisana shot a huge ball of fire that landed right in front of the Nedwuts, blasting them all off their feet to sprawl in the dirt.

The Nedwuts were soon scrambling to their feet and firing random shots as they ran for cover.

"Get your hairy asses back here!" Jack bellowed, firing a narrow stun beam that glanced off one of those hairy asses and sent its owner howling down the road only to be blasted by another of Tisana's fireballs.

Drusilla had to admire the Nedwut tenacity; they obviously had no intention of giving up without a fight. Drusilla wasn't quitting either, and after a few near misses, she knocked one of them into a nerveless heap. Two others who appeared to be unarmed tried to reach the cover of the jungle but were headed off by Cat and Leo, leaving Manx face-to-face with Klarkunk.

"You Zetithian scum!" Klarkunk snarled as he aimed his weapon.

Klarkunk was quick on the draw, but Manx was faster. Drusilla screamed as Manx fired a round that glanced off

Klarkunk's shoulder, but was enough to deflect his aim, sending the Nedwut's shot streaking past Manx's head. Unfortunately, Klarkunk wasn't one to give up easily and spun back toward Manx, ready to fire.

Another pulse beam streaked across the road, hitting Klarkunk again, just as Lester's truck burst into the clearing and screeched to a halt right in the middle of the road.

The Baradan climbed out of the ancient vehicle and surveyed the situation, his hands displaying his distress. "This violence must stop!" he exclaimed.

"We will not be interfered with again, Baradan!" Klarkunk snarled, completely ignoring the wisp of smoke rising from his shoulder. "Go back to your village with your other cowardly natives. These Zetithians are ours for the taking."

"Ha!" Tisana called out from her position. "You three are all that are left. I'd say we had the advantage here."

"Yeah, and especially since we've already disarmed most of your gang," said Jack, indicating Cat and Leo, whose pulse rifles were trained on the Nedwut leader. "You may have one fancy rifle left, but you're outnumbered, and you know it."

To everyone's surprise, skinny little Lester walked right up to Klarkunk, who was obviously too stunned by this bold move to react.

"You must put down your weapons," Lester said firmly. "Now."

Drusilla watched in amazement as the Nedwut leader lowered his weapon. Lester wasn't even armed! How was he doing that? "Don't trust them, Lester!" she cautioned. "It's a trick!"

"No trick," Lester said, his hands swirling in a dance as he spoke. "They will do as I say."

Klarkunk gazed at the Baradan's hypnotic hands as his pulse rifle fell to the ground.

"Now," said Lester, motioning toward Manx, "if you will gather all of the weapons and put them in my truck, this will be over."

Manx did as Lester requested without argument, and though Cat handed over his rifle with an expression of marked regret, he didn't argue either.

The stunned Nedwuts were beginning to stir as the other four stragglers appeared around the bend. They made a vain attempt to flee into the trees, but Lester motioned for them to approach, and they did. "Please remain where you are and do not speak," Lester said once they were all assembled in a cluster. To Drusilla, this command seemed completely unnecessary because that was just exactly what they were doing anyway. She couldn't help but laugh at the sight of the band of snarling predators standing there like a litter of chastised puppies.

"So *this* is how you do it!" Jack marveled. "I couldn't figure it out. You're a cop?"

"Enforcer," Lester replied. "It is rare that my talents are required among our own people, but since we have begun inviting offworlders, it has become more necessary." He glanced around at the two opposing factions and shook his head. "Such violence is a waste of life and resources. Peace is better for all."

"Yeah, well, we've been *trying* to put an end to it," Jack said defensively. "But these slimeballs won't cooperate."

Lester favored her with a wide orange smile. "You have not reached the source," he said. "Only then will it end."

"Tell me about it," Jack grumbled.

"You seem pretty good at this mind-control thing," Manx observed. "Don't suppose you could get them to tell you who that is?"

Lester shook his head. "I can only control actions, not get them to divulge information."

"I knew there had to be a catch," Drusilla muttered. "Wish you could give them a good case of amnesia." Then something else occurred to her. "This talent of yours. It doesn't work with eltrans, does it?"

"Sadly, no," Lester replied. "All of our people can control the lesser creatures, but only a few of us have the ability to direct the more intelligent beings. None of us have any effect on eltrans, however, which may be why we get along so poorly."

"Welcome to the real world," Drusilla said with a dry chuckle. "They're the only ones you can't manipulate. That must drive you crazy."

"Yes, it does," Lester said, looking rather bleak.

"You might try being nicer to them," Manx suggested. "Zef has always been a good friend to me. I think he only picks on you because he knows you don't like him."

"Possibly." Lester regarded Manx for a moment before he spoke again. "Dwell explained your situation to me when he called for help. You should have made your presence known when you arrived here," he said. "Had we known of your need for sanctuary, we could have protected you."

Manx grinned. "Sorry I didn't trust you more, but when you've been running as long as I have, it's hard to trust anyone."

"So, Lester," said Jack, eyeing the Nedwuts with distaste. "What are you planning to do with these guys? Just let them go?"

"I believe it would be best," Lester replied. Turning to Klarkunk, he said firmly, "You must all leave this planet."

"Don't suppose you could slip in a 'and don't hunt Zetithians anymore' while you're at it, could you?" Manx suggested.

"It would be my pleasure," said Lester, "but I have little control over future actions."

"Mind if I try asking them a few questions?" Jack asked.

"I cannot guarantee they will reply," Lester said with his wide grin. "But you may attempt it."

"Klarkunk," Jack began, standing toe-to-toe with the Nedwut leader. "Mind telling me who the hell is paying you to do this?"

Drusilla had to admire Jack's courage, but she also had an idea that it was pointless.

"Someone with far more power than you," Klarkunk spat at her.

"I could have figured that much out for myself," Jack said. "But you just confirmed my suspicion that there's only one person at the root of this."

"It will do you no good," said Klarkunk.

"You might be surprised," said Jack. "You just take your hairy rat's ass back to wherever you came from and tell your 'boss' that I'll be looking for him."

"I have no 'boss,'" Klarkunk sneered.

"Sure sounds like it to me," Jack said with a shrug. "Somebody's pulling your strings, and that puts them in charge, not you." She looked Klarkunk right in his beady little eyes and poked him in the chest with her finger. "But I guess you'll be hunted down for a bounty if you rat on him, won't you?"

"You know nothing of this matter!"

"Be that as it may, the Zetithians will survive this vendetta if I have to kill every last Nedwut in the galaxy. I can promise you that."

"Those are only words," Klarkunk said. "You do not have the power to enforce them."

"Maybe not, but I've still got something you haven't got."

"And what is that?" he said contemptuously.

"Seven Zetithians," Jack replied. "All males worth five million credits apiece. And you'll never lay so much as a finger on any of them."

''And I've got four of them," Tisana put in.

"I've only got one," Drusilla declared. "But just give me time."

Manx, Cat, and Leo exchanged wry smiles. "You won't touch any of our women, either," said Cat.

Drusilla could see that the interrogation was going nowhere, and apparently Lester agreed. "You will leave now," he told the Nedwuts.

"As simple as that," Drusilla said, shaking her head as the Nedwuts began their retreat. "And to think, Lester was the last one we ever thought to ask for help. Amazing."

"No shit," said Jack.

"There's just one thing bothering me," Drusilla said. "That last shot at Klarkunk. Who fired it?"

Jack looked at Cat and Leo and then at Tisana. They all shrugged.

"Well, *someone* did," Drusilla insisted, "and it wasn't Manx." Turning to Lester, she asked, "Is there anyone else here with an illegal weapon?"

"Illegal? No," Lester replied. "The offworlder who was attacked was provided with a weapon, just as you were."

"You mean Tash'dree," Drusilla said, still not sure why. "Oh, I get it now! You didn't need to arm any of the natives against that cat because they could control it! Too bad none of you could catch it."

"To control such a creature, we must first find it," Lester said miserably. "It did not attempt to attack any of us."

"Probably figured you would taste bad," Jack put in helpfully.

Lester's smile was sickly at best. "Possibly."

"Tash'dree!" Drusilla called out. "Are you out there?"

When the woman suddenly appeared at the edge of the clearing, Jack's reaction was immediate and intense.

"Holy sheep shit!" Jack exclaimed. Ducking her head, she turned quickly away and pulled Cat along with her.

Cat's eyes widened. "She is one of—"

"Don't say a *word*," Jack said tersely, but kept her voice down.

"Jack!" Tisana scolded. "She just saved Manx's life! What's wrong with you?"

"I don't want to talk about it," Jack said, starting down the road toward the speeders with Cat in tow.

"Jack, come back here!" Tisana called. "You can't just—"

"I understand," Tash'dree said solemnly.

Manx just stood there staring at all of them like they'd lost their minds, but Drusilla rose to the occasion, saying graciously, "Thank you so much, Tash'dree! Without you, Manx might be dead now."

Tash'dree nodded in reply. "I am very pleased to be of service to him."

"The only other armed person on the entire planet, and you just happened to be in the right place at the right time," Tisana observed, her sharp green eyes narrowing in suspicion. "Mind telling us why?"

"Zef told me you followed Drusilla when she left the house," Manx said to Tash'dree. "I'm glad you did, but—"

"If you had been killed, I would have failed in my mission," Tash'dree said simply. "I could not let that happen."

"Your mission?" Drusilla echoed.

"Perhaps this is not the best time to discuss such matters," Tash'dree said with an eye toward Lester. Darting a pointed glance at Jack, who'd had to stop when Cat dug in his heels and flatly refused to move, she added, "I would like to meet with you at a later date—and with my sister, as well. She can explain it best."

"Your sister is better now?" Lester asked anxiously.

"She remains weak, but is recovering," Tash'dree replied. "I will return with her in a few days. You will be at the lake house?"

Drusilla nodded. "I'll be there for a few more weeks," she replied. "You and your sister will be welcome."

Tash'dree bowed her head briefly before handing her pistol to Lester, and then retreated into the jungle.

"Wonder what that was all about," Tisana mused.

Drusilla had no ideas, though she suspected that Jack knew a great deal more than she was willing to admit.

"Guess we'll find out in a few days," she said with a shrug. In the meantime, she had a suggestion that she hoped would meet with everyone's approval. "Hey, Lester," she began. "I'm sure these old friends would like to spend some time together. Is it okay if they all stay at the lake house for a while?"

Lester grinned. "If it will keep them out of trouble, they are welcome to stay for the remainder of your visit."

"Yeah, we'll chip in on the rent and no worries that we'll eat up all the food," Jack put in as she rejoined the group. "We've got our own."

Cat choked, but managed to turn it into a fairly believable cough.

Jack, however, wasn't fooled for a moment. "What's the matter with our food?" she demanded.

"It isn't quite the same quality as the supplies we brought for the lake house," Tisana said, obviously doing her best to sound diplomatic.

"Those are perfectly good Suerlin marching rations," Jack insisted. "They have the best food of any army in the galaxy."

Cat winced, but Leo took Lester aside for a moment, speaking quietly, after which Lester turned to Jack.

"There is plenty of food at the house," Lester said with a gentle wave of his hands. "We may not have Terran visitors again for some time, and it shouldn't go to waste."

"Yes, and Klog is a great cook," Drusilla chimed in. "He can even squirt whipped cream out of his finger!"

"That sounds great," said Jack. "But this gang will eat you out of house and home in no time. We should contribute *something*."

With a nudge from Leo, Lester's hands resumed their hypnotic dance. "You will eat the food in the stasis chamber at the house," Lester said to Jack. "While you are here, you will not eat any of the food aboard your ship, nor will any of the rest of your crew."

"But I *love* Suerlin food!" Jack protested.

"She is difficult," Cat murmured to Lester. "Your talents may not be enough to control her."

Lester's hands moved even faster.

"Quit trying to use your wavy little hands on my mind!" Jack growled. "We'll eat whatever Klog cooks."

Lester's hands stopped. "She *was* difficult," he said to Cat.

"You didn't make me change my mind!" Jack exclaimed. "I changed it all by myself."

Leo seemed to be trying to suppress a chuckle but wasn't completely successful. Jack rounded on him. "And since when are you so darn picky, Leo?"

"Let's just say I'm looking forward to a change," he replied.

Jack rolled her eyes. "Now, Manx, I can understand. He's probably been eating raw fish and birds for years, but you guys are well fed all the time."

"I wouldn't mind eating something different for a change, but, actually, I like raw fish," Manx said sheepishly.

"Then you're gonna love sushi!" Drusilla exclaimed. "I know this great little restaurant down by the spaceport back home—"

"So, I'm really going there with you?" Manx blurted out, obviously still not believing it was really going to happen.

Drusilla just stared at him in open-mouthed disbelief.

"I believe the correct response to that is 'Do bees be? Do bears bear?'" Cat murmured to Drusilla.

"What?" Drusilla said, startled out of her shock. "What in the world does that mean?"

"Ask Jacinth," Cat said. "She has a million of them."

Jack grinned. "I just love researching old figures of speech."

"And curse words," Cat added. "She knows a million of those too."

"You should talk to Zef," Manx told Jack. "He's something of a connoisseur himself."

"He sure is," Drusilla seconded. "Like I said before, you two have a lot in common. I think yours will be a visit he'll remember fondly for the rest of his life." Drusilla then took Manx's hand and kissed it firmly. "If you think I'm leaving you here just so you can catch fish for Zef, you can forget about it. You can teach Klog how to spearfish and then you're coming back to Earth with me if I have to tie you up and drag you."

"Got some chains if you want them," Jack said helpfully. "But I don't think you'll need them."

"No, she won't," Manx said, taking Drusilla in his arms. "Unless she tries to keep me away."

"Won't *ever* want to do that," Drusilla murmured, pulling him down for a kiss. "But if you ever run away like that again, I *will* tie you up."

Manx grinned. "I promise not to," he said, "but having you tie me up sounds… interesting."

"Won't be any need for him to run away," Jack said briskly. "Nedwuts can't land on Earth." She glanced meaningfully at Lester. "And we have guns—big ones—to make sure they don't."

Lester shook his head sadly. "Such a waste of resources! Think how much food could be grown for the hungry people of the galaxy if so much wasn't spent on implements of war."

"I hear you, Lester," Jack said. "But until you can control all the bad guys, the good guys will have to fight now and then. We don't all have your talents for keeping the peace."

"While you are here on this world, you will know peace," Lester said. "It was one reason we decided to open our world to others, to demonstrate that all can live in harmony."

"Yes, but you have the mind-control thing going for you," Drusilla pointed out. "Without that, you'd be just like any other world."

"True," said Lester. "But we are thankful that we are not. Such talents as mine are rarely needed among our own people." He smiled broadly, adding, "And, hopefully, not among our guests."

"We'll be good," Tisana assured Lester. "But thanks for the food, anyway. Jack will eat anything!"

"Picky, picky, *picky,*" said Jack.

Chapter 21

DINNER THAT EVENING WAS QUITE AN EVENT. KLOG WAS IN his element and put on a lavish feast that had everyone raving. Even Jack admitted that it had Suerlin marching rations beat all to hell and back. Drusilla and Manx felt as though they now had a large family, complete with good-natured bickering and fun.

Later that night, Drusilla went out on the deck to find Manx waiting for her. Cat, Jack, Leo, and Tisana were down by the lake. The sun had already set, sending deep purple shadows across the beach where the two couples lay in the shelter of each other's arms.

"How are they?" Manx asked, gesturing toward the house.

"Dwell is telling them stories, and Klog is fussing over them like a mother hen," she replied. "Together they make a good baby-sitting team." Sighing deeply, she added, "I don't think I've ever seen cuter kids in my life."

"Would you like some of your own?" Manx murmured, his voice suggestive, but at the same time, warm and sincere. Just the thought of having children with Drusilla was turning his heart to mush, and he pulled her into his arms, breathing in her scent and purring softly.

"Yes," she replied. "But only if they're yours."

Manx felt the stinging sensation in his eyes. "I never thought I'd get the chance to have any. This life I've led... I never dreamed it would turn out this way."

"Better get used to it," Drusilla warned. "I'm never letting you out of my sight again as long as I live."

Manx sighed, and his purring grew deeper in timbre. "I can live with that."

"Jack says she'll give me a pulse pistol of my very own once we leave here," Drusilla went on. "She says she shoots Nedwuts on sight. Hopefully, I won't have to, but—"

"We still don't know where the money for the bounty is coming from," Manx said. "Jack says we'll be safe on Earth or on Terra Minor, but it doesn't matter to me where we go, as long as we are together and our children can grow up safe and strong."

"That sounds so amazing," Drusilla whispered. "All this time, I've done nothing but paint, and having children seemed like something only other women do."

"Are you ready for that?"

"I think so," Drusilla replied. "If not, I'll have plenty of time to adjust to the idea. Kids don't pop up overnight, you know."

Manx grimaced and let out a deep breath. "Um, just in case you haven't figured it out, there will be three of them."

"I know," Drusilla said. "Every time?"

Manx nodded. "Nearly always in litters of three."

"That's pretty handy now that there are so few of you, but you guys must have had quite a population problem on Zetith."

"Not really," said Manx. "It usually only happens once, sometimes twice."

"Is that your fault, or the female's?"

Manx paused for a moment to sort out his reply. "I've never been sure," he said. "The women would tell you they were incapable of having more than one or two litters, but they were never as willing to have more as Terran females seem to be."

"You mean you only have sex once or twice?" Drusilla said, aghast.

Manx couldn't help but smile. "No, but multiple litters weren't commonplace," he said. "Though Jack and Cat seem to have overcome that obstacle."

"Having triplets is enough to make any woman not want to do it again, I suppose," Drusilla said reflectively. "Maybe they used a form of birth control you men didn't know about."

"Perhaps," Manx conceded. "But you may have as many as you want." Purring contentedly, he added, "I promise to do my part with enthusiasm." Glancing down toward the beach, which was now fully dark, he said wickedly, *"They* are."

"Right now?" Drusilla gasped. "How can you tell?"

"My senses are sharper than yours," Manx replied.

"Can see pretty well in the dark, huh?"

Manx nodded.

"What are they doing, exactly?"

Turning to look more closely, he said, "Tisana and Leo are swimming, but Jack and Cat are on the boat."

"Don't suppose any of them are wearing swimsuits, are they?"

"Uh, no, they aren't."

"You've been wearing clothes ever since you came back," Drusilla pointed out.

"Don't like that, do you?" Manx purred.

"Not really," Drusilla admitted.

"Think they're asleep yet?" Manx asked with a nod toward the door.

"I'd bet on it. Dwell was telling them some Baradan fairy tale in the most soporific voice I've ever heard. And if they need anything, Klog will know what to do. I'd *still* like to know how he does that."

"Part of his charm," Manx said. "Guess he'll come down and get one of us if we're needed."

"I'll tell Dwell," Drusilla said. "But not until we get downstairs. If I tell him now, I might wake one of them."

"Wouldn't want to do that," Manx agreed. "I'm looking forward to a moonlight swim."

"So I noticed," Drusilla said archly as her hand slid to his groin. "Your purring sounds different too."

"What would you like to do?"

"Swim and then make love on the beach," she replied. "Er, no, make love, and then swim. Or both, or either."

Manx put an end to her dilemma with a deep kiss. Closing her eyes, Drusilla melted into him as her arms drifted up to encircle his neck. As Manx swept her off her feet and headed for the stairs, he murmured, "We'll make it up as we go along."

Reaching the lower level, Drusilla gave instructions to Dwell while Manx snagged a towel from the shelf and then carried his mate down to the shore.

As he reached the water's edge, he made a quick decision—one that didn't require very much thought. "Make love now, swim later," he said, flinging the towel on the sand.

For the first time, Drusilla experienced the erotic pleasure of stripping the clothes from her lover's body, seeking his bare skin to kiss and caress. "I've missed you so," she said, a sob beginning to form in her throat. "Have you ever felt like all you were doing was breathing? That your life didn't matter anymore?"

Manx nodded. "Every moment I was away from you," he replied. "Leaving you was the hardest thing I've ever done in my life. I will never do it again."

Drusilla sighed blissfully. "I certainly hope not," she said. "I don't think I could take it. It was great for painting, but really hard on the rest of me." Lightly caressing his cheek, she added, "And I didn't like having to paint you from memory. A live model is so much more—" She broke off there, unable to come up with a word that described the way she felt about painting the real Manx.

Manx grinned. "Inspiring?"

"That and so much more," Drusilla replied as their lips met. As always, the fusion of their lips and tongues set fires burning within each of them—fires unquenchable by anything other than their union as lovers.

※

Meanwhile, back on the boat, Cat was on his hands and knees fucking his wife's hungry mouth while he savored her creamy slit. His cock felt good no matter where he put it in his Jacinth's body, but this was the best place to start. It drove her completely wild, and then when she was about to catch fire, he'd turn around and bury his cock in her. She liked it all, and so did he.

Cat's nuts were hanging right at eye level and Jack

was enjoying the view as much as the taste and feel of his hot, meaty dick. The way she saw it, the only disadvantage to this position was that she couldn't tell him how good it was. She'd tell him later, like she always did, but in the meantime, moaning was about all she could do. Then he began fucking her with his tongue and her moans got even louder.

Loud enough for Leo to hear them from where he was standing a little way up the shore in water up to his chest while he floated his bewitching wife up and down on his stiff cock. He tried to swirl his hard meat inside his wife's slick body, but the sight of Tisana laid back in the water with her arms outstretched, her hair floating in the water, and her lovely breasts reflecting the moonlight had Leo's penis so hard he was having trouble moving it. "I'm really stiff," he muttered.

"You think?" Tisana giggled.

"No, I mean *too* stiff," Leo explained. "I can't get it to move the way it should."

"Do you hear me complaining?"

Leo smiled. "You never do," he said. "But there's always a first time."

"Let's move up on the beach a little," Tisana suggested, suppressing another chuckle. "I want to be able to lie back and not get water in my ears."

Leo didn't hesitate to comply because he wanted to put a little more power behind what he was doing, anyway. Upon reaching the shore, he hooked his arms under Tisana's knees, lifted her up, and drove in hard, slamming into her while his nuts bounced against her ass. He wasn't sure he liked doing it underwater; the lake water had been washing away his lubrication, and he didn't want Tisana to get sore—aside from the fact that she wasn't having as many orgasms as she normally did.

Crying out in ecstasy as the full, undiluted effect of Leo's cock syrup overcame her, Tisana begged for more, and Leo was more than willing to fulfill her wishes.

"I want to keep going all night," he whispered. "I can never get enough of you, Tisana. Never." Wanting to see more of her, he raised upright on his knees, pulling her feet up to rest on his shoulders. Slowing down, he finally regained some control of his cock and let it play inside her the way she loved. Her smooth, creamy pussy wrapped around his shaft in a firm hug as it swirled and stimulated, adding fuel to the fire that the vision before him ignited. "I may not be able to go all night," he gasped. "I—" His nuts tightened and would have driven him in harder, but his back arched and he lost his balance in the sand, flipping his cock out of her core and spraying her with his snard.

"Sorry," he said, laughing as he got back to his knees. Then he looked down at Tisana with his cream splattered all over her and came again.

"Obviously you like what you're seeing," Tisana said. "Do I look that good covered in snard?"

Leo gulped in air to reply, but his cock had other ideas and went off again, this time shooting out an arc that landed on her face. He felt another climax begin to build and made an inarticulate plea for help.

"What?"

"Put your hands on me or suck me or something!" Leo begged when he had enough breath in him to speak.

Tisana took his throbbing cock in her hands and massaged it gently before pulling him toward her to take it in her mouth. He hadn't been kidding when he said it was stiff; the veins were standing out all over it and the head was a deep shade of purple. Tisana sucked hard, pulling the ruffled edge back toward the head, a technique that Leo enjoyed enormously. He came almost instantly, filling her mouth with more of his sweet cream.

Sighing with relief, Leo rolled onto his side and lay sprawled in the sand.

"Now *that* was weird," Tisana commented. "Any idea what caused it?"

"Unless this lake is enchanted, it has to be you," Leo replied.

"Might be the moon or the purple sky," Tisana suggested.

"The moon, perhaps," Leo muttered. He felt completely sated, exhausted, and barely had the energy to move. "Something about the way you look in the moonlight."

"I meant the *effect* from the moon," Tisana said firmly. "The gravitational pull or something. It isn't as if you've never seen me in the moonlight before."

"Different moon," Leo murmured. "*Very* different moon."

Tisana laughed lightly and put her arms around him. "I suppose it might be affecting my powers."

"That must be it," Leo sighed and snuggled closer to his beautiful witch. He wasn't about to tell her the real reason.

———

Manx felt as though he was drowning, and he didn't have so much as a toe in the lake.

"Mmm," he purred against Drusilla's lips. "I should never have left you. I should have stayed and fought those Nedwuts instead of running."

"Shh," Drusilla whispered. "At least there was some comfort in knowing you were safe. When Klarkunk aimed his rifle at you, I—well, I felt *murderous*. I've never felt like that before; like the whole world was about to be destroyed right in front of my eyes."

"Don't worry about that," Manx said. "Jack seems determined to get to the bottom of this and, together, maybe we can put an end to it."

"I hope so," Drusilla said with a shudder. "When I think about what could have happened, I can understand why she shoots Nedwuts on sight."

Manx smiled. "I'm glad we're on the same side," he said. "I certainly wouldn't want to be the one she goes gunning for."

"Me either," Drusilla giggled. "She is one tough cookie."

Manx sighed. "What's a cookie—no, wait, you can tell me that later. Right now I just want to eat you alive."

Drusilla giggled again. "That's what you do with cookies, actually."

"You eat them alive?"

"No, they're baked in the oven. Sweet, chewy, and delicious."

"Sounds good, but first, I think I'd like to feast on my delicious Drusilla."

"Mmm, that sounds good too."

Manx was purring softly as his lips began their slow exploration of her face and lips, his tongue delving into the soft recesses of her mouth, the taste of her sending clouds of desire swirling through his senses. His cock stiffened with anticipation as the slick syrup began to flow and he felt it bathing his shaft, readying him for the penetration to come. Kissing her neck, he pulled up her top and found her gleaming white breasts, the nipples hard and rosy in the moonlight. Nipping at one with his fangs while he teased the other with his fingertips soon had Drusilla writhing with the need for more.

Straddling her, he pulled down her shorts, leaving them tight around her knees before forcing his dripping cock between her legs, teasing her swollen clitoris with the serrated head, raking it over her wet vaginal lips as she struggled to take him in.

"Mmm, not yet," he purred. "I'm going to fuck your entire body first."

Drusilla moaned. "I needed you so badly when Tisana gave me that potion, but I want you even more now."

"Good," Manx purred. "Then you know how I feel when I taste you; like I can't wait another moment before I have you. But I'm going to wait. I want to get my cock wet with your essence and then spread it all over you so I can lick it off."

Drusilla gasped, and Manx felt moisture flood the apex of her thighs, coating his penis, just as he wished. Pushing himself up, his body stretched out above her, and his toes buried in the sand while his stiff shaft slid between her legs.

The expression of pleasure on Drusilla's face was all Manx needed to see. "That feels *so* good…"

"It certainly does," Manx agreed. "Soft, wet—" then groaning as Drusilla squeezed her legs together, "—tight. I could stay there all night, but I'm not going to."

Pulling out, he crawled up over her and rubbed his slick cock all over her face, neck, and torso, pausing to tease her nipples and paint her breasts with his orgasmic syrup as well as her own sweet honey.

He leaned down and licked her with long, lazy strokes at first, but her skin shining in the moonlight, her scent, the taste of her, the sweat where their skin fused—it was all driving him mad, filling him with the strongest need to mate he'd ever experienced. "I don't think that potion has worn off completely," he whispered. "There's something else here that's doing something to me. I've never been so hard before."

"Well, they say absence makes the heart grow fonder," Drusilla murmured. "But if it's Tisana's potion, I'm glad because otherwise you'd have no idea what torment it was for me to feel like that and not know if I'd ever see you again."

"Trust me, Drusilla, I smelled it on the wind, and I know *exactly* how you felt."

His tongue had traced a scorching path from her nipples to her navel and was heading straight for her clitoris when it happened again; the feeling that her desire for him was more than he could comprehend. Shaking his head to clear it, he plunged his tongue into her slit and licked it from top to bottom, teasing her with his tongue, gorging himself on her. He sucked hard on her clit, pulling on it until Drusilla's body careened into orgasm. He felt her hard nub thrusting against his tongue and her fingers in his hair, gripping his head to hold him against her. He teased her until the spasms ceased and she lay sprawled out before him, her chest rising and falling as the aftershocks of her climax shook her from head to toe.

"Roll over," he said, his throat so tight he could barely speak. "I want to see that gorgeous ass of yours."

Smiling seductively, Drusilla turned on her side, shifting her hips up as she turned.

Manx fought the urge to sink his fangs into her creamy skin and dipped his penis in between her legs to cover it with more of her nectar. "I might bite," he warned, gliding the slick head across her bottom.

"I don't care," Drusilla said, backing into him. "After all, I might want to bite you too."

Manx licked her slowly, but was soon growling in frustration. She tasted like the pure essence of desire, and his penis felt as if it was about to split apart. Finally, he couldn't take it anymore; it was either mate with her or go mad.

Pushing down on the small of her back, he nudged her legs apart with his knees and then sat back on his heels, his eyes drinking in the vision before him. Her creamy slit was swollen and wet, the syrupy fluid dripping onto his knees. His stiffly up-cocked penis was poised to take the plunge, and he gripped the shaft, spreading the lubrication from the head down to the base.

"Drusilla?" he said thickly. "I can't do it yet. I—I'll come too fast. Turn around and suck me."

"Mmm," she sighed dreamily. "Manx's dick. Never thought I'd get to suck it again. I should punish you for leaving me, you know."

Manx grinned. "I think I'm punishing myself right now. It's killing me to wait."

"Never heard anyone refer to getting their cock sucked as 'waiting' before," Drusilla chuckled. "Most guys would be happy with that."

"I am not 'most guys,'" he said with a loud purr.

"No kidding," she said as she sucked him in and moaned in delight.

"Taste good?"

"Indescribably delicious," she replied.

Manx watched her go down on him again and gasped as she pulled back on the ruffled edge with her teeth. "Ohhh, bite me," he purred. "Bite me and then suck my nuts."

As Drusilla sank her teeth into his hard meat just behind the head, Manx felt the coronal points gush their magic potion into her mouth. Her orgasm followed swiftly and he heard her cry out as her body jackknifed and she let go of him. He waited breathlessly while she recovered and then sighed as she licked his scrotum with her slippery tongue. When she exhaled sharply, he had one brief moment to realize what was about to occur before she sucked it all in.

Manx saw stars that had nothing to do with the deep purple sky above him. Drusilla's mouth felt hot and all he could think of was that he wanted her to— "Pull," he said, the word seeming to burst from his lips.

He felt the tug on his testicles and his back and neck arched, sending his hair tumbling down his back to tangle in Drusilla's fingers. Her hands were gripping his ass as she took up a slow rhythm, rocking him back and forth, letting his balls slip almost out of her mouth before sucking them back in.

"You're driving me crazy," Manx groaned, but wished he hadn't said a word when Drusilla let his nuts pop out of her mouth to fall heavily against his thighs.

"I believe that's the general idea," she said.

"Oh, don't stop," he pleaded.

"Maybe you'd like to do something else?"

The vision of Drusilla's exquisite posterior swam to the surface of his memory. "Turn around."

"With pleasure," Drusilla said as she turned and lay chest down with her bottom in the air. "How's this?"

Manx made a strangled sound deep in his throat.

"What was that?" Drusilla asked.

This time he couldn't help it. He bit her—not enough to draw blood, but enough to make her squeal with delight.

"Never thought that would ever feel good," she said, wiggling her hips at him. "Come on Manx, get that big, fancy cock inside where it belongs."

It took only a second to penetrate her wet heat, and Manx knew she was exactly right. This was, indeed, where he belonged. He held her softly rounded hips in his hands and pulled her up tightly against him. His balls swayed and swung beneath her, their occasional bounce maddeningly tantalizing and infinitely pleasurable.

Manx heard Drusilla's moans of ecstasy and thrust in harder and deeper, reveling in the sound of her soft flesh slapping against his groin. He wanted to go all night, and knew he should take it more slowly, but he couldn't help it; couldn't stop driving his dick into her for all he was worth.

His body tensed and his balls sent jets of snard pouring into Drusilla's body, smoothing the way as his meaty cock thrust inside, but Manx knew it wasn't enough. He was ejaculating, but at the same time felt the overwhelming desire to continue.

"I don't want to stop!" he gasped. "Is this the potion?"

"I don't know," Drusilla replied. "Surely it's worn off by now! I took it *hours* ago—I stopped feeling the effects about the time the Nedwuts showed up—but you can keep going as long as you need to." With a soft laugh, she added, "Believe me, I have no problem with that."

Rolling her over and plunging into her soft, warm body once more, Manx kept on with short, hard strokes until he came again. Her slick inner muscles felt tight on his cock as he stretched her to the limit and filled her with his creamy snard. Drusilla eyes grew misty as he gazed into them, and, watching the euphoria begin, he knew he'd never seen anything quite so exquisite before. He listened to her cries of ecstasy as she lost all control, but knew he still wasn't finished. Not yet.

Sweat was pouring down his chest and his muscles were beginning to ache in protest, but Manx had waited all the years of his life for this moment, and knew he would wait a million more if it meant being with Drusilla. She was his one, true, and lasting love, and though he might search the galaxy until the end of his days, he knew there would be no other. Then, like a bolt of lightning, his testicles tightened and spewed forth one last time.

Sated at last, Manx rolled onto his back and lay stretched out on the warm sand, breathing heavily as he gazed up at the starry sky. Drusilla turned, pillowing her head on his chest, her arm flung across him, wrapping around his waist in a gesture of possession. He knew he belonged to her now, body and soul, and he wasn't the least bit sorry about it.

"Do me a favor," he said at last.

"Sure, anything," she replied.

"Don't take any more of Tisana's potion—"

Her head flew up in surprise. "Ever again?" she inter-jected. "You mean you didn't *like* that?"

"Until tomorrow." Manx tried to raise his arm to caress Drusilla's back and discovered he couldn't do it. "Well, no," he went on. "Tomorrow it would probably kill me. Better wait at least a week."

"I don't know," Drusilla said doubtfully. "Don't think I can go a week without—"

"I didn't mean that," he said hastily. "I mean the potion."

"Oh, good. I was afraid you meant I'd have to go a whole week without you. I think—no, I'm *sure*—I couldn't do *that*."

"Well, if I have anything to do with it, you'll never have to try."

Drusilla shook her head, still puzzled. "I know Tisana said that potion would only last three or four hours. It's been a lot longer than that."

Manx sighed. "Guess I just missed you."

"I missed you too." Drusilla said. "And I never want to have to miss you like that again as long as I live."

"Me either," he agreed. Drusilla's arm tightened posses-sively around him and Manx felt completely content. Perhaps it *hadn't* been the potion; perhaps it was just from being sepa-rated from Drusilla for so long. He'd left other women, and he'd missed them, but somehow he knew this was different. *Drusilla* was different. He was mated to her now—and probably had been from the very beginning—for life.

"Do you forgive me for leaving you?" he asked. "I know I promised I wouldn't, but—"

Drusilla's fingers touched his lips to silence him. "I understand why you did it," she said. "And, yes, I forgive you. I'd have forgiven you even if you never came back, because even if I never saw you again, I'd still love you."

Manx felt her forgiveness wash over him like a wave. "The whole time I was gone I kept trying to figure out a way to get to Earth and find you. I love you so much, Drusilla. I never want to be parted from you again." He paused for a moment, considering. "Do you have any—I mean, on Zetith, when we mated, it was for life—but other cultures have a ceremony to bond couples together. Do you have something like that on Earth?"

Drusilla nodded. "We call it a wedding," she replied. "The man asks the woman to marry him, and if she says yes, then they get married. You can have a big wedding or a small one. Everyone does it a little bit differently."

"Is there any special way the man is supposed to ask the woman?"

"No, there again, it's a matter of personal preference," she said. "No rules."

Manx looked at the sky, hoping to discover something there to help him find the right words. "Do you see all those stars up there?"

"Mmhm. Beautiful, aren't they?"

"Yes, they are, and if every last one of them belonged to me, I'd give them all up for you." Turning to face her, he gazed into her shining eyes. "But I don't have anything. Would you marry a man who has nothing?"

"No," Drusilla replied. "But I *will* marry *you*."

Chapter 22

FOR ONCE IN HIS LIFE, ZEF HAD HAD THE SENSE TO REMAIN silent, and it had given him a front row seat to something he'd never witnessed before. Not sex, necessarily, and not fun and games, but tenderness and love. If he'd had tear ducts, he would have been sobbing. No, he wasn't about to plead with Manx to stay behind; he and Drusilla belonged together, and Barada Seven was home to neither of them. He would miss them both terribly, but he would say good-bye without making a fuss.

Still, given the eltran need for conversation, he knew his life would probably be shortened when they left. Manx had been a good friend to him—the kind of friend he knew would be nearly impossible to replace. He tried to remember who among the other lake dwellers would be getting voted out soon, but he couldn't come up with one. He had been the eldest of all and any that might come to this lake would probably come too late.

Drusilla also knew this would be a problem for Zef, as did Manx, but though she spent as much time by the lake painting as she could, aside from urging him to go back to his old lake, she didn't see that there was much she could do.

"Wouldn't want to go back there even if they let me," the old eltran said firmly. "They weren't very nice to me."

"Not everyone around here has been nice to you either," she pointed out.

"You mean Lester," Zef said. "He doesn't come around that often. Hell, I'd be nicer to him if he didn't treat me like shit. Baradans just don't like eltrans, but, so far, the visitors to the lake house have been from other planets, and I've gotten along with them—well, most of them, anyway."

Tisana was sunbathing nearby. "I still don't see why they'd throw you out of your old lake, anyway," she put in. "I mean, just because you can't mate anymore doesn't make you useless, does it?"

"If you were a guy, you wouldn't be asking that question," Zef said with conviction. "Nothing is more important to a male than having a dick that works. Without it, you just don't feel right."

Tisana and Drusilla exchanged a quick glance, followed by a mutual shrug.

"But I'm okay with that now," Zef went on, "because if my dick still worked, I wouldn't have met any of you. I wouldn't have met Manx—or Jack—and I wouldn't have missed that for anything."

Drusilla and Tisana both looked at him questioningly, but it was Drusilla who spoke. "I can understand why you like Manx, but what makes Jack so special?"

"Expanded my vocabulary!" Zef said proudly. "Thanks to her, I now know over a hundred words for dung and nearly two hundred for semen, not to mention all the words for cock!" Cackling with glee, he added, "Bicho, peter, pinga, hot rod, peenie-bop, love stick, John Thomas, hot tamale, yummydoodle, sword of love... there must be a thousand or more!"

With that parting shot, Zef waved a ragged fin at them before submerging.

"Guess everyone needs a hobby," Drusilla commented.

"And I thought Norludians were strange," Tisana said absently, still gazing at the wake Zef left behind.

"Norludians?" Drusilla said curiously. "Never met any."

"You don't want to," said Tisana. "Trust me on that one."

Jack had heard of the upcoming marriage of Manx and Drusilla and was at her wit's end trying to decide what planet to have it on. She and Cat had gone back to the ship to contact the other known Zetithians, and though all of them were anxious to attend the ceremony, there were problems.

She'd been poring over the charts at the ship's navigation station for some time, but wasn't having any luck. "It can't be here," Jack told Cat firmly, pointing out their position on the star chart. "It's too remote, and Trag can't come if it's on Earth, because he didn't have sense enough to get a job piloting a ship for someone other than an arms dealer."

"But you like Lerotan," Cat reminded her.

"Just because I like him doesn't mean the landing authorities on Earth will have anything to do with him," she declared. "Terra Minor is out too, because they can't land there either."

"There must be some neutral planet," Cat began, leaning over the console to study the chart. "Somewhere in between, perhaps…"

"Ha! Not one that's safe for Zetithians. Word would get out that you were all in one spot and the damned Nedwuts would start swarming like bees to honey."

"Jacinth," Cat said gently. "Are you forgetting that this will be *their* wedding?"

Jack frowned at him. "Are you saying I should mind my own damn business?"

"Perhaps," he replied.

"You always say that," she grumbled.

"Speaking of minding your own business," he began. "There's something I've been wondering about."

Jack knew that tone of voice and was instantly on her guard. "Uh-oh, you're using contractions, Kittycat," she muttered. "Bad sign. But what do you mean?"

"You know very well what I mean," he said with an ominous glint in his eyes. "That woman, Tash'dree. She is from Statzeel."

"Your point?"

"Why would you not wish to speak with her? Your sister is living on Statzeel; she may have news of her."

"I don't think that's why she's here," Jack said evasively. Just because this discussion was inevitable didn't make it any easier. Jack hesitated a long moment before letting out a deep sigh. "If I'm right—and I'm pretty sure I am—she and her sister are here to find Manx, but not for the same reason we were."

"Go on," Cat said, his eyes beginning to glow.

"Actually, I think she'd settle for Leo," Jack mused. "If she could get him, that is."

"You believe she is looking for a Zetithian mate?"

"Not exactly," Jack said, shaking her head. "Do you remember me telling you once that I knew some women who traded semen like other women traded recipes?"

Cat replied with a nod.

"And you didn't seem to mind, so—"

"You gave some to them?"

"Uh-huh," Jack said, nodding grimly. "On Statzeel. I think Tash'dree's people must've gotten hold of it, and unless I miss my guess, they want more."

"A different bloodline?" Cat suggested.

"Yeah," Jack replied, running a nervous hand through her short locks. "Which is why they'll want it from Leo or Manx, and I'm not sure the guys will like the idea— and Drusilla and Tisana probably won't either. In fact," she went on blithely, "I'm not sure you would—now that you know about it, I mean."

Folding his arms over his chest, Cat leaned back against the console, facing his wife. "And did you think I would not guess about the Statzeelian efforts to breed the belligerence out of their males when you mentioned this 'semen trading' to me?"

"Well, no, I didn't," Jack admitted.

"Jacinth," he chided gently. "Even *their* males knew of the scheme."

Jack was incredulous. "And they went along with it?"

"They went along with more than you might think," he said with a sardonic smile. "They are not quite as stupid as they seem."

"Yes, but—"

"They see it as a necessity for their continued survival, just as I see the necessity for there to be other women to bear my children—a necessity which I believe Leo and Manx will see as well." He paused as his expression became earnest. "There are only six of us left, Jacinth. If the Zetithian species is to survive, we must sire many children. Knowing that, I was more than willing to let you give them my seed."

"But you have children you may never see," Jack protested. "Doesn't that make you mad?"

"No," Cat replied. "I see it as a privilege."

Jack sat down heavily in the navigator's seat. "Well, I'll be damned! I never thought—"

"Jacinth," Cat said, coming closer to stroke her hair, "you never *asked*."

In the meantime, Drusilla was having her own problems. She called Ralph, only to have him beg for more paintings.

"You *have* been painting, haven't you?" he said, giving her that look he always used when he was trying to be intimidating. It seldom failed to make Drusilla hide a smile because it never worked; he only appeared to be crossing his eyes.

"Well, yes," she admitted. "Some, but I've been sort of busy since I sent you those last ones."

"But my dear, they've all been sold! We didn't even have a chance to have you here for a gallery event," he lamented. "They simply flew out of here as though they had wings!"

If she knew anything about Ralph, she had to assume that they had been some very expensive wings. "I'll bring some more back, I promise," Drusilla said. "It's just that the past week or so has been… eventful."

"If it has anything to do with that ravishing creature you've been painting portraits of, I can see why you'd be busy," Ralph said with a titter. "You wouldn't tell me before, but who *is* he, and where in the galactic haze did you find him?"

"Right here on Barada Seven," Drusilla replied. "Waiting for me in the jungle."

"How romantic!" Ralph sighed. "But wait, didn't you say he was gone?"

"He came back," she said simply.

"Oh, then there *is* a romance, isn't there?"

"You could say that," Drusilla said. "We're getting married."

"Oh, my dear! Congratulations! I'm so happy for you!" He paused for a moment before adding accusingly, "You *are* coming back home for the wedding, aren't you?"

Drusilla had known that as soon as Ralph heard about the upcoming marriage, he'd want to be in on the planning—and would probably take over the entire event. "Well, it's been hard to decide. There are extenuating circumstances."

"You're pregnant?"

"Well, no, but there are some people who want to come to the wedding who can't land on Earth—or any of its colonies, either."

"Hmm, now, that's a problem," Ralph agreed, tapping his elegant chin. "I could do some checking..."

"Not that I care one way or the other, myself," Drusilla went on. "We'll be coming back to Earth to live, anyway, but—"

"Tell me again just *why* Earth is out?"

"Well, one of the guys is a pilot for some gun runners, and he can't come to Earth. There's another one who lives—well, is *based* on Darconia, but—"

"Darconia?" Ralph said scathingly. *"Darconia!* Why, that's positively dreadful! It's so... remote!"

"Hey, at least you've heard of it," Drusilla muttered,

"which is more than I can say for myself. Anyway, there's another family on Terra Minor, but they have a farm and animals and such and really can't leave—not for long, anyway."

"And just who are these people?" Ralph demanded. "And why do they have so much say in the matter?"

"It's not so much that they have a say," Drusilla replied. "It's more that they're the closest thing to family that Manx has, and—"

"His name is *Manx?*" Ralph exclaimed. "Oh, my heavens, how positively fabulous! Masculine, feline, exotic, and—"

"That'll do, Ralph," Drusilla said. "And yes, he's all of those things, but—"

"Oh, *please* tell me you aren't changing your name— are you?" Ralph said suddenly. "I mean, just *think* of all those paintings you've signed and—"

"His last name is Panteris," Drusilla said. "Manxarkodrath Panteris."

"Hmm… Manxarkodrath Panteris. Drusilla Panteris," Ralph said, letting the names roll off his tongue. "D'you know, I do believe it's better than Chevrault," he remarked. "Has a nice ring to it."

"I'm *so* glad you approve."

"I've never seen the way you write your P's, though," Ralph went on, oblivious to her sarcasm. "We may have to work on that. Your C's are so elegant."

"I'm sure I can do an elegant P, Ralph. If not, I'm sure you can coach me."

Ralph's expression suddenly changed from thoughtful to horrified. "Your dress!" he exclaimed. "You haven't chosen one yet, have you?"

Drusilla burst out laughing. "Ralph, he just asked me a few days ago, and you know there are no dress shops on Barada. The men only wear shorts and the females wear shorts with a little scarf thingy around their upper body."

"That's *all?*"

"All I've seen so far," Drusilla replied. "Not a wedding dress on the whole damn planet."

"Oh, thank God!" exclaimed Ralph with a shudder. "I know how you tend to dress, and I just—"

"Ralph," Drusilla said ominously. "I will pick out my own dress or I will get married in the nude."

"What?" Ralph said, clearly taken aback by Drusilla's direct assault. "But you can't possibly—"

"Ralph," Drusilla said firmly. "Here on Barada Seven, they loaned me a pulse pistol to defend myself and before it was all over, I shot at least one Nedwut bounty hunter—though there may have been more. I'm not really sure if I hit that last one or not."

Ralph's lips formed a soundless *"Oh."*

"And Jack is going to give me a pistol of my own so I can protect Manx."

"He needs protection?"

"Ever seen a man like him before?"

"Well, no, not in person, but that rock singer, Tycharian—you know, the front man for Princes & Slaves?—looks a bit like him." His expression changed as the light dawned. "Oh, yes, I see! He's the one from Darconia!"

"They're the same species," Drusilla said with a nod. "Nearly exterminated by Nedwuts and some other nasty folks. I have to be ready for them."

"Your point?"

"If I can do that much, I can surely pick out my own wedding dress."

"But what does shooting Nedwuts have to do with choosing the right clothes?"

"Absolutely nothing," she replied, "but it does give me the right to tell you to"—Drusilla paused and took a deep breath—"mind your own damn business."

Ralph blinked. "I never *dreamed...*"

"And Ralph," she began.

"Yes, my dear?" he said meekly.

"I want to see the receipts for those paintings that 'flew' out of the gallery."

"Of course, but—"

"*And* I want to know just exactly how much commission you took on them. We may need to renegotiate our arrangement. I'll have a family to consider pretty soon, not just myself. I have to be more careful."

Ralph couldn't have appeared more affronted if Drusilla had slapped him. "Are you suggesting that I've *cheated* you?"

"No, I just want to make sure no one ever does."

"B—but, Drusilla!" Ralph protested. "This is so unlike you!"

Drusilla grinned. "How do you like the new me?"

"I hardly know," Ralph said faintly.

"You'll get used to it—eventually." Still smiling, Drusilla leaned forward to terminate the link. "See ya later, Ralph."

———

In the end, it wasn't Ralph or Jack or even Drusilla who came up with the best location for the wedding. It was Larry.

Having listened to all the discussion and the large number of planets put forth and rejected as possible sites, he came up with an idea of his own. "Hey, Mom?" he began. "Nedwut ships are turned back when they reach Pluto's orbit, right?"

"Yes," said Jack.

"But Uncle Trag just isn't allowed to land on Earth?"

"That's right."

"If we had him on our ship, he could get inside the Terran solar system, couldn't he?"

"Yes, but what's your point?"

"We could have the wedding on the ship!" Larry announced. "People from Earth could still come, we could pick up Uncle Lynx and Aunt Bonnie on Terra Minor—"

"Or Tychar could pick them up," Jack mused, getting into the spirit. "That rock band of his has a monster of a ship. Have to, considering that some of them are Darconians. You know, it just might work. We could dock the ships together, decorate the cargo hold, and—brilliant idea, kiddo!"

"And Mom," said Larry. "Remember, you're the captain."

"So?"

"On your ship, you could perform the marriage."

"I hadn't thought of that." Jack paused for a moment, her eyes narrowing as though she was thinking hard. "Do me a favor, Larry. Run and tell Drusilla and Manx your plan. See what they think."

Larry scampered off in search of the happy couple, leaving his parents alone with the babies.

Jack looked up to find Cat staring at her in disbelief. "What are you looking at?" she demanded.

"You," Cat replied. "At least, I *believe* it is you."

"What the devil are you talking about? Of course it's me!"

"You are letting *Larry* tell them? Not taking it upon yourself?"

"It was his idea," she said with a nonchalant shrug. "I just thought he should be the one to tell them about it."

Cat wasn't fooled for a moment. "You know very well they would consider it more favorably with Larry telling them than they would if you suggested it."

Jack grinned. "Strategy, my dear Cat. Strategy."

Cat smiled back at her. Sometimes they were obscure, but her methods usually worked to her advantage in the end. That was something else he liked about her; her indomitable spirit. If one of her ploys didn't work, she'd simply try another.

Drusilla liked the idea, mainly because it wouldn't give Ralph the opportunity to interfere—not much, anyway—but Manx didn't care one way or the other.

"You really don't care?" she asked him after Larry left.

"No," Manx replied, shaking his head. "In my heart it's already done. The ceremony is for the others."

Drusilla gazed at him, her eyes misty with emotion. It never ceased to amaze her that his simplest words could affect her so profoundly. "You know what?" she said slowly. "I don't think I care either. Ralph can come aboard with his gang of decorators and do whatever he wants." Pausing for a moment, she closed her eyes and envisioned the cargo hold looking like a palace and herself in a gauzy, sequined— "But no way am I letting him pick out my dress."

Manx laughed, but Drusilla noted the light of specu-
lation in his eyes.

"And you can't do it either," she said. "It's bad luck
for you to see it before the wedding."

"Well, we certainly don't want that," he said, pulling
her into his arms. "What about kissing the bride before
the wedding?"

"Not bad luck," she replied.

"Making love?"

"Used to be something of a taboo," she admitted, "but
not unlucky."

"I'm so relieved," he purred, taking the opportunity
to lick her ear.

Drusilla felt a thrill scatter down her spine, beginning right where Manx's tongue was touching her. "You
know something?"

"What?"

"I think you've already had your full quota of bad
luck for one lifetime."

"You think my luck has been bad? I disagree. I think
I've had the best luck of any man in existence."

"Manx," Drusilla said darkly. "Your entire planet
was destroyed, your friends sold as slaves, and you've
been on the run from Nedwuts for half your life."

"But I survived," Manx reminded her. "And I'm about
to marry the most lovely, kind, adorable, wonderful,
loving, sexy, and talented woman in the galaxy. I'd say
my luck was pretty damn good."

Drusilla smiled as she threaded her fingers through
his long, silky hair and used it to pull him even closer.
"That's my line."

"You think so?"

"I know so." Gazing into his luminous green eyes, she whispered, "I love you."

Manx shook his head. "That's *my* line," he said and then he kissed her deeply, longingly, lovingly to prove it. "I think I've loved you from the first moment I saw you, arguing with Lester about carrying that huge bag."

"You saw me then?" she said. "Really?"

"Oh, yes," he replied. "I saw a lot of you before you ever saw me, and if I'd had any idea what would happen, I'd have come running out to meet you right then."

Drusilla smiled, trying to imagine her reaction to Manx running toward her in all his naked, masculine glory. "I probably would have had a screaming orgasm if you had," she said.

"Really?"

"Really, really."

It was with a great deal of trepidation that Jack sat in the corner of the living room when the two Statzeelian sisters arrived. Having dealt with their kind before, Jack wasn't surprised when they wasted no time getting to the point.

"My sister and I are members of a special breed on our world," Lutira said. "One that required many generations of selective breeding to produce. The other Statzeelians have also begun to take control of their bloodlines, but it is a very slow process. Not long ago, we discovered—quite by accident—that the introduction of Zetithian genes was very beneficial in helping us to reach our mutual goals."

Tisana shifted uncomfortably in her chair but remained silent. Jack was muttering under her breath and Drusilla could have sworn she was praying. The three men stood behind their women, but only Cat appeared relaxed.

Lutira continued. "We will not say where or how we know this, but—"

"Go ahead and say it," Jack said irritably. "He already knows."

"And we thank him for his generous contribution," Lutira said, bowing her head in Cat's direction. "However, the one bloodline may not be enough. To truly succeed, we require others, and humbly request your help in this matter."

"Let me get this straight," Drusilla said. "You want to take Manx and Leo back to Statzeel?"

"No, that will not be necessary," Tash'dree said quickly. "We only require a quantity of semen, which will be carefully distributed." Smiling at Drusilla, she said, "We had planned to bring Manx back with us, if he was willing, but we will not take him from the one he loves."

"Uh, could I say something here?" Jack said, putting up a hand.

"Certainly," said Lutira.

"Tisana and Leo already know the story," Jack began, "but Drusilla and Manx don't. Perhaps you should tell them."

"I will," said Lutira. "Statzeel was once a war-torn planet—nearly destroyed by the belligerence of our males. We sisters began an effort to breed that trait out of the population, and though we succeeded in producing a superior strain of females, the male line was a failure. Then it was discovered that if women chained themselves to their men, they could calm them by sexual means in almost any situation. This gave us more time and helped us to survive, but though our entire culture began to evolve around this practice, keeping our males chained forever was never our intention. The breeding program continues, but, as I said, it is very slow. The addition of Zetithian and human genes has helped enormously."

Turning to Cat, she went on, "Your genes appear to be dominant over most others and the children we are producing are essentially pure Zetithians. In addition to that, for our own purposes and to help save your species from extinction, we would like to collect semen from each of the other surviving Zetithian males. We have also followed your suggestion," she said with a nod toward Jack, "and have acquired a diverse selection of human sperm."

"You're going to wipe out your own species," Tisana pointed out. "Instead of Zetithians becoming extinct, Statzeelians will disappear."

"The humans are not dominant," Lutira said, "and we will only add their genes with this one generation. The Zetithian bloodlines will also be added only one time, and we will distribute them evenly among the population. We will see to it that all of those children will be male, but what happens after that will be left to chance. If the Zetithian genes overcome our own, it will occur naturally, but whatever transpires, we will then be able to set our males free and still have peace among us."

Drusilla saw the flaw in the plan and snickered audibly. "Human males are a lot better than they used to be, but if you think they'll all be good boys, think again."

"I told them that too," Jack said. "They seemed to think anything would be an improvement—and, I must admit, there are an awful lot of assholes on that planet."

"Still, if nothing else, it would provide a safe haven

for at least some of our offspring," Leo said. "What do you think, Tisana?"

"I don't mind the idea in *theory,*" she said carefully. "But just how are you planning to collect—"

Tash'dree grinned. "That will be *your* job," she said. "We will not participate in that part of the plan."

"Sounds like fun," Drusilla said with a giggle. "What do you think, Manx?"

Manx hesitated, as though carefully considering his reply. "I owe you my life," he said with a nod toward Tash'dree, "and as long as our children will be treated well—and Drusilla doesn't mind…"

"Cat's children are already precious to us," Lutira said. "As any others will be."

"Well, it sounds like you two need to come to the wedding then," Drusilla said roundly. "All the other Zetithians will be there."

"Just don't tell any Nedwuts what we're planning," Jack said nervously. "We certainly don't need them crashing the party!"

Lutira smiled. "Telling the Nedwuts is the very last thing I would ever do."

"You might warn your men, though," Cat said with a mischievous grin. "You would not be doing anything they did not already know about, but—"

Lutira looked up at him in astonishment. "Our males know nothing of our breeding program!"

"You might be surprised at what they have figured out," Cat said with a knowing smile. "Females are not the only ones who can keep a secret."

"You might as well tell them the truth, Lutira," Jack said. "They always find out anyway."

The ship was ready, Drusilla's paintings were neatly packed, but there was one last thing Manx had to do before he left Barada—possibly forever.

"It's like this, Klog," Manx said to the hovering droid. "You hold very still and when you see the fish, you throw the spear."

Klog's spear was a long spit, normally used to skewer items to be grilled, but even Manx thought it looked far more effective than his own hand-carved version. Drusilla and Zef waited nearby, watching the show.

Manx held very still, barely even breathing while he waited. As a fish swam into his range, he took careful aim and drove the spear into the water. "See? Nothing to it," he said as he held up the spear, displaying a wriggling fish impaled on the point. After tossing the fish to Zef, he motioned to Klog. "Now you try it."

Klog beeped once and hovered briefly over the shallows before moving out over deeper water.

"You're out too far," Manx cautioned. "You might not be able to—"

Klog launched his skewer which darted through the water without even making a splash.

"—see any fish," Manx finished as Klog pulled his spear from the lake.

Klog glided back over to Manx, held out the skewer, and beeped twice.

"Four fish with one throw!" Zef chortled. "Never did that well, did you, Manx?"

Manx scowled at Zef and then at Klog. "You've been holding out on me," he said darkly. "Mind telling me why, when you always seem to know what everyone wants, whether they ask for it or not, you've never caught any fish before?"

Klog responded with a buzz.

"Ah, Klog," said Zef, who had already eaten the fish Manx had speared, "over here. Yes, that's it. Well done," he said as Klog slid all four fish off the skewer and into Zef's open mouth. Crunching happily, Zef did a barrel roll in the water, displaying his well-rounded midsection as Klog floated off toward the house. "Come back and fish often!" Zef called after him. "At least twice a day."

Klog beeped once but didn't stop.

"He's a great fisherman," Zef observed, "but not much of a talker."

"You'll get fat with him feeding you," Manx warned.

"Not a problem," Zef said cheerfully. "I won't live forever and, the way I see it, I might as well die happy." Looking up at Manx, he said, "You've been a good friend to me, Manx. I've been happier here than I've ever been, thanks to you and Drusilla. Now it's your turn to go and find your own happiness."

Manx grinned and took Drusilla's hand. "Thank you, Zef," he said. "We'll do that."

"And you be sure to have lots of children," Zef went on. "Maybe come back and see me sometime. I know it's not likely, but you never know, do you?"

"No, you don't," Manx agreed. "I never thought things would turn out this way for me either. It must have been fate or something."

"Sure it was," said Zef, nodding in mock agreement, "that and your big, fancy weasel."

Manx burst out laughing. "I'm gonna miss you, Zef."

"Not half as much as I'll miss you," Zef said. "But go on, get out of here. You've got a long trip ahead of you."

They were interrupted just then by movement in the underbrush on the far side of the lake. Staring wide-eyed, they watched as a dried-out, nearly exhausted eltran crawled out of the jungle.

"Zef!" the eltran gasped as he reached the shore. "Thank God I've found you!"

"Tu'gret!" Zef shouted in greeting. "What the hell happened?"

"Got run out of the lake," the tired eltran said as he sank blissfully into the water.

"I can see that for myself!" Zef exclaimed. "What I want to know is why?"

Tu'gret snorted and shook his head. "Opened my big mouth once too often," he replied. "I'm just glad I got to you before they did, or you'd be running me off too."

"I wouldn't run you off if you were—well—" Zef paused for a moment's reflection before adding, "I wouldn't run you off for any reason at all, come to think of it."

"I hope you mean that," Tu'gret said, rolling over onto his back. Sighing happily, he said, "This is a damn fine lake you've got here."

"Ha! Don't I know it," Zef agreed. "A helluva lot better than the old one." Zef looked at his old friend curiously. "Well, let's hear it," he said gruffly. "Don't tell me you got kicked out for the same reason I was!"

"Not exactly," Tu'gret replied. "You remember Lorilei?"

"Hmph!" Zef snorted. "How could I forget her? She's the one who got pissed because I couldn't fuck her."

"Yeah, well, at least you weren't stupid enough to turn

her down," Tu'gret said ruefully. "She told everyone I only liked men after that."

"But I thought there was no such thing as a homosexual eltran," Drusilla put in.

"There isn't," Tu'gret said shortly, "but don't ever tell a female eltran—especially one like Lorilei—that she makes you wish there were *and* that you were one of them."

Drusilla clapped her hand over her mouth trying not to laugh, but she couldn't stop her giggles. Manx turned away, his shoulders shaking uncontrollably.

"It's not funny!" Tu'gret said sharply.

"Oh, yes it is," said Zef. "But who cares? C'mere, buddy! I've never been so glad to see anyone in my life!" Patting Tu'gret on the head with a ragged fin, he added, "You'll love this lake! You can swim all day, there are no women to please, you can harass the tourists, and best of all, Klog will catch fish for you! It's a fuckin' eltran paradise!"

"Well, it looks like you're in good shape now," Manx said, regaining his composure. "Thanks, Zef—for everything. Without you, I might never have had the nerve to come out of hiding and talk to Drusilla."

"And I wouldn't have found the man I'd been waiting for all my life," Drusilla said warmly.

"That's what friends are for," Zef said gruffly. "And thanks to you, I've got everything I need to live out my days in style—and with Tu'gret here, I won't be lonely. You two go on and have yourselves a good life together."

"We will," Manx promised.

～～～

And they did.

Acknowledgments

I'd like to thank Wickedly Romantic blog commenter Justine for suggesting the name Drusilla.

I'd also like to thank my son, Mike, for coming up with the name Zefa'gu and for suggesting Kang, Kor, and Kolath of *Star Trek* for the names of Cat and Jack's babies.

The ladies who follow my blog (cherylbrookserotic. blogspot.com) were also instrumental in the writing of this book, providing me with tons of support and encouragement as well as suggesting the names for the Baradan women and numerous synonyms for "weasel." It was a tough job, but *somebody* had to do it...

About the Author

Cheryl Brooks has been a critical care nurse since 1977, graduating from the Kentucky Baptist Hospital School of Nursing in 1976, and earning a BSN from Indiana University in 1986. Cheryl is an avid reader of romance novels and has been a fan of science fiction ever since watching that first episode of *Star Trek*. Always in need of a creative outlet, she has written numerous novels, with *The Cat Star Chronicles: Fugitive* being her fifth published work. She lives on a farm near Bloomfield, Indiana, with her husband, two sons, four horses, and six cats. You can visit her website at: http://cherylbrooksonline.com/, or email her at: cheryl.brooks52@yahoo.com.

**Escape to the world of
the Cat Star Chronicles,
by Cheryl Brooks**

SLAVE
WARRIOR
ROGUE
OUTCAST

Read on for a sneak peek...

From

SLAVE

I FOUND HIM IN THE SLAVE MARKET ON ORPHESEUS PRIME, AND even on such a godforsaken planet as that one, their treatment of him seemed extreme. But then again, perhaps he was an extreme subject, and the fact that there was a slave market at all was evidence of a rather backward society. Slave markets were becoming extremely rare throughout the galaxy—the legal ones, anyway.

I hitched my pack higher on my shoulder and adjusted my respirator, though even with the benefit of ultrafiltration, the place still stank to high heaven. How a planet as eternally hot and dry as this one could have ever had anything on it that could possibly rot and get into the air to cause such a stench was beyond me. Most dry climates don't support a lot of decay or fermentation, but Orpheseus was different from any desert planet I'd ever had the misfortune to visit. It smelled as though at some point all of the vegetation and animal life forms had died at once and the odor of their decay had become permanently embedded in the atmosphere.

Shuddering as a wave of nausea hit me, I walked casually closer to the line of wretched creatures lined up for pre-auction inspection, but even my unobtrusive move wasn't lost on the slave owners who were bent on selling their wares.

"Come closer!" a ragged beast urged me in a rasping, unpleasant voice as he gestured with a bony arm.

I eyed him with distaste, thinking that this thing was just ugly enough to have caused the entire planet to smell bad, though I doubted he'd been there long enough to do it. On the other hand, he didn't seem to be terribly young. Okay, so older than the hills might have been a little closer to the mark. Damn, maybe he *was* responsible, after all!

"I have here just what you have been seeking!" he said. "Help to relieve you of your burden! This one is strong and loyal and will serve you well."

I glanced dubiously at the small-statured critter there before me, and its even smaller slave. "I don't think so," I replied, thinking that the weight of my pack alone would probably have crushed the poor little thing's tiny bones to powder. I know that looks can often be deceiving, but this thing looked to me like nothing more than an oversized grasshopper. Its bulbous red eyes regarded me with an unblinking and slightly unnerving stare. "Its eyes give me the creeps, anyway," I added. "I need something that looks more… humanoid."

Dismissing them with a wave, I glanced around at the others, noting that, of the group, there were only two slaves being offered that were even bipedal: one reminded me of a cross between a cow and a chimpanzee, and the other, well, the other was the one who had first caught my eye—possibly because out of all the slaves there, he was the one seeming to require the most restraint, and also because he was completely naked.

I studied him out of the corner of my eye, noting that the other prospective buyers seemed to be giving him a wide berth. His owner, an ugly Cylopean—and Cylopeans are *all* ugly, but this one would have stood out in a crowd of them—was exhorting the masses to purchase his slave.

"Come!" he shouted in heavily accented Standard Tongue, "my slave is strong and will serve you well. I part with him only out of extreme financial need, for he is as a brother to me, and it pains me greatly to lose him."

His pain wasn't as great as the slave's, obviously. I eyed the Cylopean skeptically. Surely he couldn't imagine that anyone would have suspected that his "brother" would require a genital restraint in order to drag him to the market to part him from his current master!

Rolling my eyes with disdain, I muttered, "Go ahead and admit it. You're selling him because you can't control him."

"Oh, no, my good sir!" the Cylopean exclaimed, seemingly aghast at my suggestion. "He is strong! He is willing! He is even intelligent!"

I stifled a snicker. The slave was obviously smart enough to have this one buffaloed, I thought, chuckling to myself as it occurred to me that no one around here would even know what a buffalo was, let alone the euphemism associated with the animal.

I blew out a breath hard enough to fog the eye screen on my respirator. Damn, but I was a long way from home! Earth was at least five hundred long light-years away. How the hell had I managed to end up here, searching for a lost sister whom I sometimes suspected of not wanting to be found? I'd followed her trail from planet to planet for six years now, and had always been just a few steps behind her. I was beginning to consider giving up the search, but the memory of the terror in her wild blue eyes as she was torn from my arms on Dexia Four kept me going.

And now, she had been—or so I'd been informed—taken to Statzeel, a planet where all women were slaves and upon which I didn't dare set foot, knowing that I, too, would become enslaved. The denizens of Statzeel would undoubtedly not make the same mistake that the slave trader had, for I was most definitely female, and, as such, vulnerable to the same fate that had befallen my lovely little sister. That I wasn't the delicate, winsome creature Ranata was wouldn't matter, for a female on Statzeel was a slave by definition. Free women simply did not exist there.

Which was why I needed a male slave of my own. One to pose as my owner—one that I could trust to a certain extent, though I was beginning to believe that such a creature couldn't possibly exist, and certainly not on Orpheseus Prime! I was undoubtedly wasting my time, I thought as I looked back at the slave. He was tall, dirty, and probably stank every bit as much as his owner did. I was going to have to check the filter in that damn respirator—either that or go back and beat the shit out of the scheming little scoundrel who'd taken me for ten qidnits when he sold it to me. I should have simply stolen it, but getting myself in trouble with what law there was on that nasty little planet wouldn't have done either my sister, or myself, a lick of good.

As I glanced at the man standing there before me, he raised his head ever so slightly to regard me out of the corner of one glittering, obsidian eye. Something passed between us at that moment—something almost palpable and real—making me wonder if the people of his race might have had psychic powers of some kind. That he was most definitely not human was quite evident, though at first glance he might have appeared to be, and could possibly have passed for one to the uneducated. There weren't many humans this far out for comparison, which was undoubtedly why I'd been able to get wind of Ranata's whereabouts from time to time. She seemed to have left a lasting impression wherever she was taken.

Just as this slave would do, even with the upswept eyebrows that marked him as belonging to some other alien world. His black, waving hair hung to his waist, though matted and dirty and probably crawling with vermin. I had no doubt that his owner hadn't lied when he had said that the slave was strong, for he was collared and shackled—hand, foot, and genitals. I'd been through many slave markets in my search, but I'd rarely seen any slave who was bound the way this one was, which spoke not only of strength, but also of a belligerent, and probably untrainable, nature. The muscles were all right there to see, and while they were not overly bulky—appearing, instead, to be more tough and sinewy—their level of strength was unquestionable.

This man had seen some rough work and even rougher treatment, for jagged scars laced his back and a long, straight scar sliced across his left cheekbone as though it had been made with a sword. He had a piercing in his penis, which appeared to have been done recently, for the ring through it was crusted over with dried blood. A chain ran from the metallic collar around his neck, through the ring in his cock, to another metal band that encircled his penis and testicles at the base. The pain that such a device could inflict on a man was horrifying, even to me, and I'd had to inflict a lot of pain in the course of my travels—though never to someone so defenseless and completely within my power as a slave. My never-ending search for Ranata had left me nearly as tough and battle-scarred as the slave was, and I'd often had to fight to the death in order to stay alive. So far, however, I'd never stooped to torturing a slave, and sincerely hoped I never would. This slave owner obviously had no such qualms, and it made me want to take a shot at him, just on general principles.

Call me an old softy if you will, but I must admit that I considered buying this slave, if for no other reason than to set him free of his restraints. I might feed him first, though—and perhaps buy him some clothes.... I cocked my head to one side as I considered him again. You're a fool if you think feeding this thing will tame it, I told myself. A bona-fide fool…

SLAVE

BY CHERYL BROOKS

"I found him in the slave market on Orpheseus Prime, and even on such a god-forsaken planet as that one, their treatment of him seemed extreme."

Cat may be the last of a species whose sexual talents were the envy of the galaxy. Even filthy, chained, and beaten, his feline gene gives him a special aura.

Jacinth is on a rescue mission… and she needs a man she can trust with her life.

PRAISE FOR CHERYL BROOKS' *SLAVE*:

"A sexy adventure with a hero you can't resist!"

—Candace Havens, author of *Charmed & Deadly*

"Fascinating world customs, a bit of mystery, and the relationship between the hero and heroine make this a very sensual romance."

—*Romantic Times*

978-1-4022-1192-8 • $6.99 U.S. / $8.99 CAN

WARRIOR

by Cheryl Brooks

"He came to me in the dead of winter,
his body burning with fever."

Even near death, his sensuality is amazing...

Leo arrives on Tisana's doorstep a beaten slave from a near extinct race with feline genes. As soon as Leo recovers his strength, he'll use his extraordinary sexual talents to bewitch Tisana and make a bolt for freedom...

Praise for The Cat Star Chronicles:

"A compelling tale of danger, intrigue, and sizzling romance!"
—Candace Havens, author of *Charmed & Deadly*

"Hot enough to start a fire. Add in a thrilling new world and my reading experience was complete."
—*Romance Junkies*

978-1-4022-1440-0 • $6.99 U.S. / $7.99 CAN

ROGUE

BY CHERYL BROOKS

Tychar crawled toward me on his hands and knees like a tiger stalking his prey. "I, for one, am glad you came," he purred. "And I promise you, Kyra, you will never want to leave Darconia."

"Cheryl Brooks knows how to keep the heat on and the reader turning pages!"

—Sydney Croft, author of *Seduced by the Storm*

978-1-4022-1762-3 • $6.99 U.S. / $7.99 CAN

OUTCAST

BY CHERYL BROOKS

Sold into slavery in a harem, Lynx is a favorite because his feline gene gives him remarkable sexual powers. But after ten years, Lynx is exhausted and is thrown out of the harem without a penny. Then he meets Bonnie, who's determined not to let such a beautiful and sensual young man go to waste…

PRAISE FOR THE CAT STAR CHRONICLES:

"Leaves the reader eager for the next story featuring these captivating aliens." —*Romantic Times*

"One of the sweetest love stories…one of the hottest heroes ever conceived and…one of the most exciting and adventurous quests that I have ever had the pleasure of reading." —*Single Titles*

"One of the most sensually imaginative books that I've ever read… A magical story of hope, love and devotion" —*Yankee Romance Reviews*

978-1-4022-1896-5 • $6.99 U.S. / $7.99 CAN

Hex Appeal

BY LINDA WISDOM

> "Kudos to Linda Wisdom for a
> series that's pure magic!"

—Vicki Lewis Thompson,
New York Times bestselling author of *Wild & Hexy*

JAZZ AND NICK'S DREAM ROMANCE HAS
TURNED INTO A NIGHTMARE...

FEISTY WITCH JASMINE TREMAINE AND DROP-DEAD GORGEOUS
vampire cop Nikolai Gregorovich have a hot thing going,
but it's tough to keep it together when nightmare visions
turn their passion into bickering.

With a little help from their friends, Nick and Jazz are in a
race against time to uncover whoever it is that's poisoning
their dreams, and their relationship...

978-1-4022-1400-4 • $6.99 U.S. / $7.99 CAN

WILD HIGHLAND MAGIC

BY KENDRA LEIGH CASTLE

She's a Scottish Highlands werewolf

Growing up in America, Catrionna MacInnes always tried desperately to control her powers and pretend to be normal…

He's a wizard prince with a devastating secret

The minute Cat lays eyes on Bastian, she knows she's met her destiny. In their first encounter, she unwittingly binds him to her for life, and now they're both targets for the evil enemies out to destroy their very souls.

Praise for Kendra Leigh Castle:

"Fans of straight up romance looking for a little extra something will be bitten." —*Publishers Weekly*

978-1-4022-1856-9 • $7.99 U.S. / $8.99 CAN

Destiny
of the Wolf

BY TERRY SPEAR

Praise for Terry Spear's *Heart of the Wolf*:

"The chemistry crackles off the page."
—*Publisher's Weekly*

"The characters are well drawn and believable, which makes the contemporary plotline of love and life among the lupus garou seem, well, realistic." —*Romantic Times*

"Full of action, adventure, suspense, and romance… one of the best werewolf stories I've read!" —*Fallen Angel Reviews*

ALL SHE WANTS IS THE TRUTH

Lelandi is determined to discover the truth about her beloved sister's mysterious death. But everyone thinks she's making a bid for her sister's widowed mate…

HE'S A PACK LEADER TORMENTED BY MEMORIES

Darien finds himself bewitched by Lelandi, and when someone attempts to silence her, he realizes that protecting the beautiful stranger may be the only way to protect his pack…and himself…

978-1-4022-1668-8 · $6.99 U.S. / $7.99 CAN

IN OVER HER HEAD

by Judi Fennell

"Holy mackerel! *In Over Her Head* is a
fantastically fun romantic catch!"

—Michelle Rowen, author of *Bitten & Smitten*

○ ○ ○ ○ ○ ○ **HE LIVES UNDER THE SEA** ○ ○ ○ ○ ○ ○

Reel Tritone is the rebellious royal second son of the ruler
of a vast undersea kingdom. A Merman, born with legs
instead of a tail, he's always been fascinated by humans,
especially one young woman he once saw swimming near
his family's reef...

○ ○ ○ ○ ○ **SHE'S TERRIFIED OF THE OCEAN** ○ ○ ○ ○ ○

Ever since the day she swam out too far and heard voices
in the water, marina owner Erica Peck won't go swimming
for anything—until she's forced into the water by a shady
ex-boyfriend searching for stolen diamonds, and is nearly
eaten by a shark...luckily Reel is nearby to save her, and
discovers she's the woman he's been searching for...

978-1-4022-2001-2 • $6.99 U.S. / $7.99 CAN